Shojo Beat

Story & Art by
Aya Nakahara

3

love ★ com

contents ③

The Story So Far...

First-year high school student Risa Koizumi is 5'7". She and Atsushi Ôtani (5'1") are considered their class's lopsided comedy duo, and have so much in common that a "love fortune" machine tells them they're 100% compatible—but in fact all they do is bicker. Right now, they're competing over who can hook up with someone first, and Ôtani's ex-girlfriend shows up and says that she has something to tell him! It looks like they might get back together, but it turns out that she has a new boyfriend, and all she wanted to tell Ôtani was that his height wasn't the reason she had dumped him.

Meanwhile, Risa's childhood friend Haruka suddenly appears and starts going after her! He constantly puts down Ôtani, who's always by Risa's side, and Risa for some reason finds herself defending him. When Haruka asks her if she's in love with Ôtani, Risa gets very flustered...!

♥ To really get all the details, check out *Lovely Complex* volumes 1 and 2, available at bookstores everywhere!!

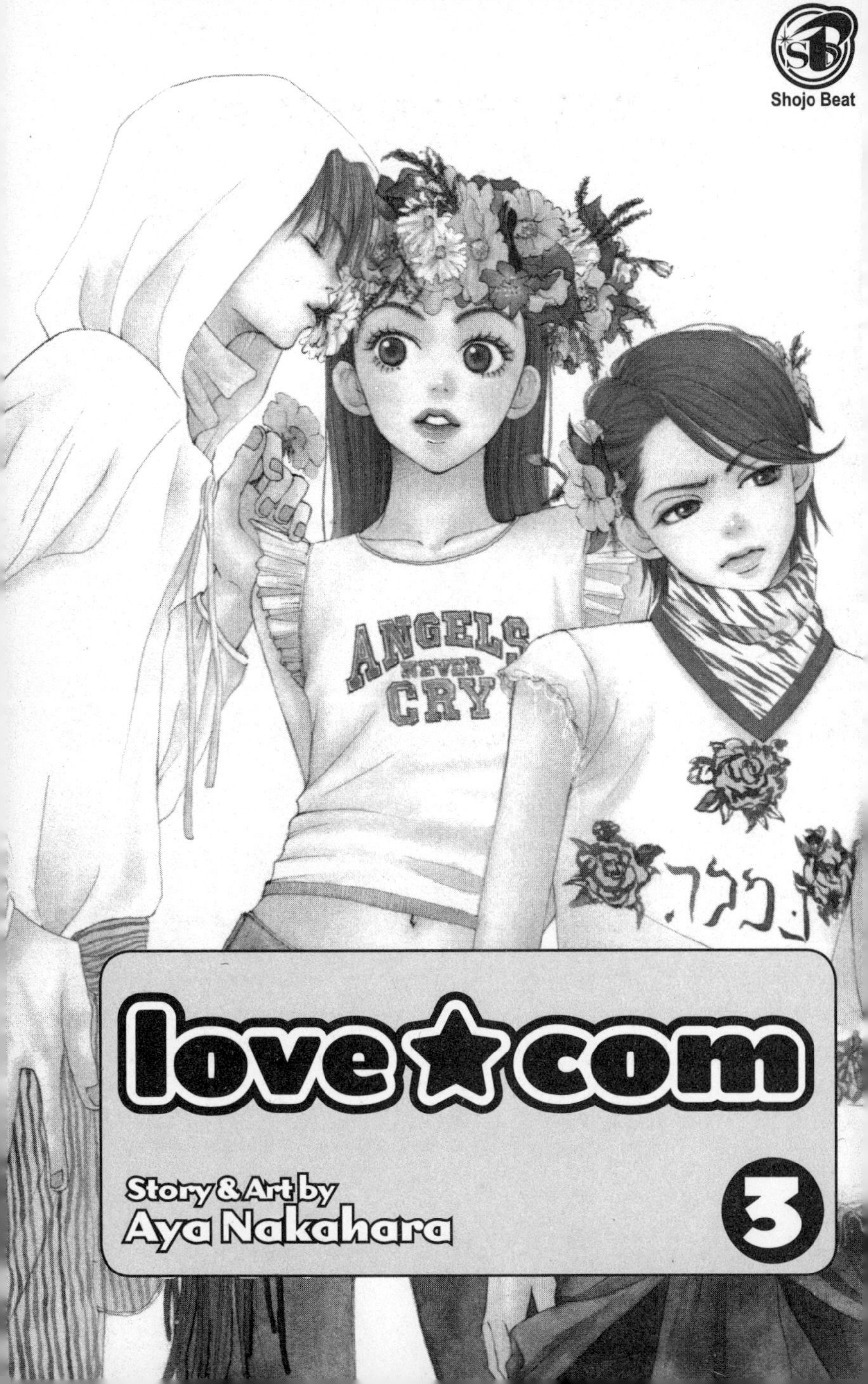
Shojo Beat
ANGELS NEVER CRY
love★com
Story & Art by
Aya Nakahara
3

LOVELY
COMPLEX

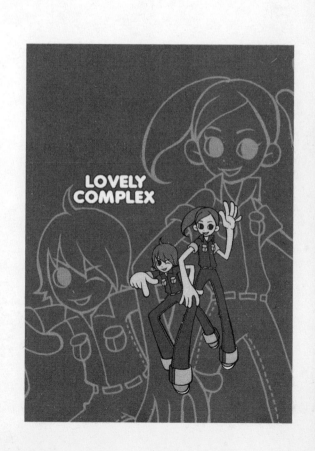

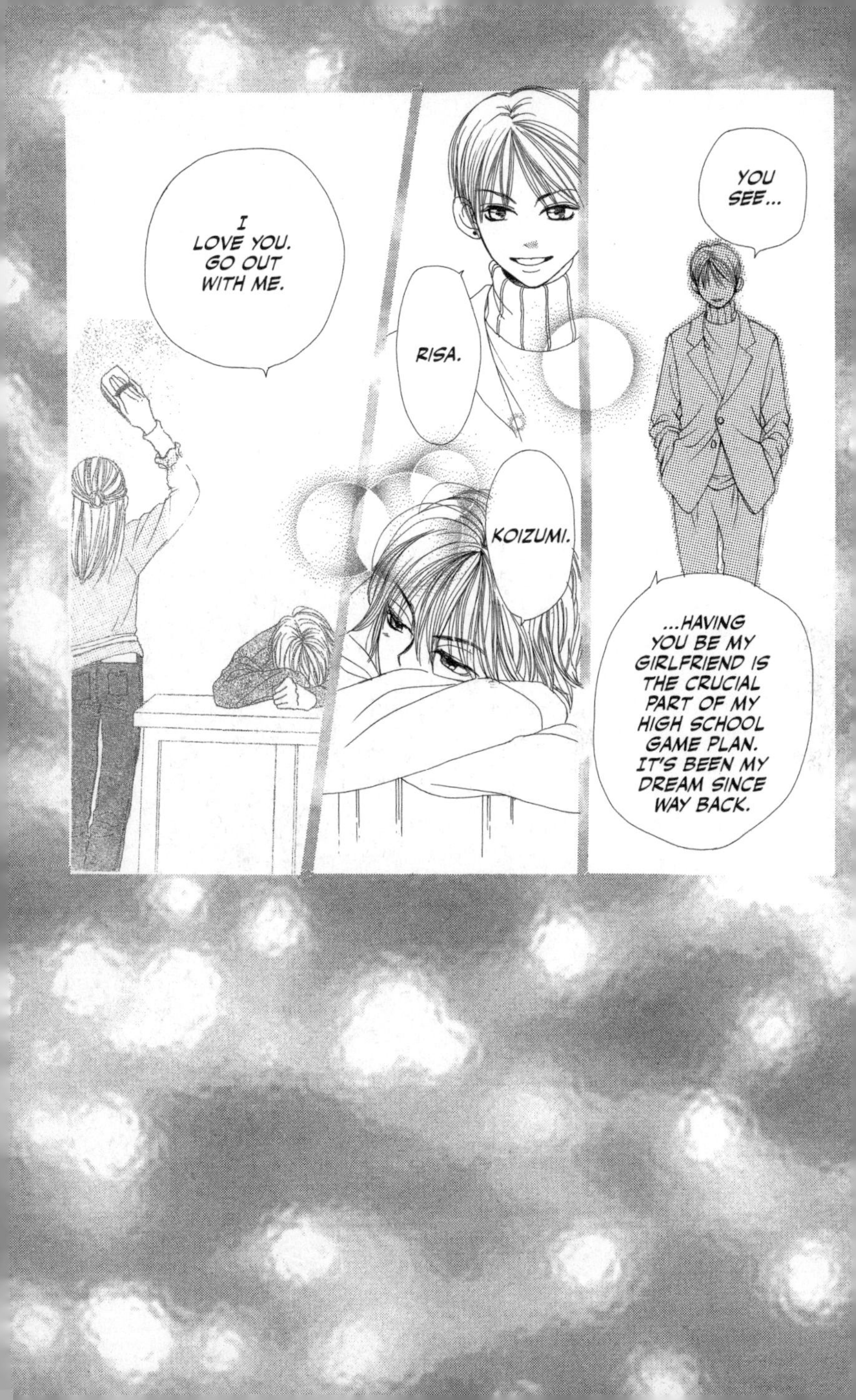
YOU SEE...
...HAVING YOU BE MY GIRLFRIEND IS THE CRUCIAL PART OF MY HIGH SCHOOL GAME PLAN. IT'S BEEN MY DREAM SINCE WAY BACK.
RISA.
KOIZUMI.
I LOVE YOU. GO OUT WITH ME.

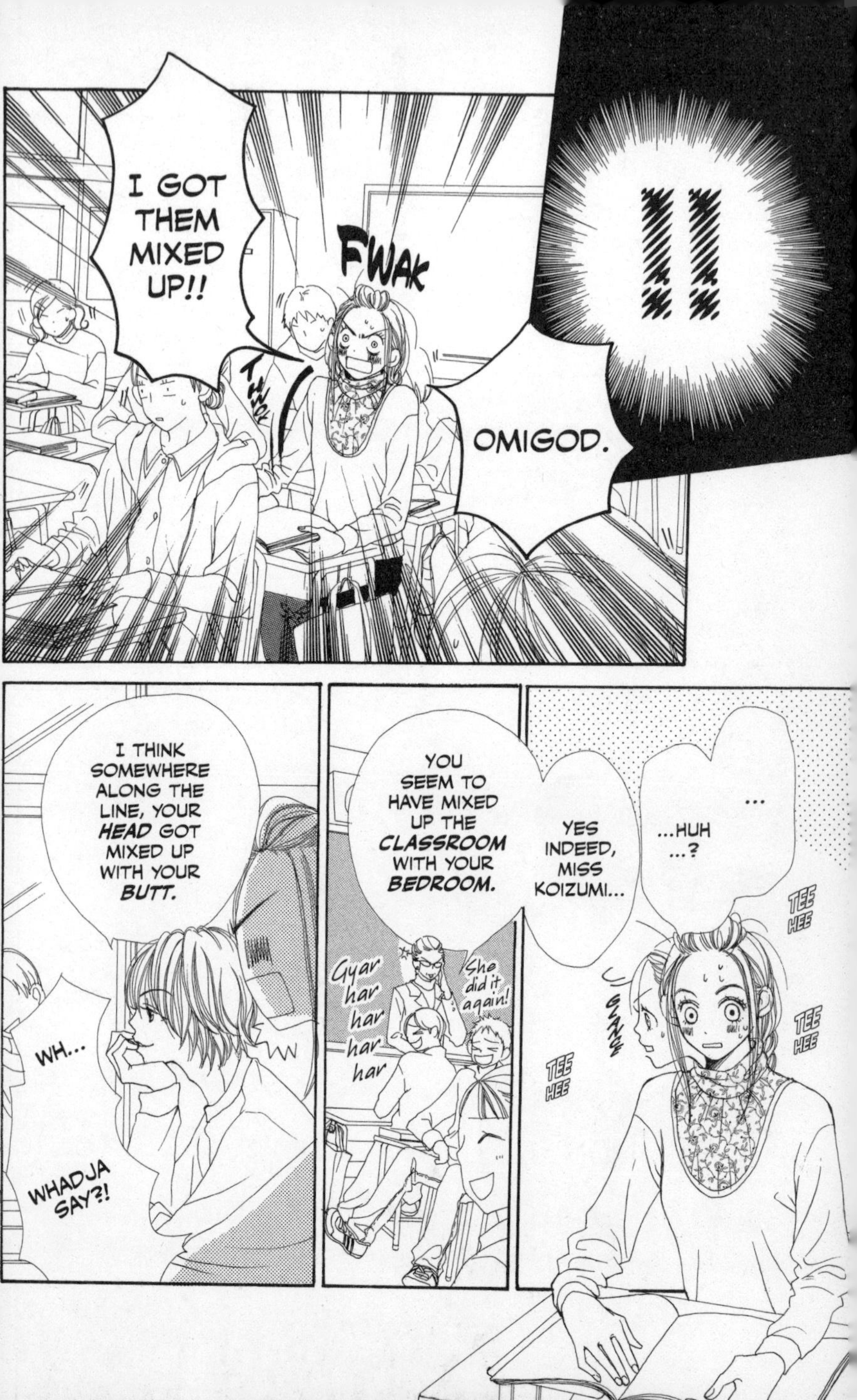
!!
OMIGOD.
FWAK
THWOK
I GOT THEM MIXED UP!!
...
...HUH ...?
TEE HEE
TEE HEE
GLANCE
TEE HEE
YES INDEED, MISS KOIZUMI...
YOU SEEM TO HAVE MIXED UP THE CLASSROOM WITH YOUR BEDROOM.
She did it again!
Gyar har har har har
I THINK SOMEWHERE ALONG THE LINE, YOUR HEAD GOT MIXED UP WITH YOUR BUTT.
WH...
WHADJA SAY?!

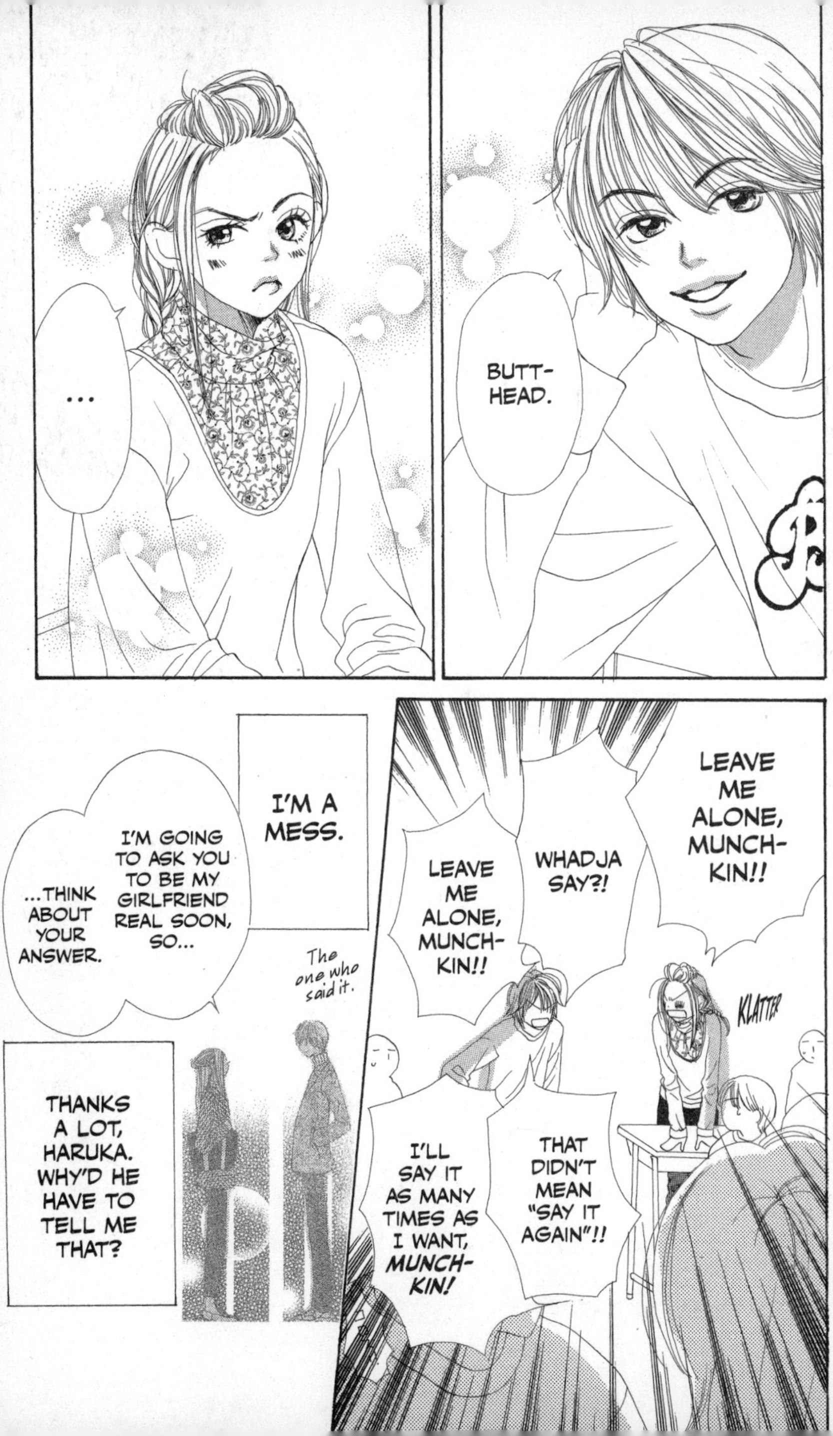
BUTT-HEAD.
...
LEAVE ME ALONE, MUNCH-KIN!!
WHADJA SAY?!
LEAVE ME ALONE, MUNCH-KIN!!
KLATTER
THAT DIDN'T MEAN "SAY IT AGAIN"!!
I'LL SAY IT AS MANY TIMES AS I WANT, *MUNCH-KIN!*
I'M A MESS.
I'M GOING TO ASK YOU TO BE MY GIRLFRIEND REAL SOON, SO...
...THINK ABOUT YOUR ANSWER.
The one who said it.
THANKS A LOT, HARUKA. WHY'D HE HAVE TO TELL ME THAT?

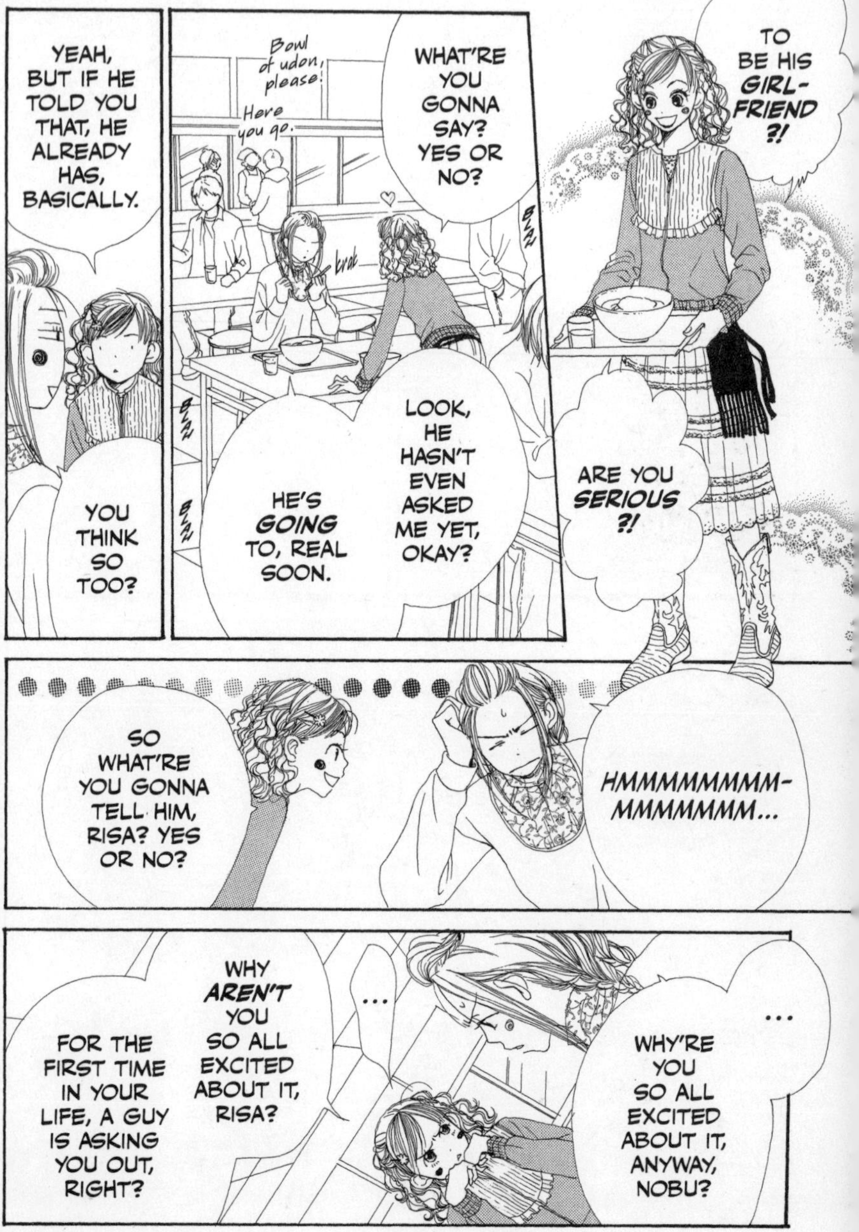
TO BE HIS *GIRLFRIEND* ?!
ARE YOU *SERIOUS* ?!
WHAT'RE YOU GONNA SAY? YES OR NO?
Bowl of udon, please!
Here you go.
krak
BLAH
LOOK, HE HASN'T EVEN ASKED ME YET, OKAY?
HE'S *GOING* TO, REAL SOON.
BLAH
BLAH
YEAH, BUT IF HE TOLD YOU THAT, HE ALREADY HAS, BASICALLY.
YOU THINK SO TOO?
HMMMMMMMM-MMMMMMM...
SO WHAT'RE YOU GONNA TELL HIM, RISA? YES OR NO?
...
WHY'RE YOU SO ALL EXCITED ABOUT IT, ANYWAY, NOBU?
...
WHY *AREN'T* YOU SO ALL EXCITED ABOUT IT, RISA?
FOR THE FIRST TIME IN YOUR LIFE, A GUY IS ASKING YOU OUT, RIGHT?

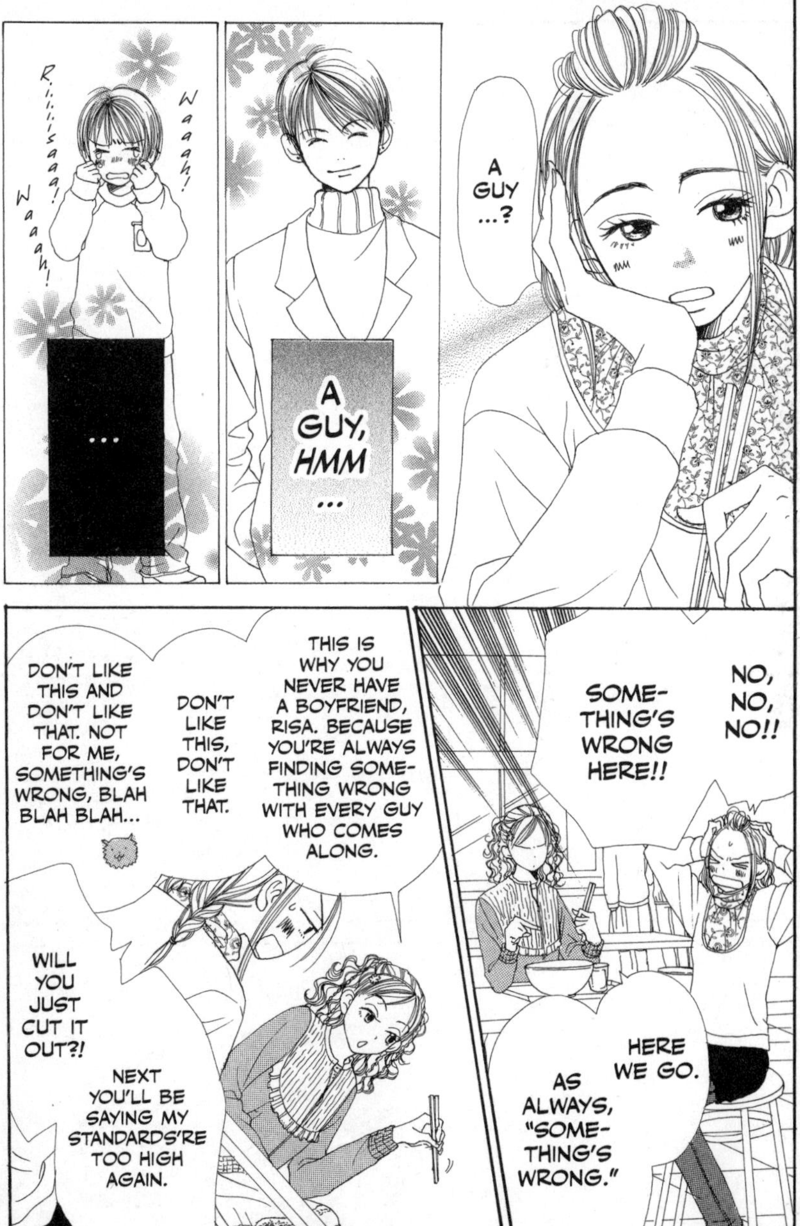

A GUY ...?
A GUY, HMM ...
Waaaah!
R.i.i.i.i.saaaa!
Waaaah!
...
NO, NO, NO!!
SOME-THING'S WRONG HERE!!
HERE WE GO.
AS ALWAYS, "SOME-THING'S WRONG."
THIS IS WHY YOU NEVER HAVE A BOYFRIEND, RISA. BECAUSE YOU'RE ALWAYS FINDING SOME-THING WRONG WITH EVERY GUY WHO COMES ALONG.
DON'T LIKE THIS, DON'T LIKE THAT.
DON'T LIKE THIS AND DON'T LIKE THAT. NOT FOR ME, SOMETHING'S WRONG, BLAH BLAH BLAH...
WILL YOU JUST CUT IT OUT?!
NEXT YOU'LL BE SAYING MY STANDARDS'RE TOO HIGH AGAIN.

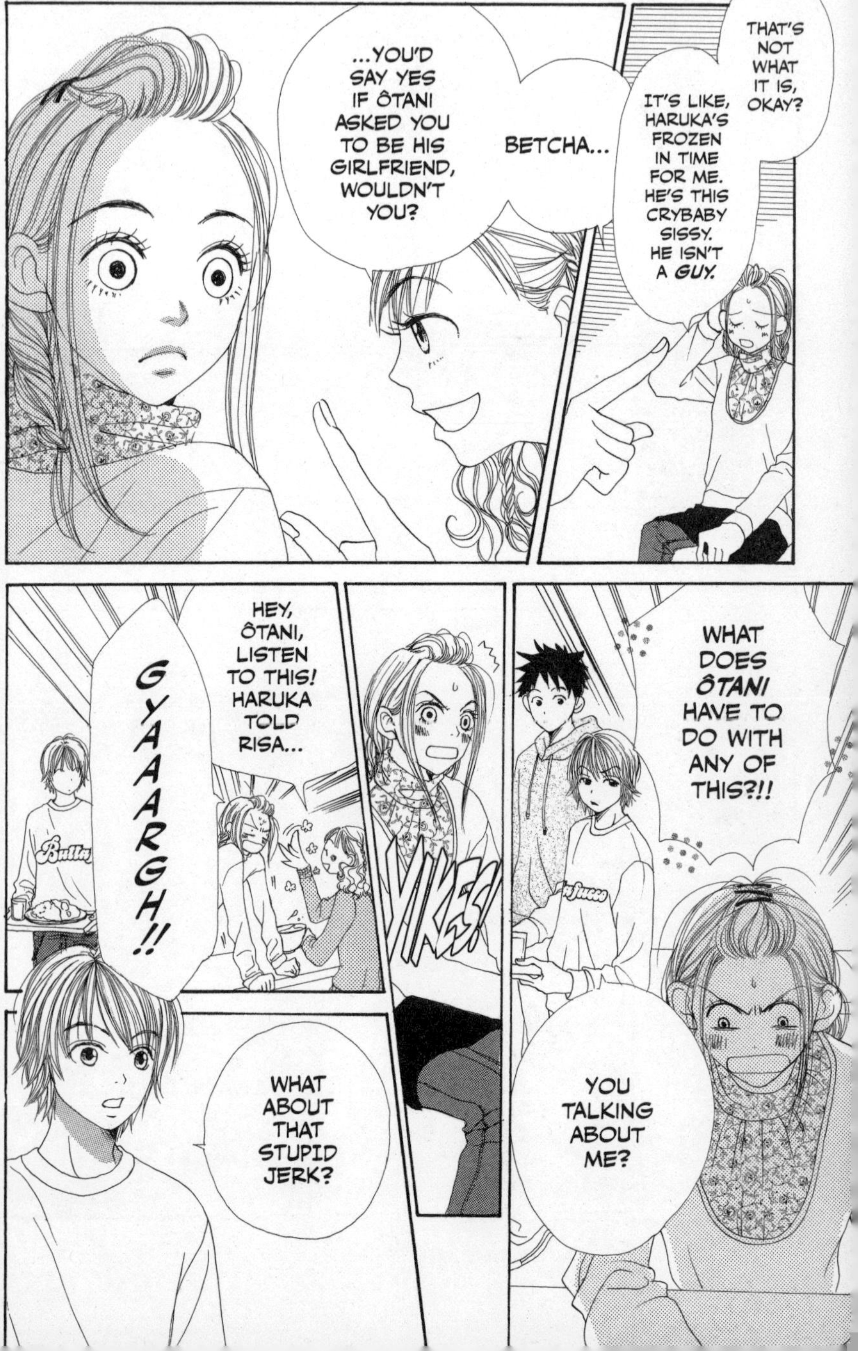
THAT'S NOT WHAT IT IS, OKAY?
IT'S LIKE, HARUKA'S FROZEN IN TIME FOR ME. HE'S THIS CRYBABY SISSY. HE ISN'T A *GUY.*
BETCHA...
...YOU'D SAY YES IF ÔTANI ASKED YOU TO BE HIS GIRLFRIEND, WOULDN'T YOU?
WHAT DOES *ÔTANI* HAVE TO DO WITH ANY OF THIS?!!
YOU TALKING ABOUT ME?
YIKES!
HEY, ÔTANI, LISTEN TO THIS! HARUKA TOLD RISA...
GYAAARGH!!
WHAT ABOUT THAT STUPID JERK?

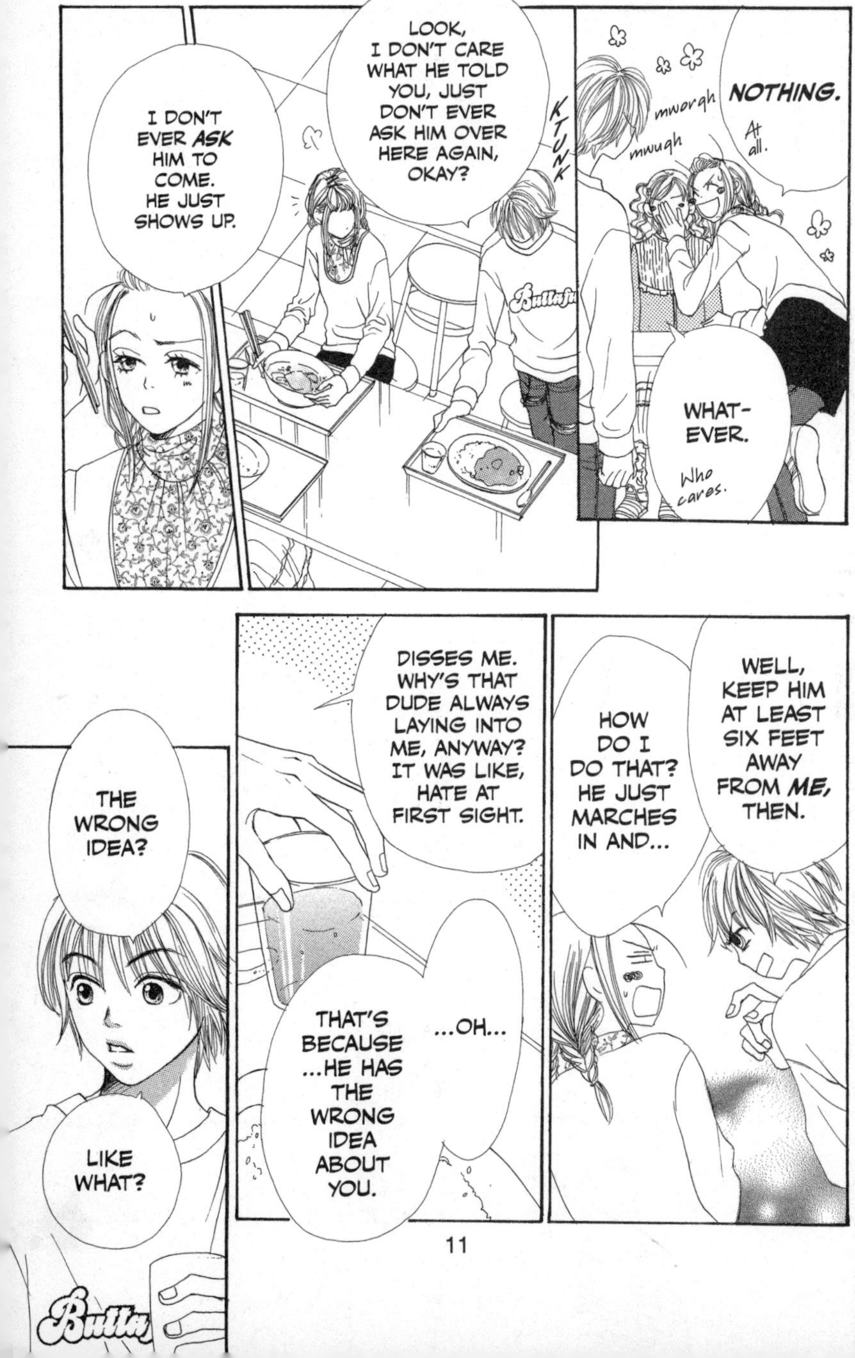
NOTHING.
At all.
mworgh
mwugh
WHAT-EVER.
Who cares.
LOOK, I DON'T CARE WHAT HE TOLD YOU, JUST DON'T EVER ASK HIM OVER HERE AGAIN, OKAY?
KTUNK
I DON'T EVER ASK HIM TO COME. HE JUST SHOWS UP.
WELL, KEEP HIM AT LEAST SIX FEET AWAY FROM ME, THEN.
HOW DO I DO THAT? HE JUST MARCHES IN AND...
DISSES ME. WHY'S THAT DUDE ALWAYS LAYING INTO ME, ANYWAY? IT WAS LIKE, HATE AT FIRST SIGHT.
...OH...
THAT'S BECAUSE ...HE HAS THE WRONG IDEA ABOUT YOU.
THE WRONG IDEA?
LIKE WHAT?

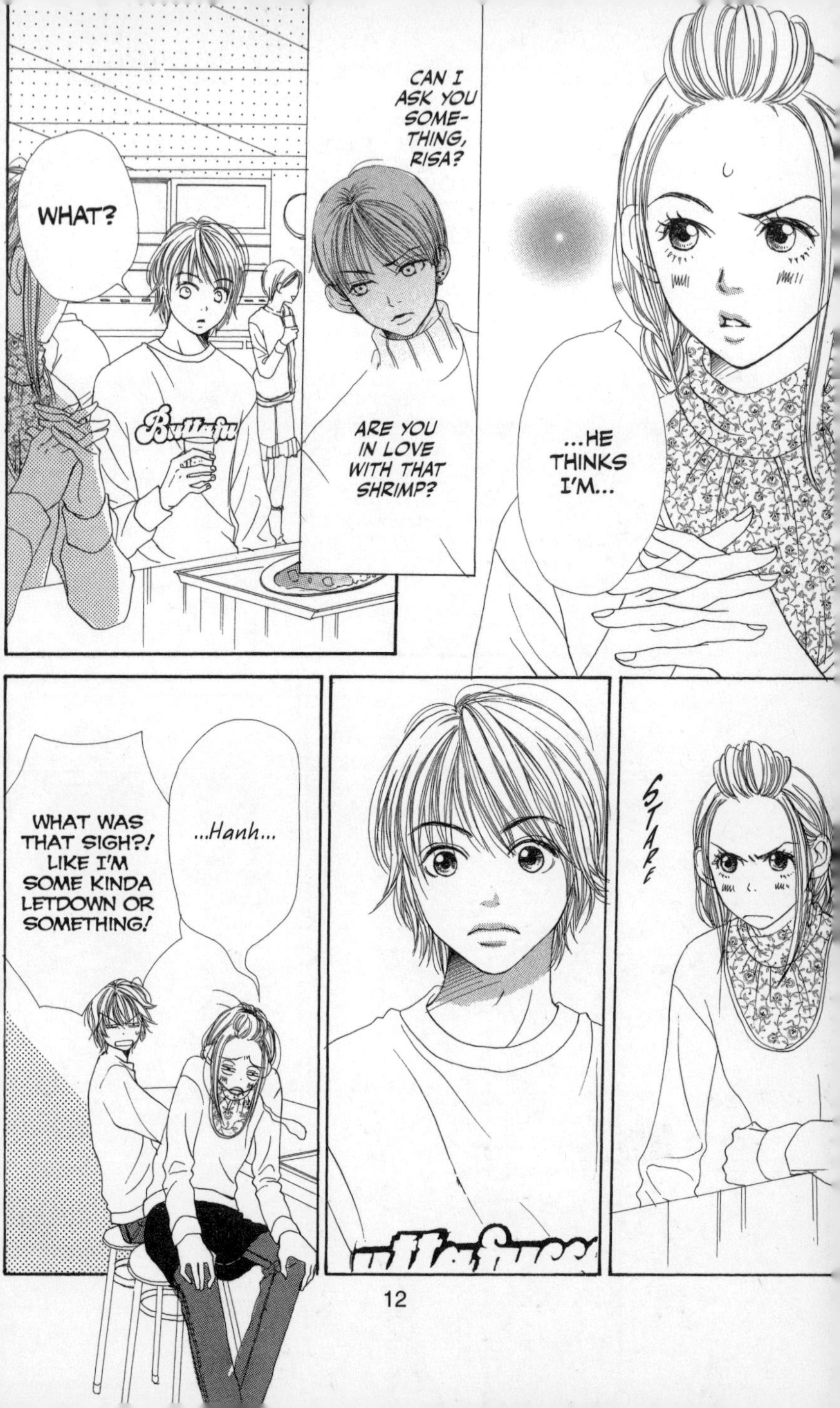
...HE THINKS I'M...
CAN I ASK YOU SOMETHING, RISA?
ARE YOU IN LOVE WITH THAT SHRIMP?
WHAT?
STARE
...Hanh...
WHAT WAS THAT SIGH?! LIKE I'M SOME KINDA LETDOWN OR SOMETHING!

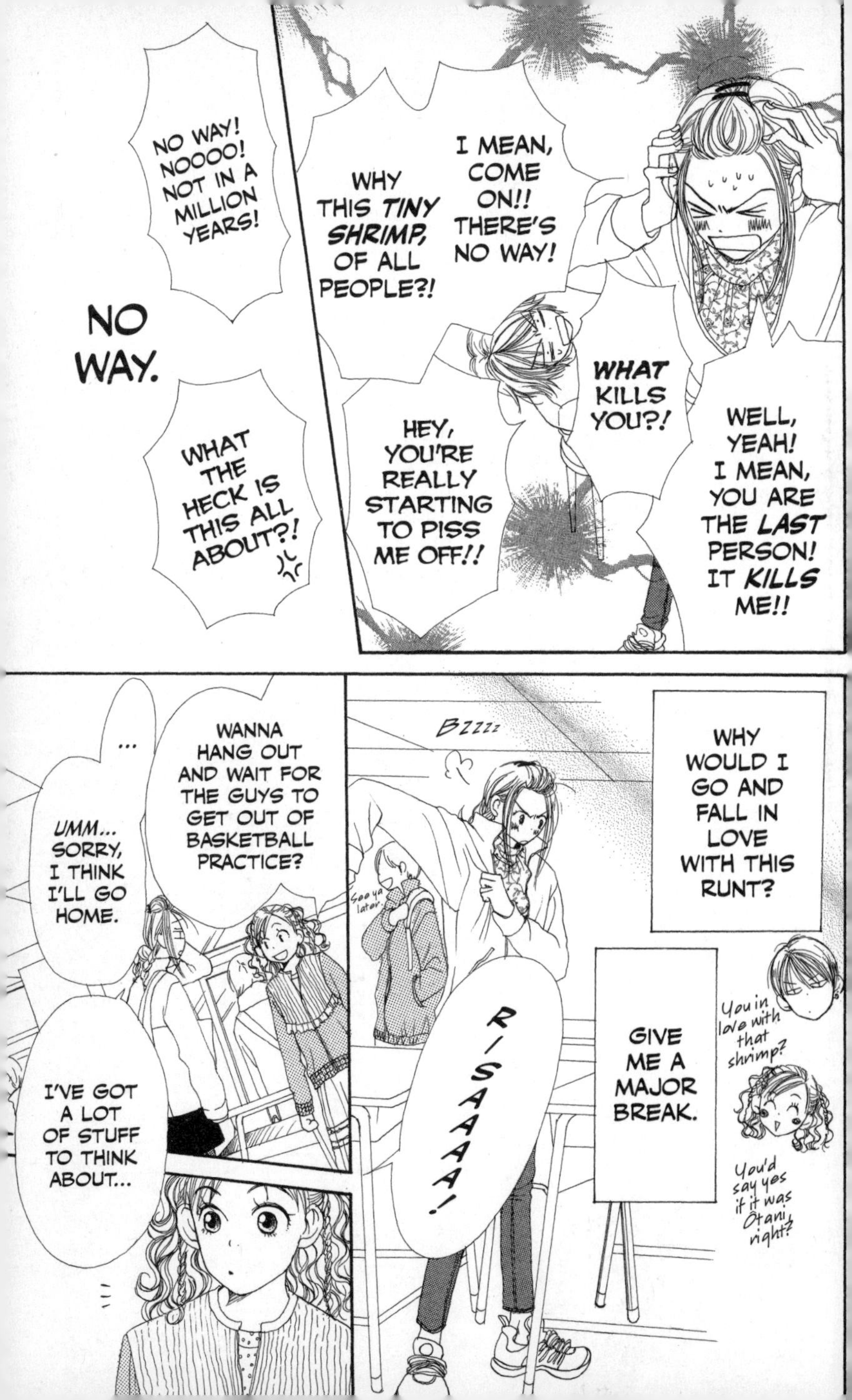
I MEAN, COME ON!! THERE'S NO WAY!
WHY THIS TINY SHRIMP, OF ALL PEOPLE?!
WELL, YEAH! I MEAN, YOU ARE THE LAST PERSON! IT KILLS ME!!
WHAT KILLS YOU?!
HEY, YOU'RE REALLY STARTING TO PISS ME OFF!!
NO WAY! NOOOO! NOT IN A MILLION YEARS!
NO WAY.
WHAT THE HECK IS THIS ALL ABOUT?!
WHY WOULD I GO AND FALL IN LOVE WITH THIS RUNT?
BZZZZ
See ya later.
You in love with that shrimp?
GIVE ME A MAJOR BREAK.
You'd say yes if it was Ōtani right?
RISAAAAA!
WANNA HANG OUT AND WAIT FOR THE GUYS TO GET OUT OF BASKETBALL PRACTICE?
...
UMM... SORRY, I THINK I'LL GO HOME.
I'VE GOT A LOT OF STUFF TO THINK ABOUT...

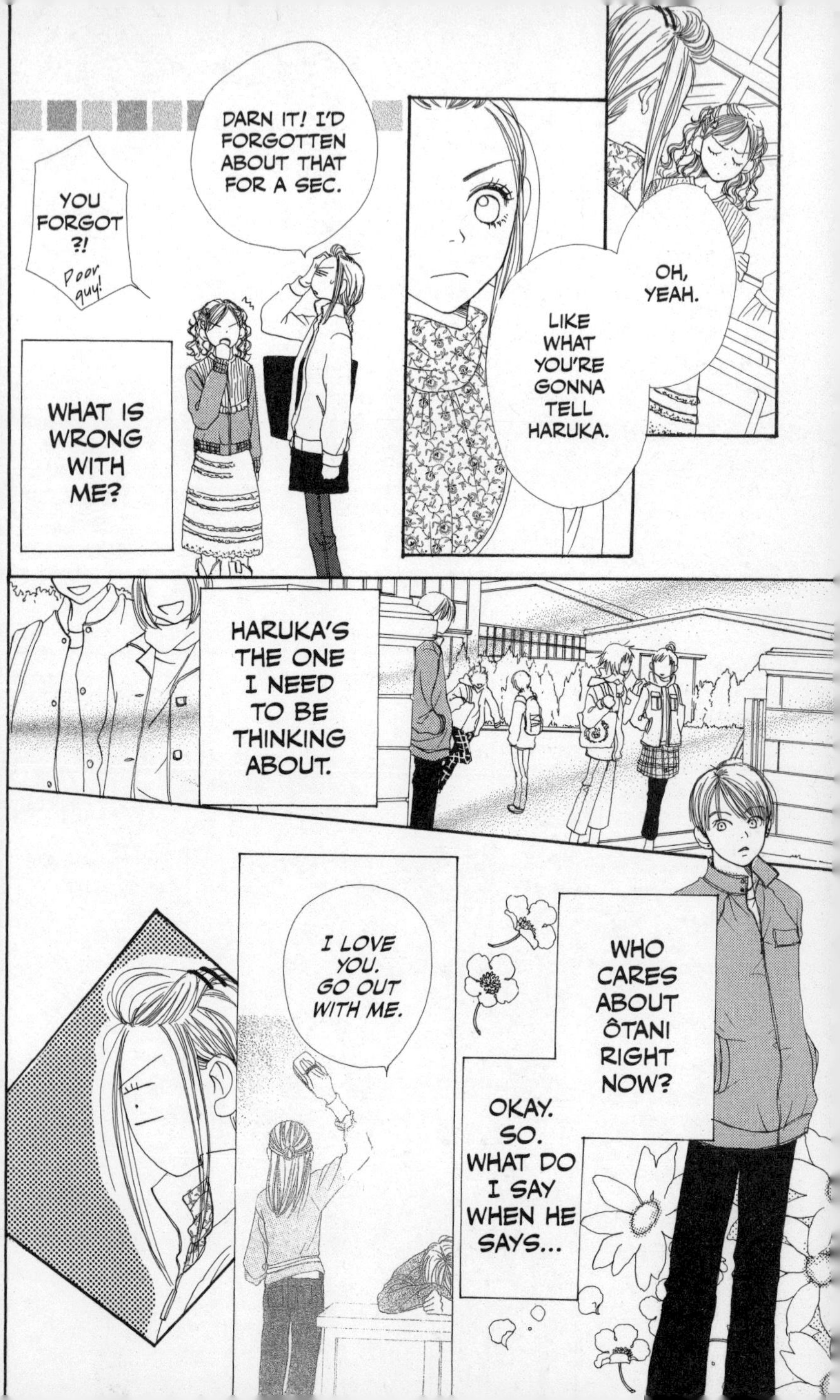
OH, YEAH.
LIKE WHAT YOU'RE GONNA TELL HARUKA.
DARN IT! I'D FORGOTTEN ABOUT THAT FOR A SEC.
YOU FORGOT?!
Poor guy!
WHAT IS WRONG WITH ME?
HARUKA'S THE ONE I NEED TO BE THINKING ABOUT.
WHO CARES ABOUT ÔTANI RIGHT NOW?
OKAY. SO. WHAT DO I SAY WHEN HE SAYS...
I LOVE YOU. GO OUT WITH ME.

1

Hello.
Nakahara here.
We're up to Vol. 3.

I got another year older over the summer. It feels like...with every year I age, I lose more and more zing. You could say I'm "mellowing," I suppose, but that doesn't quite seem to be it... More like I'm getting worn out... Or dull and listless... <sigh> umph...

And at the same time, it kinda feels like the manga I'm drawing are getting all hyper for no reason. <sigh> umph...

I'm starting to enjoy the taste of seaweed and tofu these days... chwumf chwumf

Gee, I really oughta hustle a little more... <sigh> umph...

Back in the old days, I used to have the energy to fill up every last corner of these spaces... <sigh> umph.

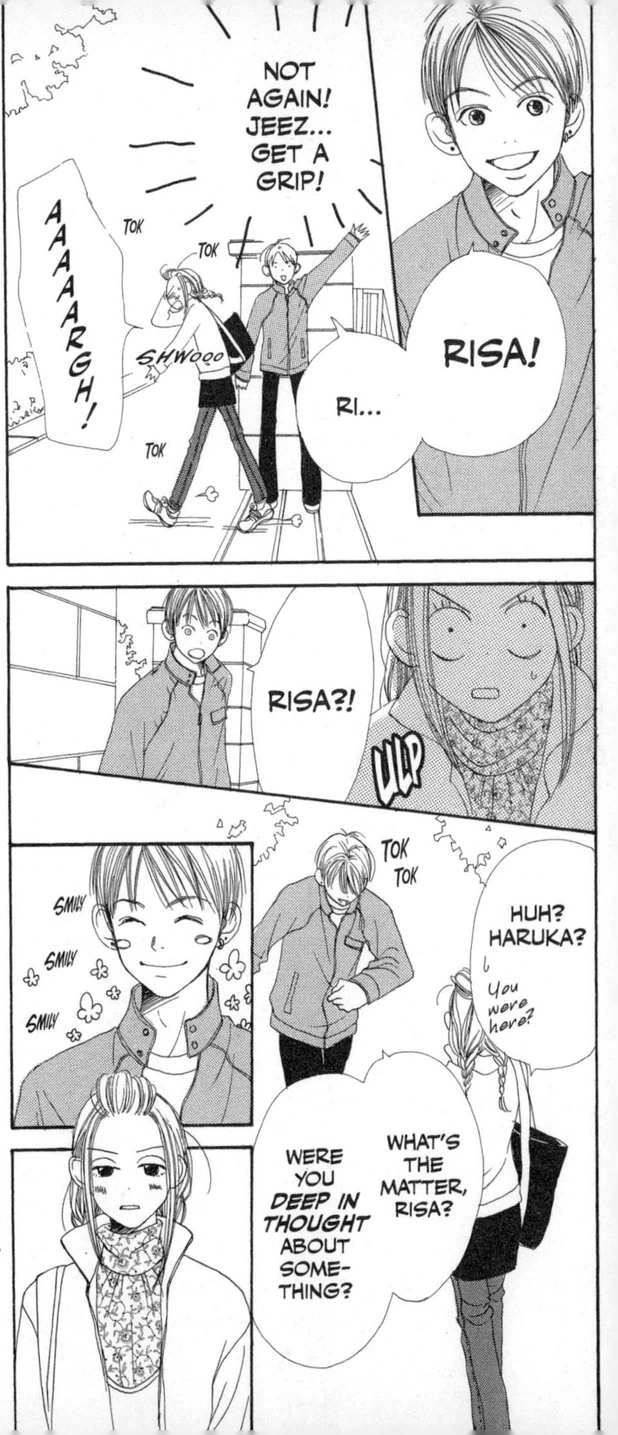
RI...
RISA!
AAAAARGH!
TOK
TOK
SHWOOO
TOK
NOT AGAIN! JEEZ... GET A GRIP!
ULP
RISA?!
TOK TOK
HUH? HARUKA?
You were here?
SMILY
SMILY
SMILY
WHAT'S THE MATTER, RISA?
WERE YOU DEEP IN THOUGHT ABOUT SOMETHING?

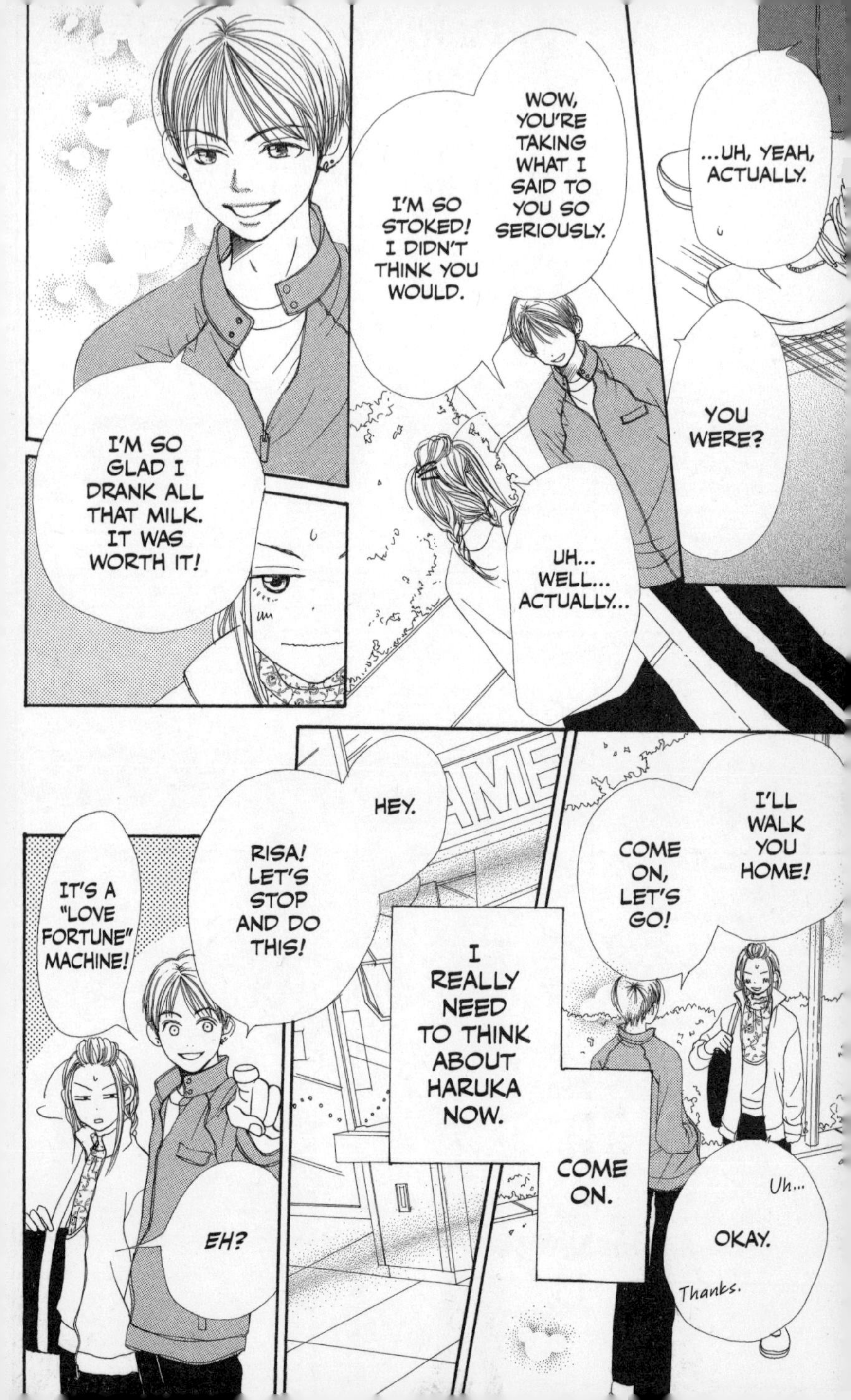
...UH, YEAH, ACTUALLY.
YOU WERE?
WOW, YOU'RE TAKING WHAT I SAID TO YOU SO SERIOUSLY.
I'M SO STOKED! I DIDN'T THINK YOU WOULD.
UH... WELL... ACTUALLY...
I'M SO GLAD I DRANK ALL THAT MILK. IT WAS WORTH IT!
I'LL WALK YOU HOME!
COME ON, LET'S GO!
Uh...
OKAY.
Thanks.
I REALLY NEED TO THINK ABOUT HARUKA NOW.
COME ON.
HEY.
RISA! LET'S STOP AND DO THIS!
IT'S A "LOVE FORTUNE" MACHINE!
EH?

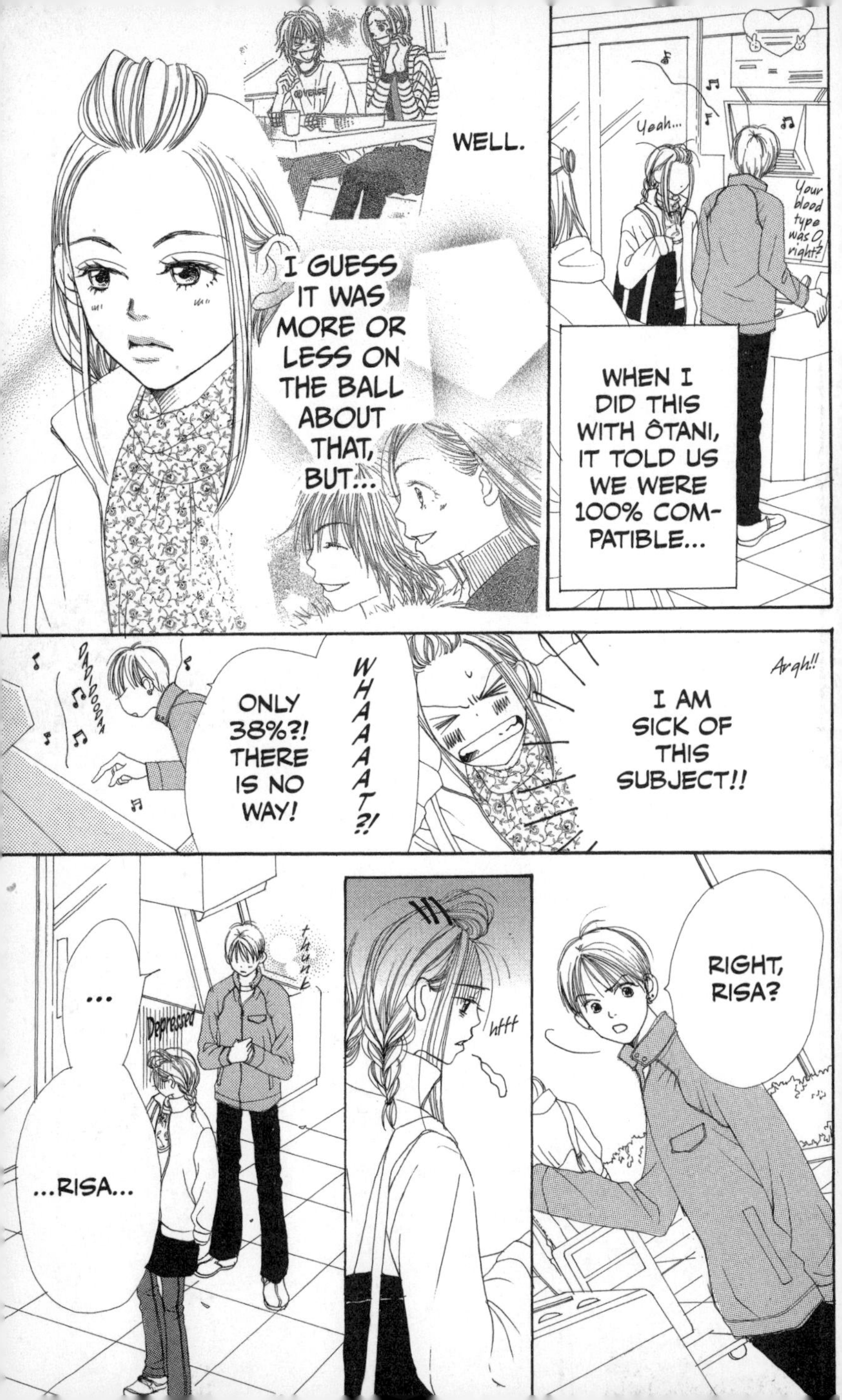
Your blood type was O, right?
Yeah...
WHEN I DID THIS WITH ÔTANI, IT TOLD US WE WERE 100% COMPATIBLE...
WELL.
I GUESS IT WAS MORE OR LESS ON THE BALL ABOUT THAT, BUT...
Argh!!
I AM SICK OF THIS SUBJECT!!
WHAAAAAT?!
ONLY 38%?! THERE IS NO WAY!
DADIDOOODAA
RIGHT, RISA?
hfff
thunk
Depressed
...
...RISA...

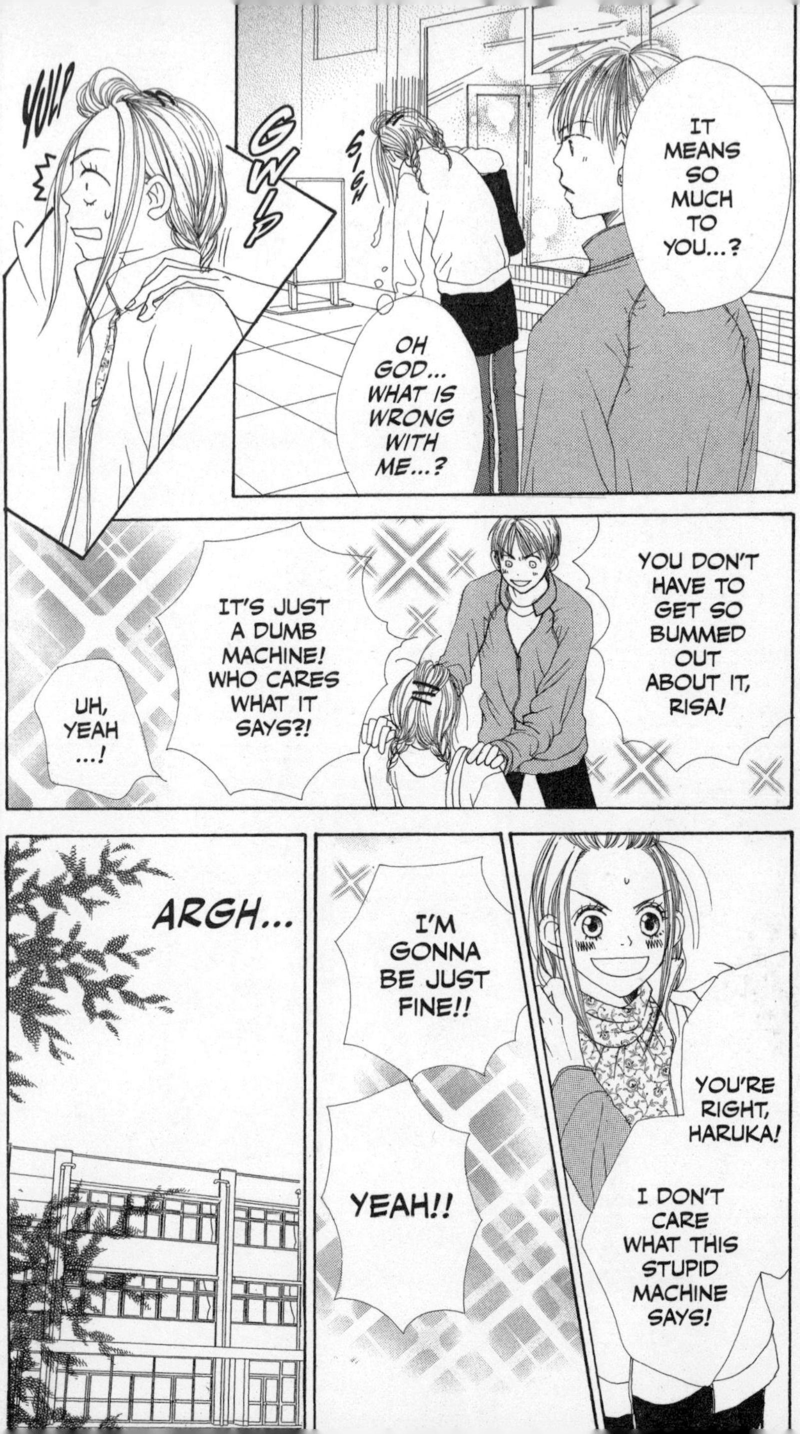
IT MEANS SO MUCH TO YOU...?
SIGH
OH GOD... WHAT IS WRONG WITH ME...?
YELP
YOU DON'T HAVE TO GET SO BUMMED OUT ABOUT IT, RISA!
IT'S JUST A DUMB MACHINE! WHO CARES WHAT IT SAYS?!
UH, YEAH ...!
YOU'RE RIGHT, HARUKA!
I DON'T CARE WHAT THIS STUPID MACHINE SAYS!
I'M GONNA BE JUST FINE!!
YEAH!!
ARGH...

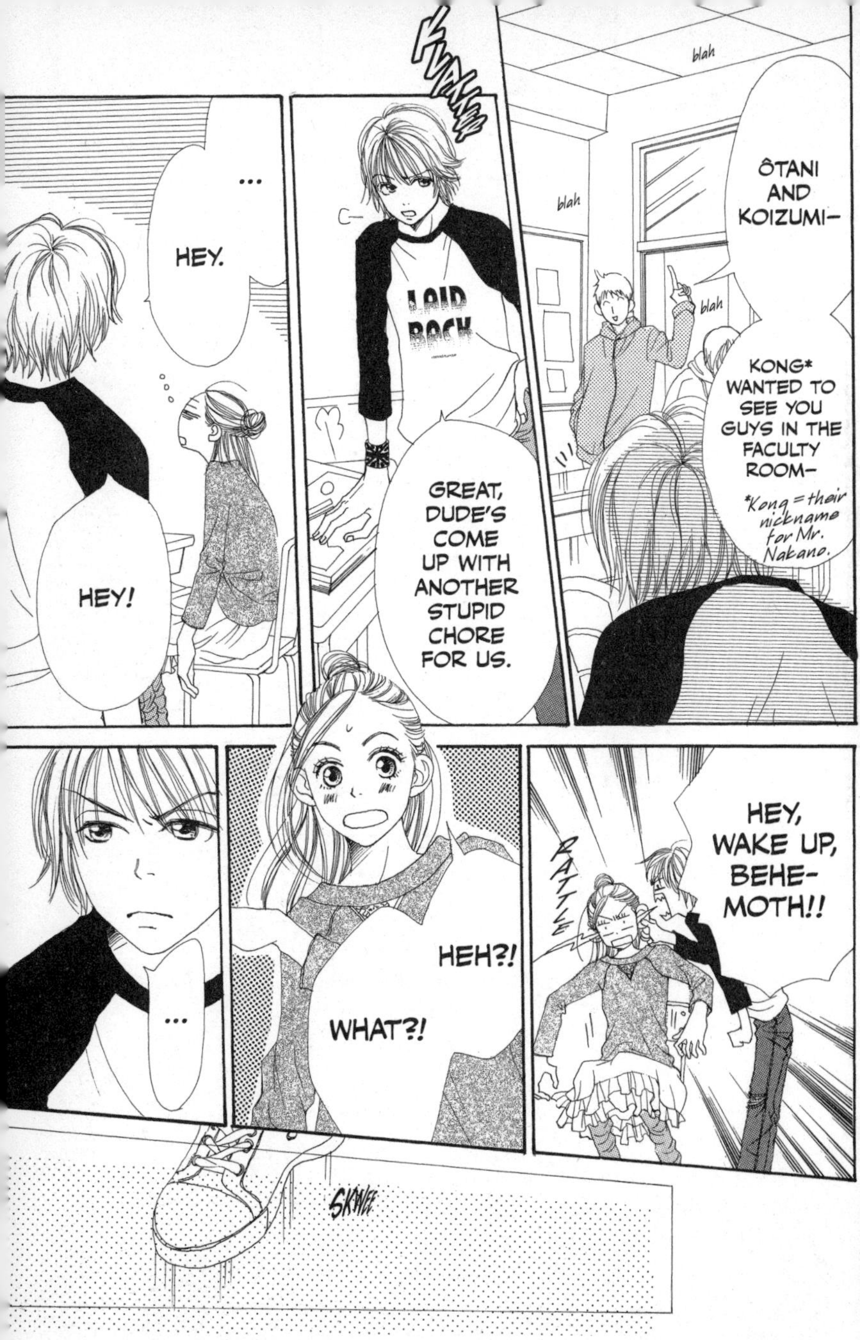

blah
blah
blah
ÔTANI AND KOIZUMI—
KONG* WANTED TO SEE YOU GUYS IN THE FACULTY ROOM—
*Kong = their nickname for Mr. Nakano.
C—
GREAT, DUDE'S COME UP WITH ANOTHER STUPID CHORE FOR US.
...
HEY.
HEY!
RATTLE
HEY, WAKE UP, BEHE-MOTH!!
HEH?!
WHAT?!
...
SKWEE

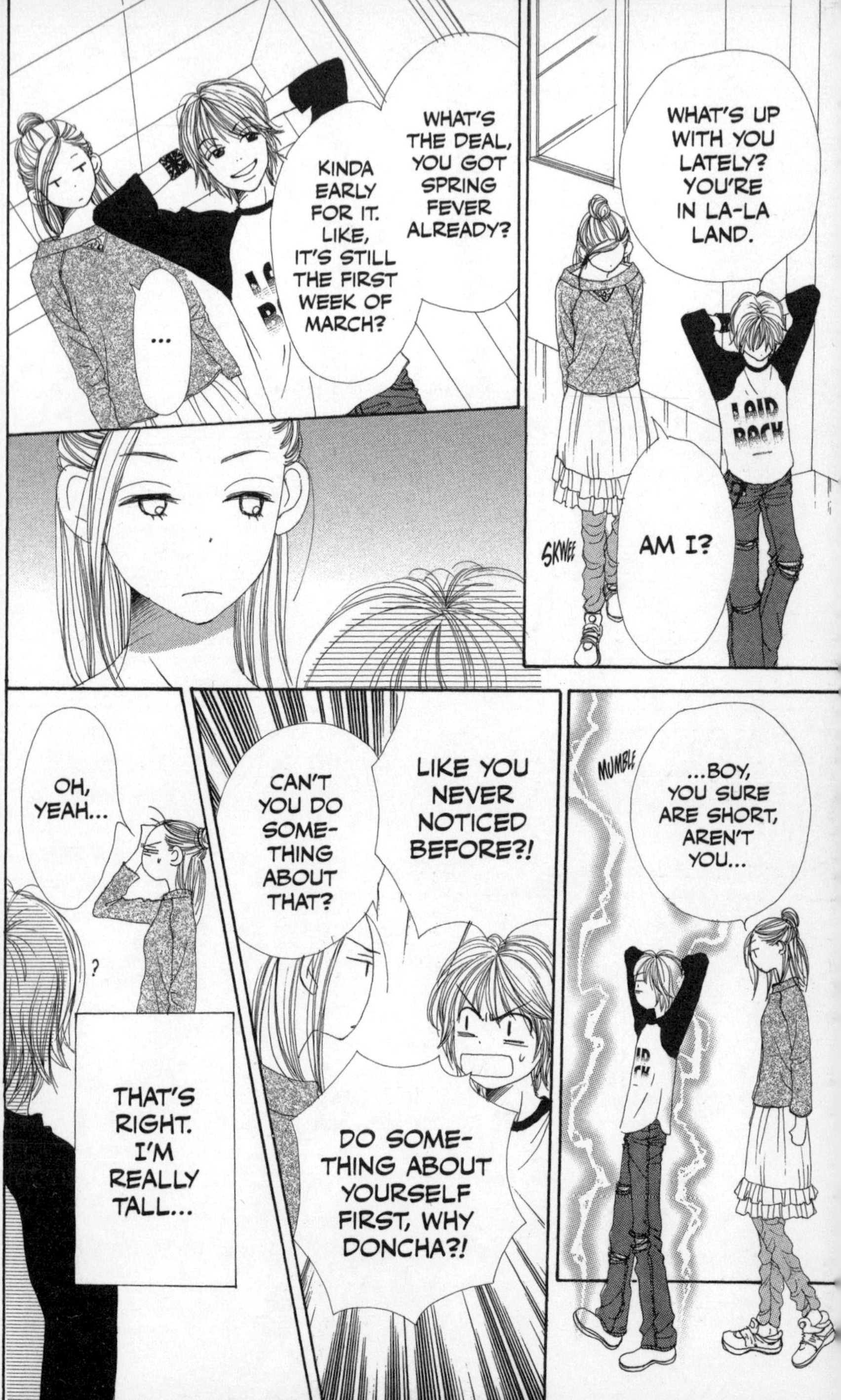
WHAT'S UP WITH YOU LATELY? YOU'RE IN LA-LA LAND.
SKWEE
AM I?
WHAT'S THE DEAL, YOU GOT SPRING FEVER ALREADY?
KINDA EARLY FOR IT. LIKE, IT'S STILL THE FIRST WEEK OF MARCH?
...
...BOY, YOU SURE ARE SHORT, AREN'T YOU...
MUMBLE
LIKE YOU NEVER NOTICED BEFORE?!
CAN'T YOU DO SOME-THING ABOUT THAT?
DO SOME-THING ABOUT YOURSELF FIRST, WHY DONCHA?!
OH, YEAH...
?
THAT'S RIGHT. I'M REALLY TALL...

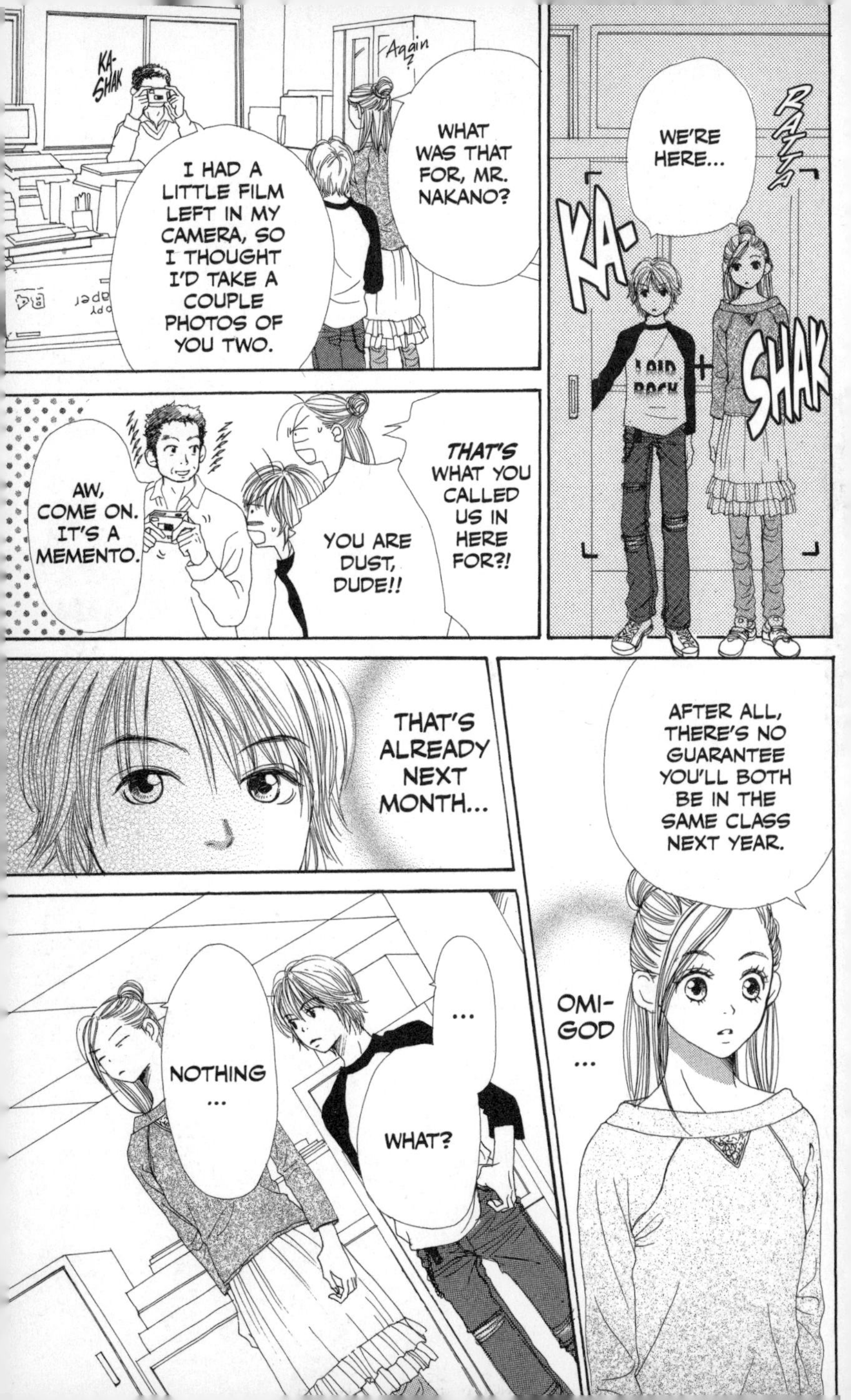
RATTA
WE'RE HERE...
KA-SHAK
Aagin?
WHAT WAS THAT FOR, MR. NAKANO?
KA-SHAK
I HAD A LITTLE FILM LEFT IN MY CAMERA, SO I THOUGHT I'D TAKE A COUPLE PHOTOS OF YOU TWO.
THAT'S WHAT YOU CALLED US IN HERE FOR?!
YOU ARE DUST, DUDE!!
AW, COME ON. IT'S A MEMENTO.
AFTER ALL, THERE'S NO GUARANTEE YOU'LL BOTH BE IN THE SAME CLASS NEXT YEAR.
OMI-GOD...
THAT'S ALREADY NEXT MONTH...
...
WHAT?
NOTHING...

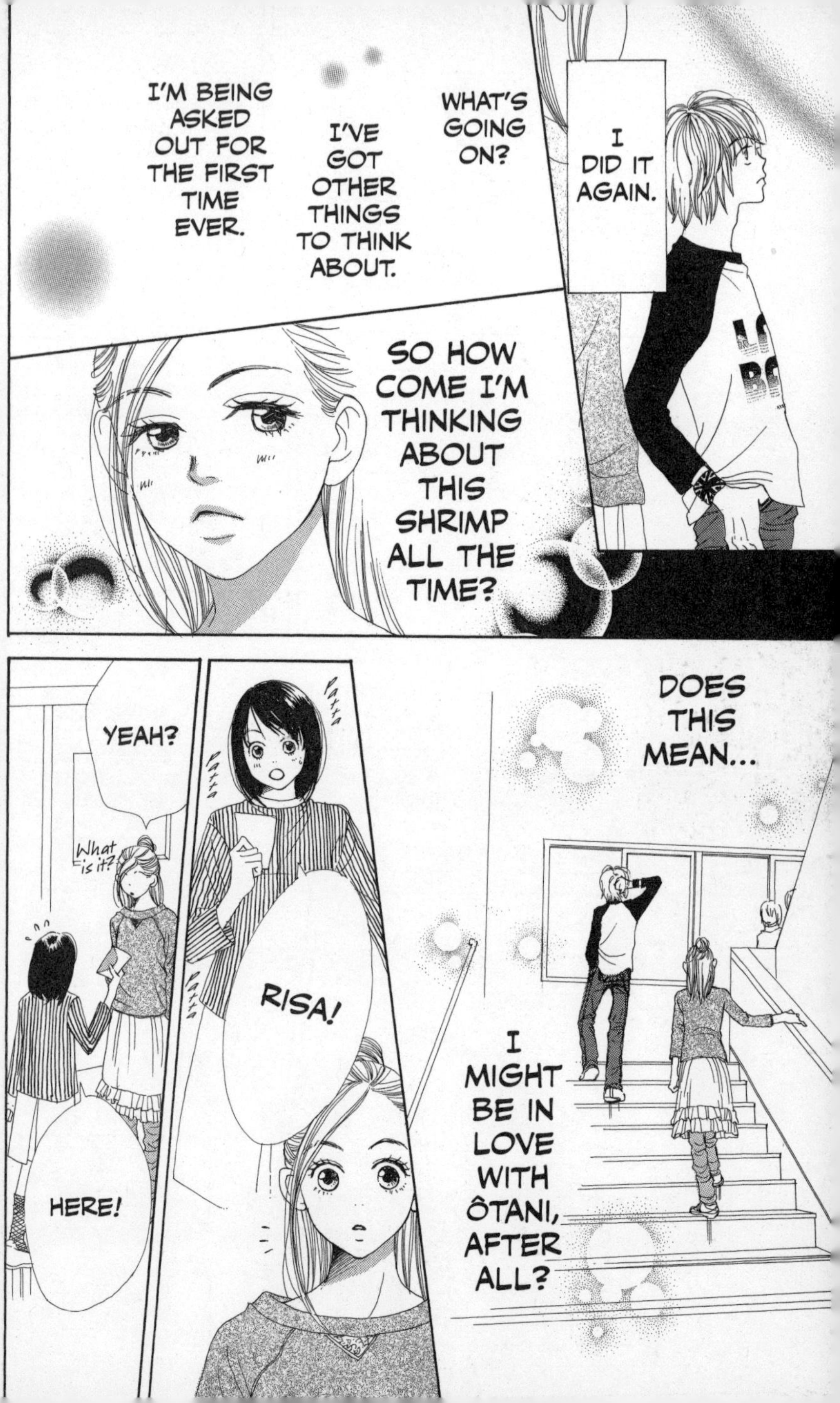
I DID IT AGAIN.
WHAT'S GOING ON?
I'VE GOT OTHER THINGS TO THINK ABOUT.
I'M BEING ASKED OUT FOR THE FIRST TIME EVER.
SO HOW COME I'M THINKING ABOUT THIS SHRIMP ALL THE TIME?
DOES THIS MEAN...
I MIGHT BE IN LOVE WITH ÔTANI, AFTER ALL?
RISA!
YEAH?
What is it?
HERE!

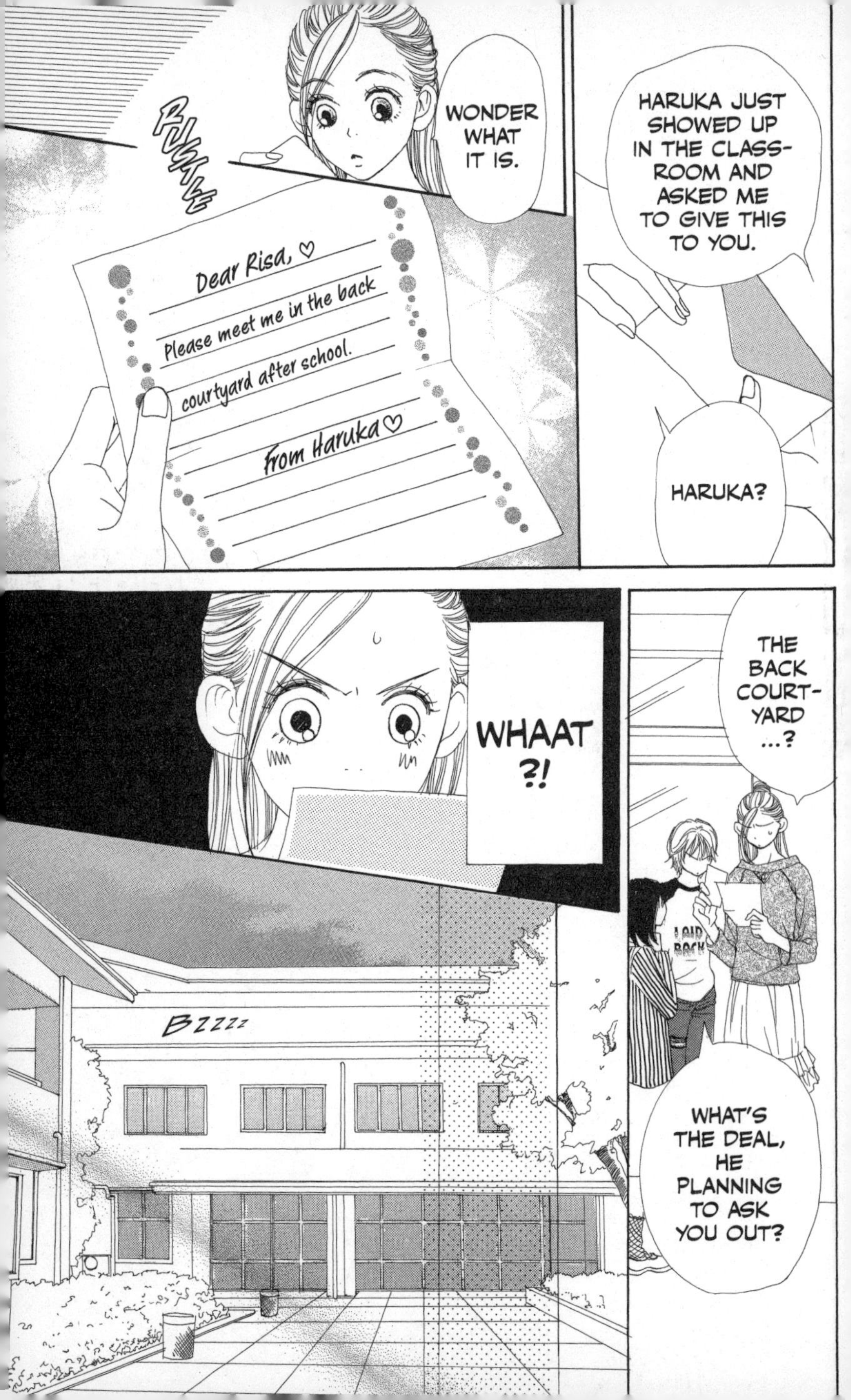
HARUKA JUST SHOWED UP IN THE CLASS-ROOM AND ASKED ME TO GIVE THIS TO YOU.
HARUKA?
WONDER WHAT IT IS.
Dear Risa, ♡
Please meet me in the back courtyard after school.
From Haruka♡
THE BACK COURT-YARD ...?
WHAT'S THE DEAL, HE PLANNING TO ASK YOU OUT?
LAID BACK
WHAAT ?!
BZZZZ

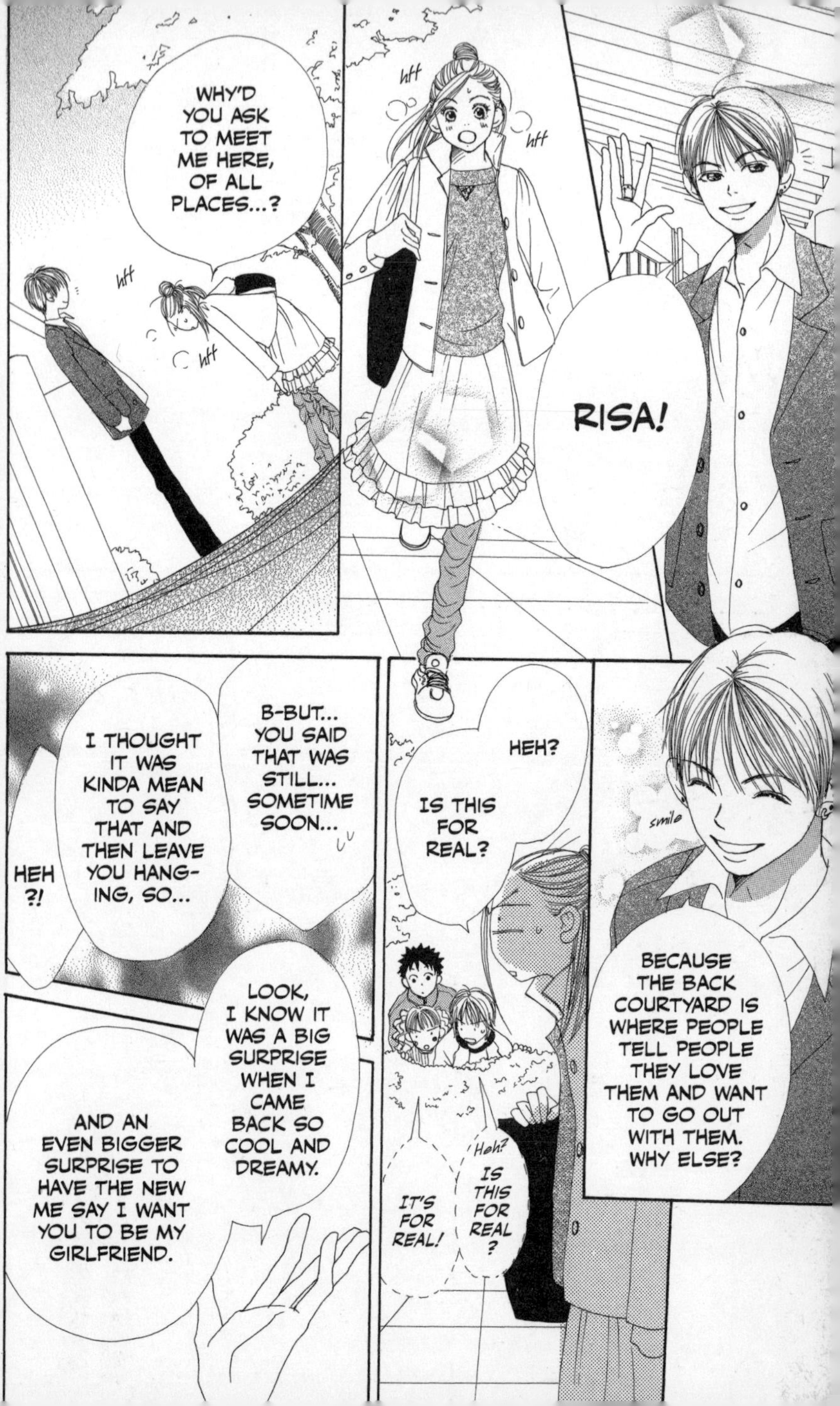
RISA!
hff
hff
WHY'D YOU ASK TO MEET ME HERE, OF ALL PLACES...?
hff
hff
smile
BECAUSE THE BACK COURTYARD IS WHERE PEOPLE TELL PEOPLE THEY LOVE THEM AND WANT TO GO OUT WITH THEM. WHY ELSE?
HEH?
IS THIS FOR REAL?
Heh? IS THIS FOR REAL?
IT'S FOR REAL!
B-BUT... YOU SAID THAT WAS STILL... SOMETIME SOON...
I THOUGHT IT WAS KINDA MEAN TO SAY THAT AND THEN LEAVE YOU HANGING, SO...
HEH ?!
LOOK, I KNOW IT WAS A BIG SURPRISE WHEN I CAME BACK SO COOL AND DREAMY.
AND AN EVEN BIGGER SURPRISE TO HAVE THE NEW ME SAY I WANT YOU TO BE MY GIRLFRIEND.

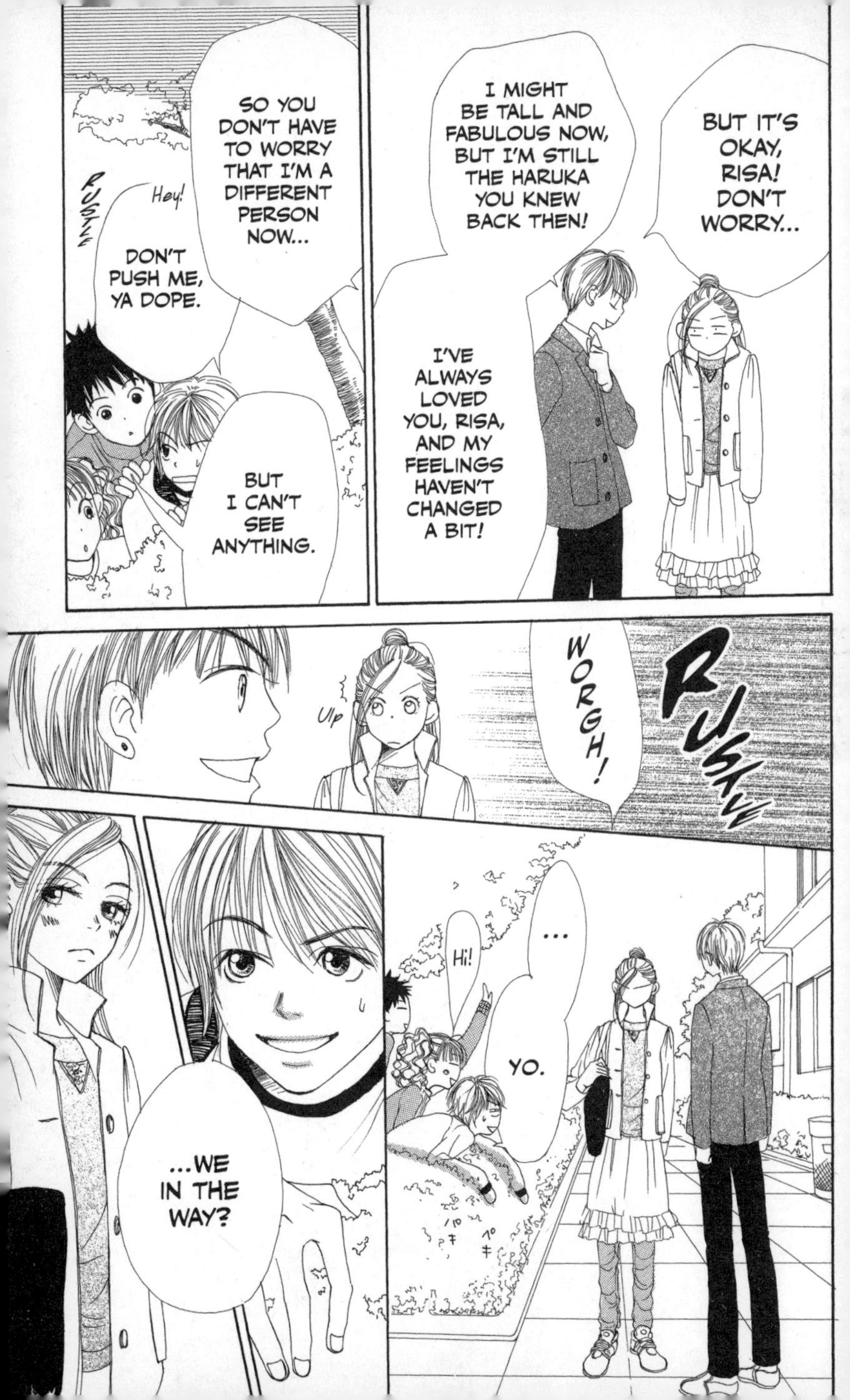
BUT IT'S OKAY, RISA! DON'T WORRY...
I MIGHT BE TALL AND FABULOUS NOW, BUT I'M STILL THE HARUKA YOU KNEW BACK THEN!
I'VE ALWAYS LOVED YOU, RISA, AND MY FEELINGS HAVEN'T CHANGED A BIT!
SO YOU DON'T HAVE TO WORRY THAT I'M A DIFFERENT PERSON NOW...
RUSTLE
Hey!
DON'T PUSH ME, YA DOPE.
BUT I CAN'T SEE ANYTHING.
WORGH!
Ulp
...
Hi!
YO.
...WE IN THE WAY?

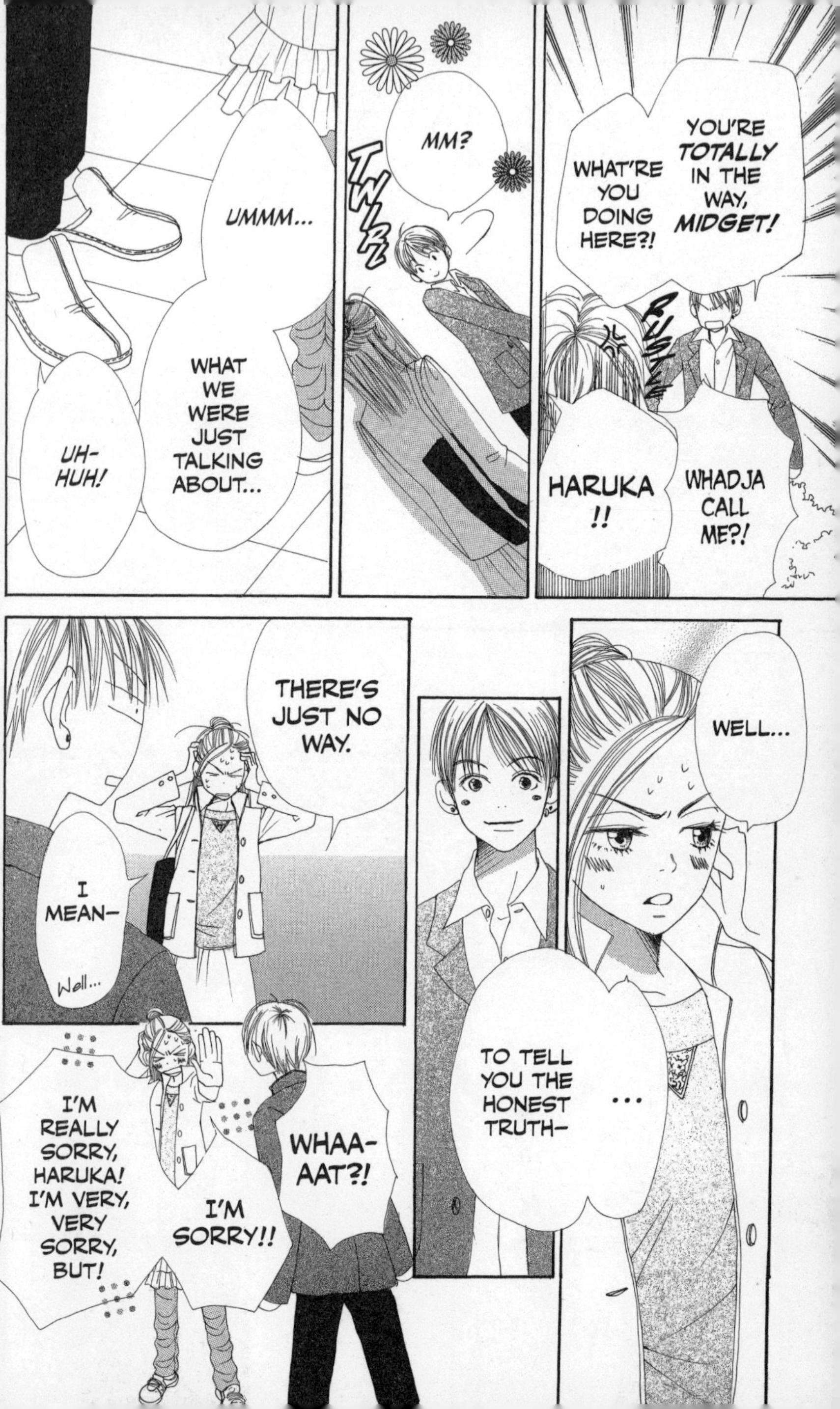
YOU'RE TOTALLY IN THE WAY, MIDGET!
WHAT'RE YOU DOING HERE?!
RUSTLE
WHADJA CALL ME?!
HARUKA !!
MM?
TWIRL
UMMM...
WHAT WE WERE JUST TALKING ABOUT...
UH-HUH!
WELL...
...
TO TELL YOU THE HONEST TRUTH-
THERE'S JUST NO WAY.
I MEAN-
Well...
WHAA-AAT?!
I'M SORRY!!
I'M REALLY SORRY, HARUKA! I'M VERY, VERY SORRY, BUT!

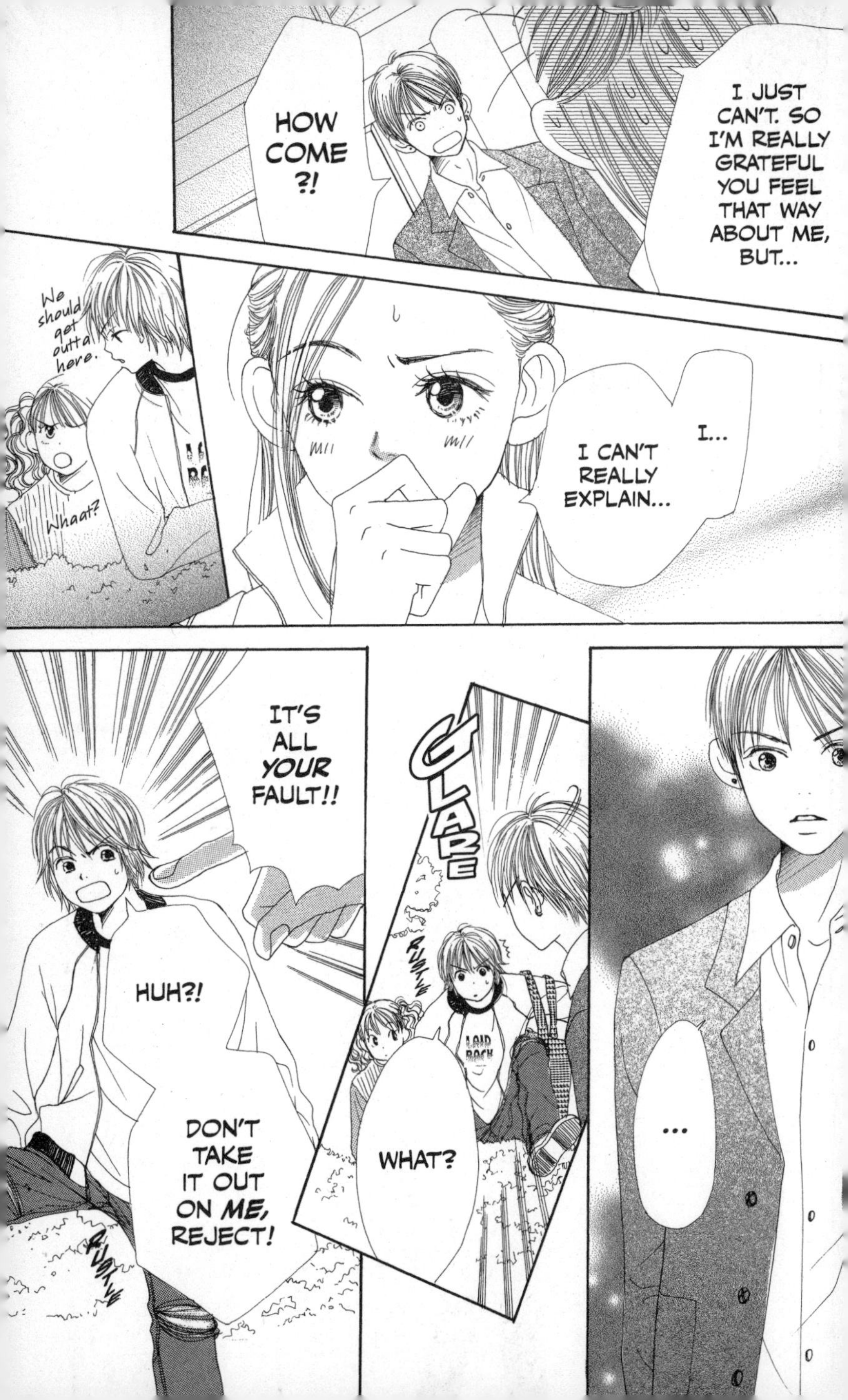
I JUST CAN'T. SO I'M REALLY GRATEFUL YOU FEEL THAT WAY ABOUT ME, BUT...
HOW COME ?!
I...
I CAN'T REALLY EXPLAIN...
We should get outta here.
Whaat?
...
GLARE
RUSTLE
WHAT?
IT'S ALL *YOUR* FAULT!!
HUH?!
DON'T TAKE IT OUT ON *ME*, REJECT!
RUSTLE

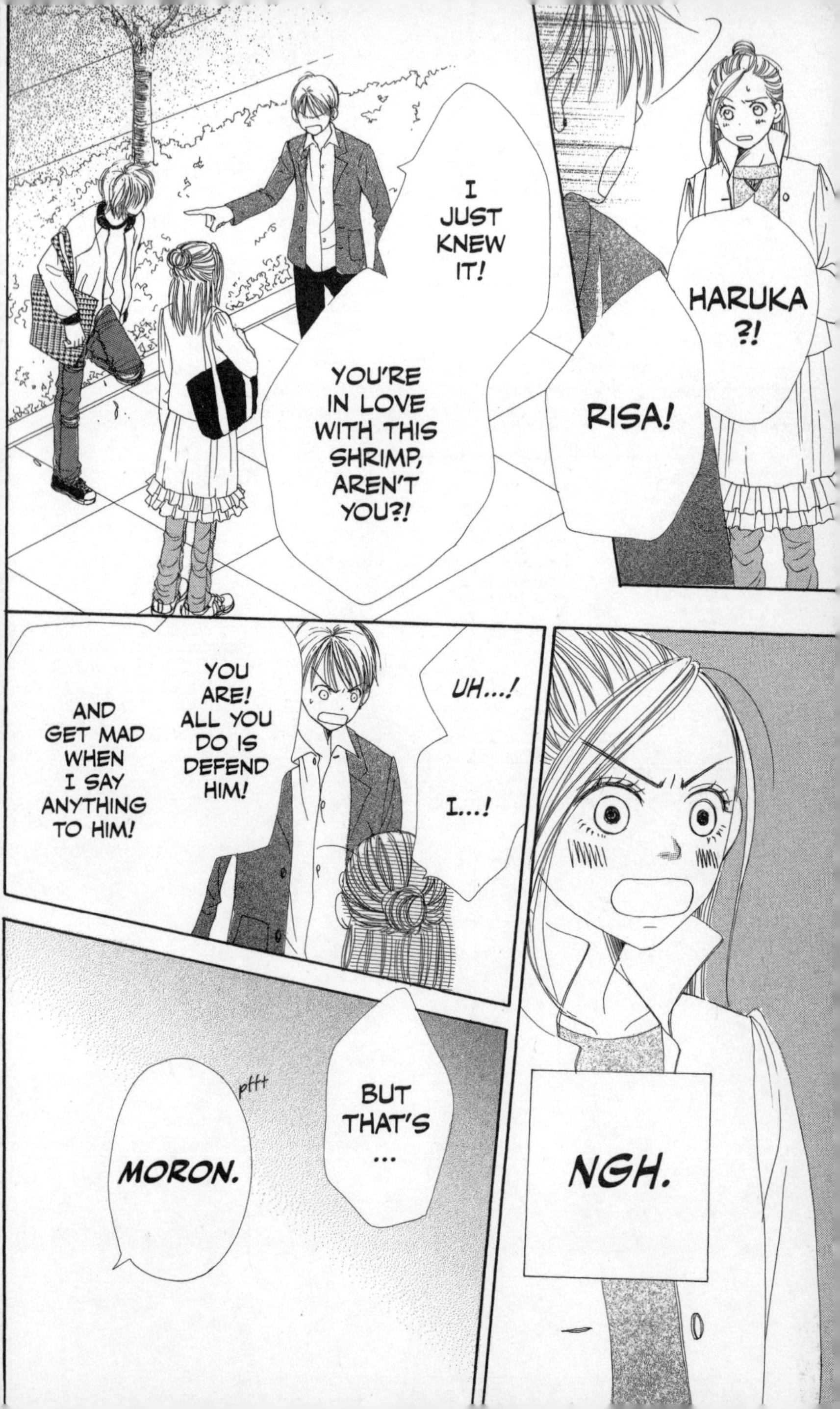
HARUKA ?!
RISA!
I JUST KNEW IT!
YOU'RE IN LOVE WITH THIS SHRIMP, AREN'T YOU?!
NGH.
UH...!
I...!
YOU ARE! ALL YOU DO IS DEFEND HIM!
AND GET MAD WHEN I SAY ANYTHING TO HIM!
BUT THAT'S ...
pfft
MORON.

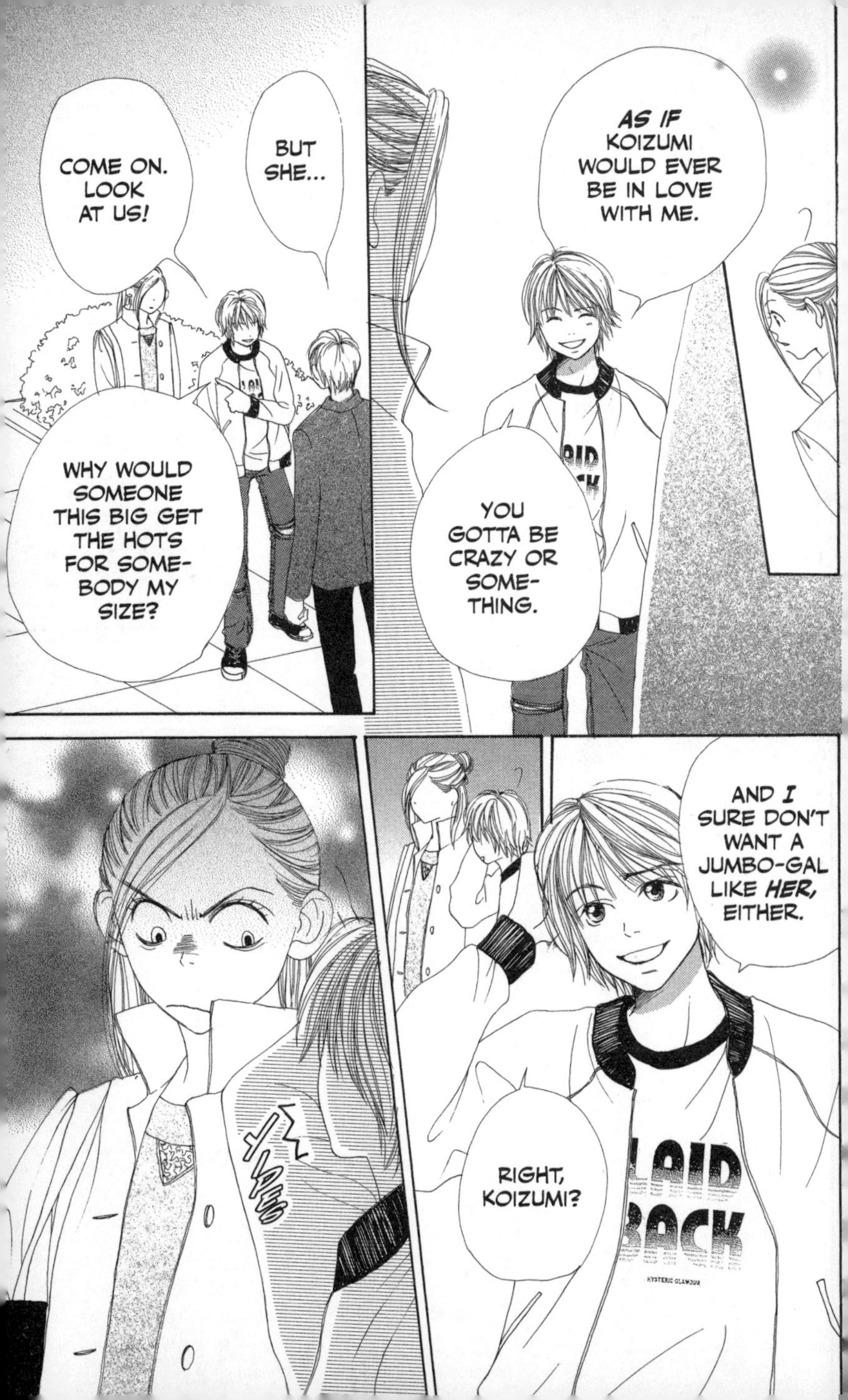

AS IF KOIZUMI WOULD EVER BE IN LOVE WITH ME.
YOU GOTTA BE CRAZY OR SOME-THING.
BUT SHE...
COME ON. LOOK AT US!
WHY WOULD SOMEONE THIS BIG GET THE HOTS FOR SOME-BODY MY SIZE?
AND *I* SURE DON'T WANT A JUMBO-GAL LIKE *HER*, EITHER.
RIGHT, KOIZUMI?

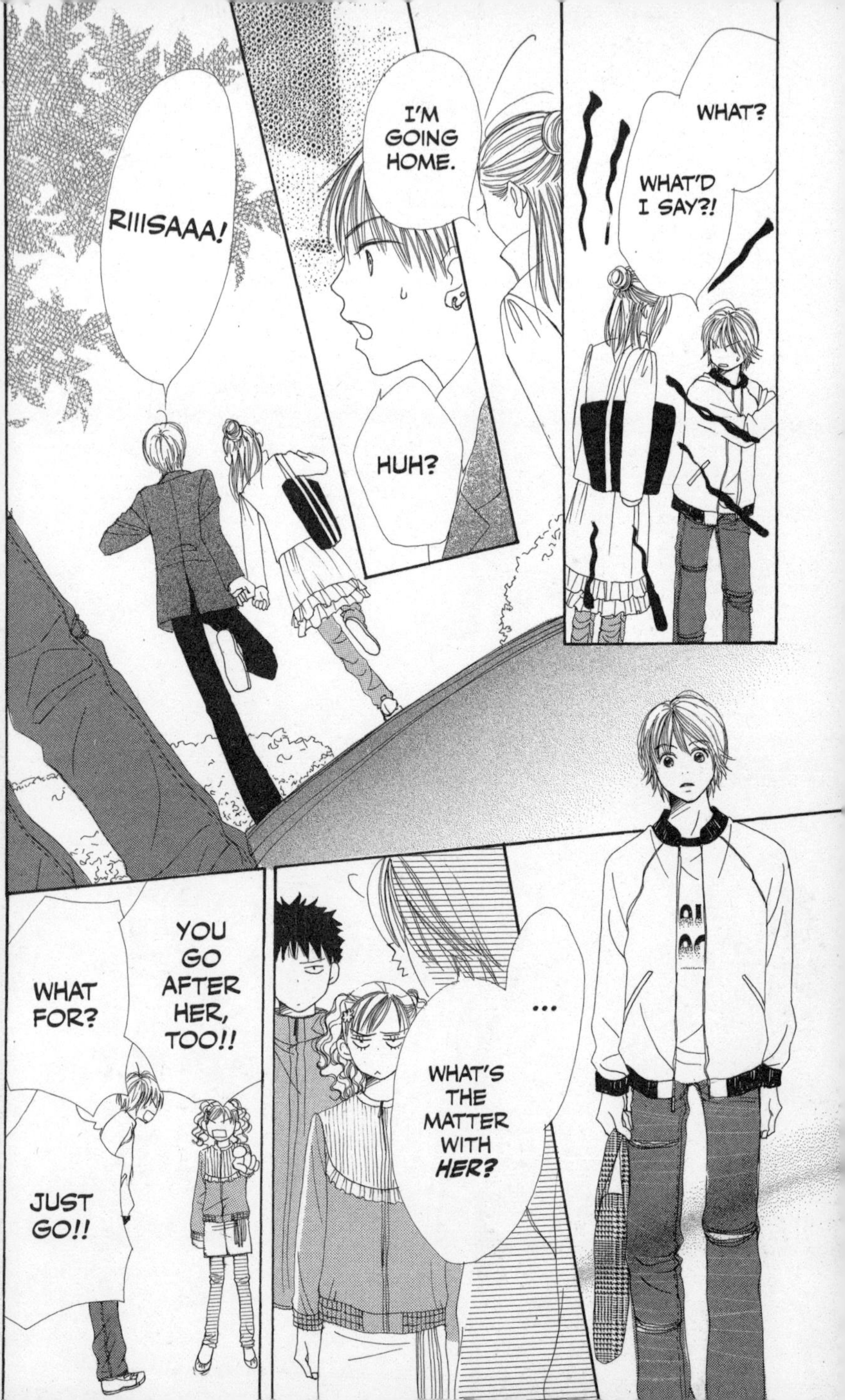
WHAT?
WHAT'D I SAY?!
I'M GOING HOME.
HUH?
RIIISAAA!
...
WHAT'S THE MATTER WITH *HER?*
YOU GO AFTER HER, TOO!!
WHAT FOR?
JUST GO!!

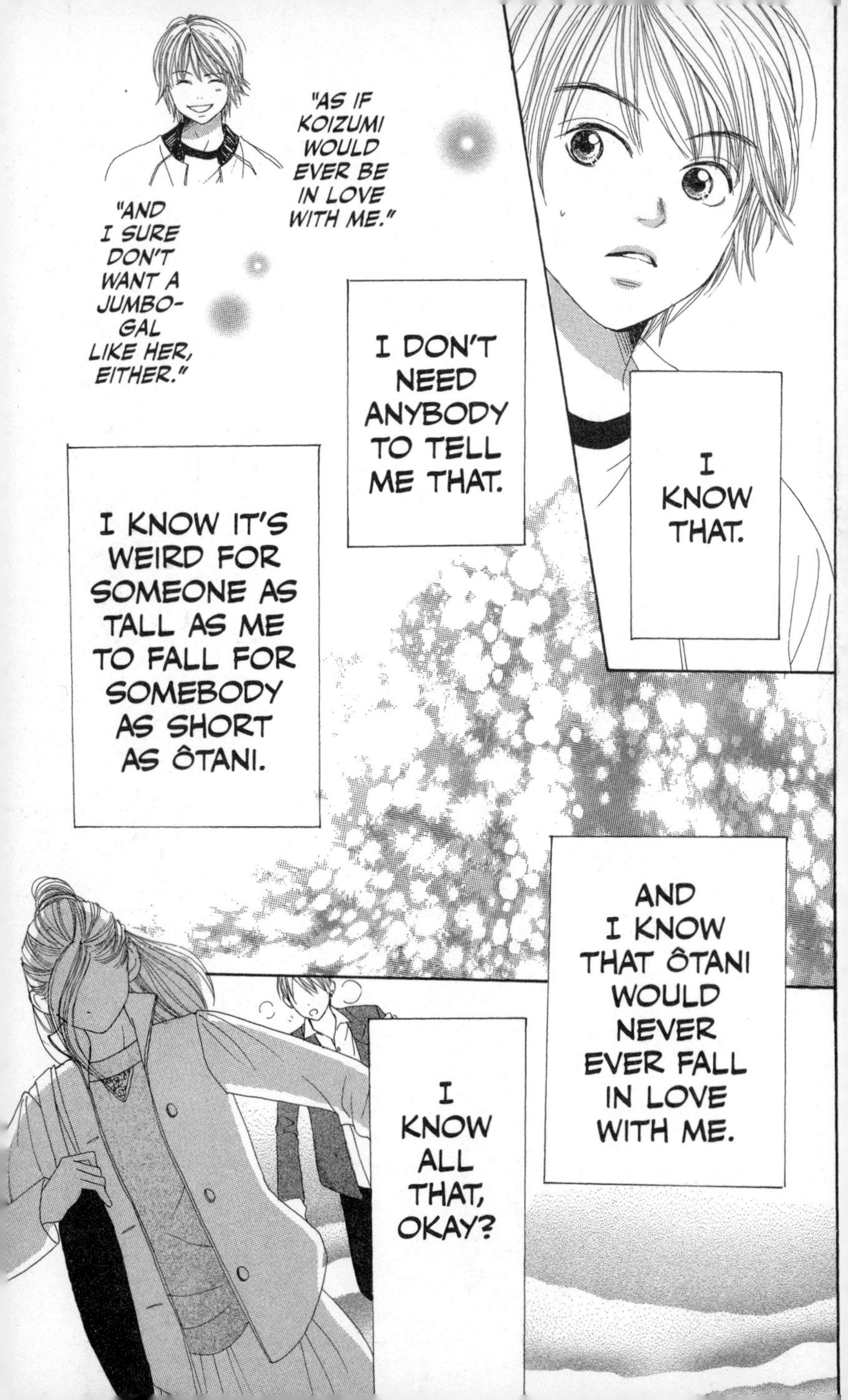
I KNOW THAT.
I DON'T NEED ANYBODY TO TELL ME THAT.
"AS IF KOIZUMI WOULD EVER BE IN LOVE WITH ME."
"AND I SURE DON'T WANT A JUMBO-GAL LIKE HER, EITHER."
I KNOW IT'S WEIRD FOR SOMEONE AS TALL AS ME TO FALL FOR SOMEBODY AS SHORT AS ÔTANI.
AND I KNOW THAT ÔTANI WOULD NEVER EVER FALL IN LOVE WITH ME.
I KNOW ALL THAT, OKAY?

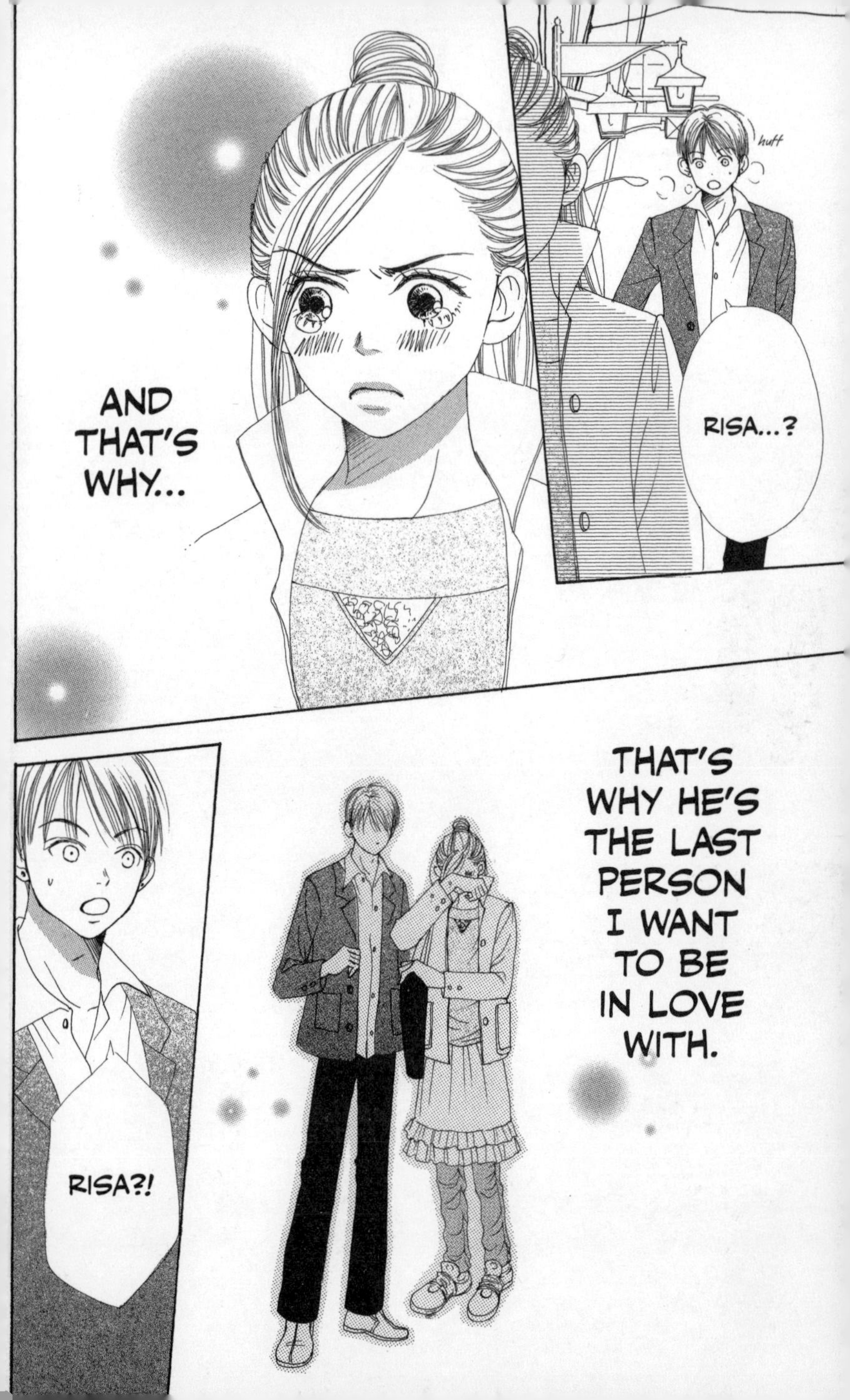
huff
RISA...?
AND THAT'S WHY...
THAT'S WHY HE'S THE LAST PERSON I WANT TO BE IN LOVE WITH.
RISA?!

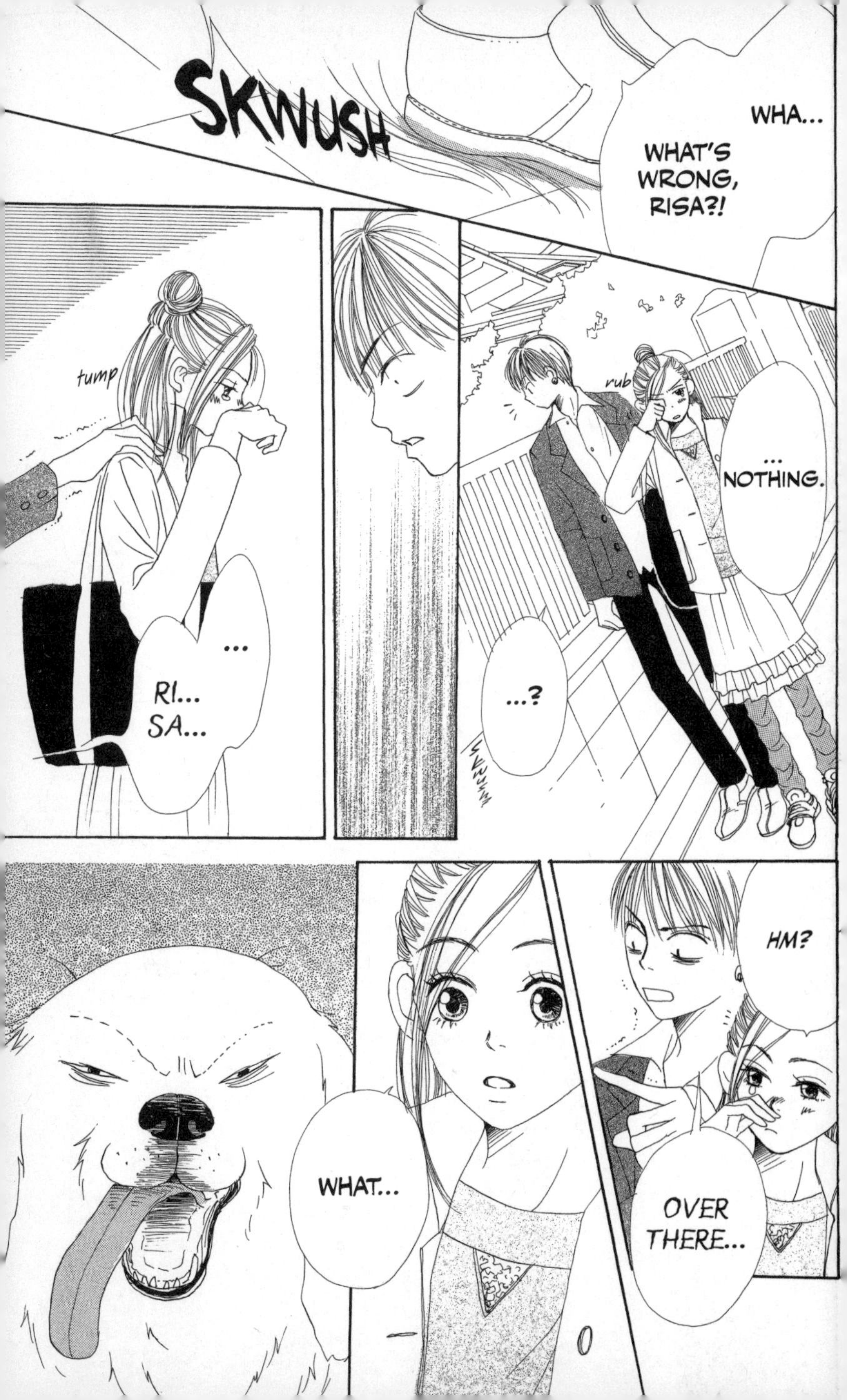
WHA...
WHAT'S WRONG, RISA?!
SKWUSH
rub
... NOTHING.
...?
tump
... RI... SA...
HM?
OVER THERE...
WHAT...

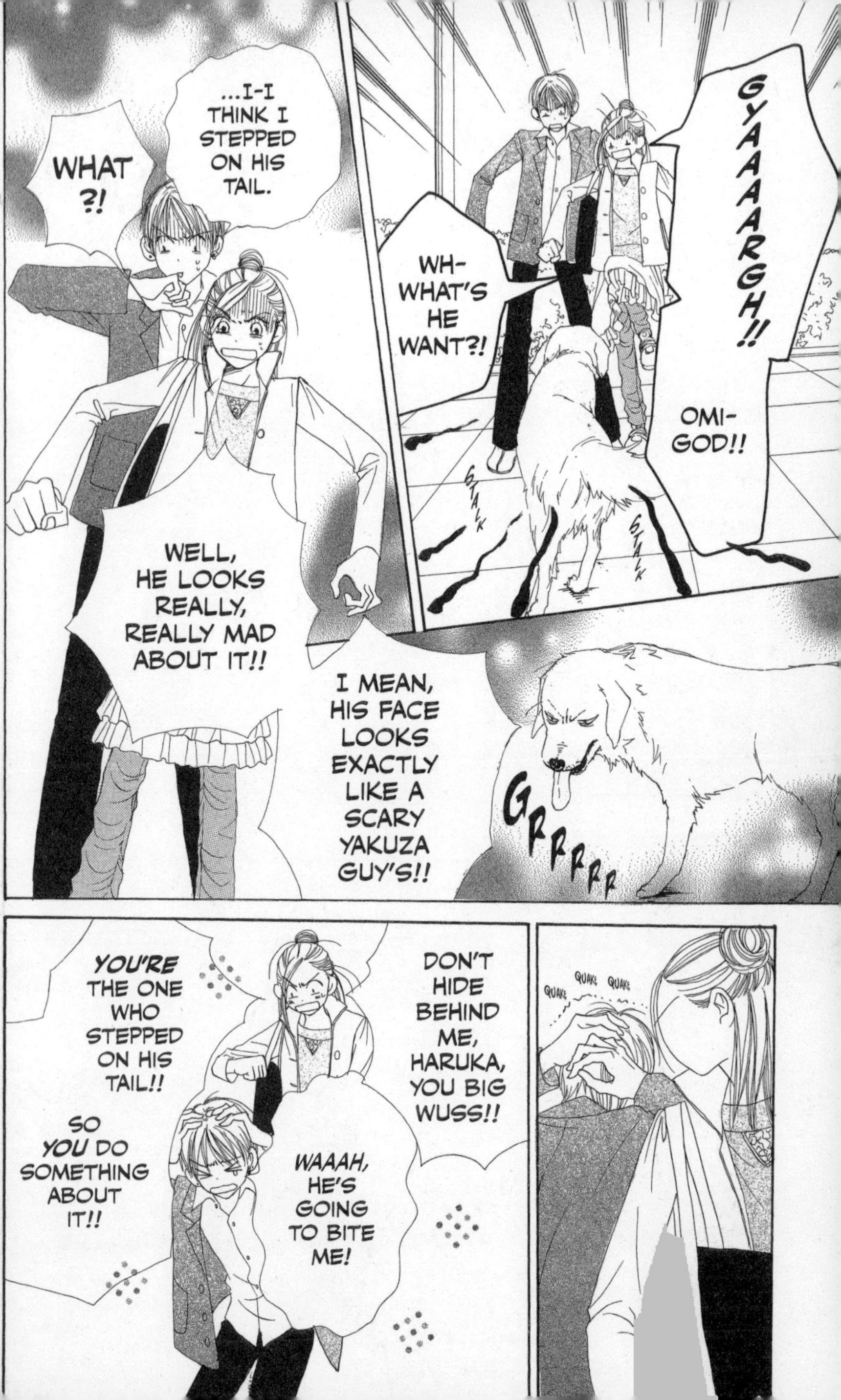
GYAAAARGH!!
OMI-GOD!!
WH-WHAT'S HE WANT?!
STALK
STALK
...I-I THINK I STEPPED ON HIS TAIL.
WHAT?!
WELL, HE LOOKS REALLY, REALLY MAD ABOUT IT!!
I MEAN, HIS FACE LOOKS EXACTLY LIKE A SCARY YAKUZA GUY'S!!
GRRRRR
QUAKE QUAKE QUAKE
DON'T HIDE BEHIND ME, HARUKA, YOU BIG WUSS!!
WAAAH, HE'S GOING TO BITE ME!
YOU'RE THE ONE WHO STEPPED ON HIS TAIL!!
SO *YOU* DO SOMETHING ABOUT IT!!

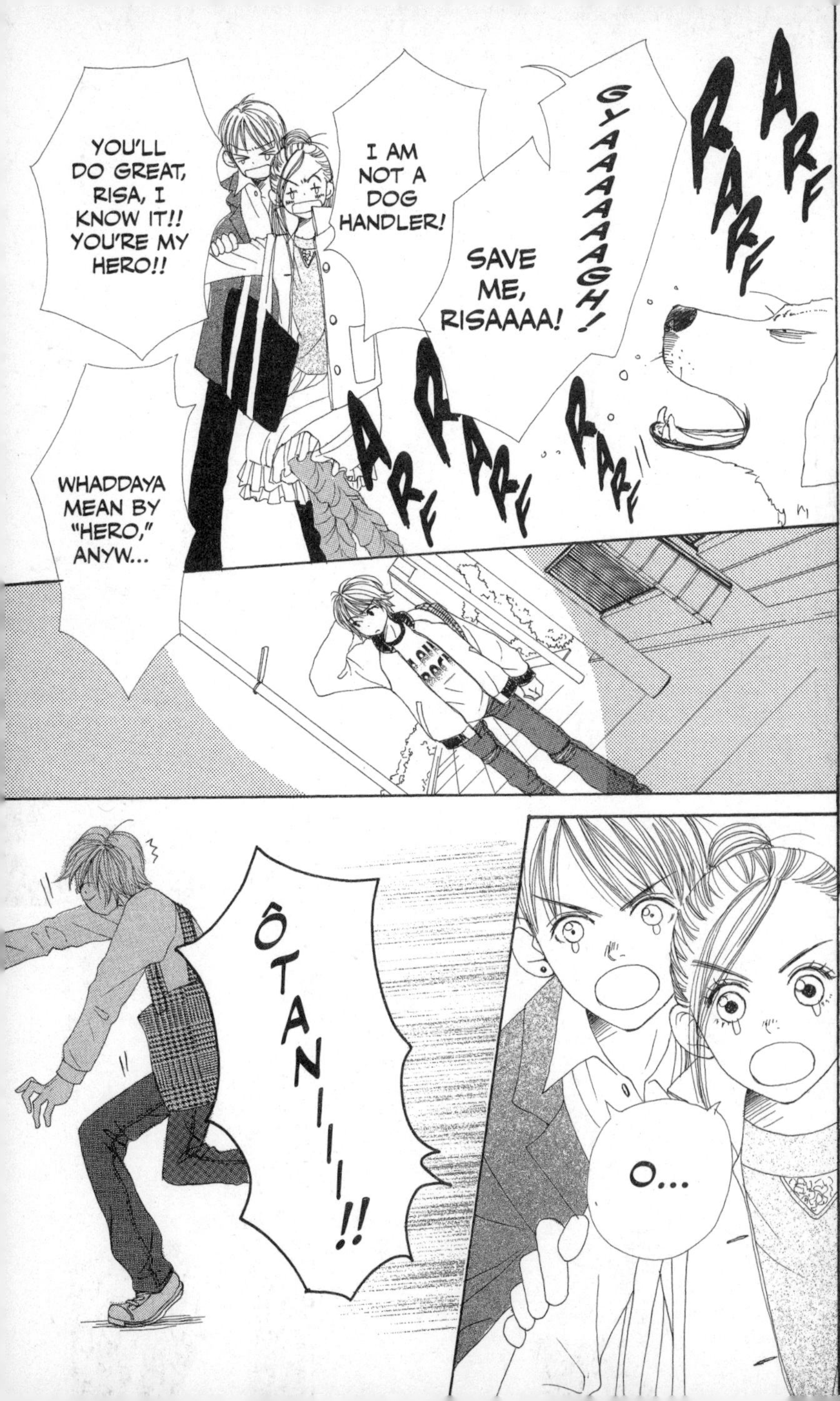
RARF RARF
GYAAAAAAAGH!
SAVE ME, RISAAAA!
RARF RARF RARF
I AM NOT A DOG HANDLER!
YOU'LL DO GREAT, RISA, I KNOW IT!! YOU'RE MY HERO!!
WHADDAYA MEAN BY "HERO," ANYW...
O...
ÔTANIII!!

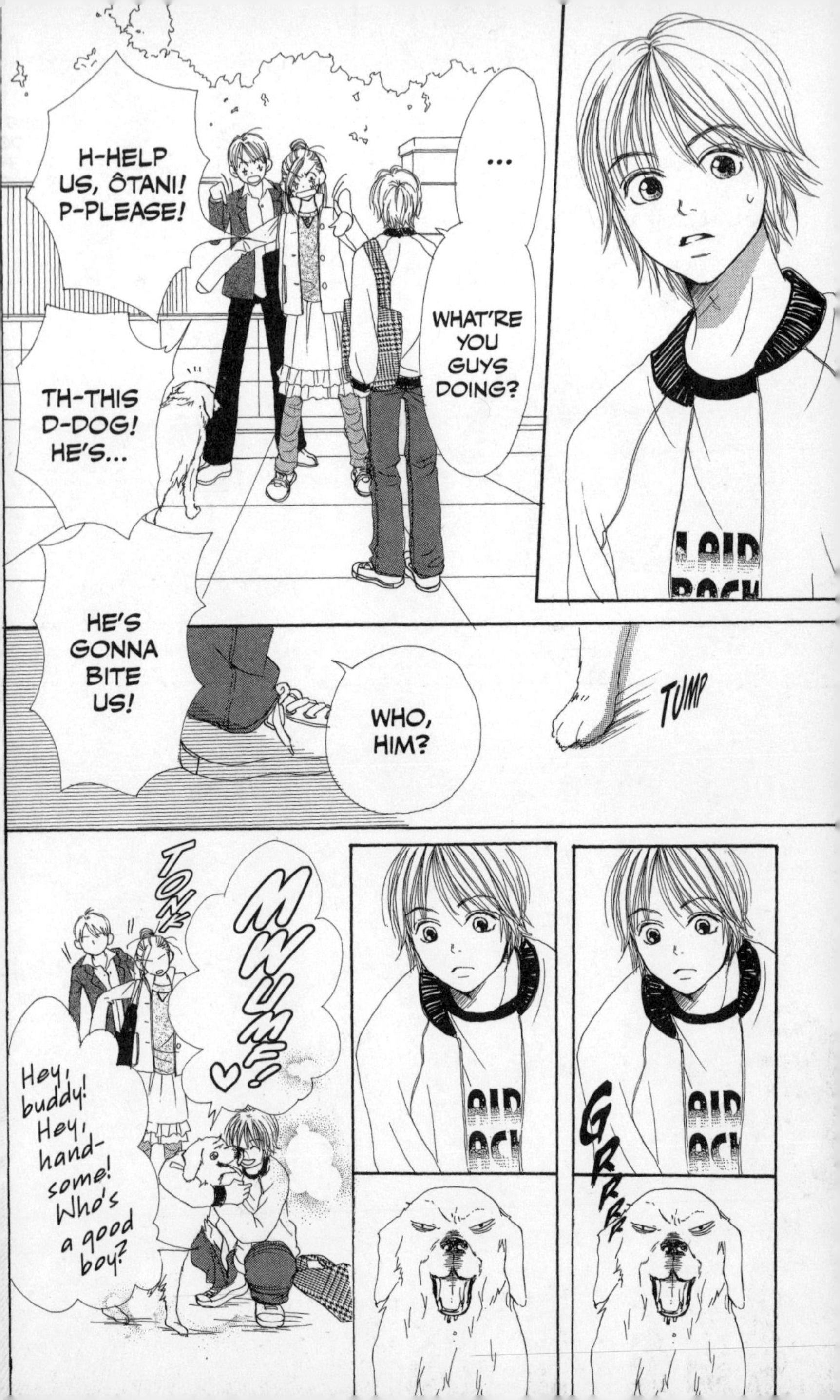
...
WHAT'RE YOU GUYS DOING?
H-HELP US, ÔTANI! P-PLEASE!
TH-THIS D-DOG! HE'S...
HE'S GONNA BITE US!
TUMP
WHO, HIM?
GRRR
TONY
MWUMF! ♥
Hey, buddy! Hey, handsome! Who's a good boy?

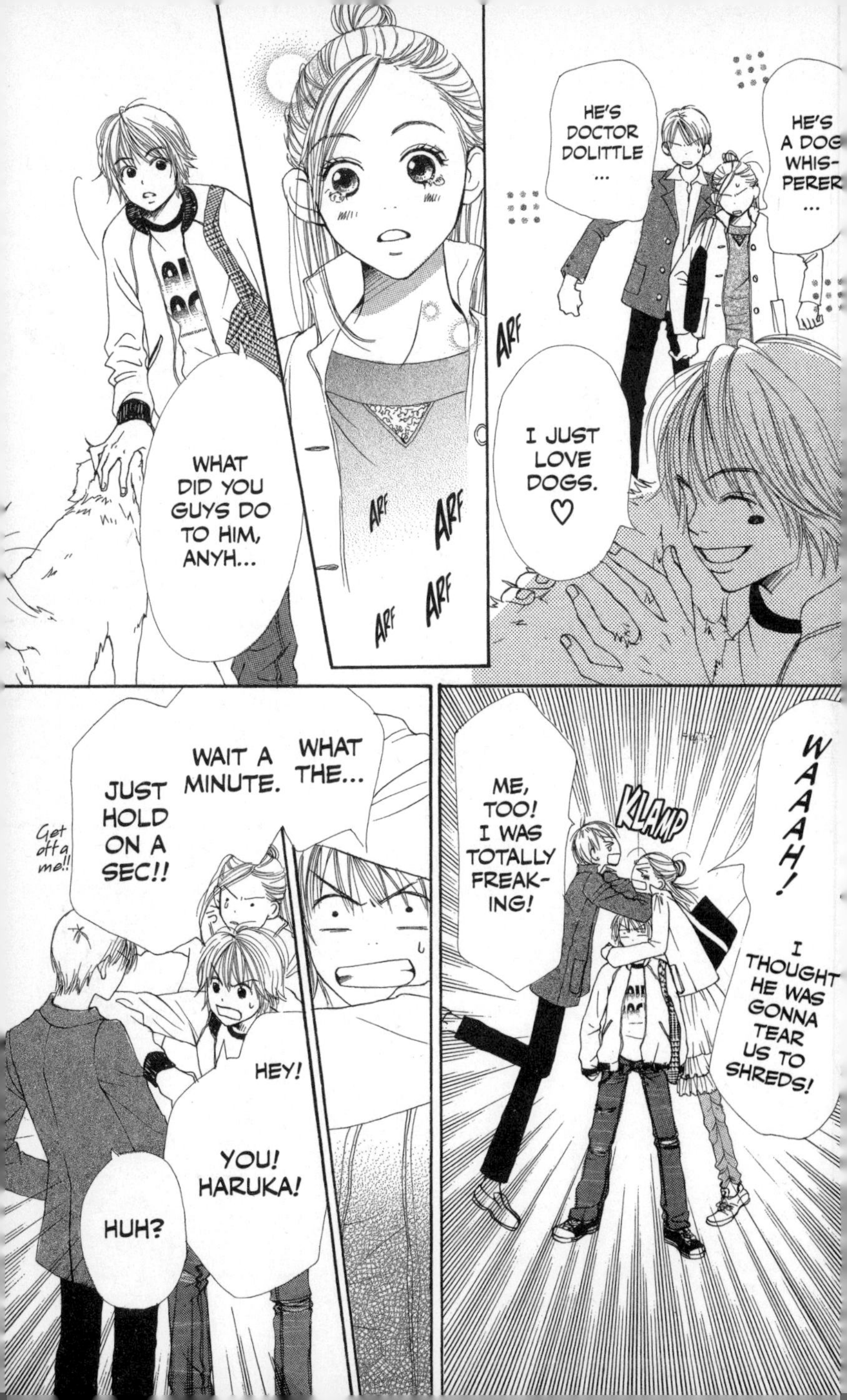
HE'S A DOG WHIS-PERER...
HE'S DOCTOR DOLITTLE...
ARF
I JUST LOVE DOGS. ♡
ARF
ARF
ARF
ARF
WHAT DID YOU GUYS DO TO HIM, ANYH...
WAAAAH!
KLAMP
ME, TOO! I WAS TOTALLY FREAK-ING!
I THOUGHT HE WAS GONNA TEAR US TO SHREDS!
WHAT THE...
WAIT A MINUTE.
JUST HOLD ON A SEC!!
Get offa me!!
HEY!
YOU! HARUKA!
HUH?

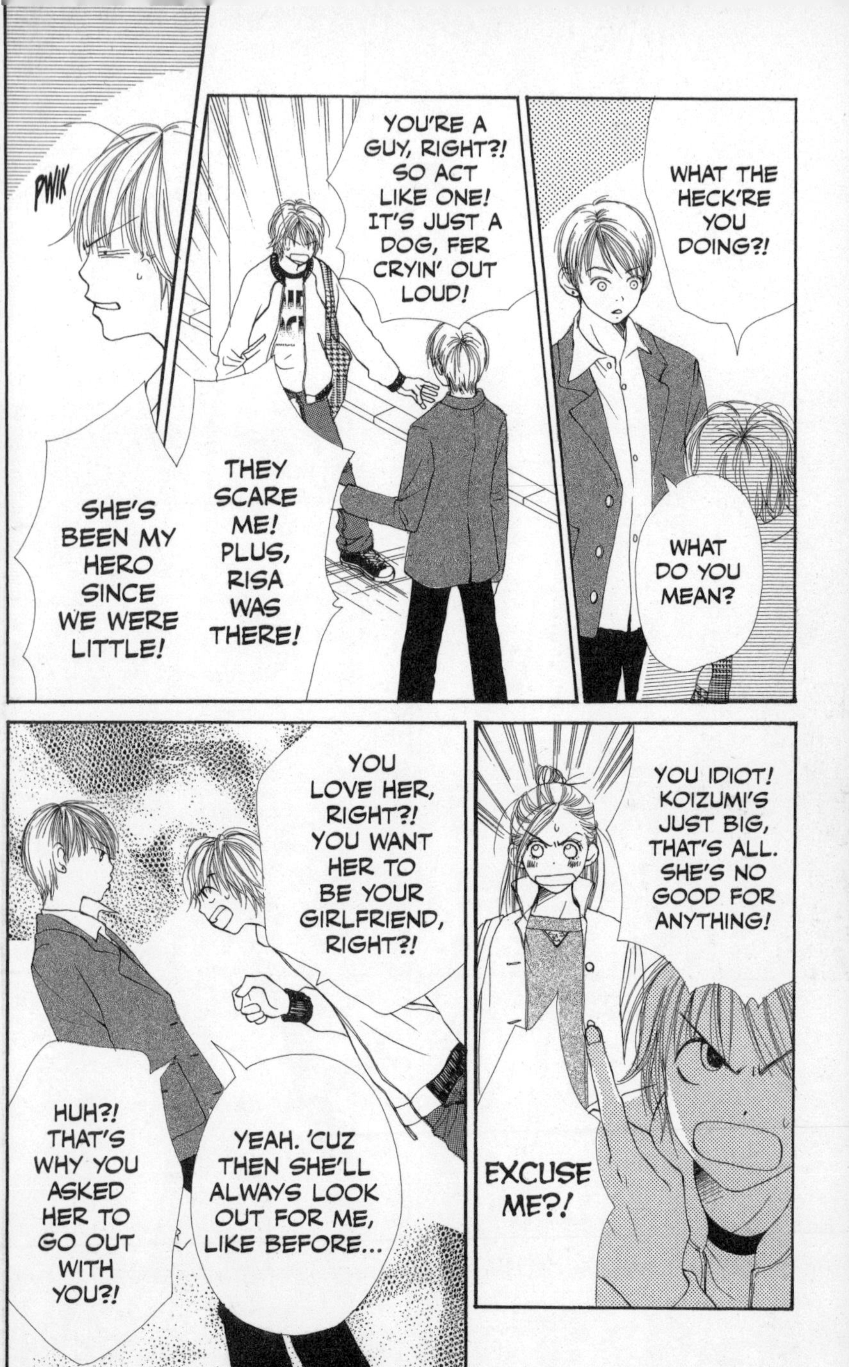
WHAT THE HECK'RE YOU DOING?!
WHAT DO YOU MEAN?
YOU'RE A GUY, RIGHT?! SO ACT LIKE ONE! IT'S JUST A DOG, FER CRYIN' OUT LOUD!
THEY SCARE ME! PLUS, RISA WAS THERE!
PWIK
SHE'S BEEN MY HERO SINCE WE WERE LITTLE!
YOU IDIOT! KOIZUMI'S JUST BIG, THAT'S ALL. SHE'S NO GOOD FOR ANYTHING!
EXCUSE ME?!
YOU LOVE HER, RIGHT?! YOU WANT HER TO BE YOUR GIRLFRIEND, RIGHT?!
HUH?! THAT'S WHY YOU ASKED HER TO GO OUT WITH YOU?!
YEAH. 'CUZ THEN SHE'LL ALWAYS LOOK OUT FOR ME, LIKE BEFORE...

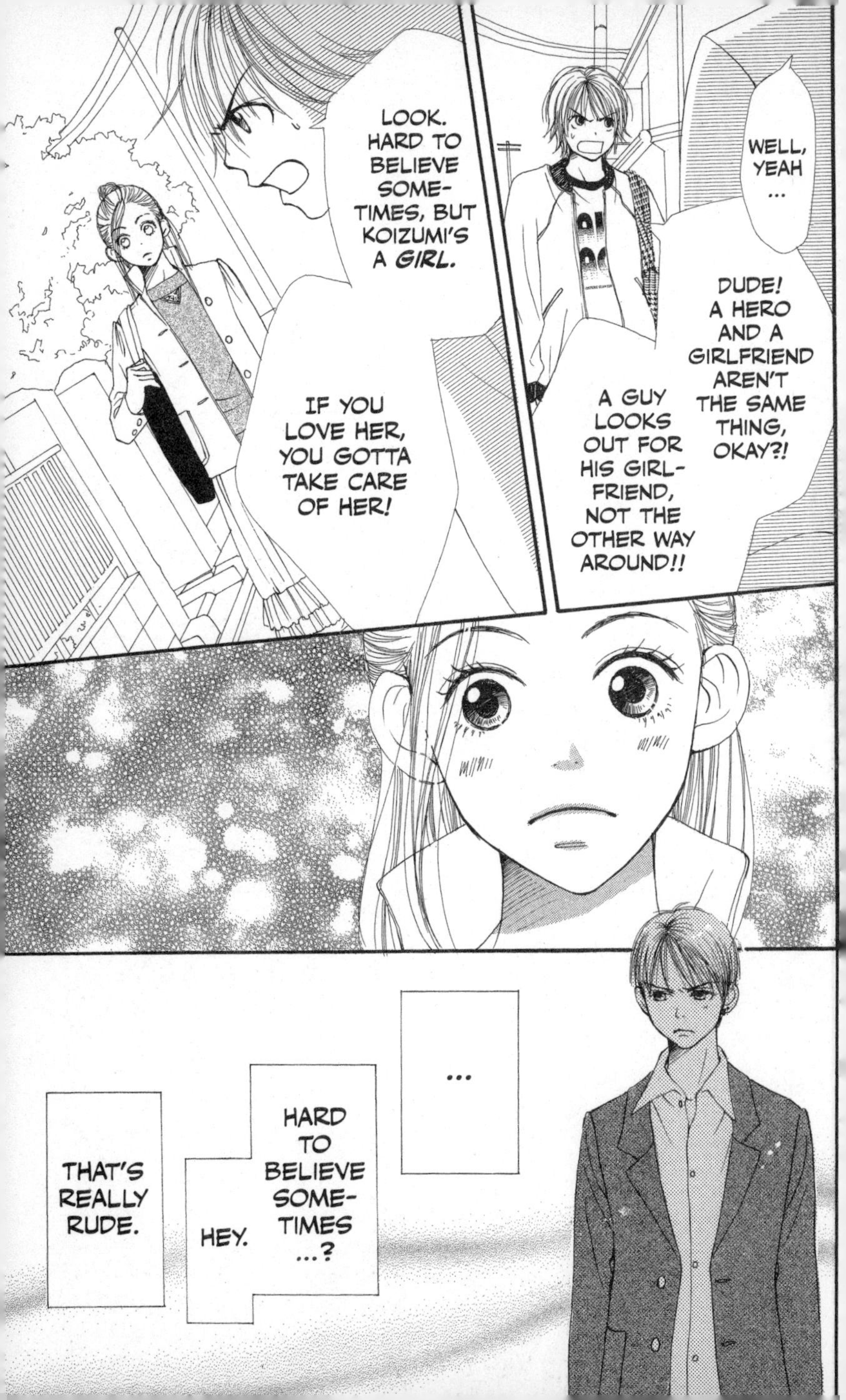

WELL, YEAH...
DUDE! A HERO AND A GIRLFRIEND AREN'T THE SAME THING, OKAY?!
A GUY LOOKS OUT FOR HIS GIRLFRIEND, NOT THE OTHER WAY AROUND!!
LOOK. HARD TO BELIEVE SOMETIMES, BUT KOIZUMI'S A *GIRL*.
IF YOU LOVE HER, YOU GOTTA TAKE CARE OF HER!
...
HARD TO BELIEVE SOMETIMES...?
HEY.
THAT'S REALLY RUDE.

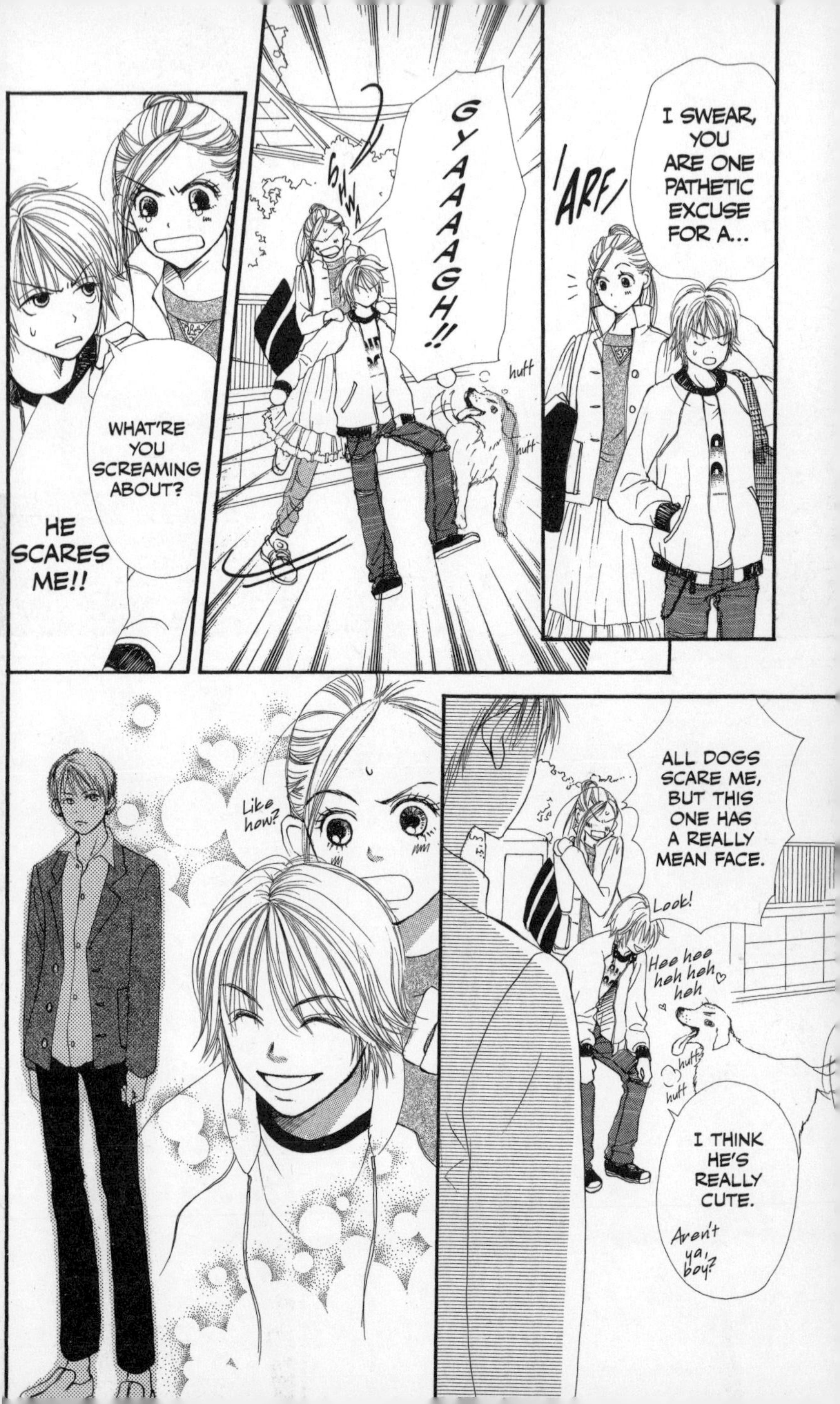
I SWEAR, YOU ARE ONE PATHETIC EXCUSE FOR A...
ARF!
GYAAAAAGH!!
huff
huff
WHAT'RE YOU SCREAMING ABOUT?
HE SCARES ME!!
ALL DOGS SCARE ME, BUT THIS ONE HAS A REALLY MEAN FACE.
Look!
Hee hee heh heh heh
huff
huff
I THINK HE'S REALLY CUTE.
Aren't ya, boy?
Like how?

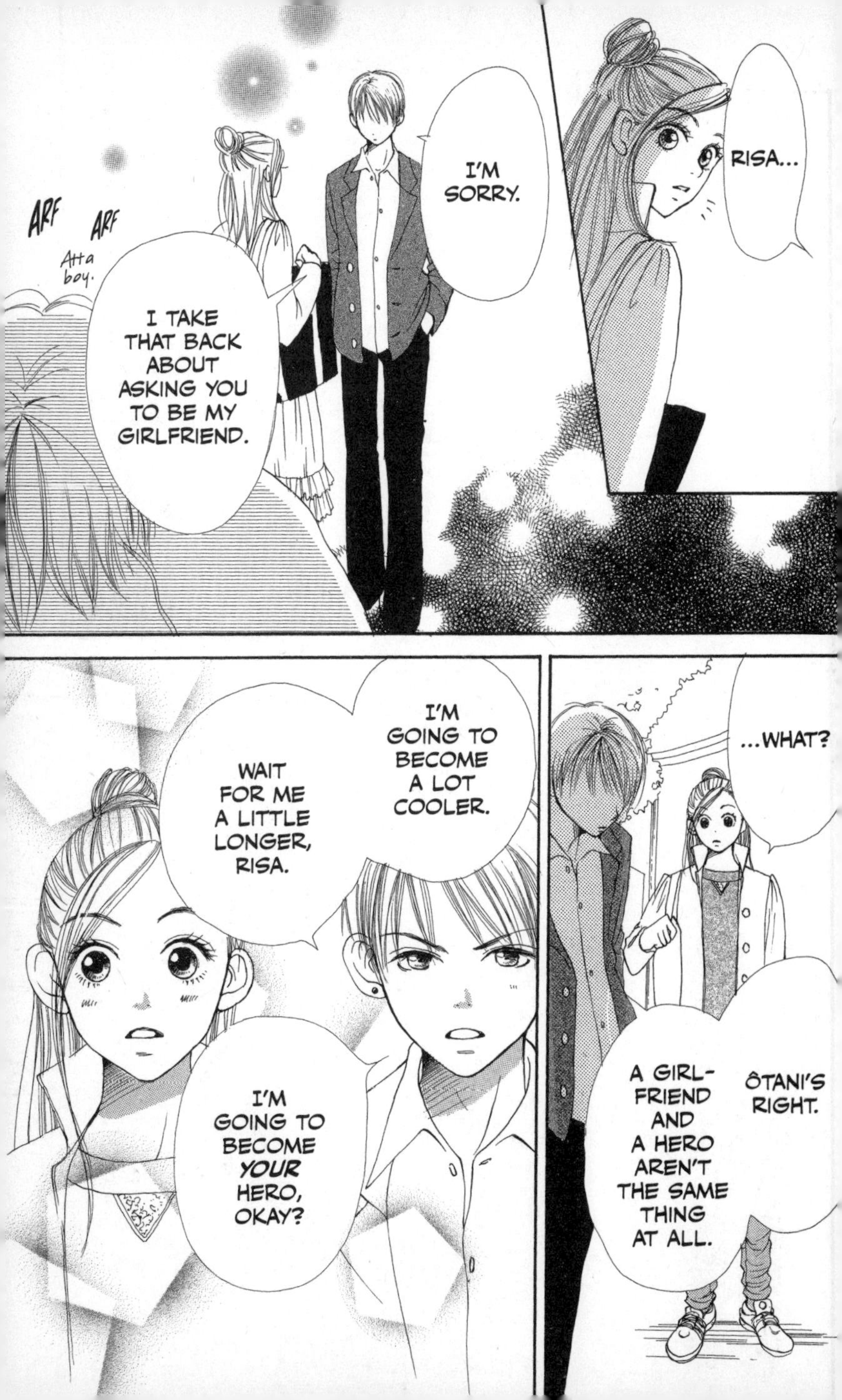

RISA...
I'M SORRY.
ARF
ARF
Atta boy.
I TAKE THAT BACK ABOUT ASKING YOU TO BE MY GIRLFRIEND.
...WHAT?
ŌTANI'S RIGHT.
A GIRL-FRIEND AND A HERO AREN'T THE SAME THING AT ALL.
I'M GOING TO BECOME A LOT COOLER.
WAIT FOR ME A LITTLE LONGER, RISA.
I'M GOING TO BECOME *YOUR* HERO, OKAY?

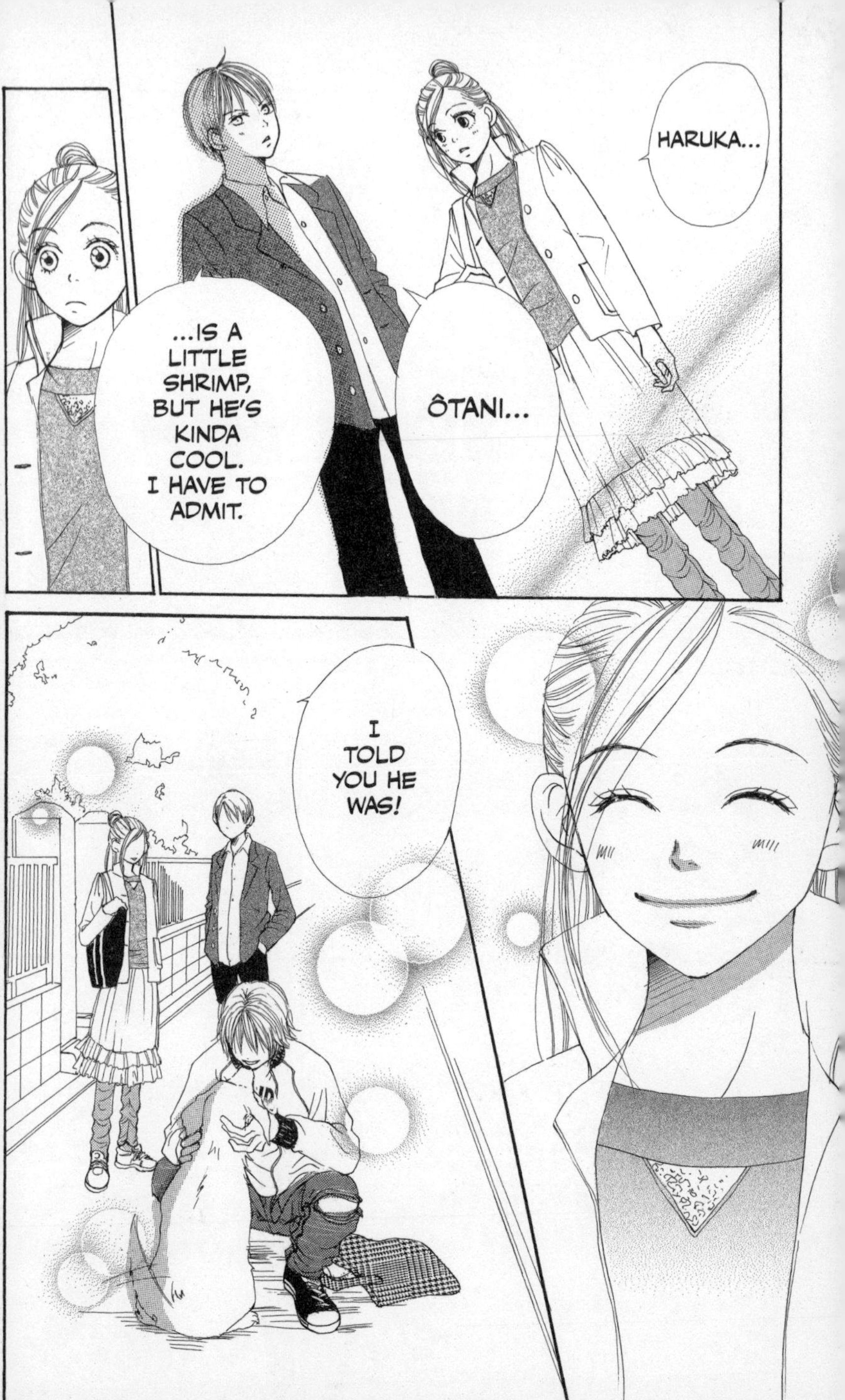
HARUKA...
ÔTANI...
...IS A LITTLE SHRIMP, BUT HE'S KINDA COOL. I HAVE TO ADMIT.
I TOLD YOU HE WAS!

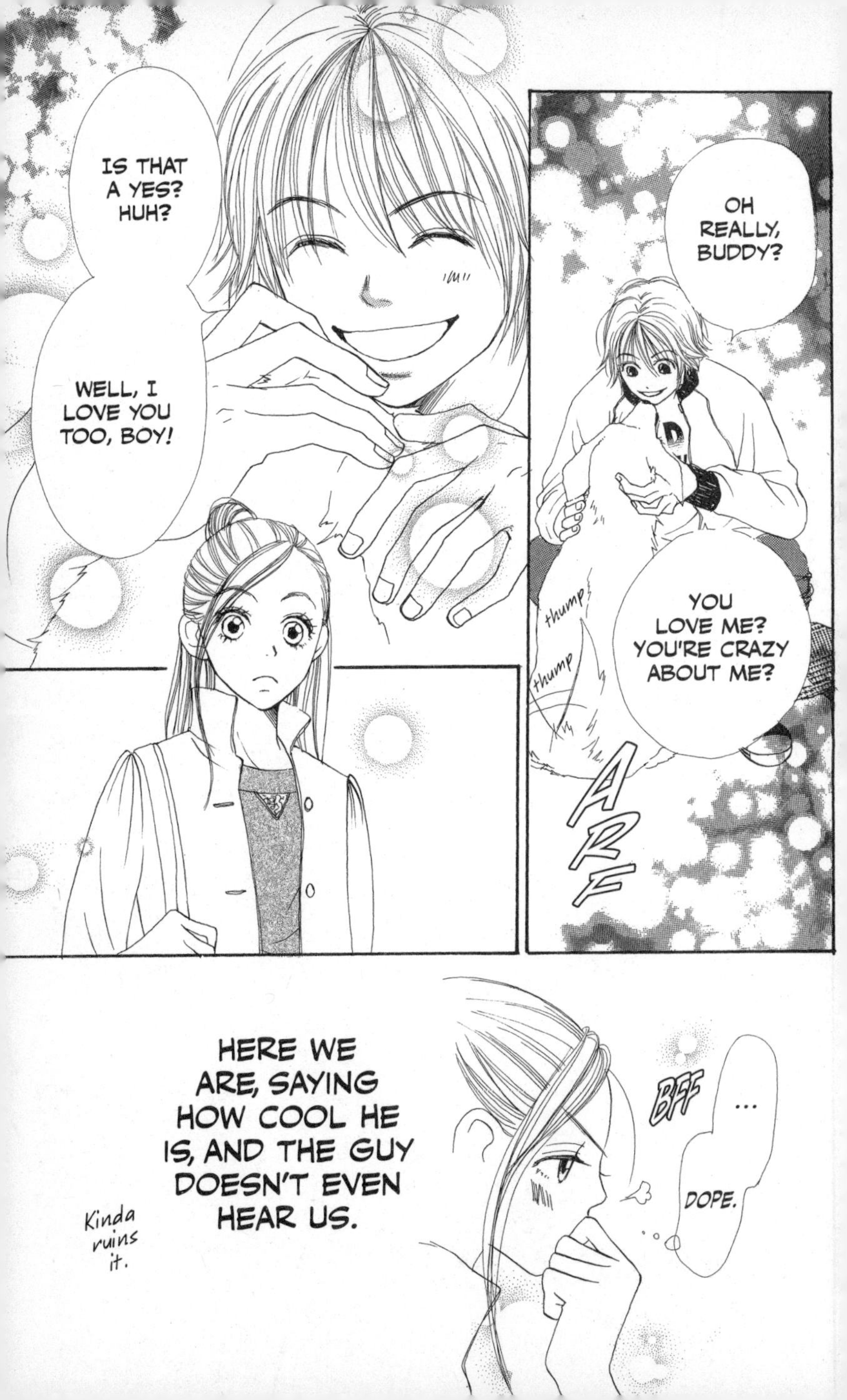
OH REALLY, BUDDY?
YOU LOVE ME? YOU'RE CRAZY ABOUT ME?
thump
thump
ARF
IS THAT A YES? HUH?
WELL, I LOVE YOU TOO, BOY!
BFF
...
DOPE.
HERE WE ARE, SAYING HOW COOL HE IS, AND THE GUY DOESN'T EVEN HEAR US.
Kinda ruins it.

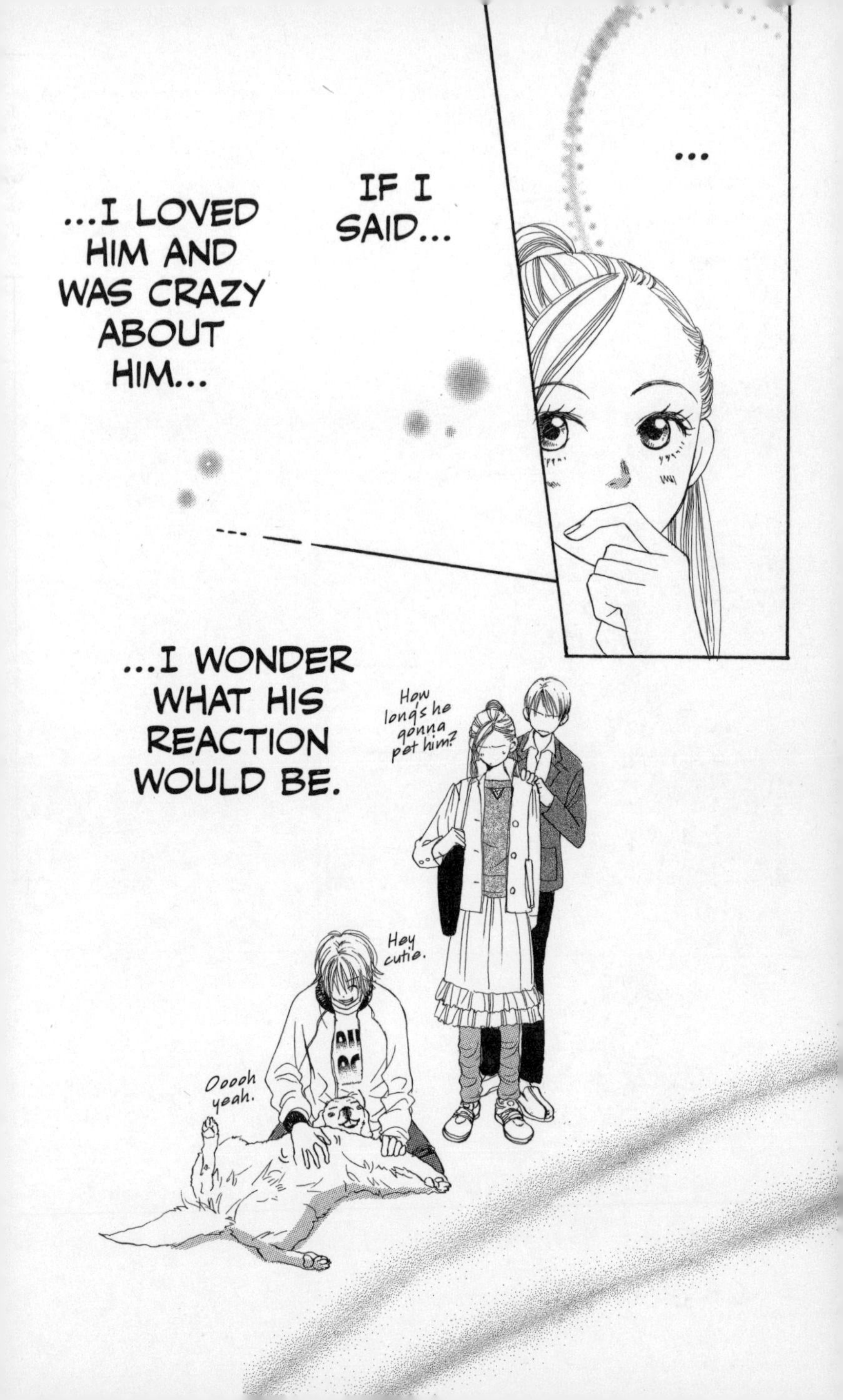
...
IF I SAID...
...I LOVED HIM AND WAS CRAZY ABOUT HIM...
...I WONDER WHAT HIS REACTION WOULD BE.
How long's he gonna pet him?
Hey cutie.
Ooooh yeah.

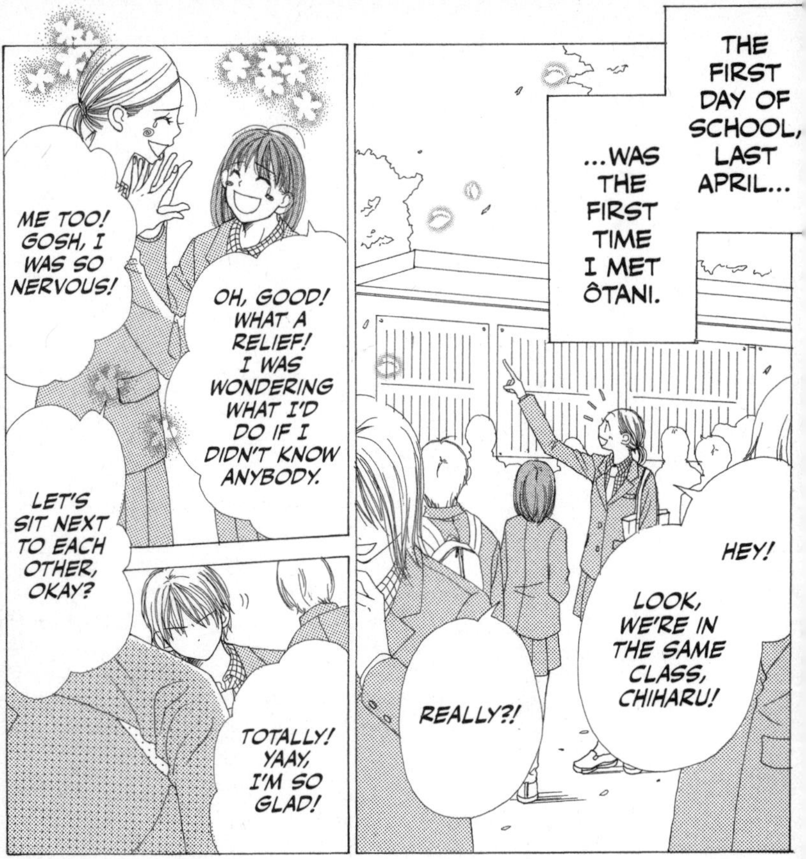
THE FIRST DAY OF SCHOOL, LAST APRIL...
...WAS THE FIRST TIME I MET ÔTANI.
HEY!
LOOK, WE'RE IN THE SAME CLASS, CHIHARU!
REALLY?!
OH, GOOD! WHAT A RELIEF! I WAS WONDERING WHAT I'D DO IF I DIDN'T KNOW ANYBODY.
ME TOO! GOSH, I WAS SO NERVOUS!
LET'S SIT NEXT TO EACH OTHER, OKAY?
TOTALLY! YAAY, I'M SO GLAD!

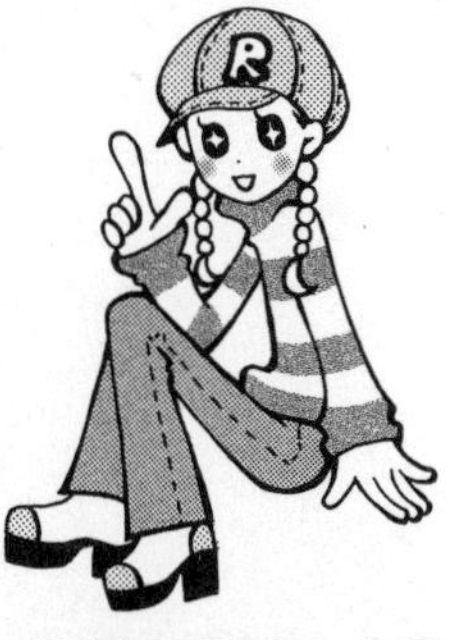

CHAPTER 10

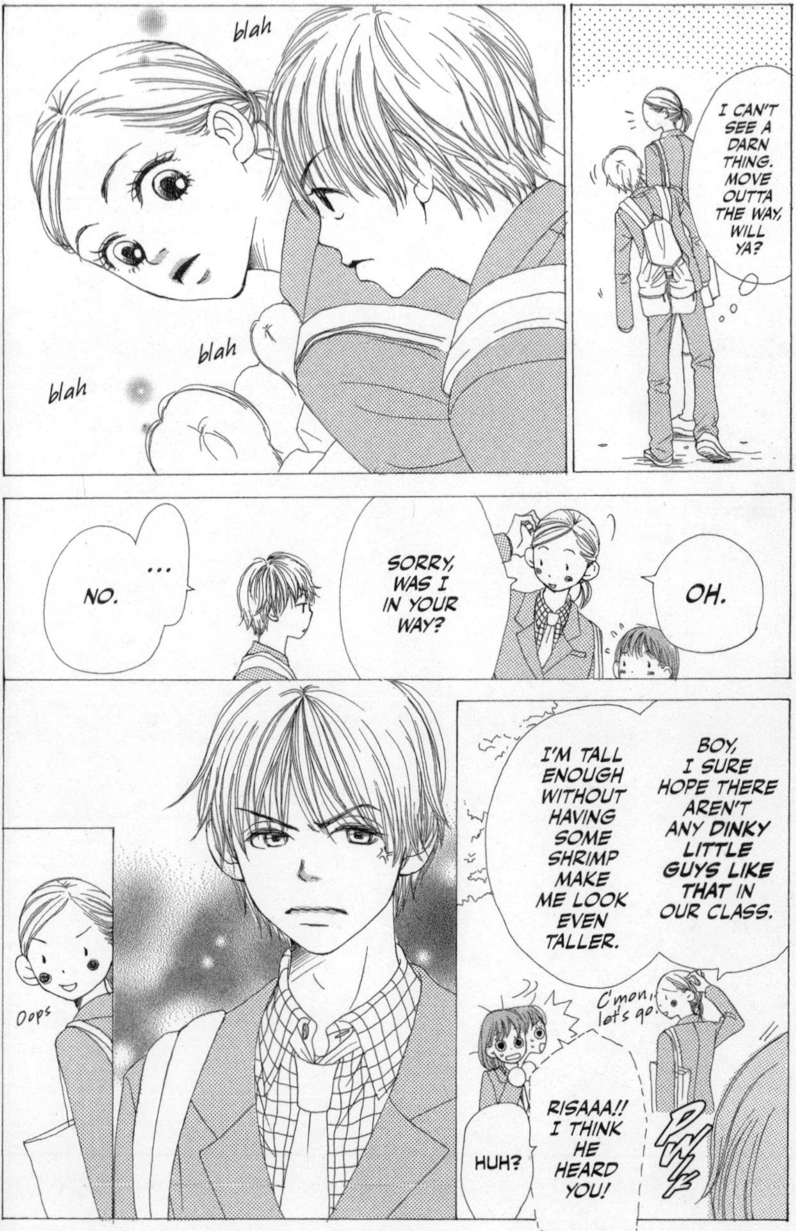
I CAN'T SEE A DARN THING. MOVE OUTTA THE WAY, WILL YA?
blah
blah
blah
OH.
SORRY, WAS I IN YOUR WAY?
... NO.
BOY, I SURE HOPE THERE AREN'T ANY DINKY LITTLE GUYS LIKE THAT IN OUR CLASS.
I'M TALL ENOUGH WITHOUT HAVING SOME SHRIMP MAKE ME LOOK EVEN TALLER.
C'mon, let's go.
RISAAA!! I THINK HE HEARD YOU!
HUH?
Oops

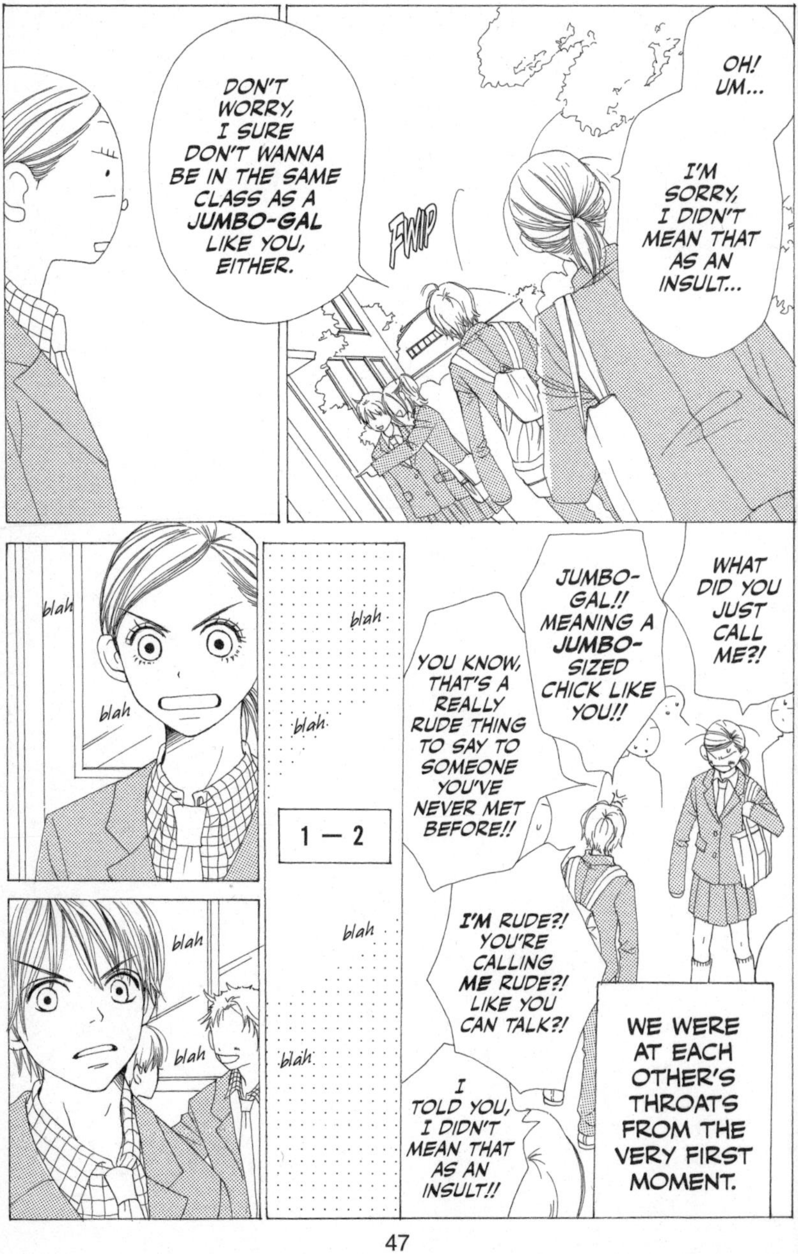
OH! UM...
I'M SORRY, I DIDN'T MEAN THAT AS AN INSULT...
FWIP
DON'T WORRY, I SURE DON'T WANNA BE IN THE SAME CLASS AS A JUMBO-GAL LIKE YOU, EITHER.
WHAT DID YOU JUST CALL ME?!
JUMBO-GAL!! MEANING A JUMBO-SIZED CHICK LIKE YOU!!
YOU KNOW, THAT'S A REALLY RUDE THING TO SAY TO SOMEONE YOU'VE NEVER MET BEFORE!!
I'M RUDE?! YOU'RE CALLING ME RUDE?! LIKE YOU CAN TALK?!
I TOLD YOU, I DIDN'T MEAN THAT AS AN INSULT!!
WE WERE AT EACH OTHER'S THROATS FROM THE VERY FIRST MOMENT.
blah
blah
1 — 2
blah
blah
blah
blah
blah
blah

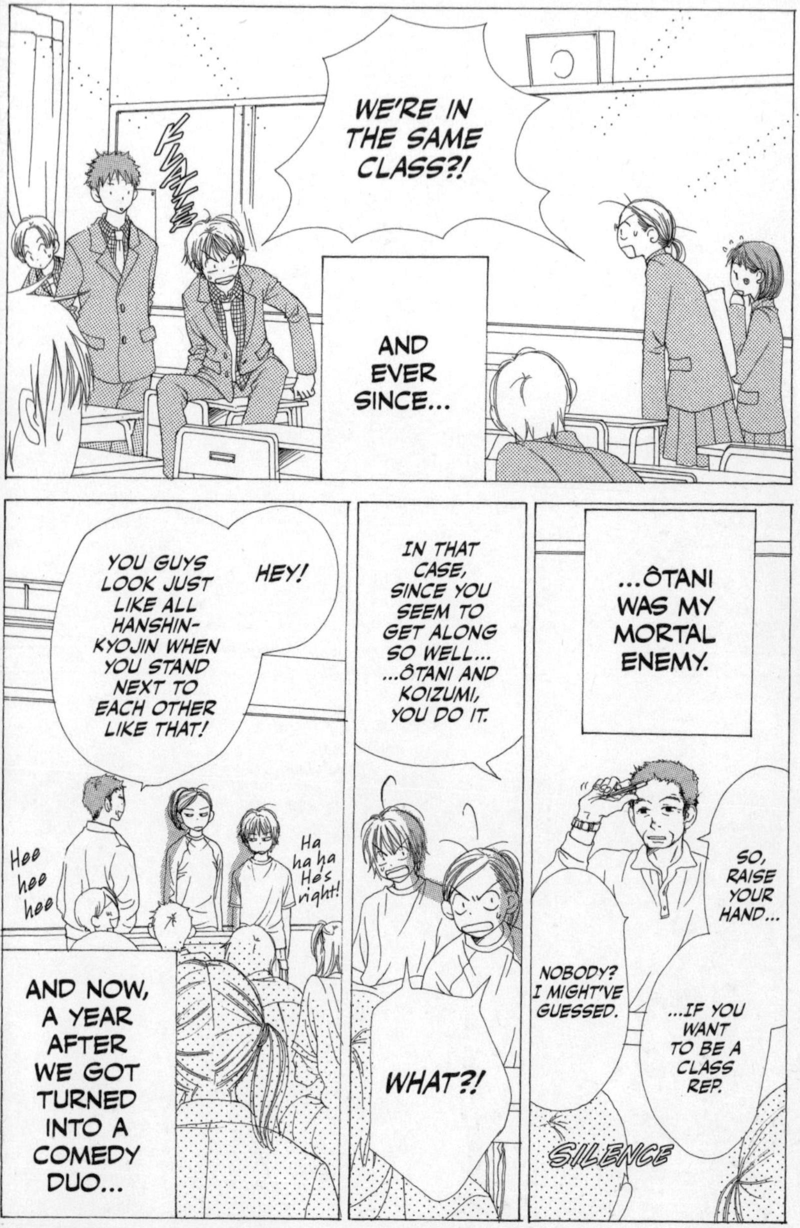

WE'RE IN THE SAME CLASS?!
AND EVER SINCE...
...ÔTANI WAS MY MORTAL ENEMY.
SO, RAISE YOUR HAND...
...IF YOU WANT TO BE A CLASS REP.
NOBODY? I MIGHT'VE GUESSED.
SILENCE
IN THAT CASE, SINCE YOU SEEM TO GET ALONG SO WELL... ...ÔTANI AND KOIZUMI, YOU DO IT.
WHAT?!
HEY!
YOU GUYS LOOK JUST LIKE ALL HANSHIN-KYOJIN WHEN YOU STAND NEXT TO EACH OTHER LIKE THAT!
Ha ha ha He's right!
Hee hee hee
AND NOW, A YEAR AFTER WE GOT TURNED INTO A COMEDY DUO...

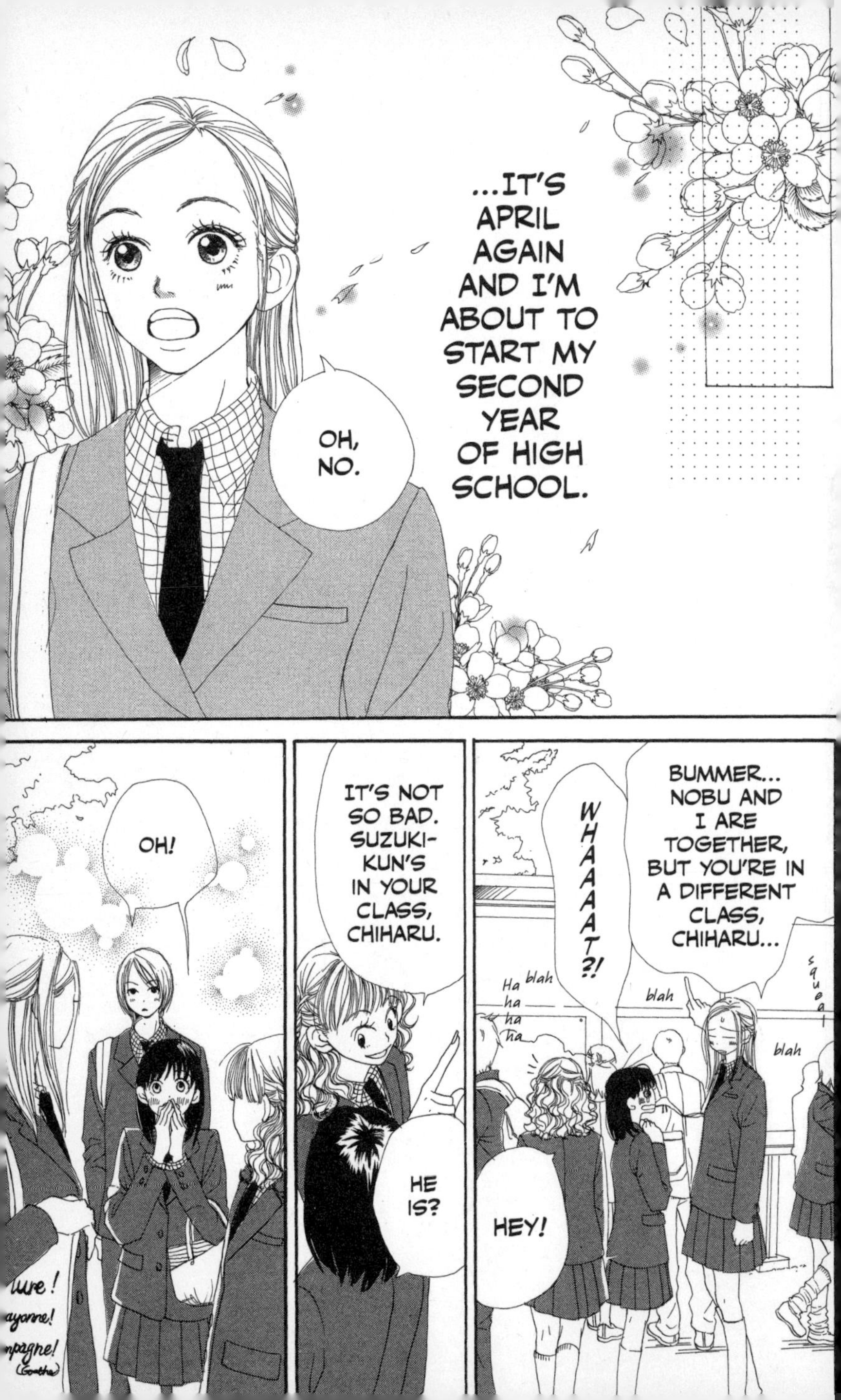
...IT'S APRIL AGAIN AND I'M ABOUT TO START MY SECOND YEAR OF HIGH SCHOOL.
OH, NO.
BUMMER... NOBU AND I ARE TOGETHER, BUT YOU'RE IN A DIFFERENT CLASS, CHIHARU...
squeal
blah
WHAAAAAT?!
blah
Ha ha ha ha
blah
HEY!
IT'S NOT SO BAD. SUZUKI-KUN'S IN YOUR CLASS, CHIHARU.
HE IS?
OH!

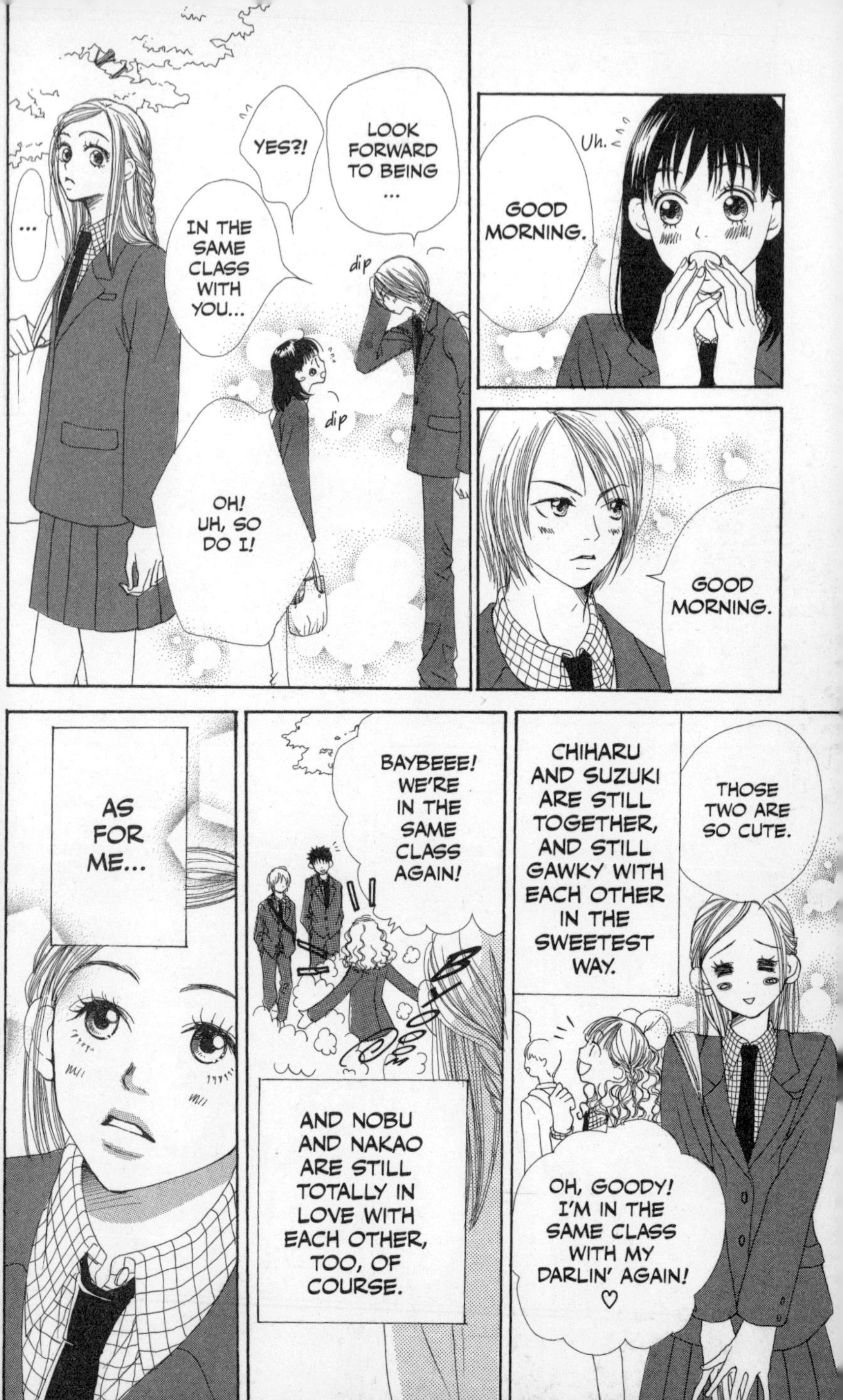
Uh.
GOOD MORNING.
GOOD MORNING.
LOOK FORWARD TO BEING ...
YES?!
IN THE SAME CLASS WITH YOU...
dip
dip
OH! UH, SO DO I!
...
THOSE TWO ARE SO CUTE.
CHIHARU AND SUZUKI ARE STILL TOGETHER, AND STILL GAWKY WITH EACH OTHER IN THE SWEETEST WAY.
OH, GOODY! I'M IN THE SAME CLASS WITH MY DARLIN' AGAIN! ♡
BAYBEEE! WE'RE IN THE SAME CLASS AGAIN!
AND NOBU AND NAKAO ARE STILL TOTALLY IN LOVE WITH EACH OTHER, TOO, OF COURSE.
AS FOR ME...

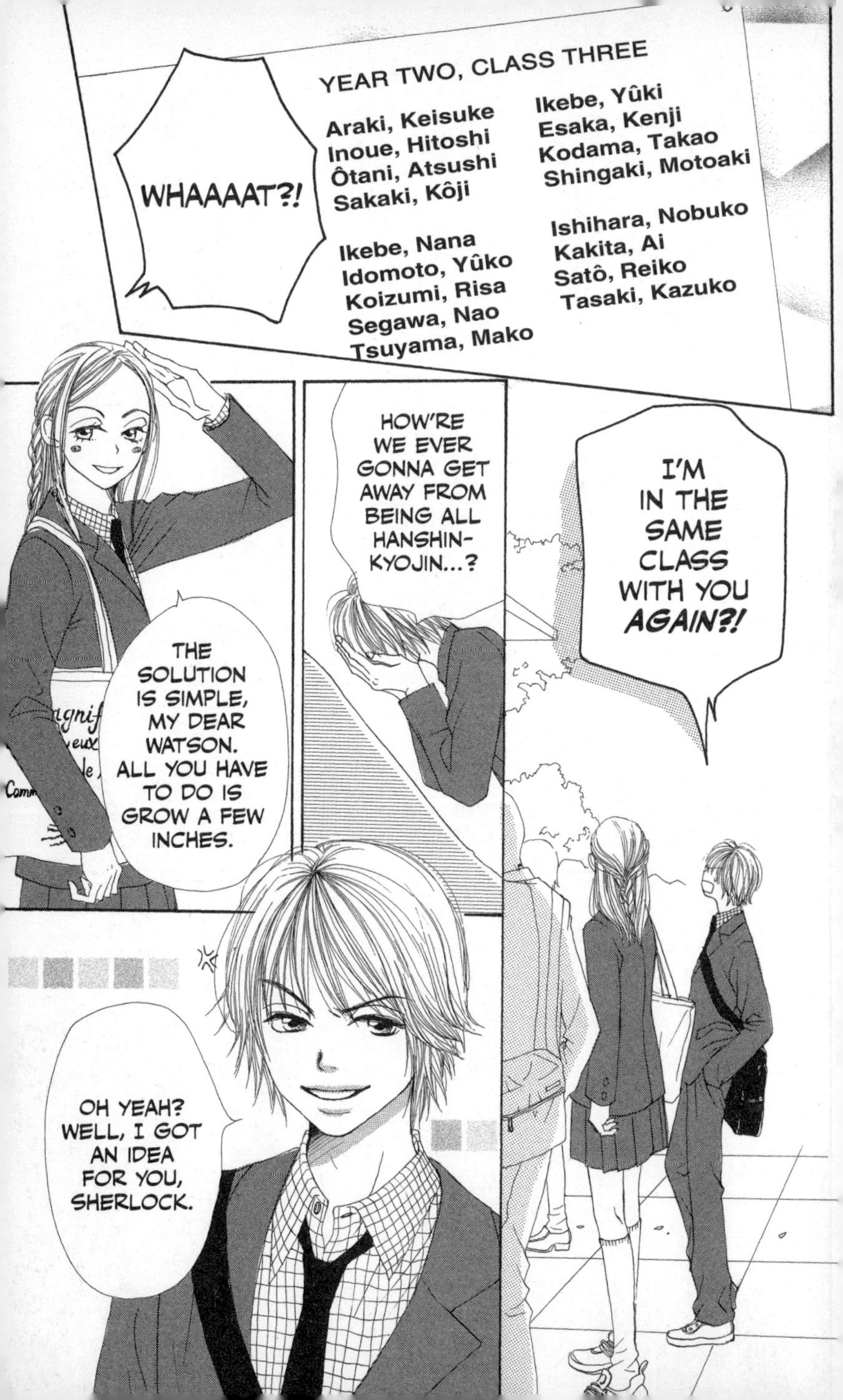
YEAR TWO, CLASS THREE
Araki, Keisuke
Inoue, Hitoshi
Ôtani, Atsushi
Sakaki, Kôji
Ikebe, Yûki
Esaka, Kenji
Kodama, Takao
Shingaki, Motoaki
Ikebe, Nana
Idomoto, Yûko
Koizumi, Risa
Segawa, Nao
Tsuyama, Mako
Ishihara, Nobuko
Kakita, Ai
Satô, Reiko
Tasaki, Kazuko
WHAAAAT?!
I'M IN THE SAME CLASS WITH YOU *AGAIN?!*
HOW'RE WE EVER GONNA GET AWAY FROM BEING ALL HANSHIN-KYOJIN...?
THE SOLUTION IS SIMPLE, MY DEAR WATSON. ALL YOU HAVE TO DO IS GROW A FEW INCHES.
OH YEAH? WELL, I GOT AN IDEA FOR YOU, SHERLOCK.

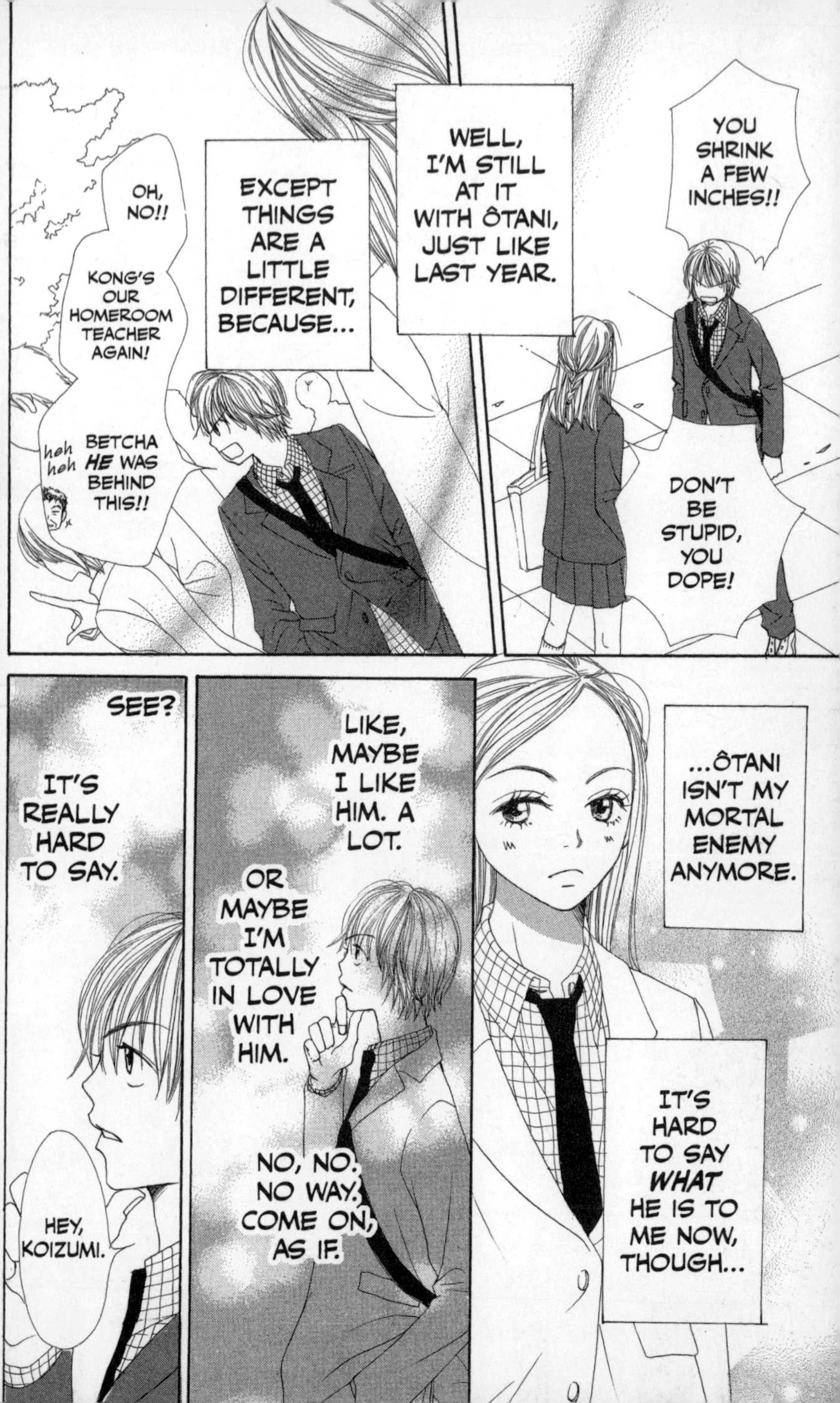
WELL, I'M STILL AT IT WITH ÔTANI, JUST LIKE LAST YEAR.
YOU SHRINK A FEW INCHES!!
DON'T BE STUPID, YOU DOPE!
EXCEPT THINGS ARE A LITTLE DIFFERENT, BECAUSE...
OH, NO!!
KONG'S OUR HOMEROOM TEACHER AGAIN!
BETCHA *HE* WAS BEHIND THIS!!
heh heh
...ÔTANI ISN'T MY MORTAL ENEMY ANYMORE.
IT'S HARD TO SAY *WHAT* HE IS TO ME NOW, THOUGH...
LIKE, MAYBE I LIKE HIM. A LOT.
OR MAYBE I'M TOTALLY IN LOVE WITH HIM.
NO, NO. NO WAY. COME ON, AS IF.
SEE?
IT'S REALLY HARD TO SAY.
HEY, KOIZUMI.

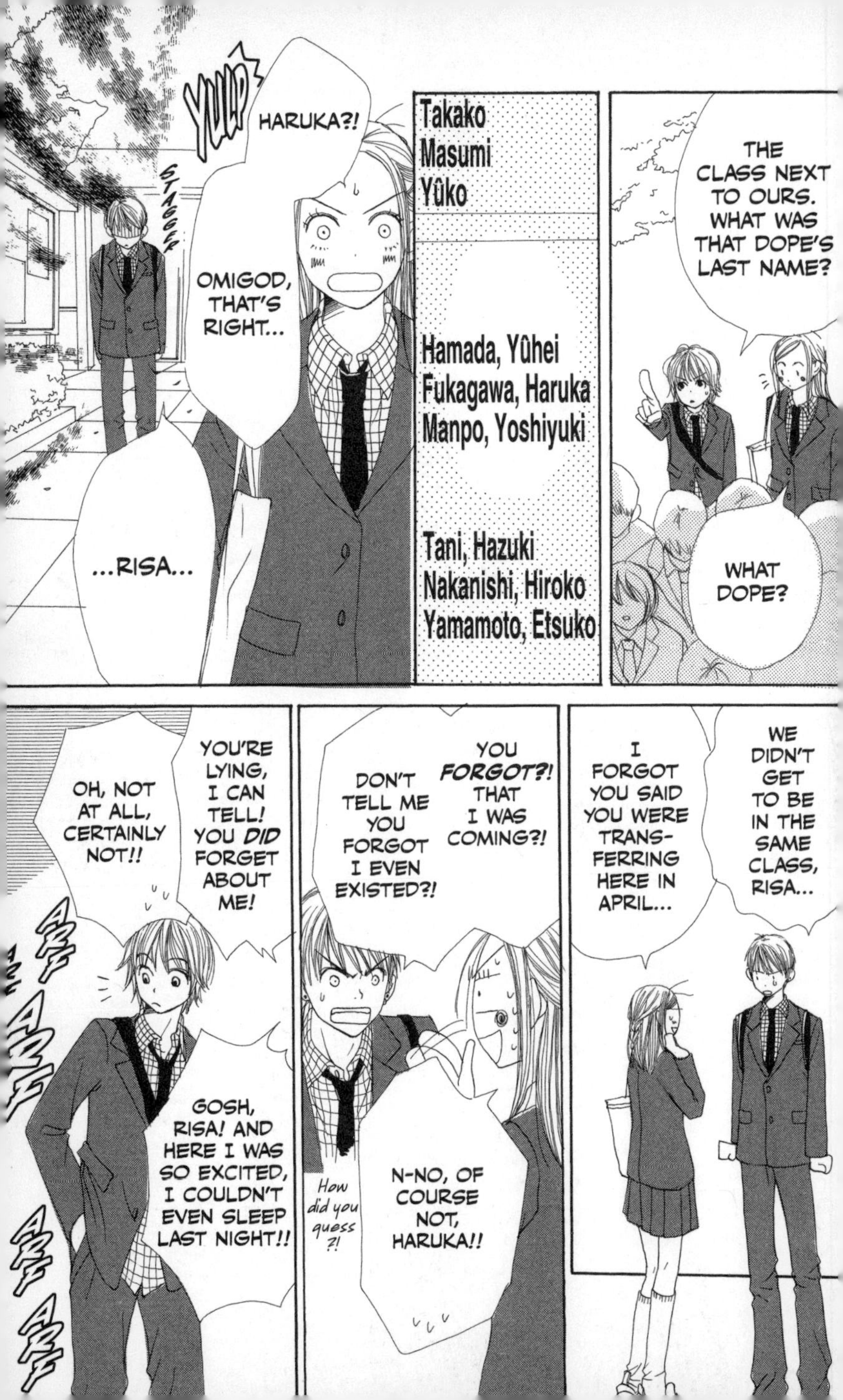
THE CLASS NEXT TO OURS. WHAT WAS THAT DOPE'S LAST NAME?
WHAT DOPE?
Takako
Masumi
Yûko
Hamada, Yûhei
Fukagawa, Haruka
Manpo, Yoshiyuki
Tani, Hazuki
Nakanishi, Hiroko
Yamamoto, Etsuko
YULP!
HARUKA?!
OMIGOD, THAT'S RIGHT...
STAGGER
...RISA...
WE DIDN'T GET TO BE IN THE SAME CLASS, RISA...
I FORGOT YOU SAID YOU WERE TRANS-FERRING HERE IN APRIL...
YOU *FORGOT?!* THAT I WAS COMING?!
DON'T TELL ME YOU FORGOT I EVEN EXISTED?!
N-NO, OF COURSE NOT, HARUKA!!
How did you guess?!
YOU'RE LYING, I CAN TELL! YOU *DID* FORGET ABOUT ME!
OH, NOT AT ALL, CERTAINLY NOT!!
GOSH, RISA! AND HERE I WAS SO EXCITED, I COULDN'T EVEN SLEEP LAST NIGHT!!

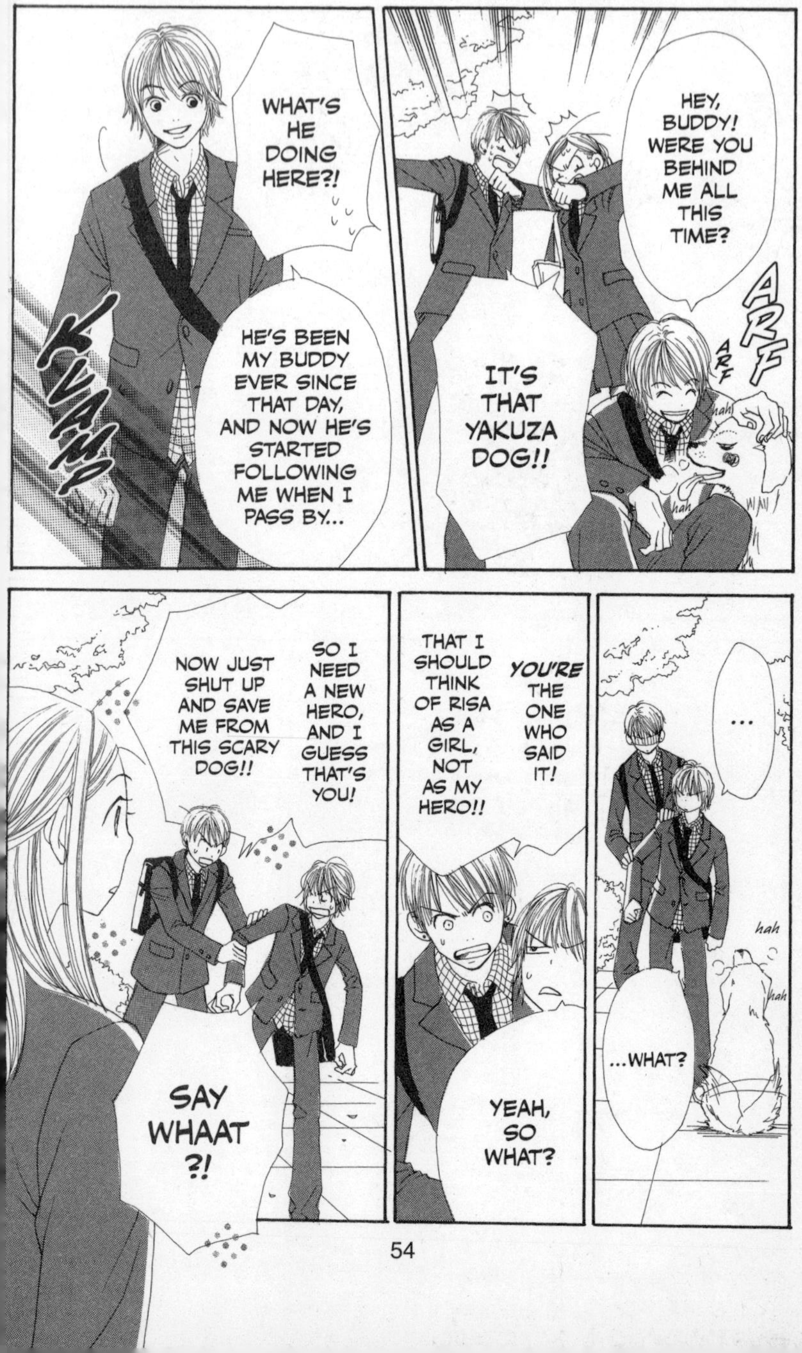
HEY, BUDDY! WERE YOU BEHIND ME ALL THIS TIME?
ARF
ARF
hah
hah
IT'S THAT YAKUZA DOG!!
WHAT'S HE DOING HERE?!
KVAMP
HE'S BEEN MY BUDDY EVER SINCE THAT DAY, AND NOW HE'S STARTED FOLLOWING ME WHEN I PASS BY...
...
hah
hah
...WHAT?
YOU'RE THE ONE WHO SAID IT!
THAT I SHOULD THINK OF RISA AS A GIRL, NOT AS MY HERO!!
YEAH, SO WHAT?
SO I NEED A NEW HERO, AND I GUESS THAT'S YOU!
NOW JUST SHUT UP AND SAVE ME FROM THIS SCARY DOG!!
SAY WHAAT ?!

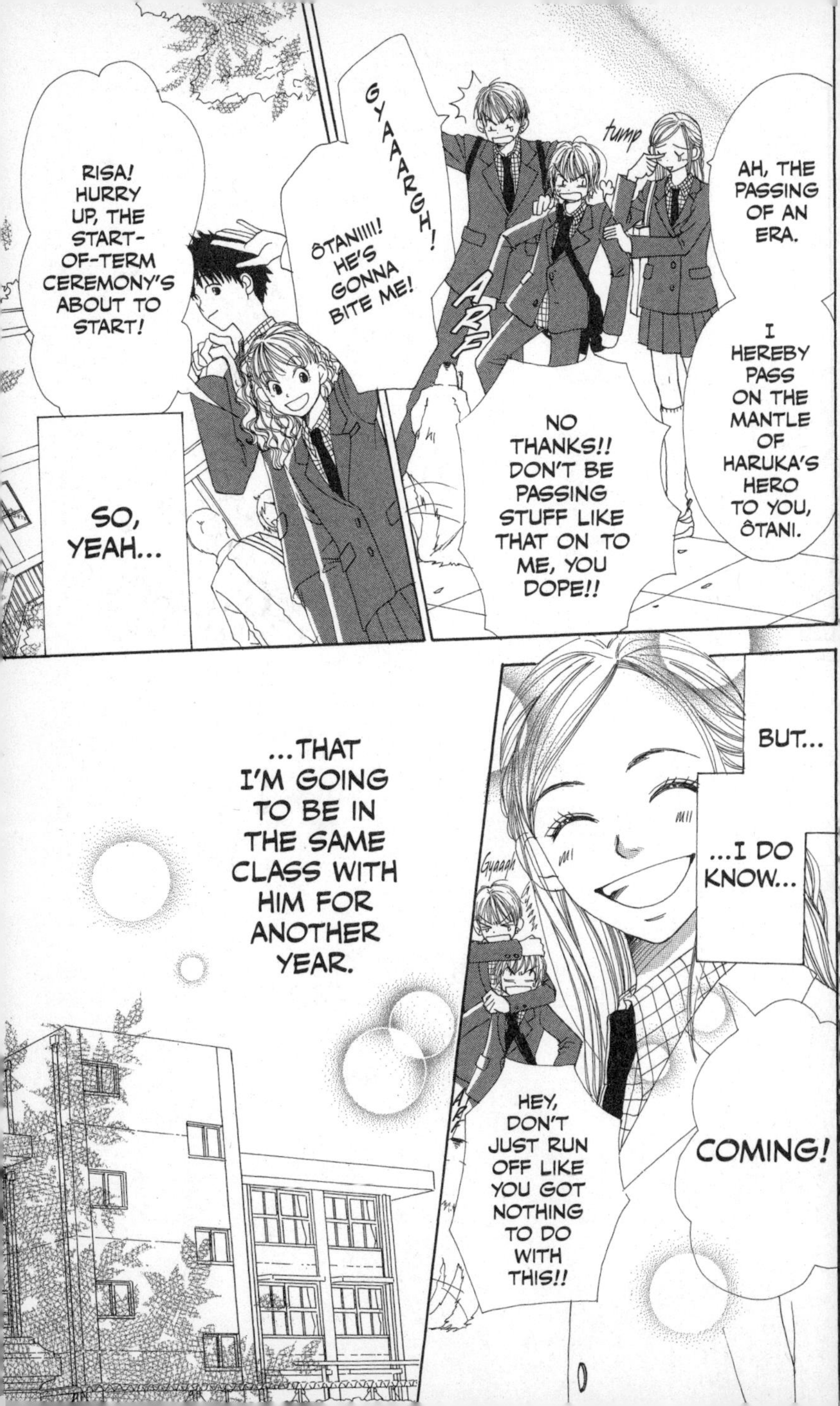
AH, THE PASSING OF AN ERA.
I HEREBY PASS ON THE MANTLE OF HARUKA'S HERO TO YOU, ŌTANI.
tump
GYAAAARGH!
ŌTANIIIII! HE'S GONNA BITE ME!
ARF
NO THANKS!! DON'T BE PASSING STUFF LIKE THAT ON TO ME, YOU DOPE!!
RISA! HURRY UP, THE START-OF-TERM CEREMONY'S ABOUT TO START!
SO, YEAH...
BUT...
...I DO KNOW...
Gyaaah
ARF
HEY, DON'T JUST RUN OFF LIKE YOU GOT NOTHING TO DO WITH THIS!!
COMING!
...THAT I'M GOING TO BE IN THE SAME CLASS WITH HIM FOR ANOTHER YEAR.

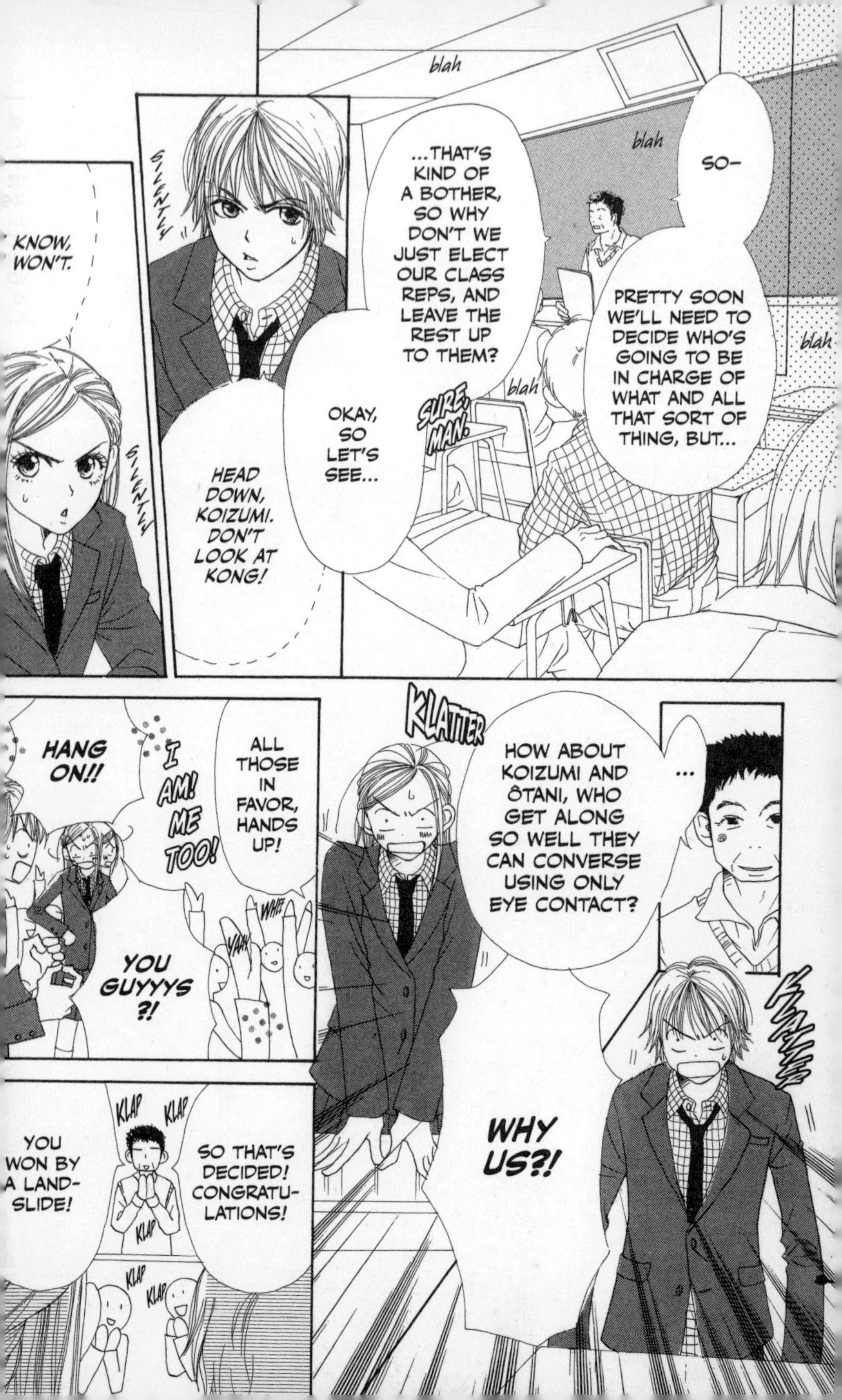
blah
blah
SO–
PRETTY SOON WE'LL NEED TO DECIDE WHO'S GOING TO BE IN CHARGE OF WHAT AND ALL THAT SORT OF THING, BUT...
blah
...THAT'S KIND OF A BOTHER, SO WHY DON'T WE JUST ELECT OUR CLASS REPS, AND LEAVE THE REST UP TO THEM?
blah
SURE, MAN.
OKAY, SO LET'S SEE...
HEAD DOWN, KOIZUMI. DON'T LOOK AT KONG!
KNOW, WON'T.
...
HOW ABOUT KOIZUMI AND ÔTANI, WHO GET ALONG SO WELL THEY CAN CONVERSE USING ONLY EYE CONTACT?
KLATTER
WHY US?!
ALL THOSE IN FAVOR, HANDS UP!
I AM! ME TOO!
WHEE
YAAY
HANG ON!!
YOU GUYYYS?!
SO THAT'S DECIDED! CONGRATULATIONS!
KLAP
KLAP
KLAP
KLAP
KLAP
YOU WON BY A LAND-SLIDE!

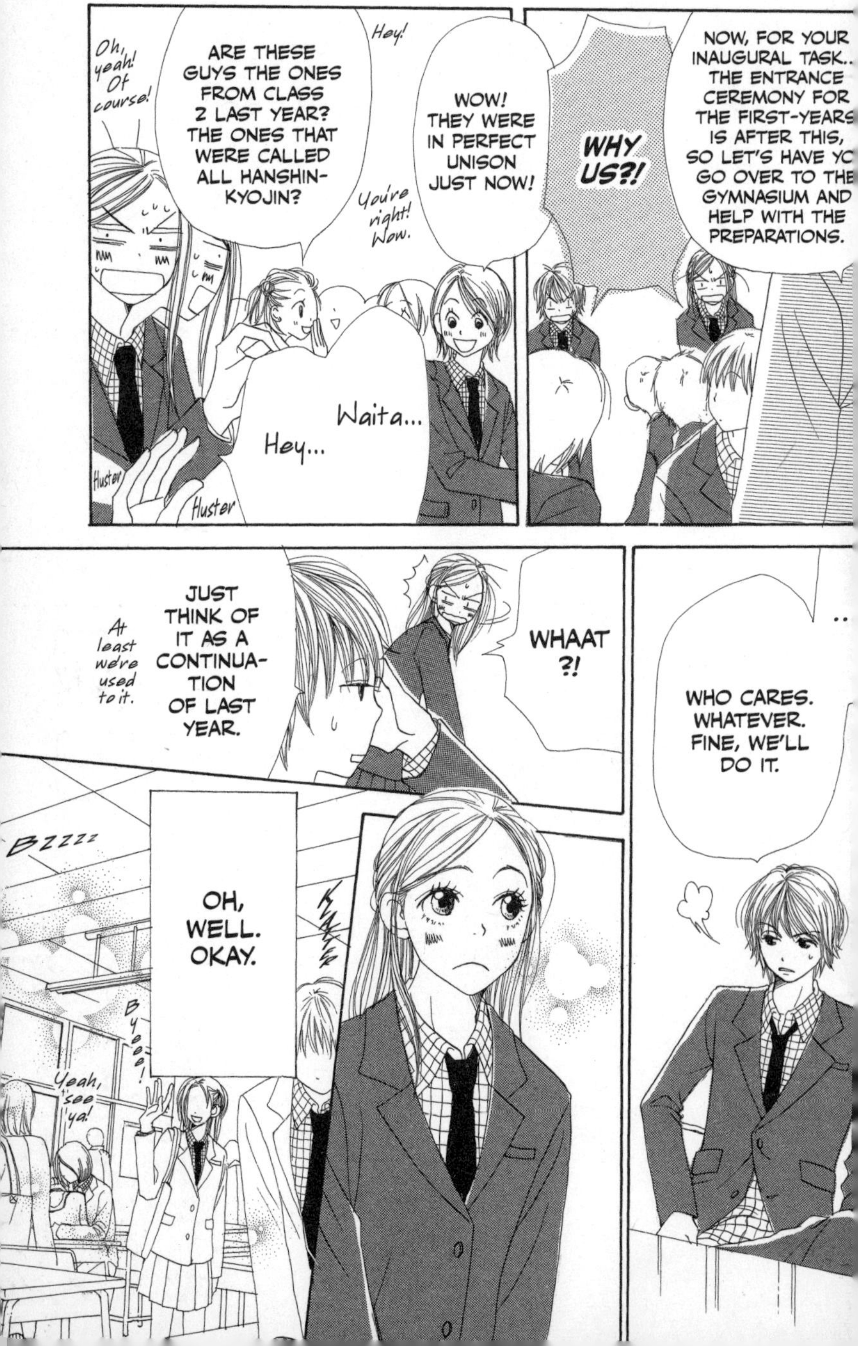

NOW, FOR YOUR INAUGURAL TASK... THE ENTRANCE CEREMONY FOR THE FIRST-YEARS IS AFTER THIS, SO LET'S HAVE YO GO OVER TO THE GYMNASIUM AND HELP WITH THE PREPARATIONS.
WHY US?!
Hey!
WOW! THEY WERE IN PERFECT UNISON JUST NOW!
ARE THESE GUYS THE ONES FROM CLASS 2 LAST YEAR? THE ONES THAT WERE CALLED ALL HANSHIN-KYOJIN?
Oh, yeah! Of course!
You're right! Wow.
Waita...
Hey...
fluster
fluster
..
WHO CARES. WHATEVER. FINE, WE'LL DO IT.
WHAAT ?!
JUST THINK OF IT AS A CONTINUATION OF LAST YEAR.
At least we're used to it.
OH, WELL. OKAY.
BZZZZ
Byeee!
Yeah, see ya!

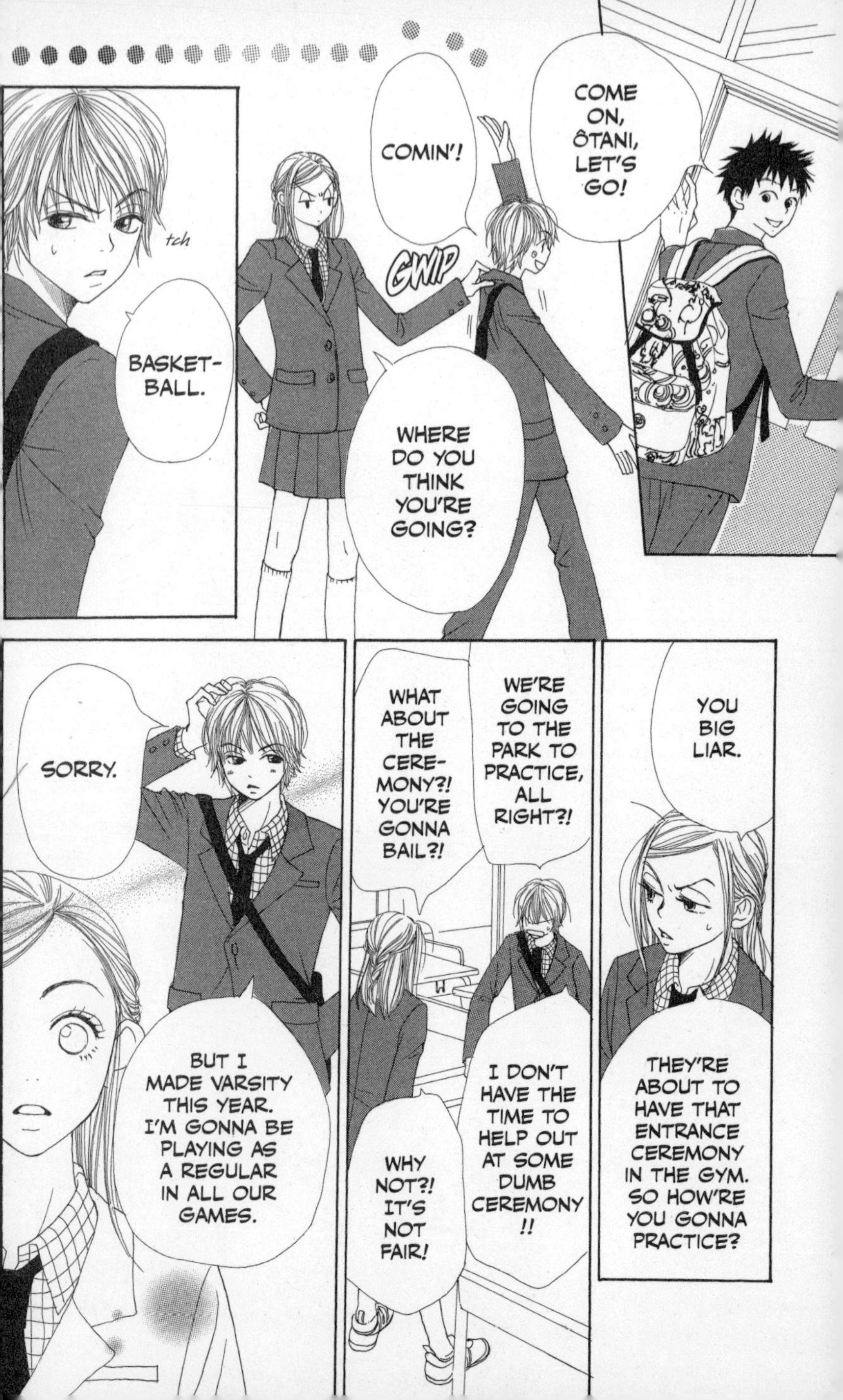

COME ON, ŌTANI, LET'S GO!
COMIN'!
GWIP
WHERE DO YOU THINK YOU'RE GOING?
tch
BASKET-BALL.
YOU BIG LIAR.
THEY'RE ABOUT TO HAVE THAT ENTRANCE CEREMONY IN THE GYM. SO HOW'RE YOU GONNA PRACTICE?
WE'RE GOING TO THE PARK TO PRACTICE, ALL RIGHT?!
WHAT ABOUT THE CERE-MONY?! YOU'RE GONNA BAIL?!
I DON'T HAVE THE TIME TO HELP OUT AT SOME DUMB CEREMONY!!
WHY NOT?! IT'S NOT FAIR!
SORRY.
BUT I MADE VARSITY THIS YEAR. I'M GONNA BE PLAYING AS A REGULAR IN ALL OUR GAMES.

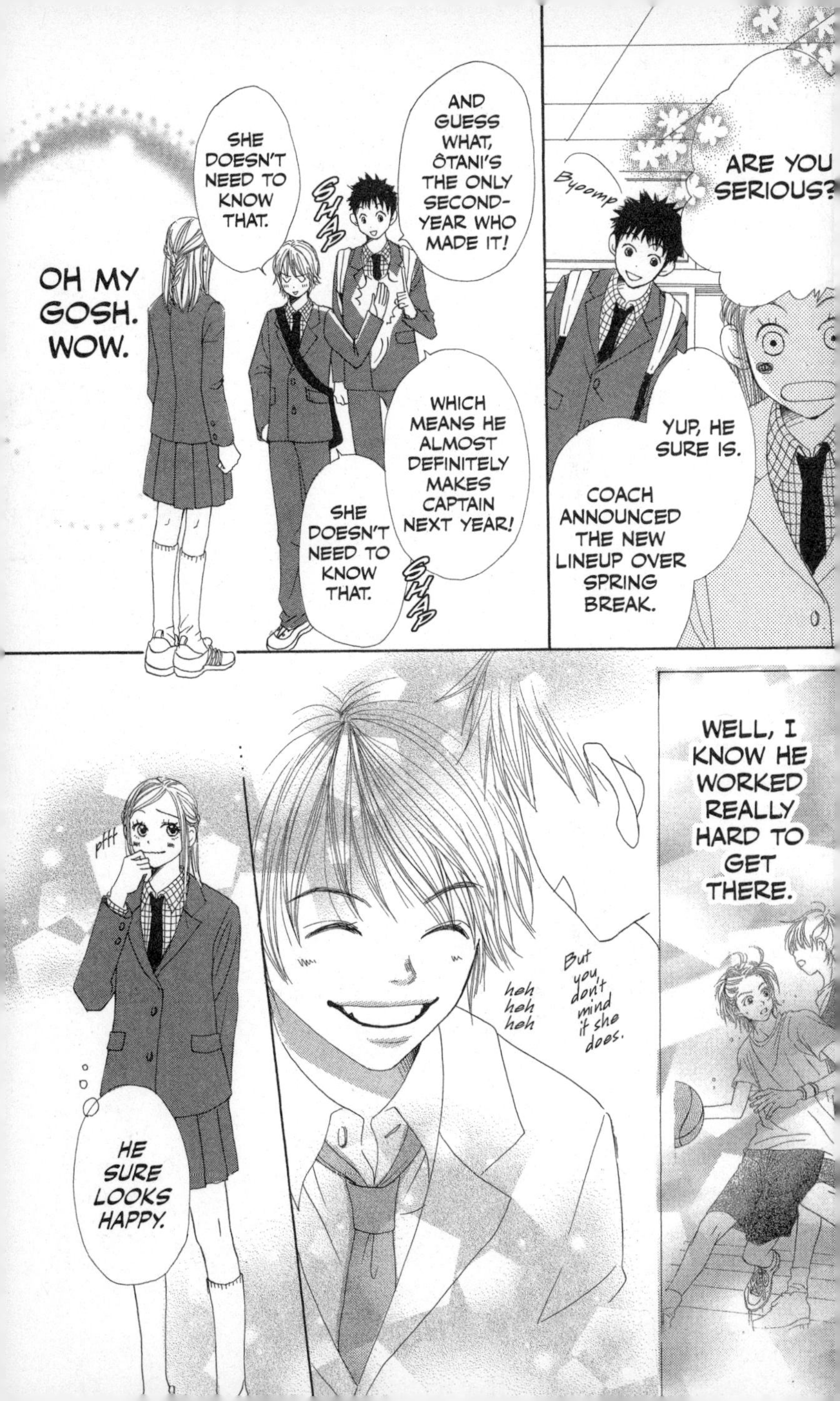
ARE YOU SERIOUS?
Byoomp
YUP, HE SURE IS.
COACH ANNOUNCED THE NEW LINEUP OVER SPRING BREAK.
AND GUESS WHAT, ÔTANI'S THE ONLY SECOND-YEAR WHO MADE IT!
SHAP
SHE DOESN'T NEED TO KNOW THAT.
OH MY GOSH. WOW.
WHICH MEANS HE ALMOST DEFINITELY MAKES CAPTAIN NEXT YEAR!
SHAP
SHE DOESN'T NEED TO KNOW THAT.
WELL, I KNOW HE WORKED REALLY HARD TO GET THERE.
But you don't mind if she does.
heh heh heh
pfff
HE SURE LOOKS HAPPY.

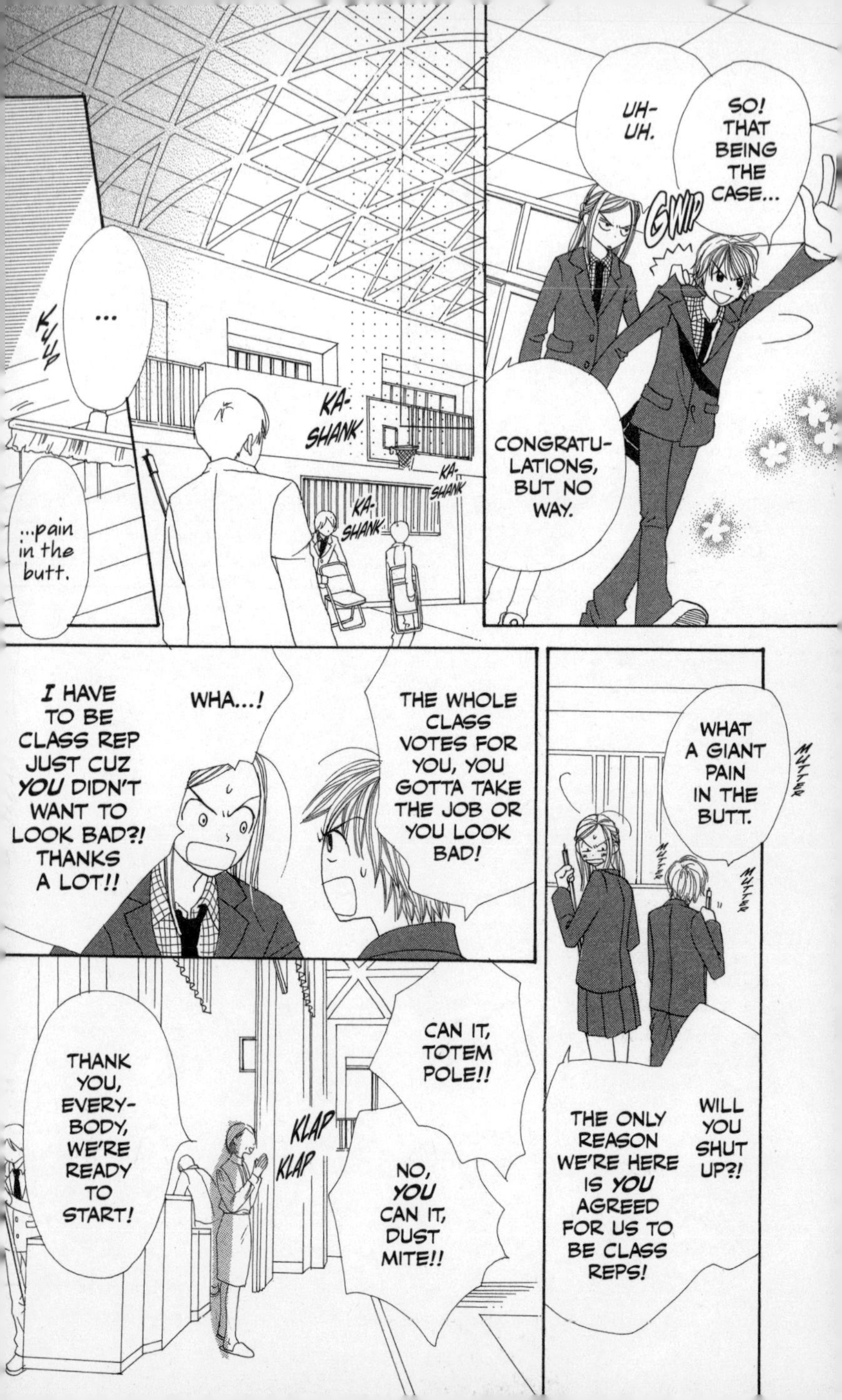
SO! THAT BEING THE CASE...
UH-UH.
GWIP
CONGRATULATIONS, BUT NO WAY.
...
KUUP
KA-SHANK
KA-SHANK
KA-SHANK
...pain in the butt.
WHAT A GIANT PAIN IN THE BUTT.
MUTTER
MUTTER
MUTTER
WILL YOU SHUT UP?!
THE ONLY REASON WE'RE HERE IS YOU AGREED FOR US TO BE CLASS REPS!
THE WHOLE CLASS VOTES FOR YOU, YOU GOTTA TAKE THE JOB OR YOU LOOK BAD!
WHA...!
I HAVE TO BE CLASS REP JUST CUZ YOU DIDN'T WANT TO LOOK BAD?! THANKS A LOT!!
CAN IT, TOTEM POLE!!
NO, YOU CAN IT, DUST MITE!!
KLAP
KLAP
THANK YOU, EVERYBODY, WE'RE READY TO START!

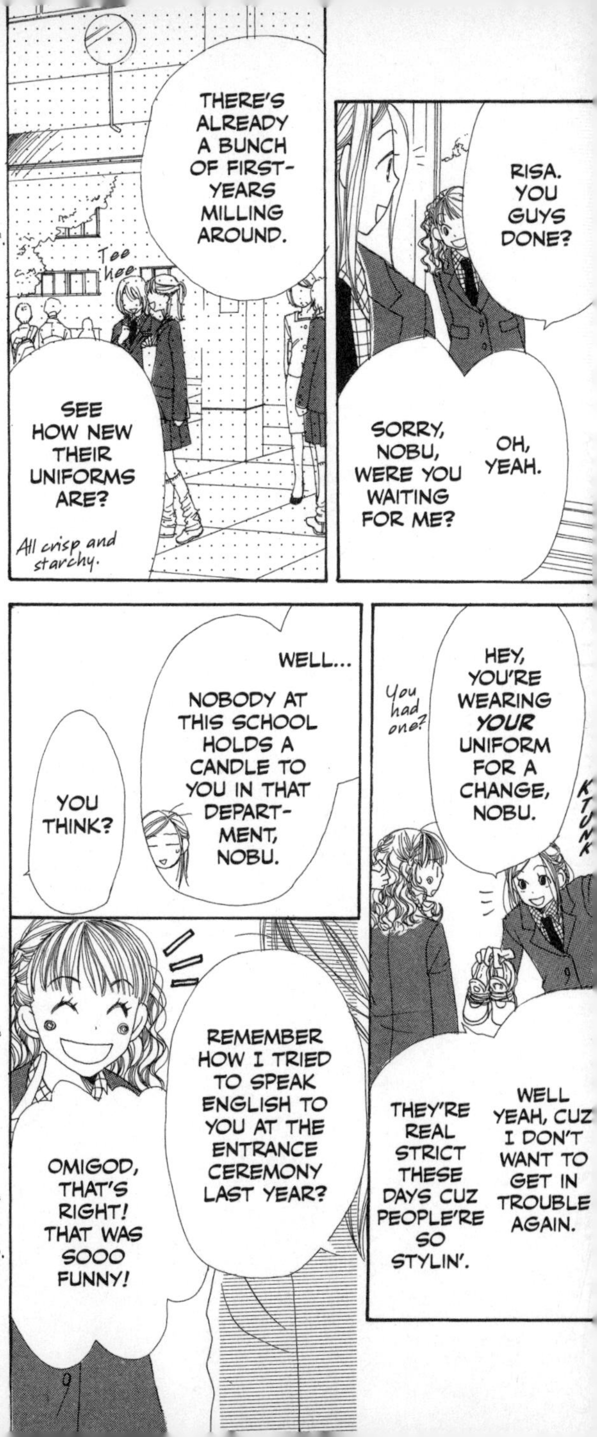

RISA. YOU GUYS DONE?
OH, YEAH.
SORRY, NOBU, WERE YOU WAITING FOR ME?
THERE'S ALREADY A BUNCH OF FIRST-YEARS MILLING AROUND.
Tee hee
SEE HOW NEW THEIR UNIFORMS ARE?
All crisp and starchy.
HEY, YOU'RE WEARING *YOUR* UNIFORM FOR A CHANGE, NOBU.
You had one?
KTUNK
WELL YEAH, CUZ I DON'T WANT TO GET IN TROUBLE AGAIN.
THEY'RE REAL STRICT THESE DAYS CUZ PEOPLE'RE SO STYLIN'.
WELL...
NOBODY AT THIS SCHOOL HOLDS A CANDLE TO YOU IN THAT DEPARTMENT, NOBU.
YOU THINK?
REMEMBER HOW I TRIED TO SPEAK ENGLISH TO YOU AT THE ENTRANCE CEREMONY LAST YEAR?
OMIGOD, THAT'S RIGHT! THAT WAS SOOO FUNNY!

-②

So anyway, I turned 74 on July 28th. Well that's a lie, but that day, which really was my birthday, I did an autograph session for the first time in my life. When it got decided that I would do this, people in my family said stuff like "Who'd come to something like that? What'll you do if nobody comes?," in other words coming right out and voicing my deepest qualms, but when the day arrived a lot of people took the time and trouble to come. Thank you so much! I'm not very good at that kind of thing so I was really stiff and nervous, and I'm sure I did all kinds of things wrong, but I was really happy that I got to meet so many of the people out there who read my manga. Thank you again for coming. Ikuemi-sensei and Chiyo Morinaga and Ayako Yoshimura came and stood in line for my autograph that day, too. I sneaked a little poop cartoon next to my autograph for theirs.

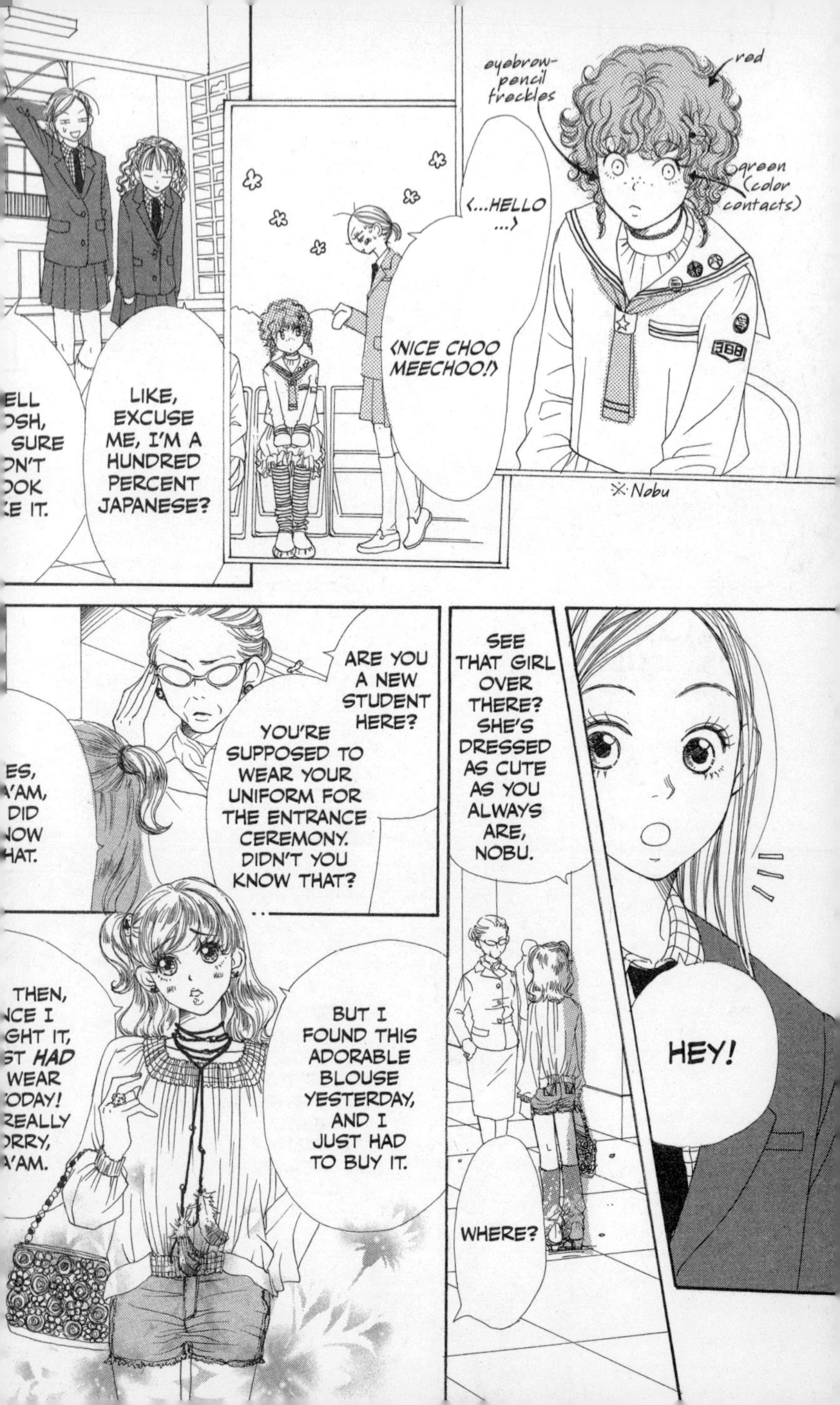

red
eyebrow-pencil freckles
green (color contacts)
‹...HELLO ...›
※Nobu
‹NICE CHOO MEECHOO!›
LIKE, EXCUSE ME, I'M A HUNDRED PERCENT JAPANESE?
ELL OSH, SURE ON'T OOK E IT.
HEY!
SEE THAT GIRL OVER THERE? SHE'S DRESSED AS CUTE AS YOU ALWAYS ARE, NOBU.
WHERE?
ARE YOU A NEW STUDENT HERE?
YOU'RE SUPPOSED TO WEAR YOUR UNIFORM FOR THE ENTRANCE CEREMONY. DIDN'T YOU KNOW THAT?
...
ES, 'AM, DID NOW HAT.
BUT I FOUND THIS ADORABLE BLOUSE YESTERDAY, AND I JUST HAD TO BUY IT.
THEN, NCE I GHT IT, ST *HAD* WEAR ODAY! REALLY ORRY, 'AM.

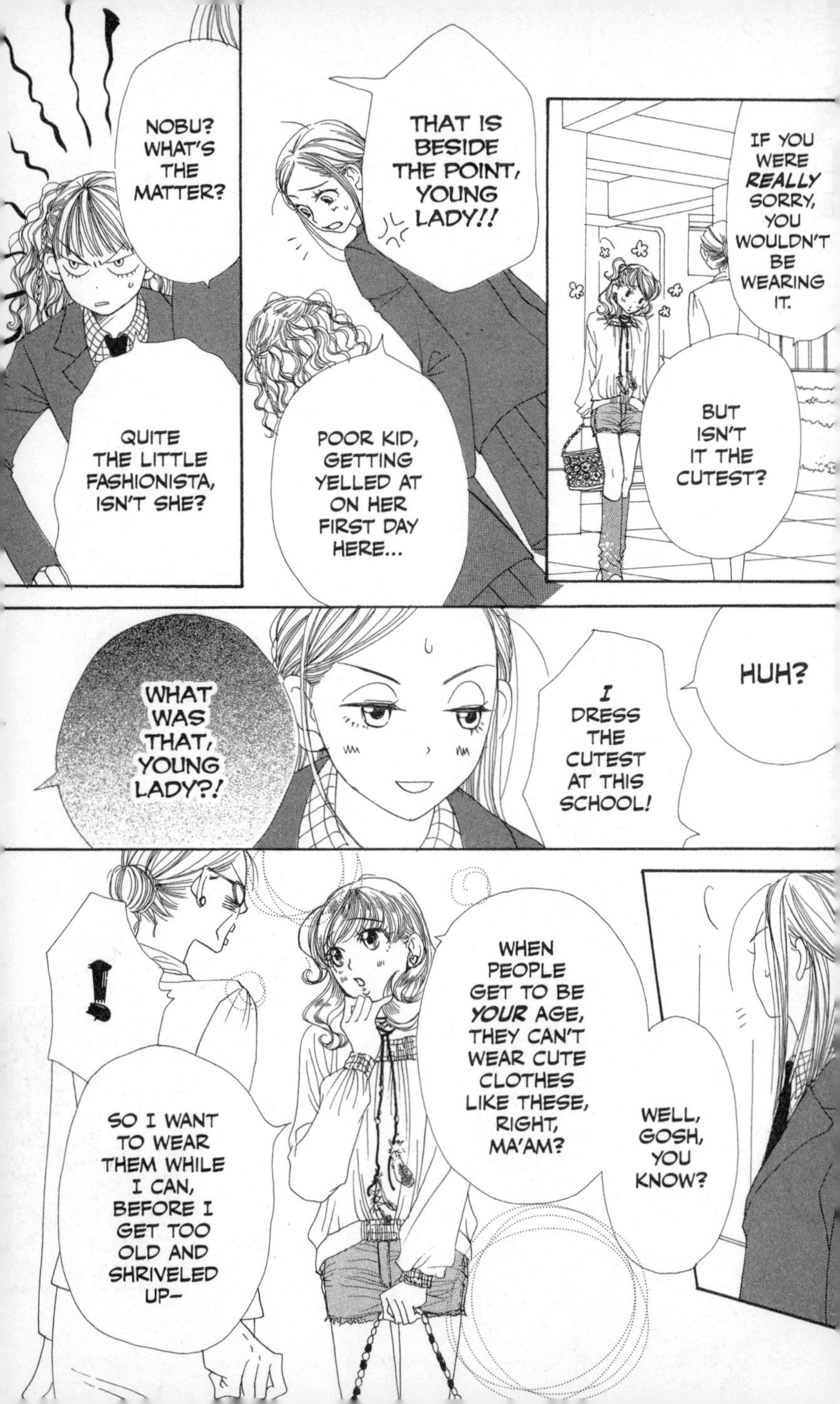
IF YOU WERE *REALLY* SORRY, YOU WOULDN'T BE WEARING IT.
BUT ISN'T IT THE CUTEST?
THAT IS BESIDE THE POINT, YOUNG LADY!!
POOR KID, GETTING YELLED AT ON HER FIRST DAY HERE...
NOBU? WHAT'S THE MATTER?
QUITE THE LITTLE FASHIONISTA, ISN'T SHE?
HUH?
I DRESS THE CUTEST AT THIS SCHOOL!
WHAT WAS THAT, YOUNG LADY?!
WHEN PEOPLE GET TO BE *YOUR* AGE, THEY CAN'T WEAR CUTE CLOTHES LIKE THESE, RIGHT, MA'AM?
WELL, GOSH, YOU KNOW?
!
SO I WANT TO WEAR THEM WHILE I CAN, BEFORE I GET TOO OLD AND SHRIVELED UP–

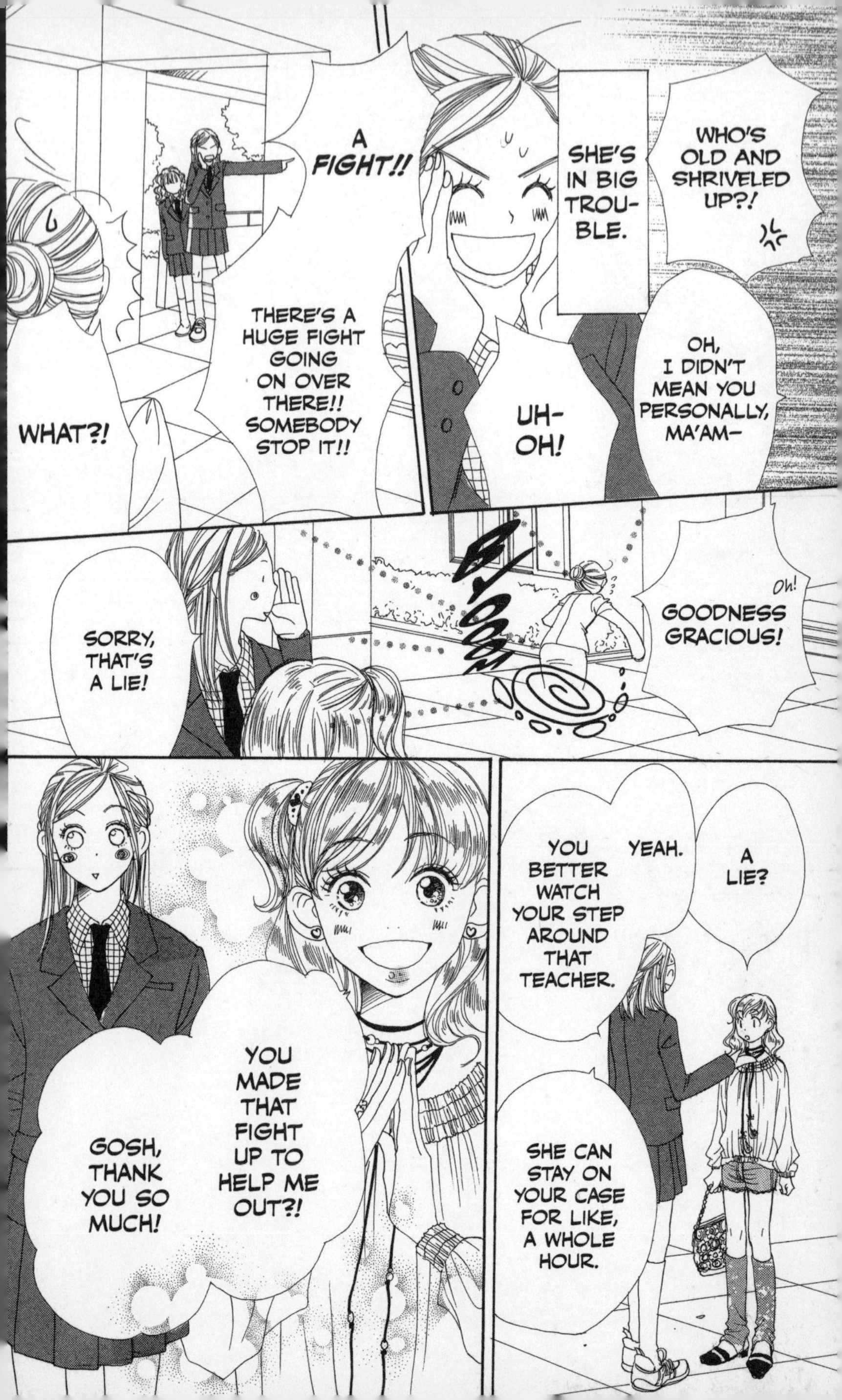
WHO'S OLD AND SHRIVELED UP?!
SHE'S IN BIG TROUBLE.
OH, I DIDN'T MEAN YOU PERSONALLY, MA'AM–
UH-OH!
A FIGHT!!
THERE'S A HUGE FIGHT GOING ON OVER THERE!! SOMEBODY STOP IT!!
WHAT?!
Oh!
GOODNESS GRACIOUS!
SORRY, THAT'S A LIE!
A LIE?
YEAH.
YOU BETTER WATCH YOUR STEP AROUND THAT TEACHER.
SHE CAN STAY ON YOUR CASE FOR LIKE, A WHOLE HOUR.
YOU MADE THAT FIGHT UP TO HELP ME OUT?!
GOSH, THANK YOU SO MUCH!

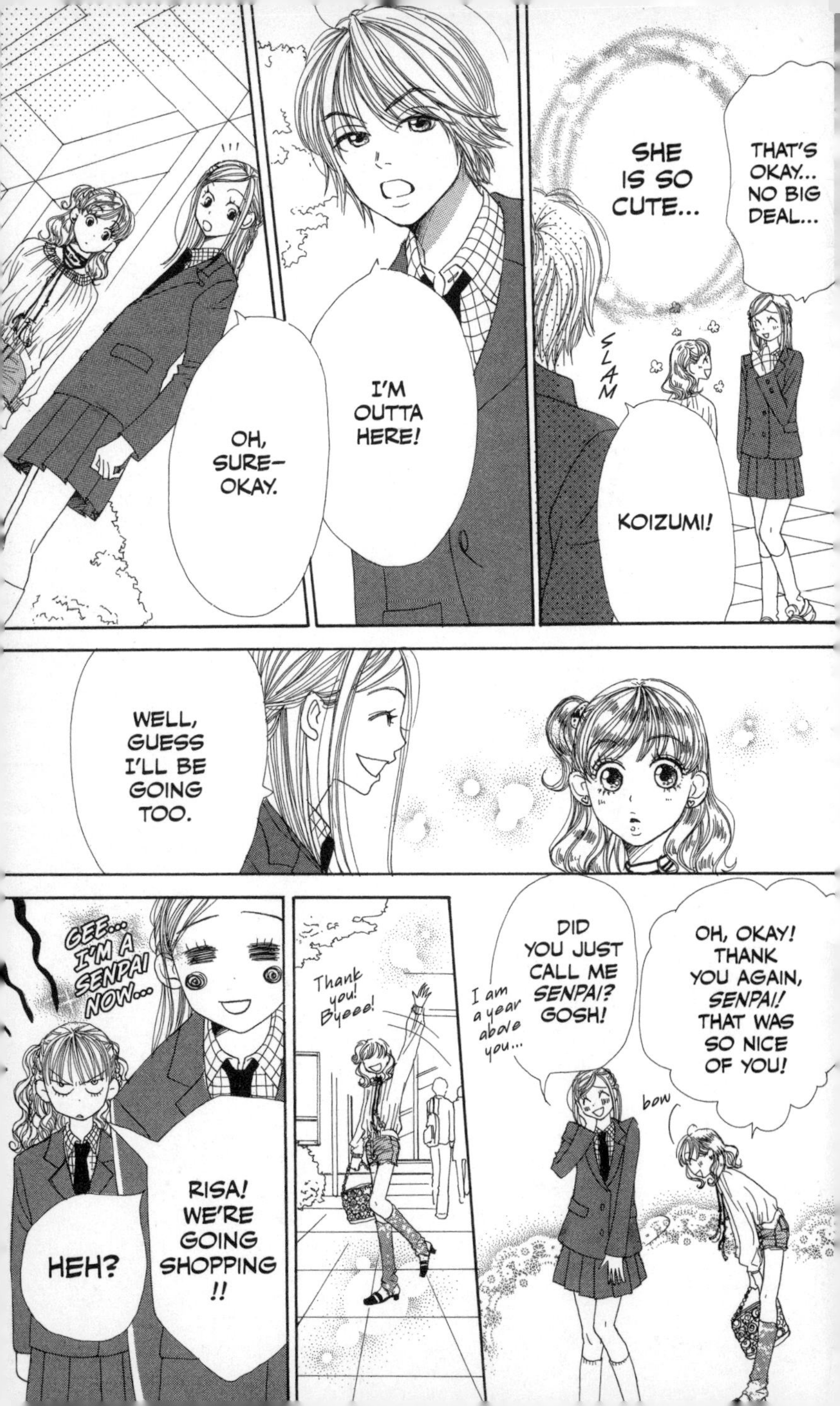
THAT'S OKAY... NO BIG DEAL...
SHE IS SO CUTE...
SLAM
KOIZUMI!
I'M OUTTA HERE!
OH, SURE-OKAY.
WELL, GUESS I'LL BE GOING TOO.
OH, OKAY! THANK YOU AGAIN, SENPAI! THAT WAS SO NICE OF YOU!
bow
DID YOU JUST CALL ME SENPAI? GOSH!
I am a year above you...
Thank you! Byeee!
GEE... I'M A SENPAI NOW...
RISA! WE'RE GOING SHOPPING!!
HEH?

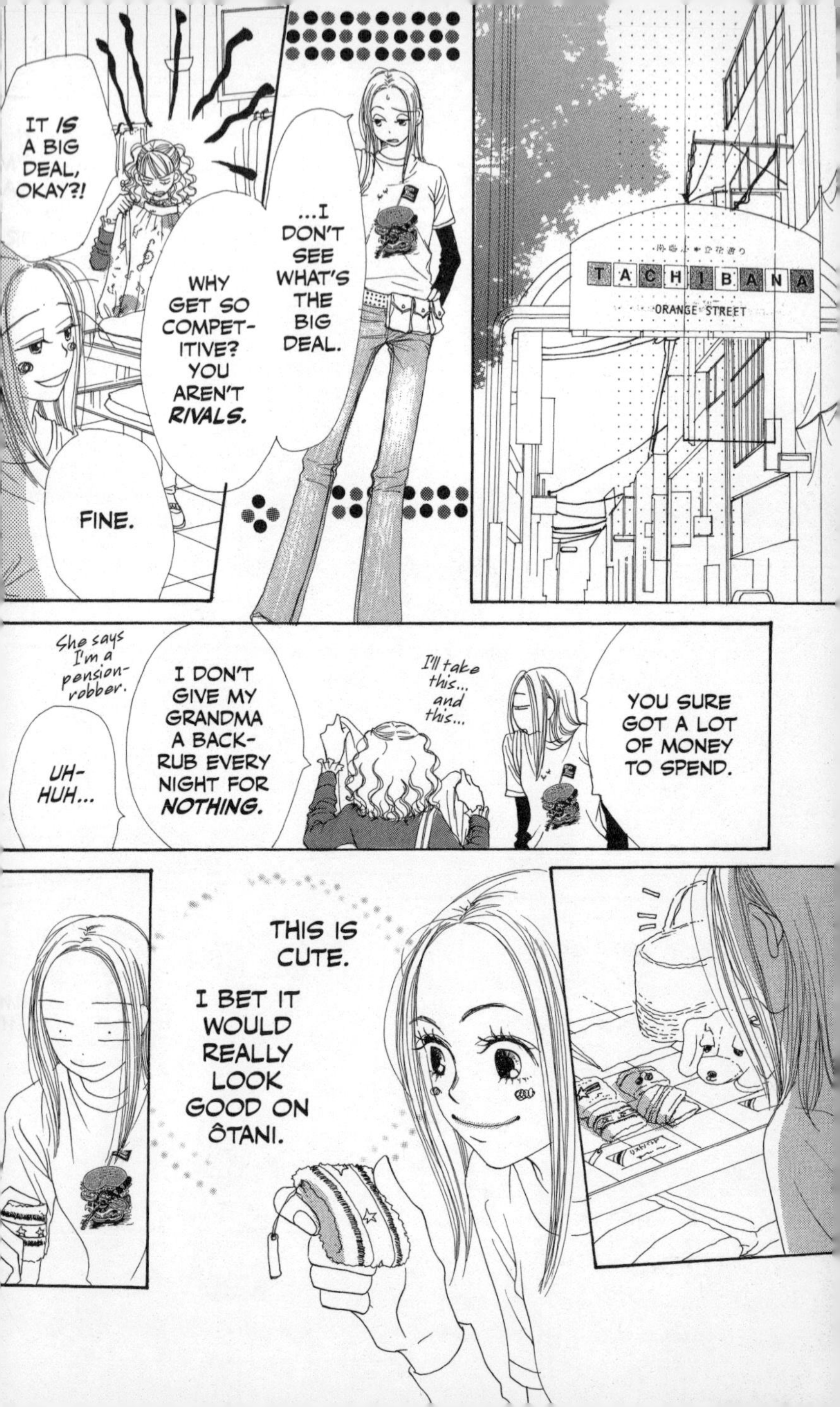
TACHIBANA
ORANGE STREET
...I DON'T SEE WHAT'S THE BIG DEAL.
IT *IS* A BIG DEAL, OKAY?!
WHY GET SO COMPETITIVE? YOU AREN'T *RIVALS.*
FINE.
YOU SURE GOT A LOT OF MONEY TO SPEND.
I'll take this... and this...
I DON'T GIVE MY GRANDMA A BACK-RUB EVERY NIGHT FOR *NOTHING.*
She says I'm a pension-robber.
UH-HUH...
THIS IS CUTE.
I BET IT WOULD REALLY LOOK GOOD ON ÔTANI.

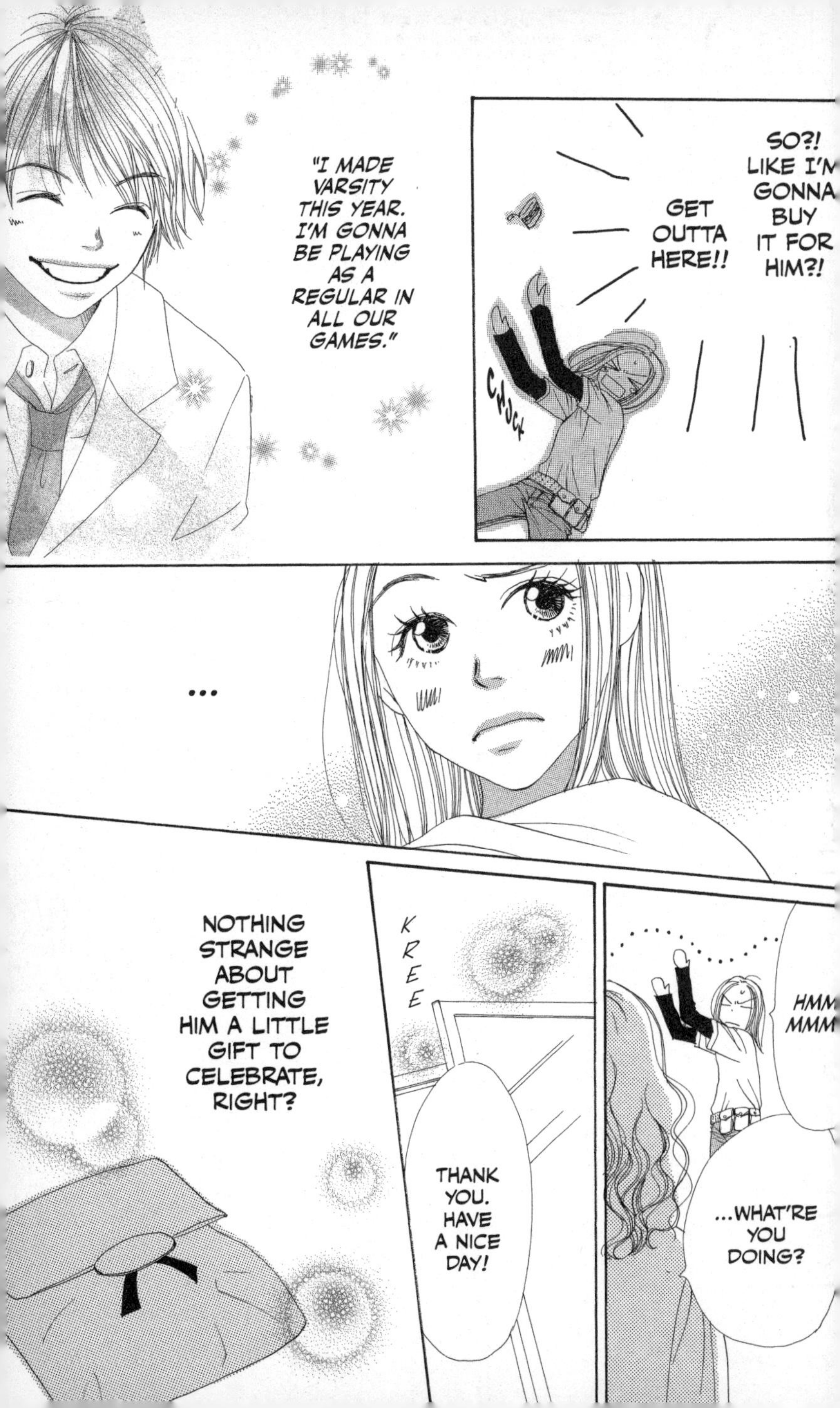
SO?! LIKE I'M GONNA BUY IT FOR HIM?!
GET OUTTA HERE!!
CHUCK
"I MADE VARSITY THIS YEAR. I'M GONNA BE PLAYING AS A REGULAR IN ALL OUR GAMES."
...
HMM MMM
...WHAT'RE YOU DOING?
KREE
THANK YOU. HAVE A NICE DAY!
NOTHING STRANGE ABOUT GETTING HIM A LITTLE GIFT TO CELEBRATE, RIGHT?

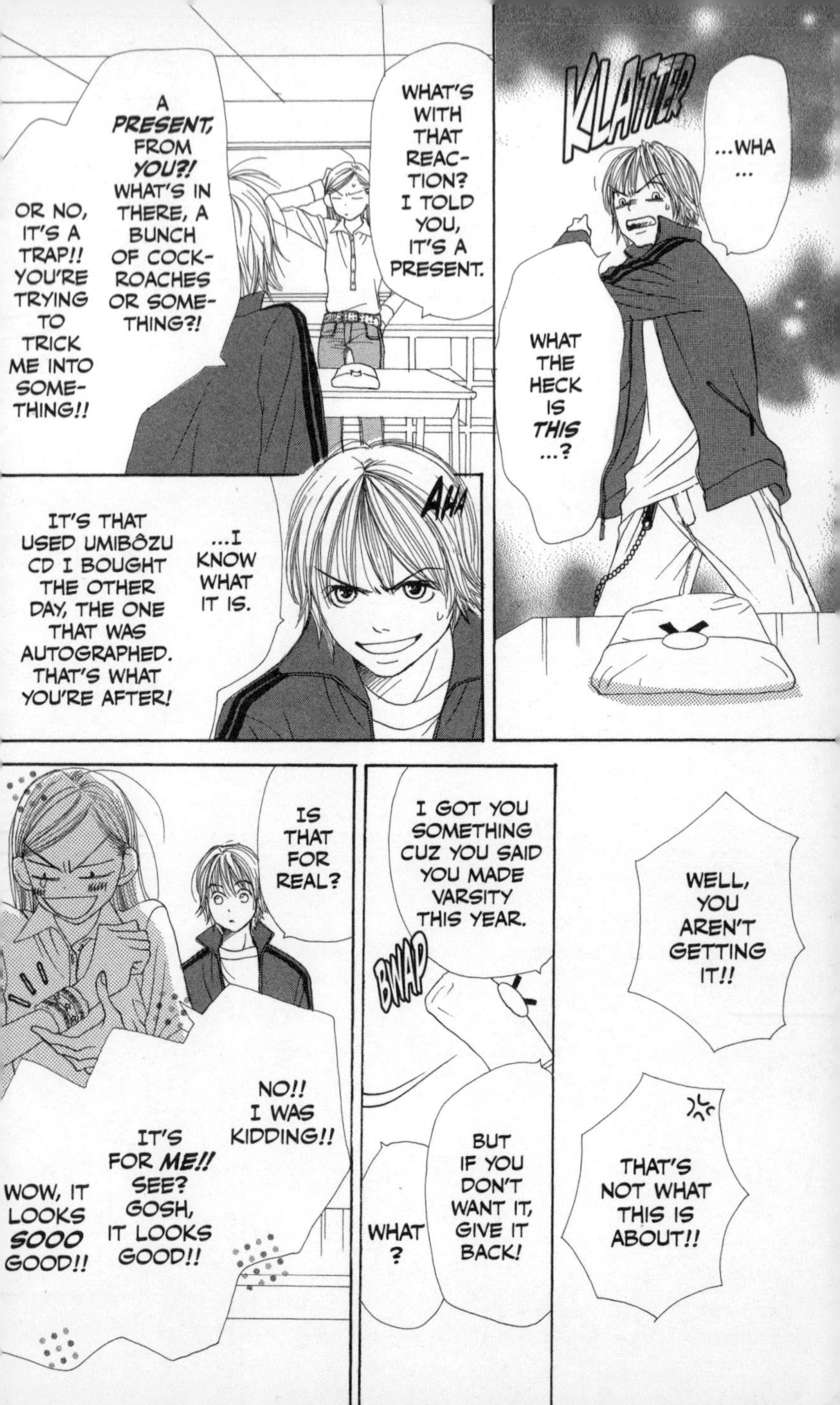
KLATTER
...WHA ...
WHAT THE HECK IS THIS ...?
WHAT'S WITH THAT REACTION? I TOLD YOU, IT'S A PRESENT.
A PRESENT, FROM YOU?! WHAT'S IN THERE, A BUNCH OF COCKROACHES OR SOMETHING?!
OR NO, IT'S A TRAP!! YOU'RE TRYING TO TRICK ME INTO SOMETHING!!
AHA
...I KNOW WHAT IT IS.
IT'S THAT USED UMIBÔZU CD I BOUGHT THE OTHER DAY, THE ONE THAT WAS AUTOGRAPHED. THAT'S WHAT YOU'RE AFTER!
WELL, YOU AREN'T GETTING IT!!
THAT'S NOT WHAT THIS IS ABOUT!!
I GOT YOU SOMETHING CUZ YOU SAID YOU MADE VARSITY THIS YEAR.
BWAP
BUT IF YOU DON'T WANT IT, GIVE IT BACK!
WHAT ?
IS THAT FOR REAL?
NO!! I WAS KIDDING!!
IT'S FOR ME!! SEE? GOSH, IT LOOKS GOOD!!
WOW, IT LOOKS SOOO GOOD!!

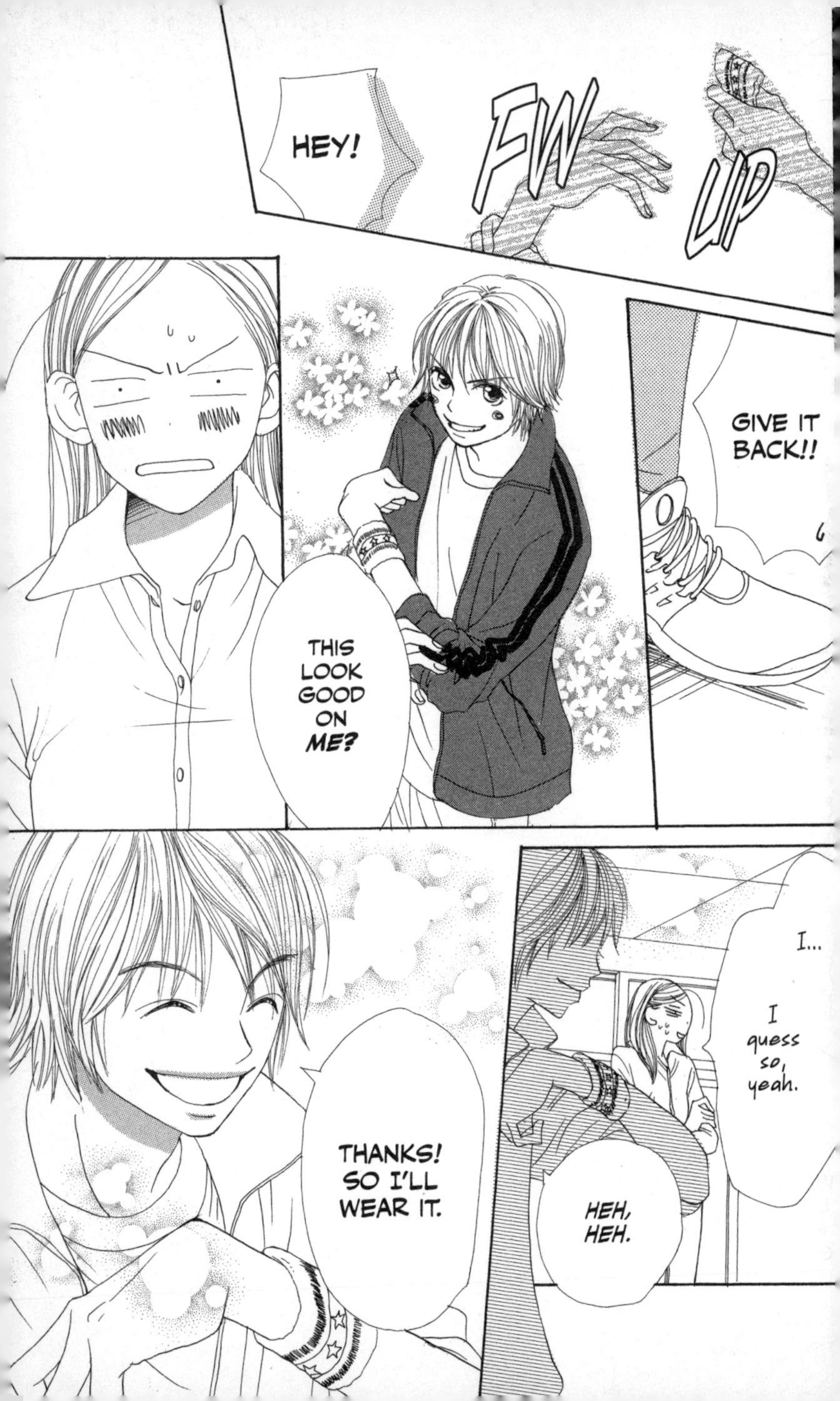
FW
UP
HEY!
GIVE IT BACK!!
THIS LOOK GOOD ON *ME?*
I...
I guess so, yeah.
HEH, HEH.
THANKS! SO I'LL WEAR IT.

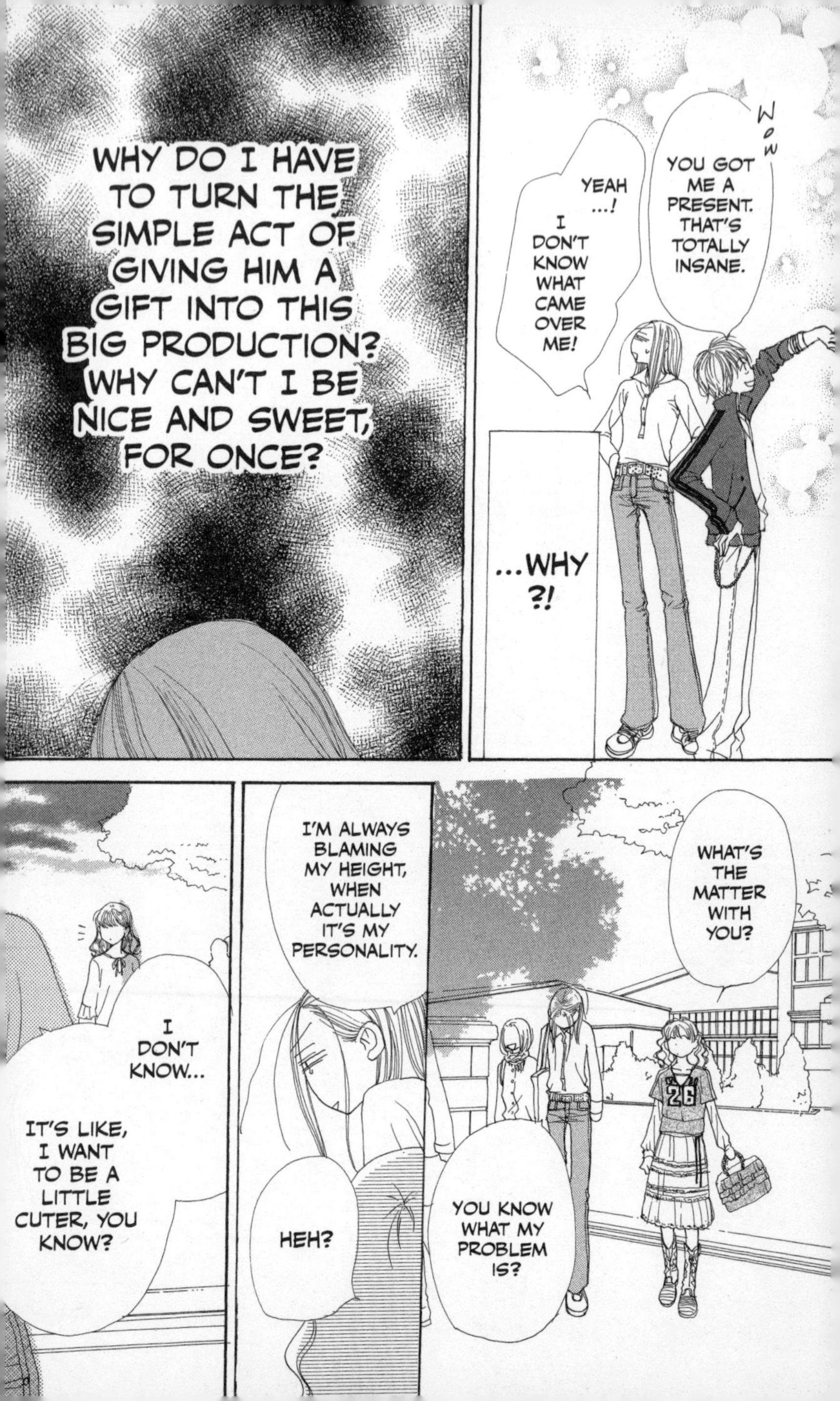
WOW
YOU GOT ME A PRESENT. THAT'S TOTALLY INSANE.
YEAH ...!
I DON'T KNOW WHAT CAME OVER ME!
...WHY ?!
WHY DO I HAVE TO TURN THE SIMPLE ACT OF GIVING HIM A GIFT INTO THIS BIG PRODUCTION? WHY CAN'T I BE NICE AND SWEET, FOR ONCE?
WHAT'S THE MATTER WITH YOU?
YOU KNOW WHAT MY PROBLEM IS?
I'M ALWAYS BLAMING MY HEIGHT, WHEN ACTUALLY IT'S MY PERSONALITY.
HEH?
I DON'T KNOW...
IT'S LIKE, I WANT TO BE A LITTLE CUTER, YOU KNOW?

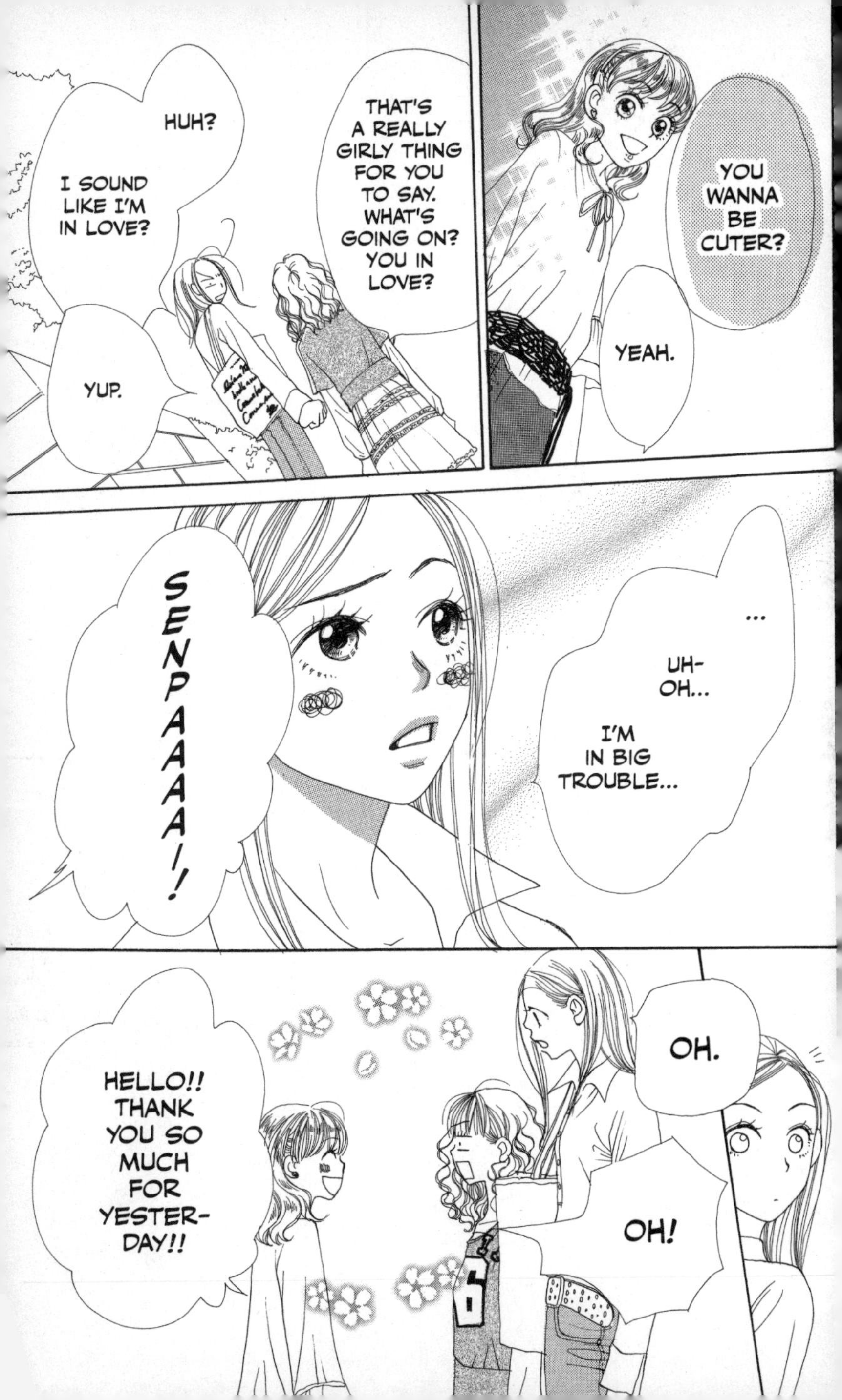
YOU WANNA BE CUTER?
YEAH.
THAT'S A REALLY GIRLY THING FOR YOU TO SAY. WHAT'S GOING ON? YOU IN LOVE?
HUH?
I SOUND LIKE I'M IN LOVE?
YUP.
...
UH-OH...
I'M IN BIG TROUBLE...
SENPAAAAAI!!
OH.
OH!
HELLO!! THANK YOU SO MUCH FOR YESTER-DAY!!

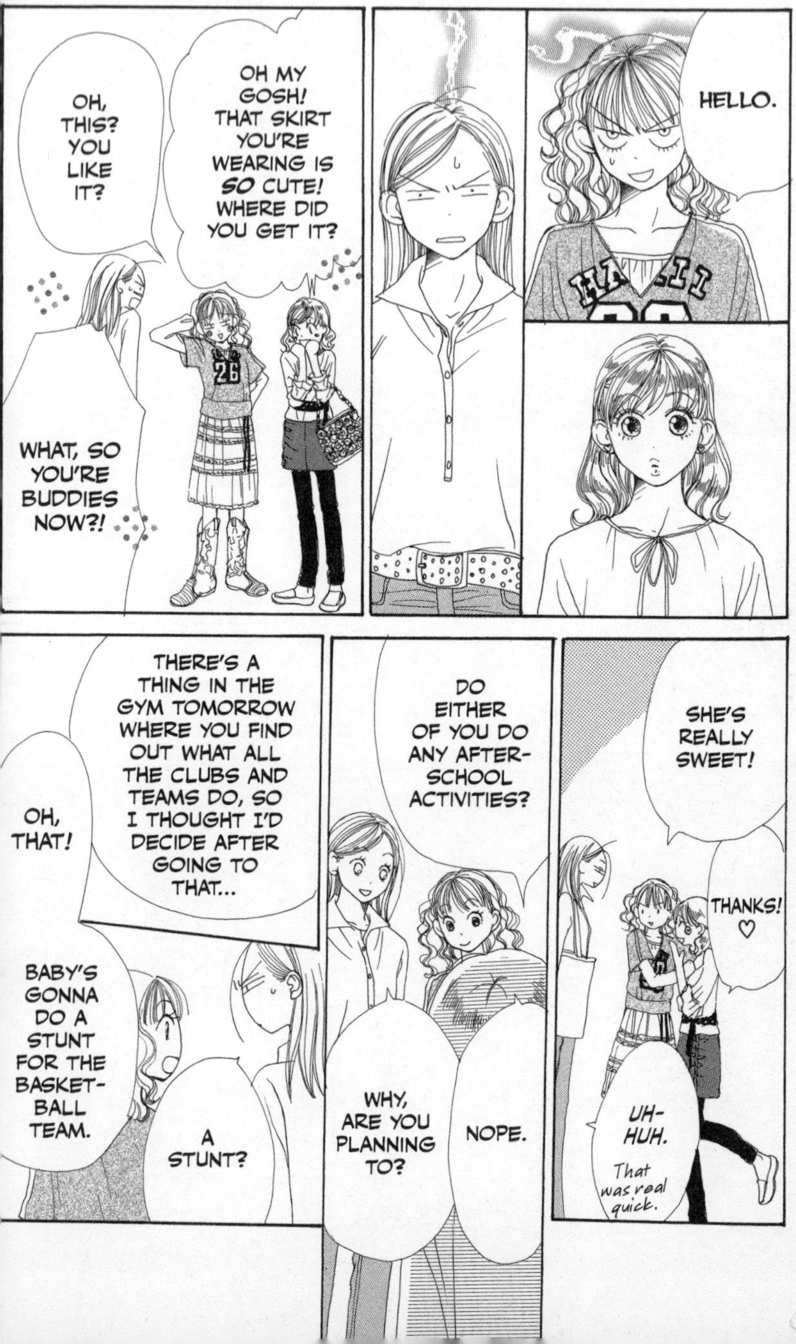
HELLO.
OH MY GOSH! THAT SKIRT YOU'RE WEARING IS *SO* CUTE! WHERE DID YOU GET IT?
OH, THIS? YOU LIKE IT?
WHAT, SO YOU'RE BUDDIES NOW?!
SHE'S REALLY SWEET!
THANKS! ♡
UH-HUH.
That was real quick.
DO EITHER OF YOU DO ANY AFTER-SCHOOL ACTIVITIES?
NOPE.
WHY, ARE YOU PLANNING TO?
THERE'S A THING IN THE GYM TOMORROW WHERE YOU FIND OUT WHAT ALL THE CLUBS AND TEAMS DO, SO I THOUGHT I'D DECIDE AFTER GOING TO THAT...
OH, THAT!
BABY'S GONNA DO A STUNT FOR THE BASKET-BALL TEAM.
A STUNT?

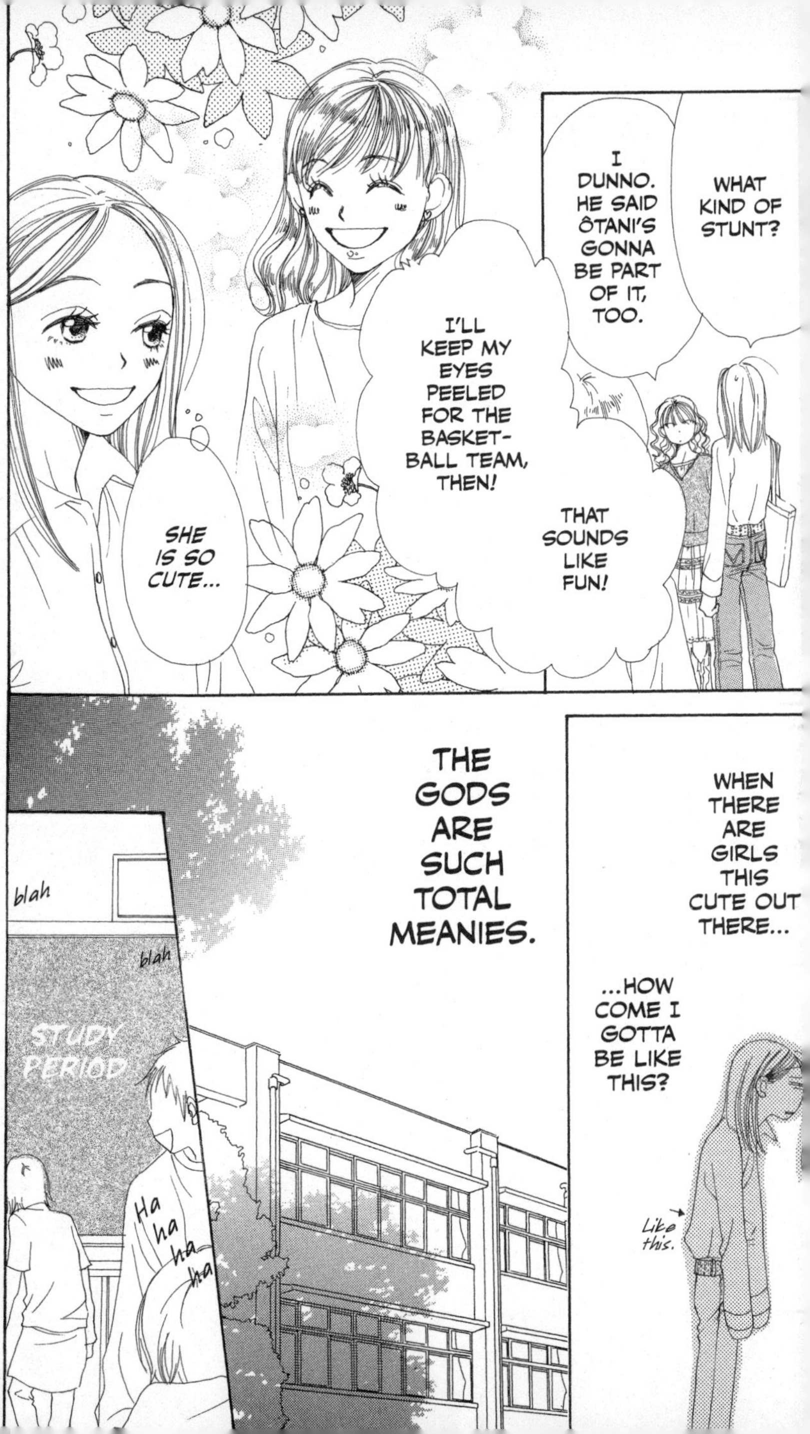
WHAT KIND OF STUNT?
I DUNNO. HE SAID ÔTANI'S GONNA BE PART OF IT, TOO.
THAT SOUNDS LIKE FUN!
I'LL KEEP MY EYES PEELED FOR THE BASKET-BALL TEAM, THEN!
SHE IS SO CUTE...
WHEN THERE ARE GIRLS THIS CUTE OUT THERE...
...HOW COME I GOTTA BE LIKE THIS?
Like this.
THE GODS ARE SUCH TOTAL MEANIES.
blah
blah
STUDY PERIOD
Ha ha ha ha

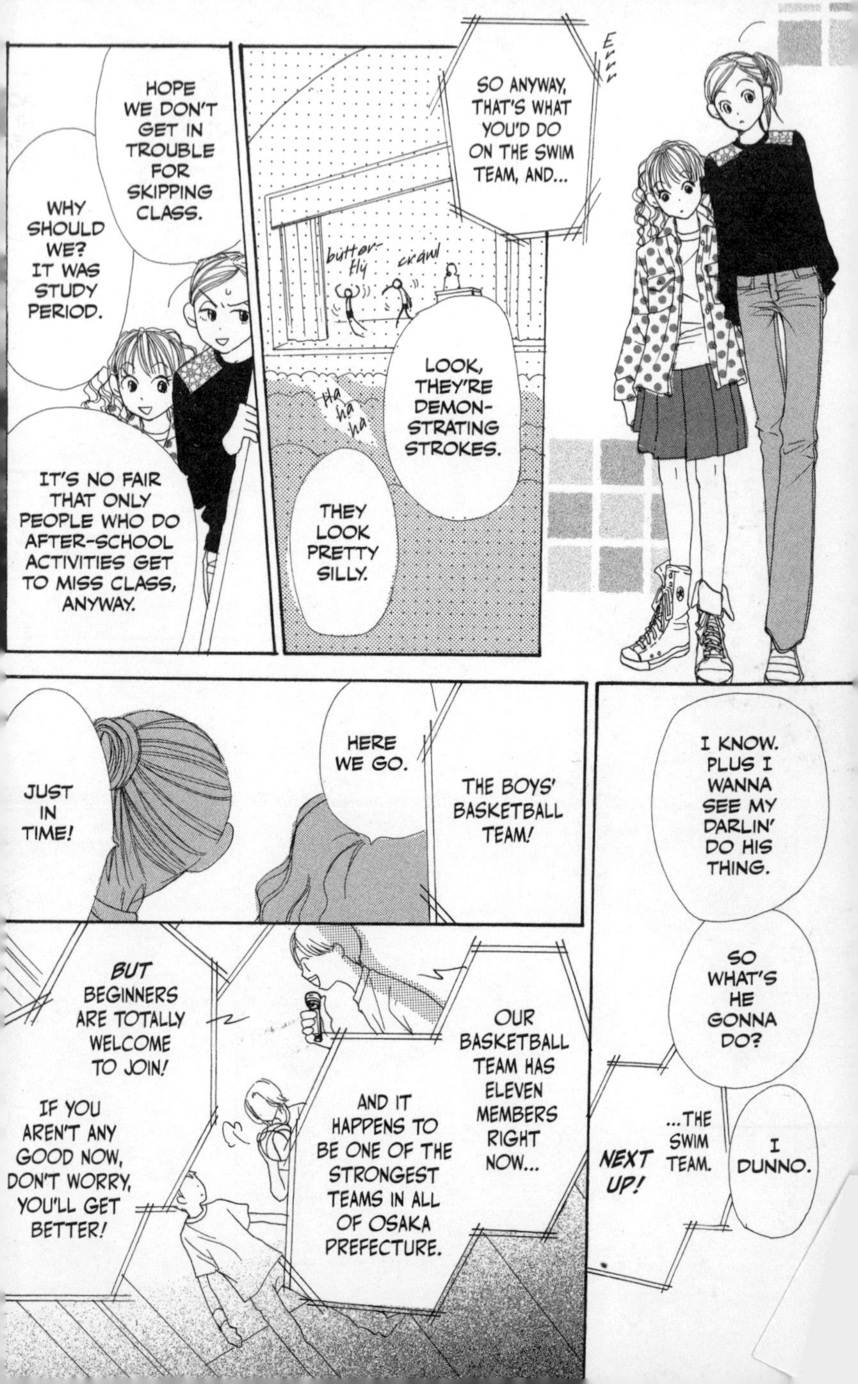
Errr
SO ANYWAY, THAT'S WHAT YOU'D DO ON THE SWIM TEAM, AND...
LOOK, THEY'RE DEMON-STRATING STROKES.
butter-fly
crawl
Ha ha ha
THEY LOOK PRETTY SILLY.
HOPE WE DON'T GET IN TROUBLE FOR SKIPPING CLASS.
WHY SHOULD WE? IT WAS STUDY PERIOD.
IT'S NO FAIR THAT ONLY PEOPLE WHO DO AFTER-SCHOOL ACTIVITIES GET TO MISS CLASS, ANYWAY.
I KNOW. PLUS I WANNA SEE MY DARLIN' DO HIS THING.
SO WHAT'S HE GONNA DO?
I DUNNO.
...THE SWIM TEAM.
NEXT UP!
HERE WE GO.
THE BOYS' BASKETBALL TEAM!
JUST IN TIME!
OUR BASKETBALL TEAM HAS ELEVEN MEMBERS RIGHT NOW...
AND IT HAPPENS TO BE ONE OF THE STRONGEST TEAMS IN ALL OF OSAKA PREFECTURE.
BUT BEGINNERS ARE TOTALLY WELCOME TO JOIN!
IF YOU AREN'T ANY GOOD NOW, DON'T WORRY, YOU'LL GET BETTER!

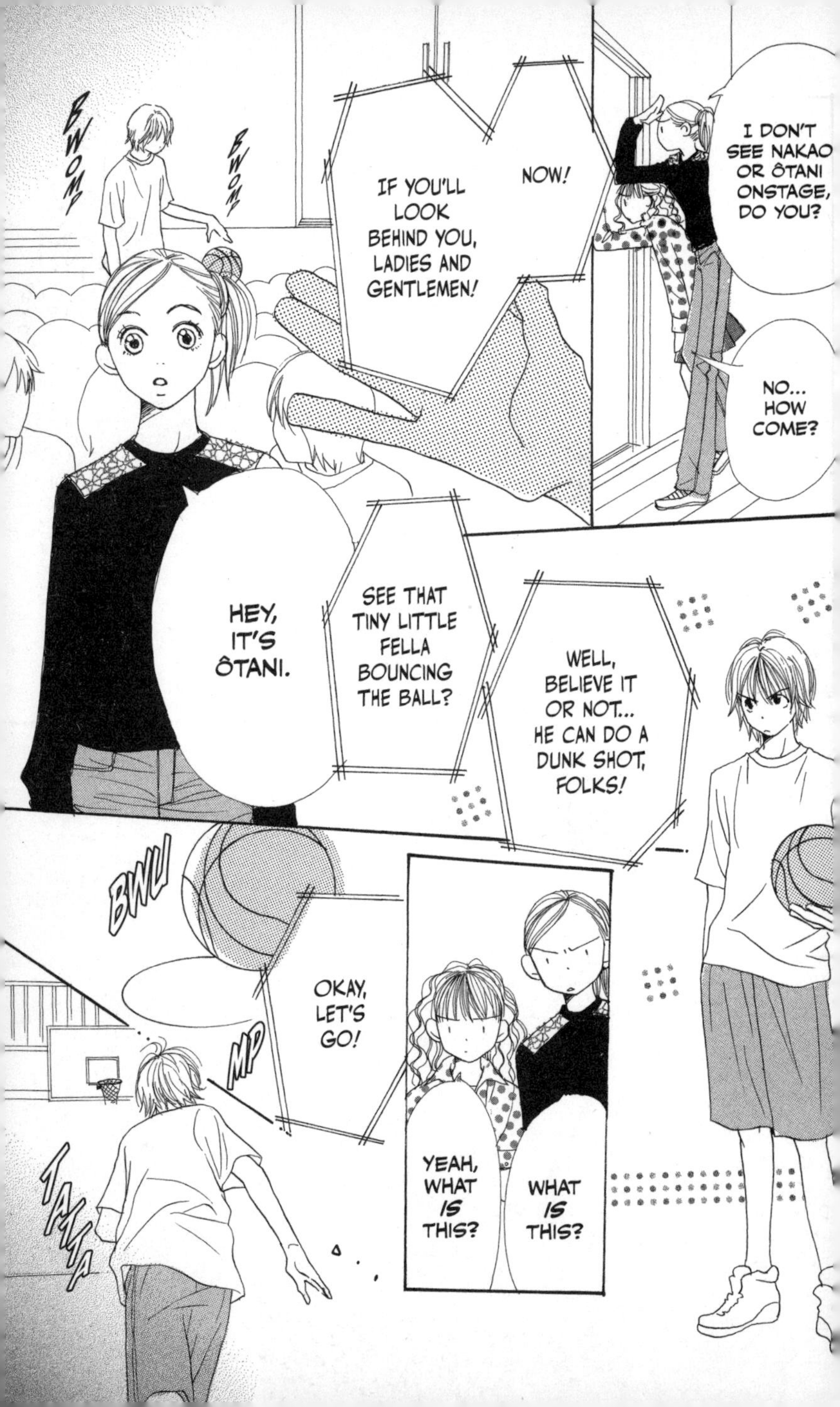
I DON'T SEE NAKAO OR ÔTANI ONSTAGE, DO YOU?
NO... HOW COME?
NOW!
IF YOU'LL LOOK BEHIND YOU, LADIES AND GENTLEMEN!
BWOMP
BWOMP
SEE THAT TINY LITTLE FELLA BOUNCING THE BALL?
WELL, BELIEVE IT OR NOT... HE CAN DO A DUNK SHOT, FOLKS!
HEY, IT'S ÔTANI.
WHAT IS THIS?
YEAH, WHAT IS THIS?
OKAY, LET'S GO!
BWU
MP

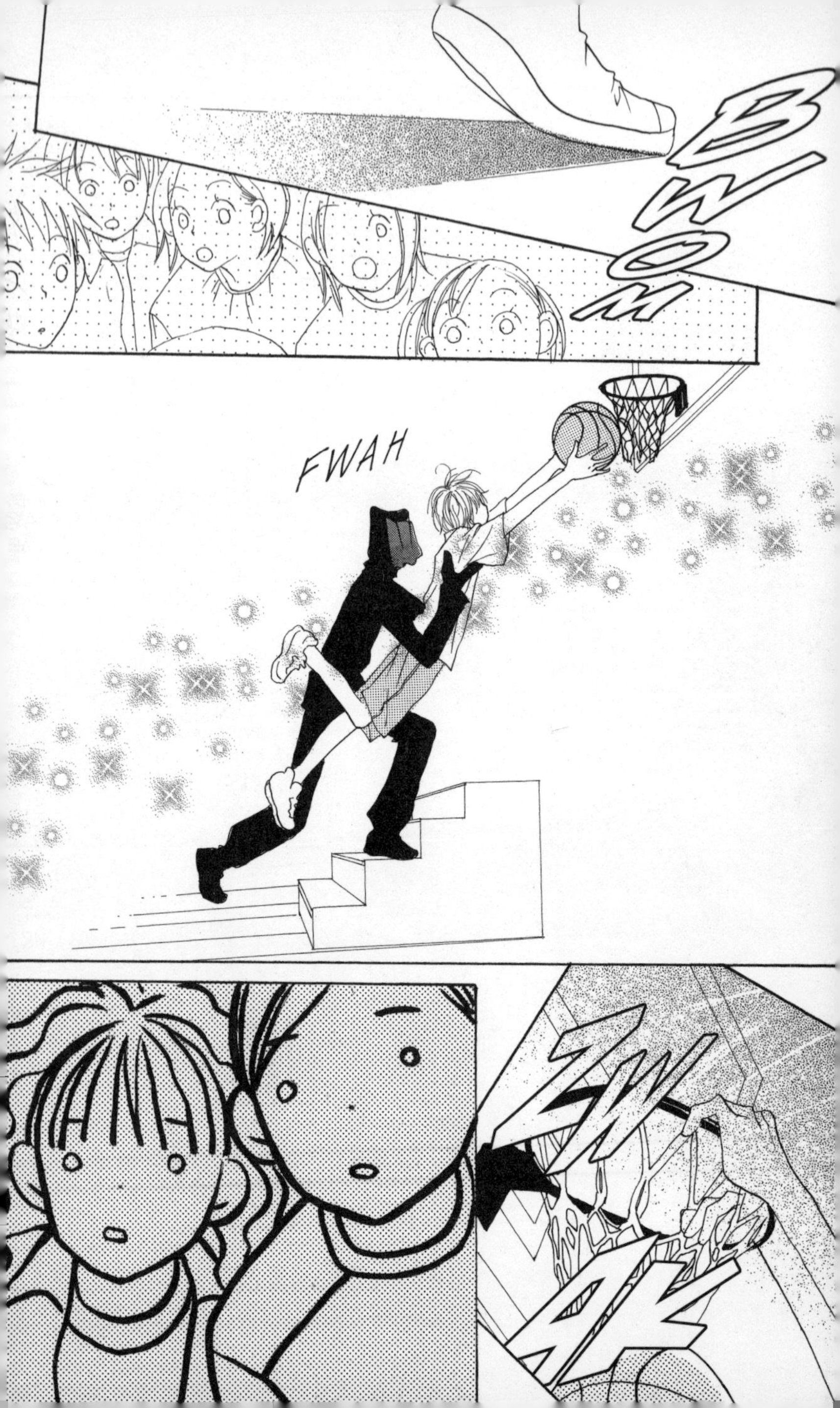
BWOM
FWAH

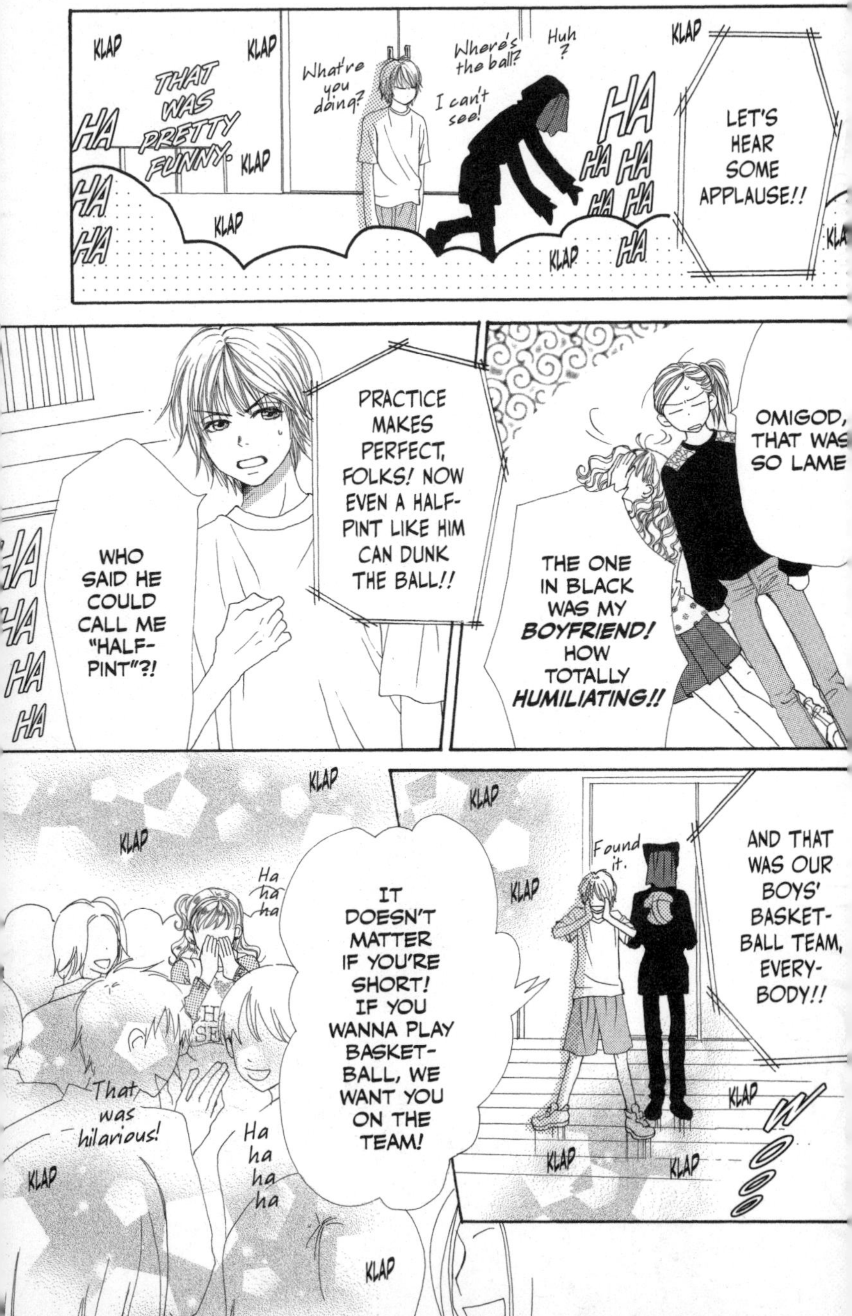

KLAP
LET'S HEAR SOME APPLAUSE!!
KLA
HA HA HA HA HA HA
KLAP
Huh?
Where's the ball?
I can't see!
What're you doing?
KLAP
THAT WAS PRETTY FUNNY.
KLAP
KLAP
HA HA HA
KLAP
OMIGOD, THAT WAS SO LAME
THE ONE IN BLACK WAS MY BOYFRIEND! HOW TOTALLY HUMILIATING!!
PRACTICE MAKES PERFECT, FOLKS! NOW EVEN A HALF-PINT LIKE HIM CAN DUNK THE BALL!!
WHO SAID HE COULD CALL ME "HALF-PINT"?!
HA HA HA HA
AND THAT WAS OUR BOYS' BASKETBALL TEAM, EVERYBODY!!
KLAP
Found it.
KLAP
KLAP
WOOOO
KLAP
KLAP
KLAP
IT DOESN'T MATTER IF YOU'RE SHORT! IF YOU WANNA PLAY BASKETBALL, WE WANT YOU ON THE TEAM!
Ha ha ha
KLAP
That was hilarious!
Ha ha ha ha
KLAP
KLAP

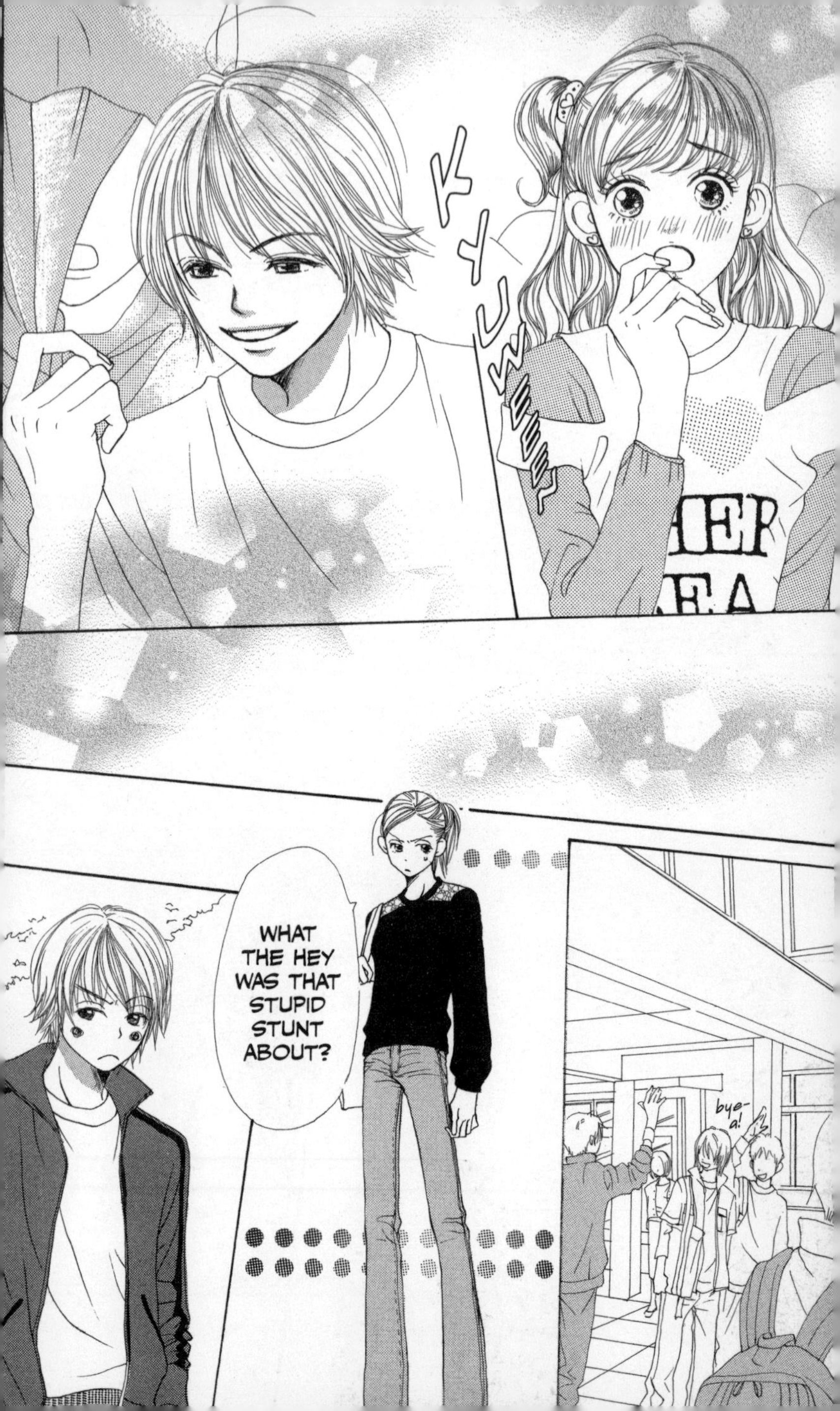
bye-a!
WHAT THE HEY WAS THAT STUPID STUNT ABOUT?

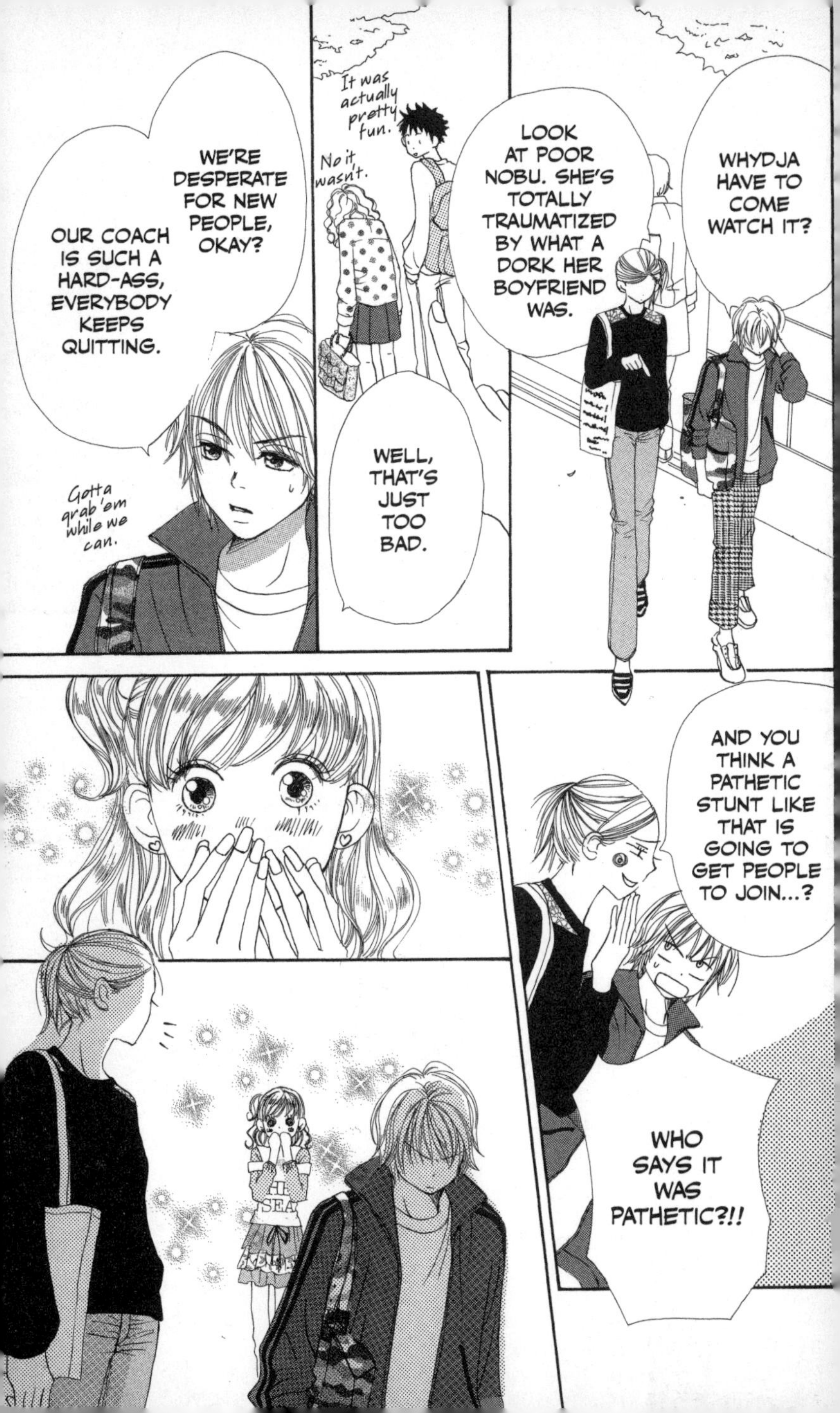
WHYDJA HAVE TO COME WATCH IT?
LOOK AT POOR NOBU. SHE'S TOTALLY TRAUMATIZED BY WHAT A DORK HER BOYFRIEND WAS.
It was actually pretty fun.
No it wasn't.
WELL, THAT'S JUST TOO BAD.
WE'RE DESPERATE FOR NEW PEOPLE, OKAY?
OUR COACH IS SUCH A HARD-ASS, EVERYBODY KEEPS QUITTING.
Gotta grab'em while we can.
AND YOU THINK A PATHETIC STUNT LIKE THAT IS GOING TO GET PEOPLE TO JOIN...?
WHO SAYS IT WAS PATHETIC?!!

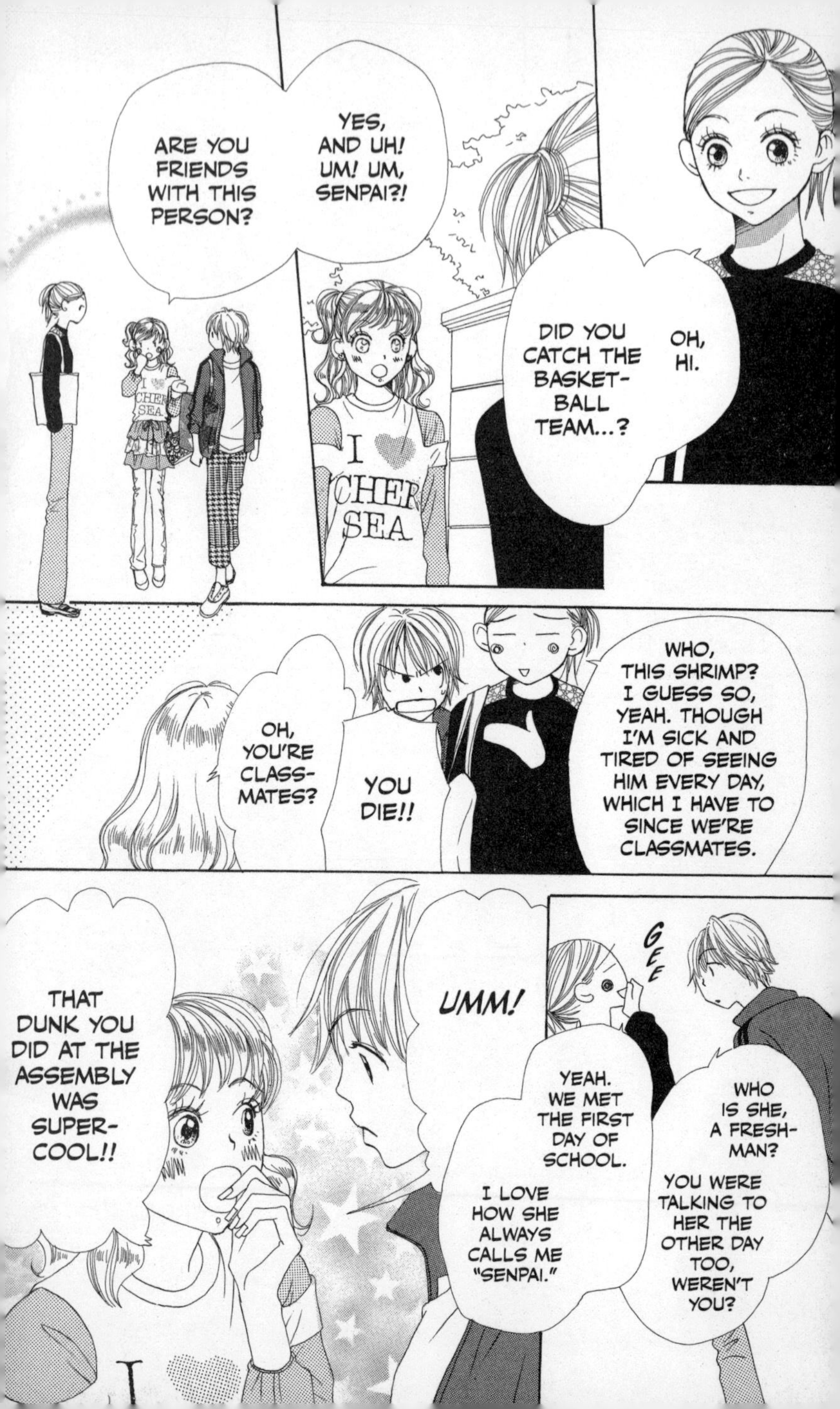
OH, HI.
DID YOU CATCH THE BASKET-BALL TEAM...?
YES, AND UH! UM! UM, SENPAI?!
ARE YOU FRIENDS WITH THIS PERSON?
WHO, THIS SHRIMP? I GUESS SO, YEAH. THOUGH I'M SICK AND TIRED OF SEEING HIM EVERY DAY, WHICH I HAVE TO SINCE WE'RE CLASSMATES.
YOU DIE!!
OH, YOU'RE CLASS-MATES?
GEE
WHO IS SHE, A FRESH-MAN?
YOU WERE TALKING TO HER THE OTHER DAY TOO, WEREN'T YOU?
YEAH. WE MET THE FIRST DAY OF SCHOOL.
I LOVE HOW SHE ALWAYS CALLS ME "SENPAI."
UMM!
THAT DUNK YOU DID AT THE ASSEMBLY WAS SUPER-COOL!!

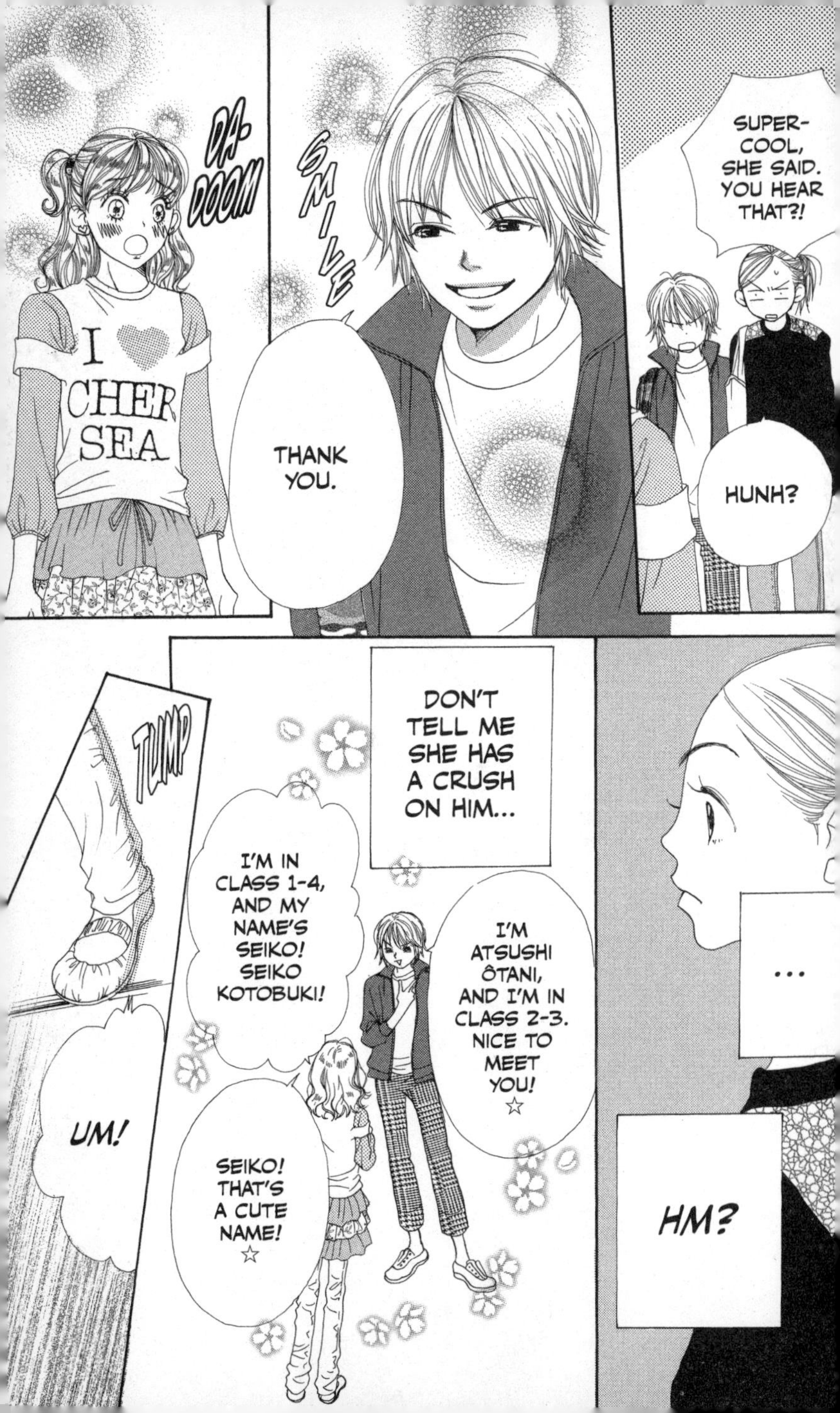
SUPER-COOL, SHE SAID. YOU HEAR THAT?!
HUNH?
SMILE
THANK YOU.
DA-DOOM
...
HM?
DON'T TELL ME SHE HAS A CRUSH ON HIM...
I'M ATSUSHI ÔTANI, AND I'M IN CLASS 2-3. NICE TO MEET YOU! ☆
I'M IN CLASS 1-4, AND MY NAME'S SEIKO! SEIKO KOTOBUKI!
SEIKO! THAT'S A CUTE NAME! ☆
TUMP
UM!

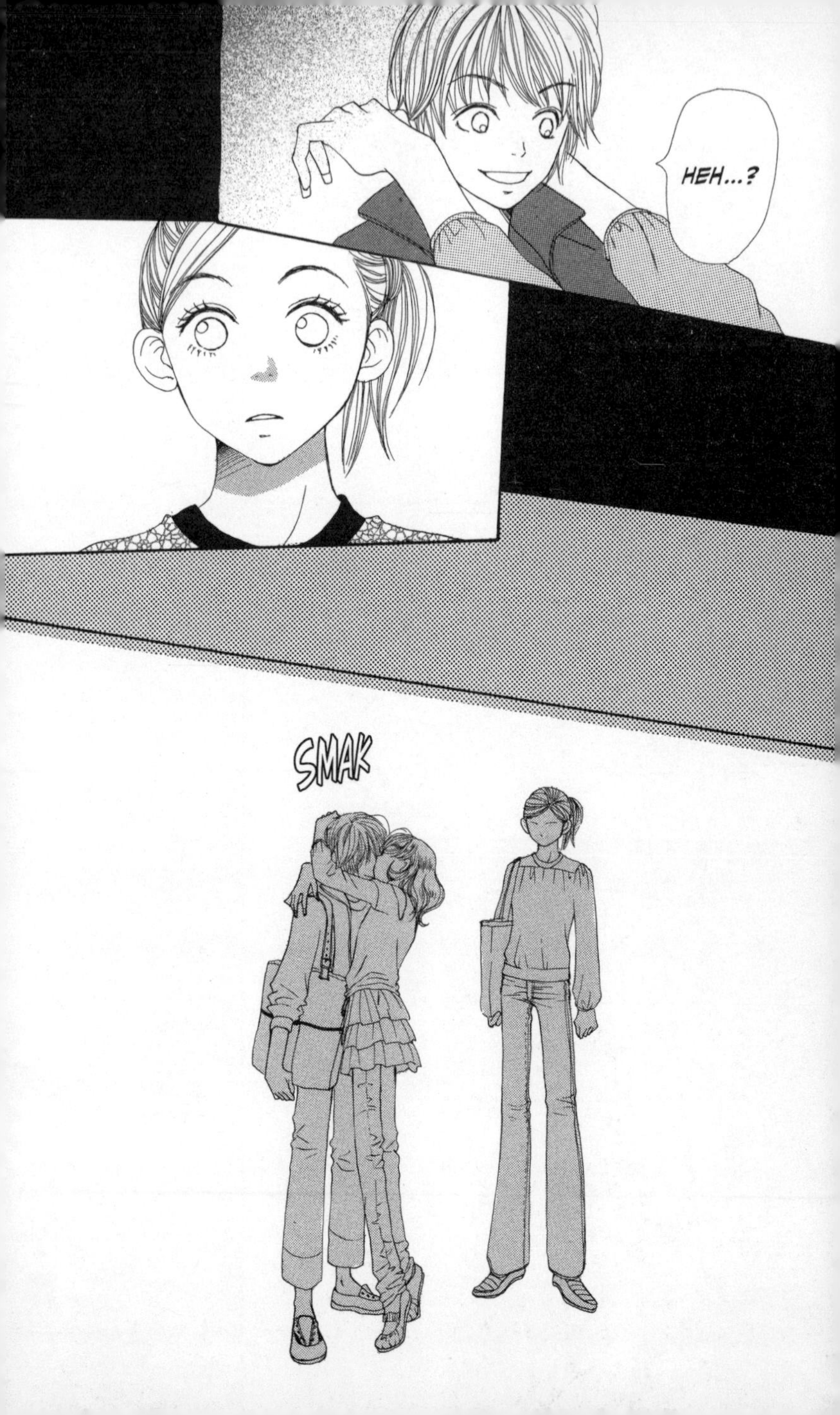
HEH...?
SMAK

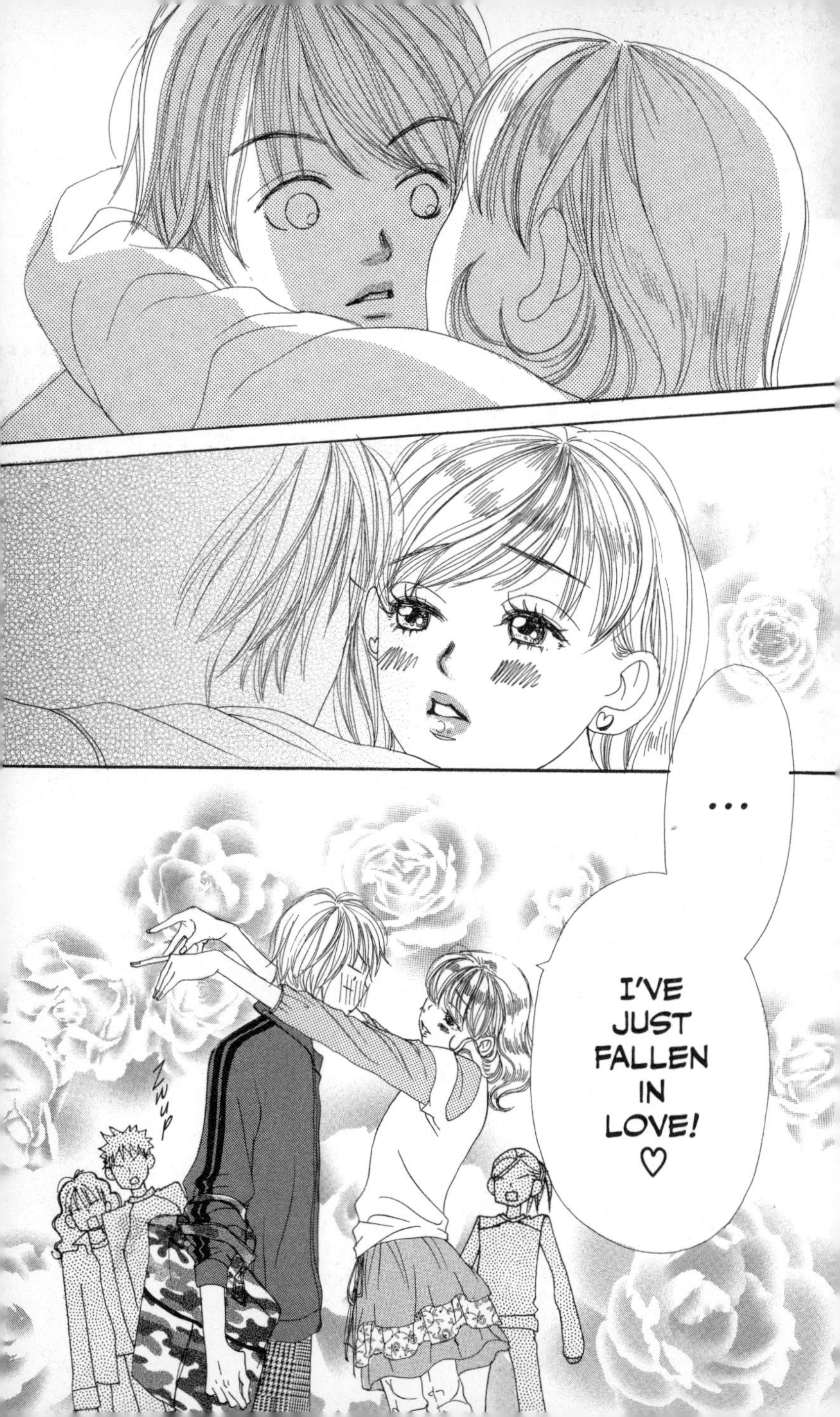
...
I'VE JUST FALLEN IN LOVE! ♡
ZWUP

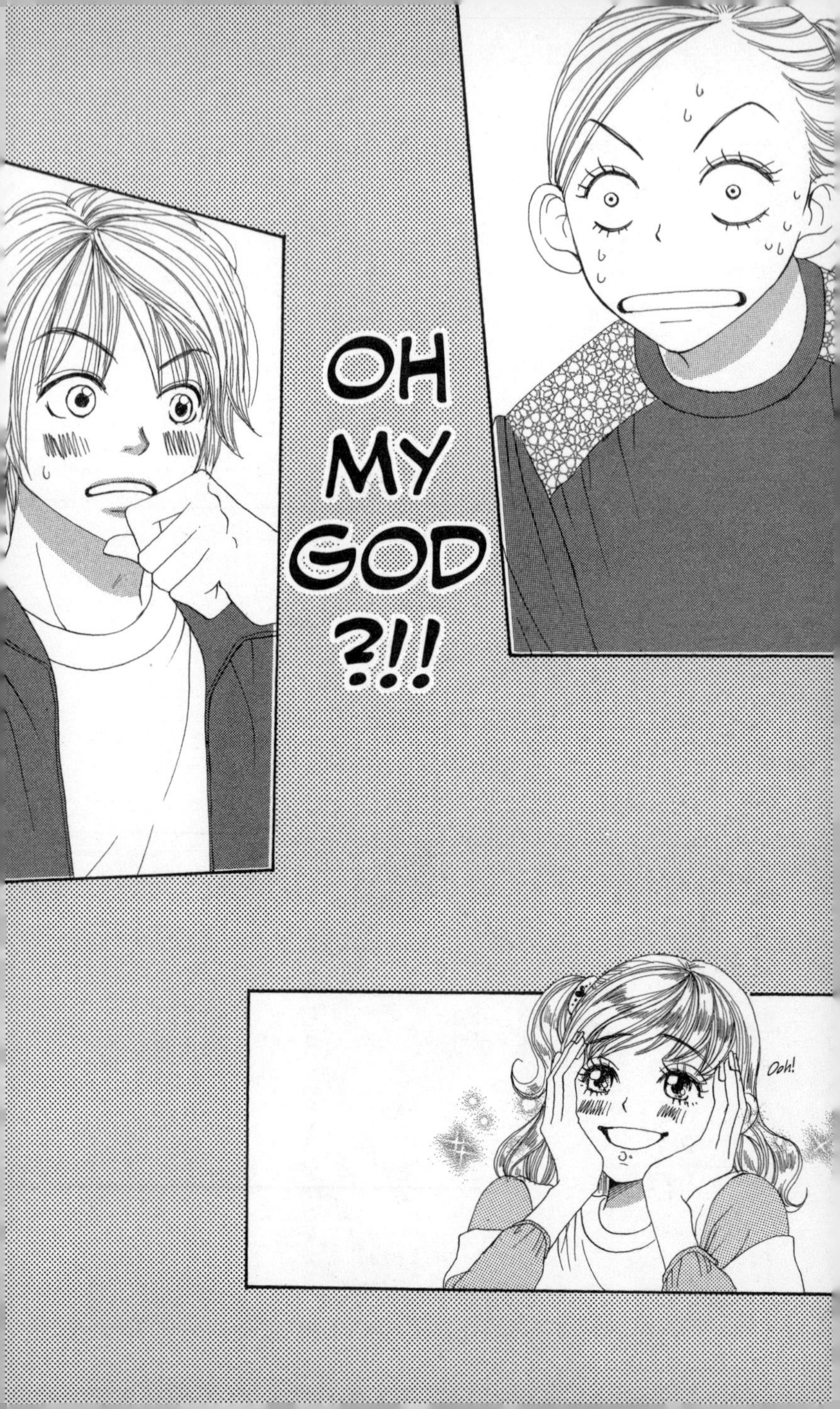
OH MY GOD ?!!
Ooh!

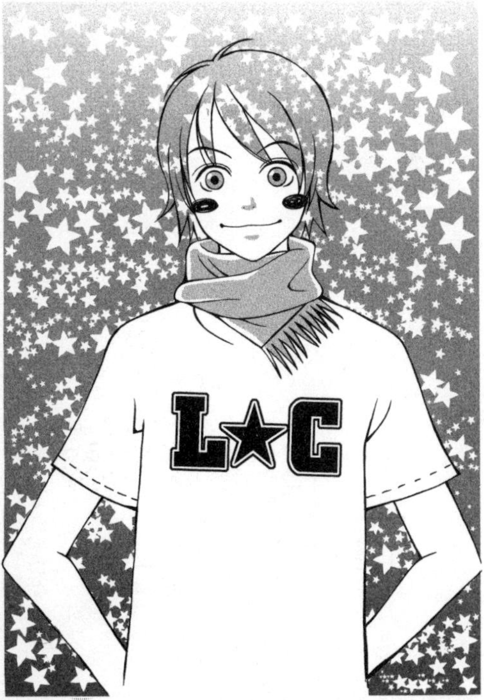
L★C

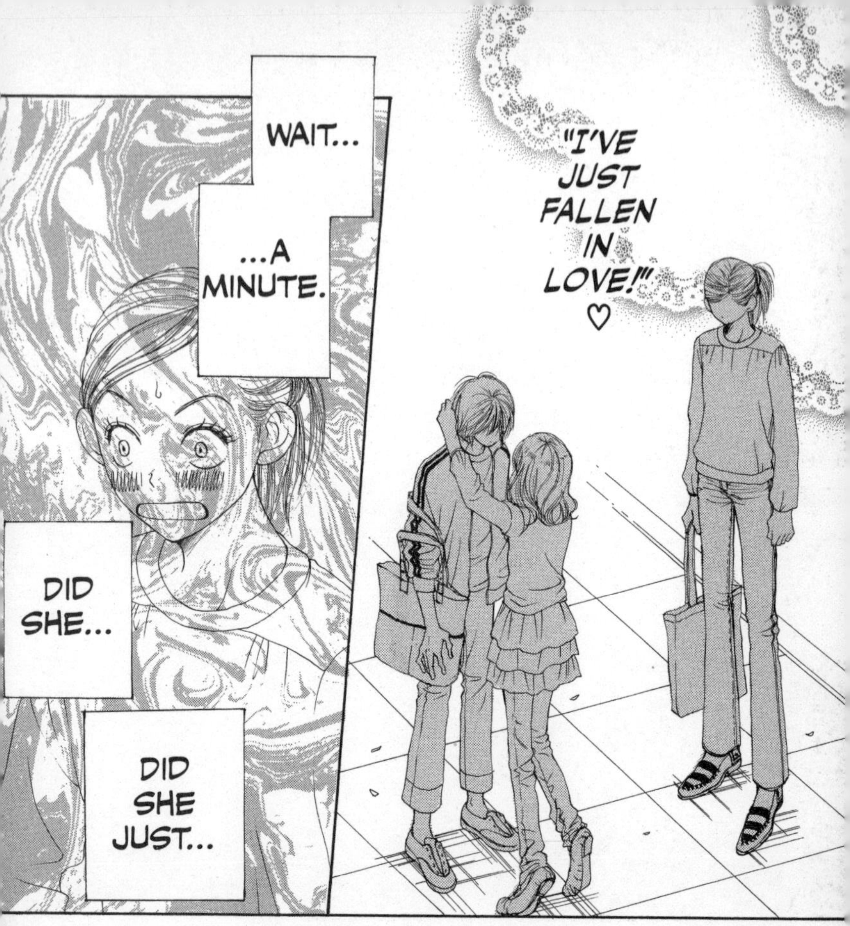
"I'VE JUST FALLEN IN LOVE!" ♡
WAIT...
...A MINUTE.
DID SHE...
DID SHE JUST...

CHAPTER 11

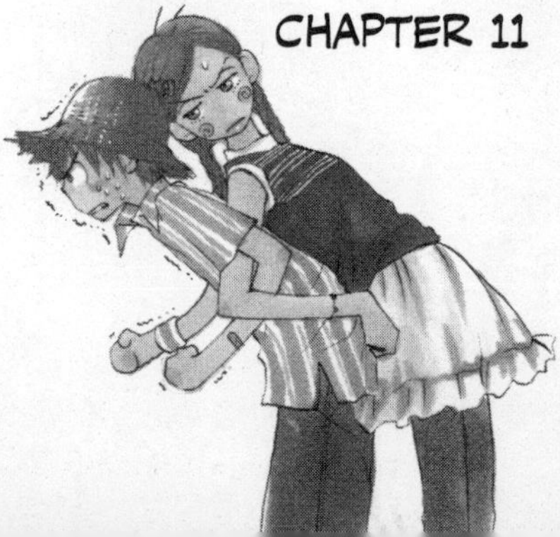

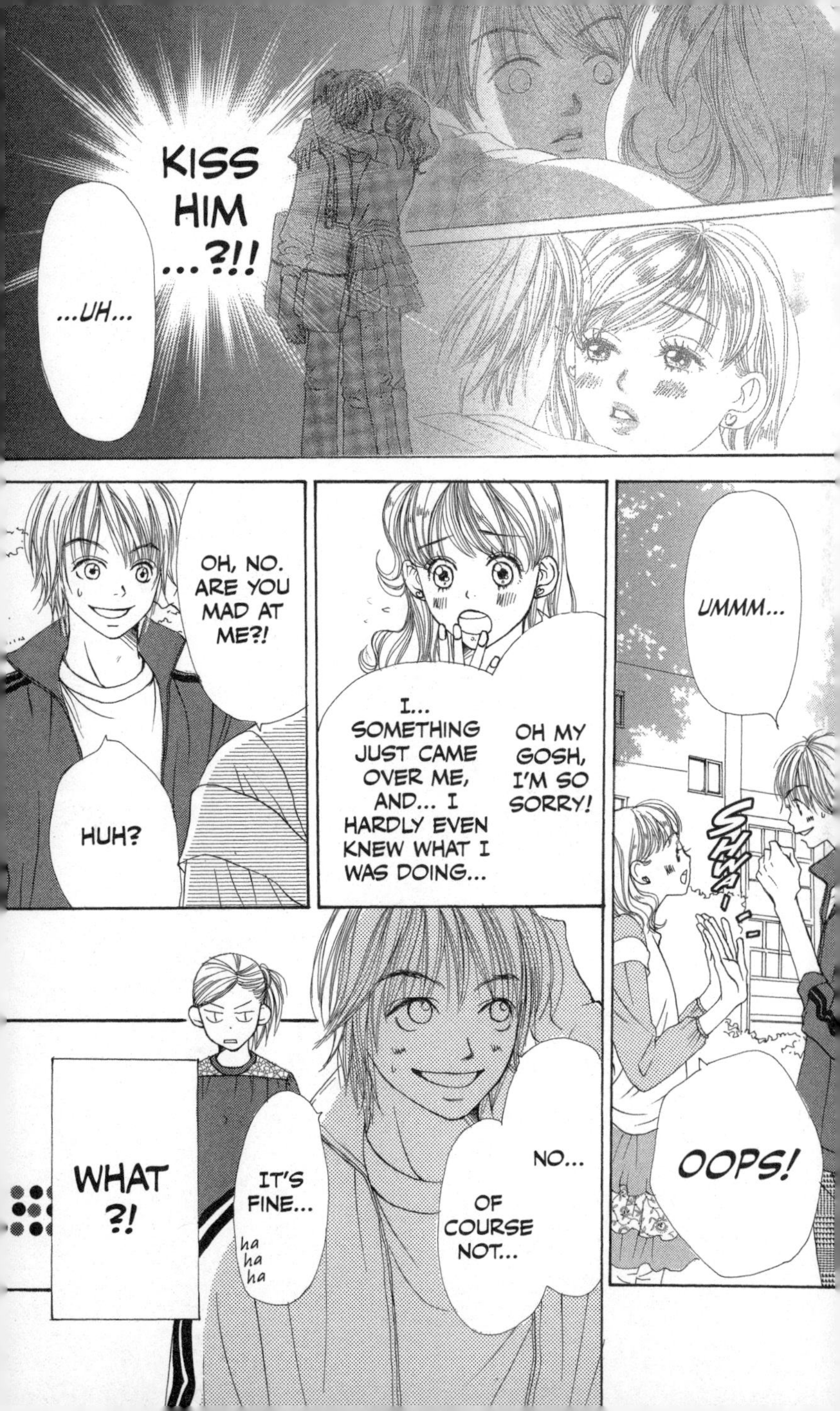
KISS HIM ...?!!
...UH...
UMMM...
SHWA
OOPS!
OH MY GOSH, I'M SO SORRY!
I... SOMETHING JUST CAME OVER ME, AND... I HARDLY EVEN KNEW WHAT I WAS DOING...
OH, NO. ARE YOU MAD AT ME?!
HUH?
NO... OF COURSE NOT...
IT'S FINE...
ha ha ha
WHAT ?!

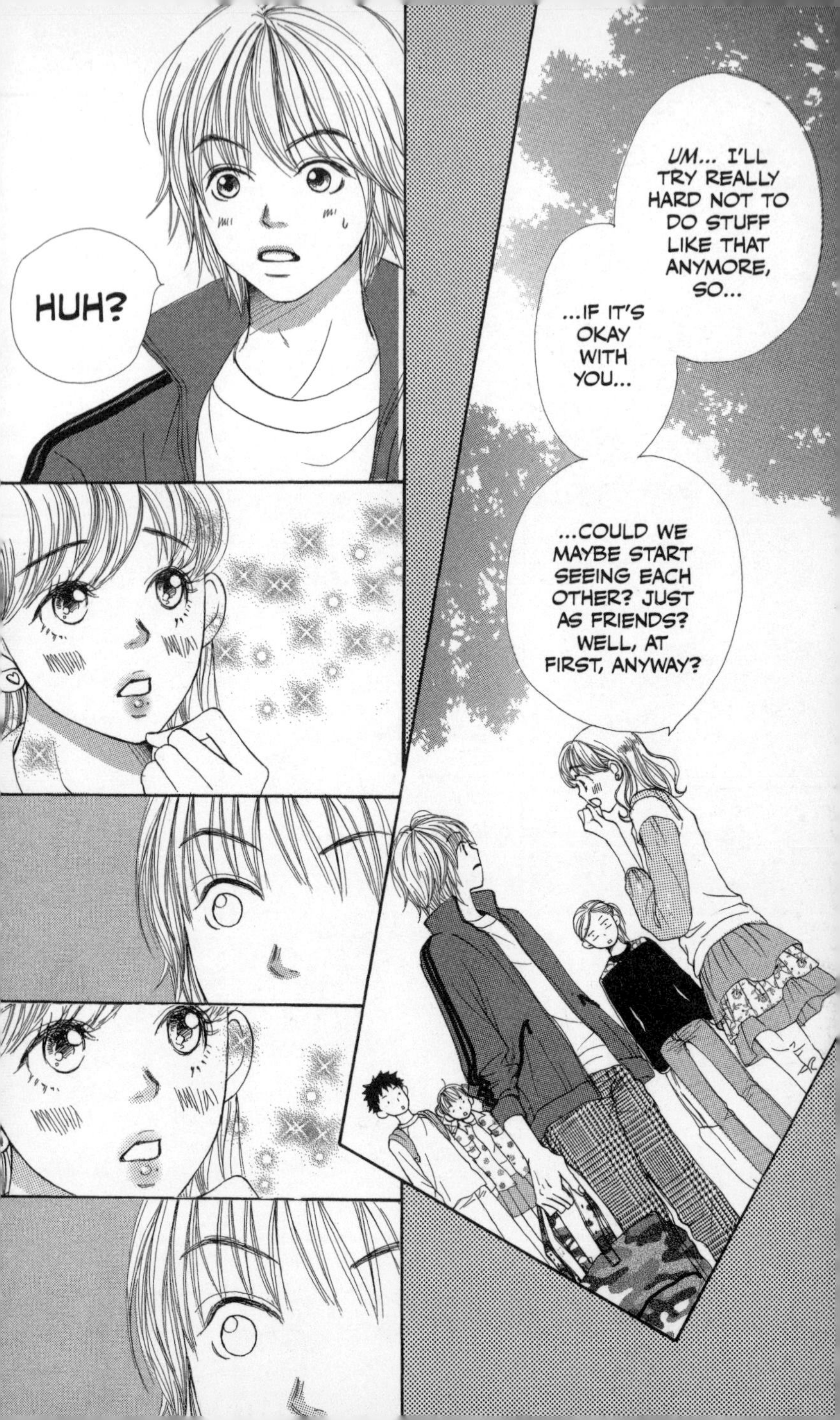
UM... I'LL TRY REALLY HARD NOT TO DO STUFF LIKE THAT ANYMORE, SO...
...IF IT'S OKAY WITH YOU...
...COULD WE MAYBE START SEEING EACH OTHER? JUST AS FRIENDS? WELL, AT FIRST, ANYWAY?
HUH?

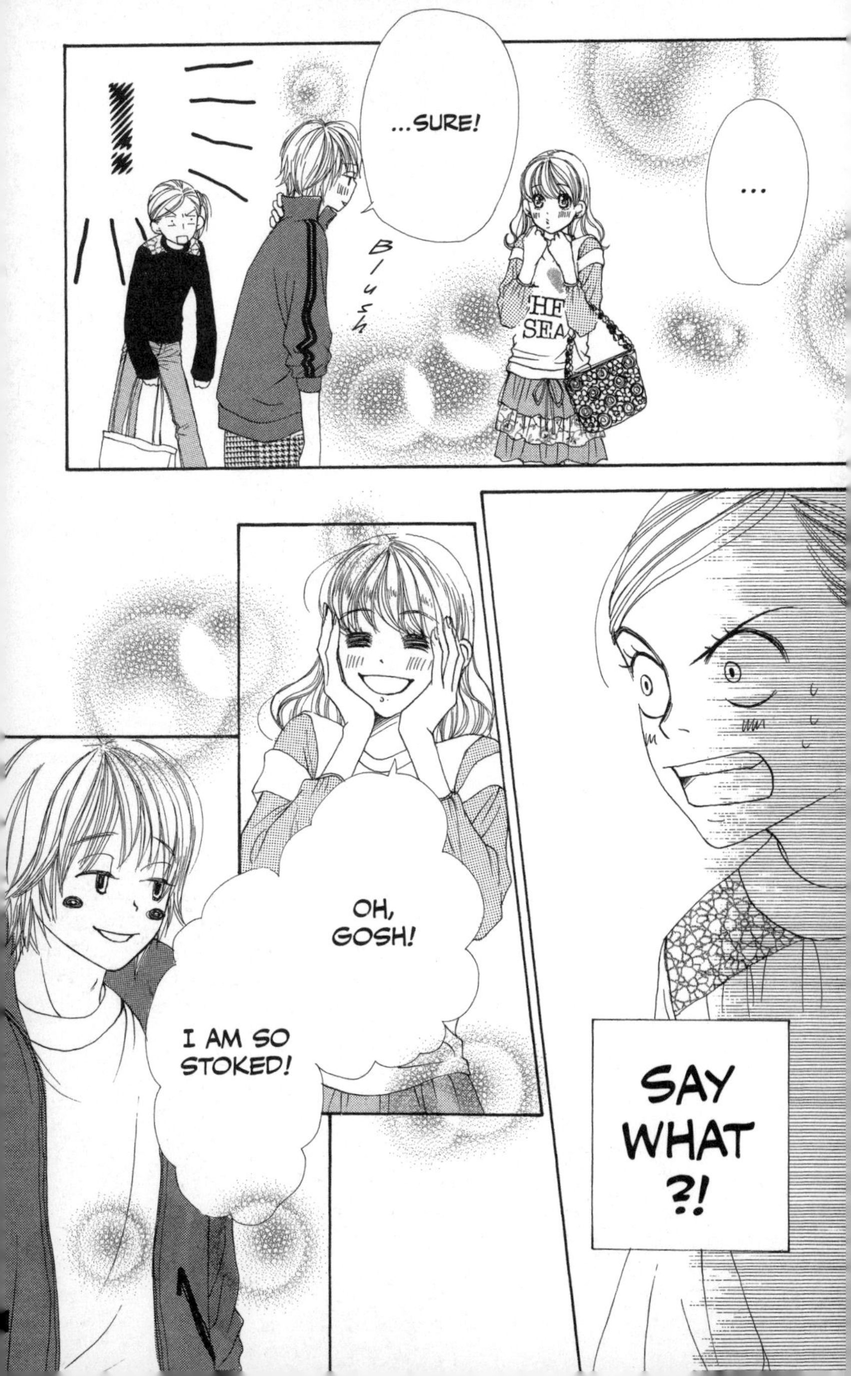
...
...SURE!
BLUSH
SAY WHAT ?!
OH, GOSH!
I AM SO STOKED!

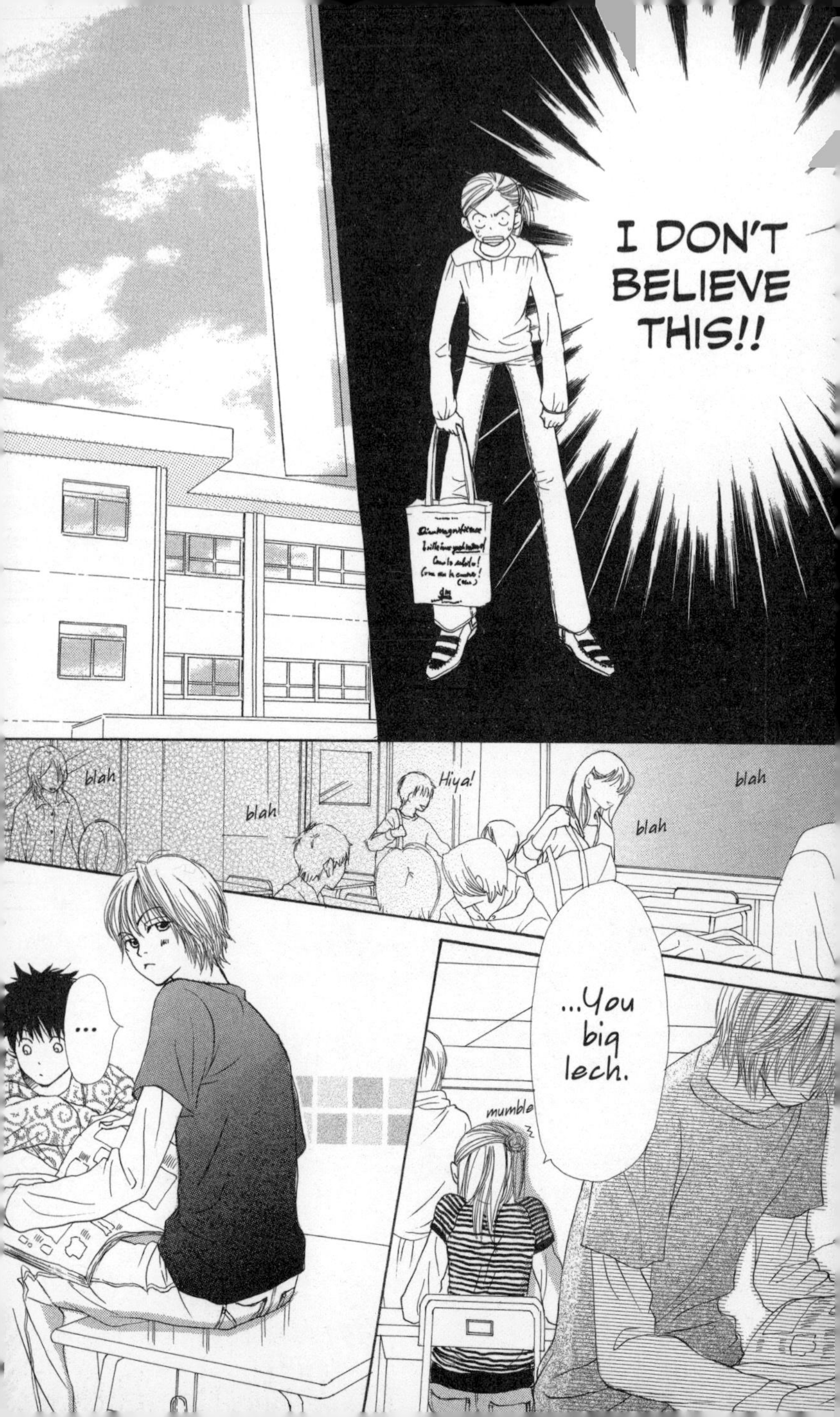
I DON'T BELIEVE THIS!!
blah
blah
Hiya!
blah
blah
...You big lech.
mumble
...

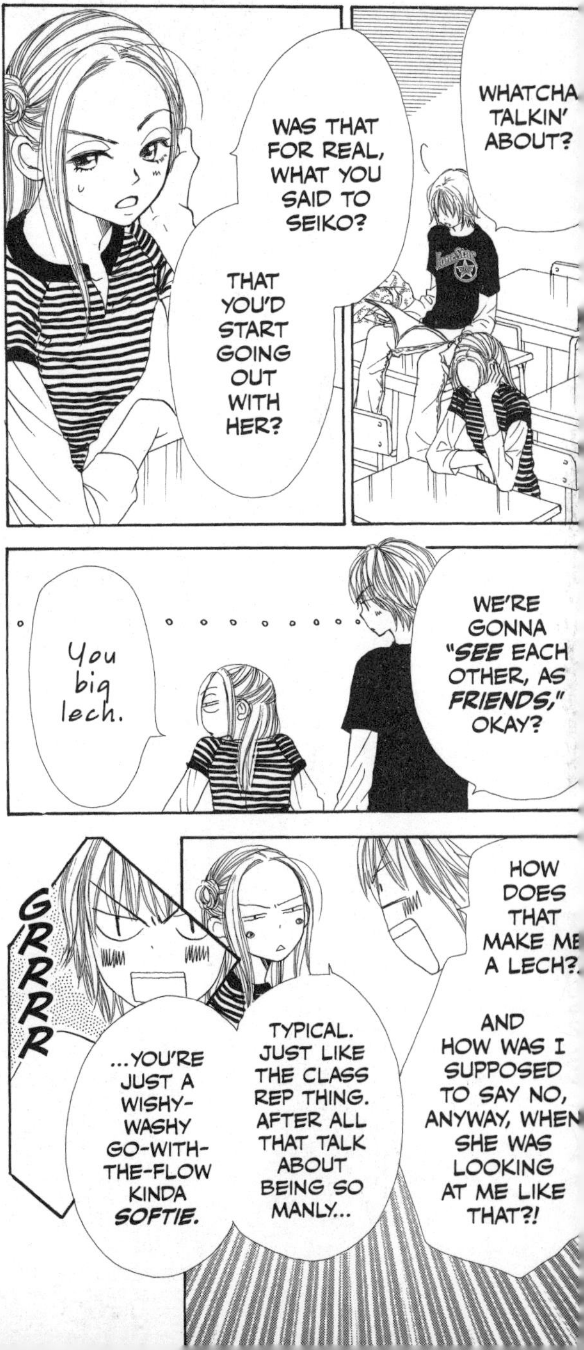
WHATCHA TALKIN' ABOUT?
WAS THAT FOR REAL, WHAT YOU SAID TO SEIKO?
THAT YOU'D START GOING OUT WITH HER?
WE'RE GONNA "SEE EACH OTHER, AS FRIENDS," OKAY?
You big lech.
HOW DOES THAT MAKE ME A LECH?
AND HOW WAS I SUPPOSED TO SAY NO, ANYWAY, WHEN SHE WAS LOOKING AT ME LIKE THAT?!
TYPICAL. JUST LIKE THE CLASS REP THING. AFTER ALL THAT TALK ABOUT BEING SO MANLY...
...YOU'RE JUST A WISHY-WASHY GO-WITH-THE-FLOW KINDA SOFTIE.
GRRRR

3

This summer went by real fast 'cuz I was so busy doing all kinds of stuff. Like going to see a lot of bands. The Ulfuls have been doing this big outdoor show every summer for the past two or three years, in Osaka only, and I never miss that...except last year I did, because of work, so this year I made up for it by going nuts for two years' worth. Every time I go to that, I'm like, "I am so glad I'm from Osaka!!" Those guys electrify me. bzz bzz bzz
The only time I have any energy is when I go to concerts. <sigh> umph.
Oh, and the other day I went to this outdoor festival called "Rush Ball 2002" where they had bands playing all day from around noon until 8 p.m. or so. That's a lot of bands. So I only went around halfway through, in the late afternoon. What a slacker!
But I got to see lots of people I really love, like Tamio Okuda and Bump of Chicken and Tokyo Ska Paradise Orchestra, all in one day, so that was pretty great.

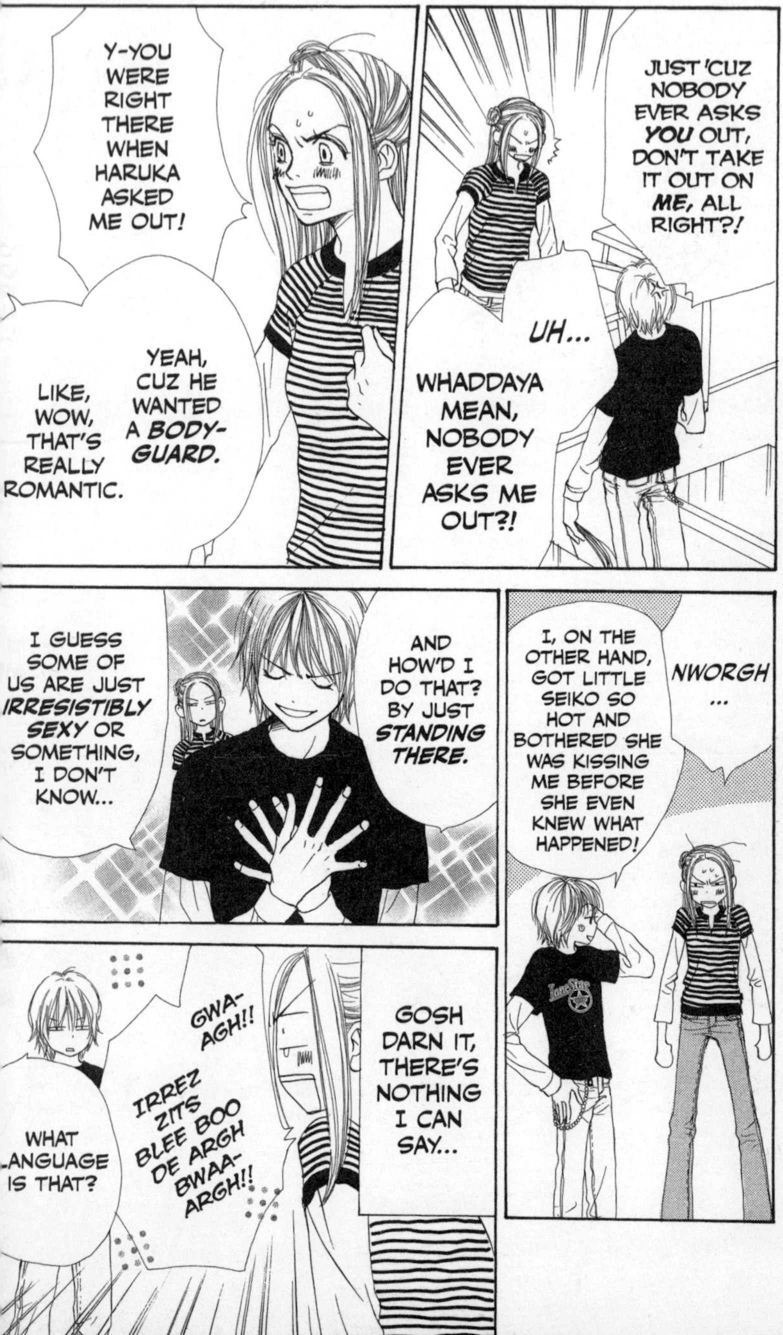
JUST 'CUZ NOBODY EVER ASKS *YOU* OUT, DON'T TAKE IT OUT ON *ME*, ALL RIGHT?!
UH...
WHADDAYA MEAN, NOBODY EVER ASKS ME OUT?!
Y-YOU WERE RIGHT THERE WHEN HARUKA ASKED ME OUT!
YEAH, CUZ HE WANTED A *BODY-GUARD.*
LIKE, WOW, THAT'S REALLY ROMANTIC.
I, ON THE OTHER HAND, GOT LITTLE SEIKO SO HOT AND BOTHERED SHE WAS KISSING ME BEFORE SHE EVEN KNEW WHAT HAPPENED!
NWORGH ...
AND HOW'D I DO THAT? BY JUST *STANDING THERE.*
I GUESS SOME OF US ARE JUST *IRRESISTIBLY SEXY* OR SOMETHING, I DON'T KNOW...
GOSH DARN IT, THERE'S NOTHING I CAN SAY...
GWA-AGH!!
IRREZ ZITS BLEE BOO DE ARGH BWAA-ARGH!!
WHAT LANGUAGE IS THAT?

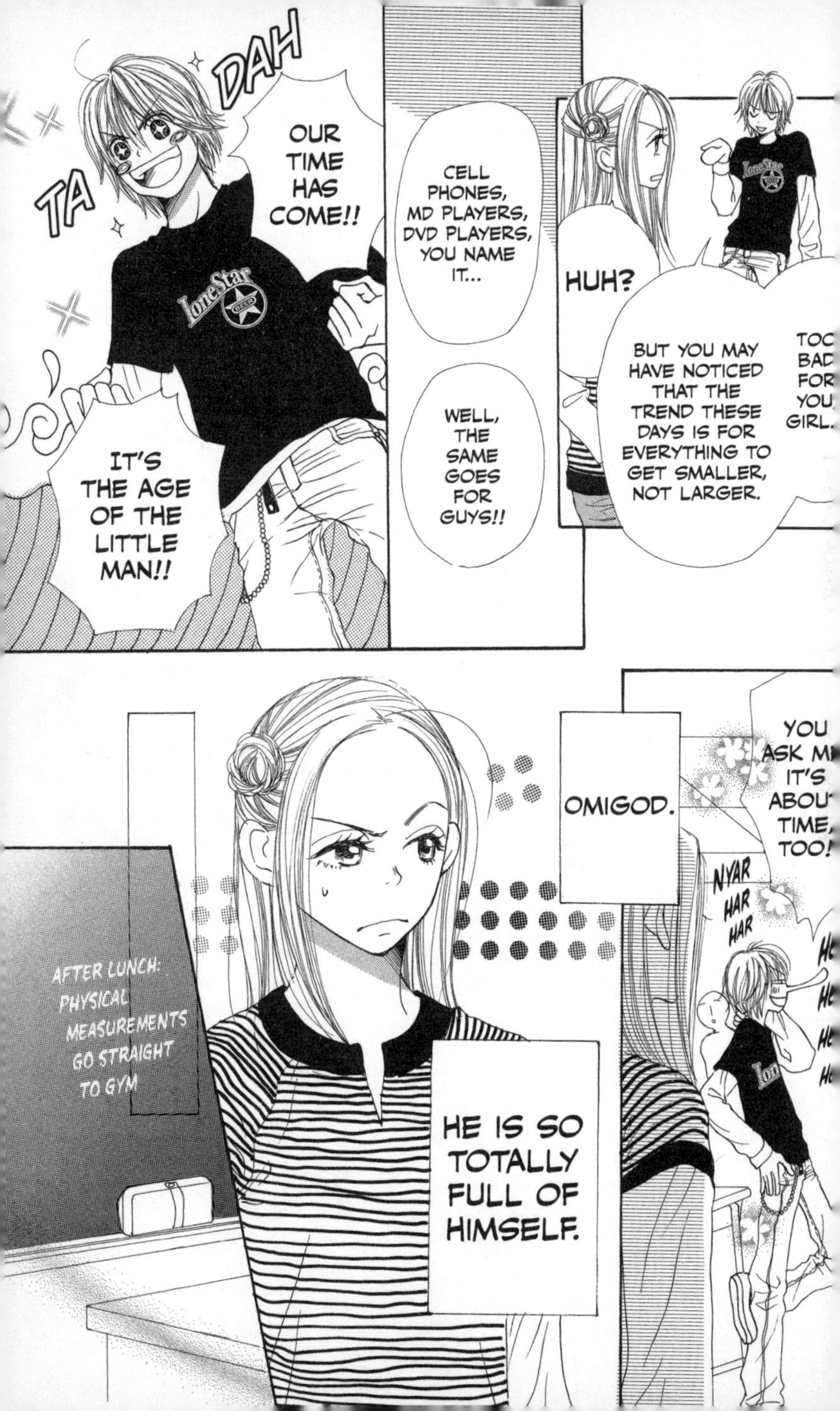
TOO BAD FOR YOU, GIRL.
BUT YOU MAY HAVE NOTICED THAT THE TREND THESE DAYS IS FOR EVERYTHING TO GET SMALLER, NOT LARGER.
HUH?
CELL PHONES, MD PLAYERS, DVD PLAYERS, YOU NAME IT...
WELL, THE SAME GOES FOR GUYS!!
TA DAH
OUR TIME HAS COME!!
IT'S THE AGE OF THE LITTLE MAN!!
YOU ASK ME IT'S ABOUT TIME, TOO!
NYAR HAR HAR
OMIGOD.
AFTER LUNCH: PHYSICAL MEASUREMENTS GO STRAIGHT TO GYM
HE IS SO TOTALLY FULL OF HIMSELF.

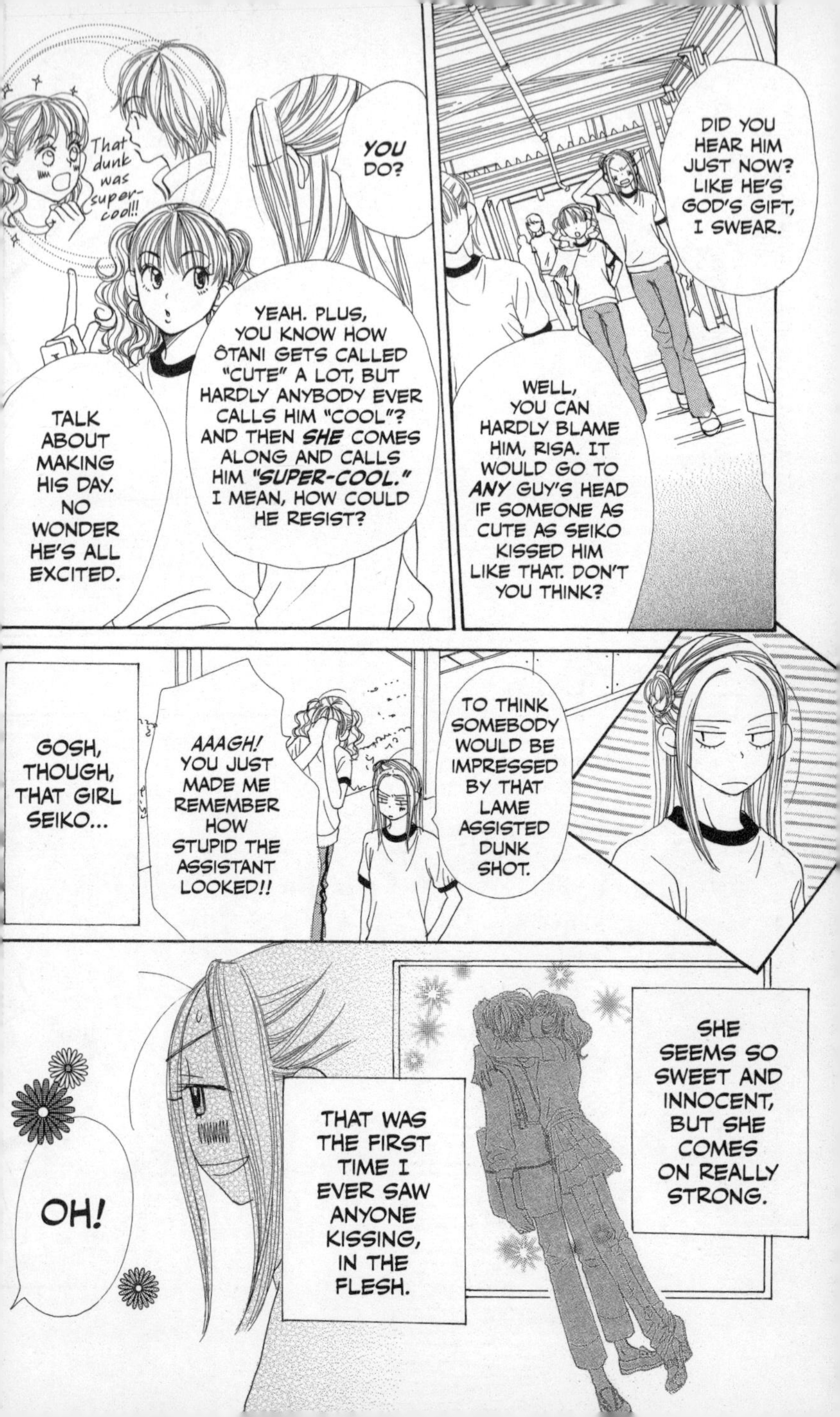
DID YOU HEAR HIM JUST NOW? LIKE HE'S GOD'S GIFT, I SWEAR.
WELL, YOU CAN HARDLY BLAME HIM, RISA. IT WOULD GO TO *ANY* GUY'S HEAD IF SOMEONE AS CUTE AS SEIKO KISSED HIM LIKE THAT. DON'T YOU THINK?
YOU DO?
That dunk was super-cool!!
YEAH. PLUS, YOU KNOW HOW ŌTANI GETS CALLED "CUTE" A LOT, BUT HARDLY ANYBODY EVER CALLS HIM "COOL"? AND THEN *SHE* COMES ALONG AND CALLS HIM *"SUPER-COOL."* I MEAN, HOW COULD HE RESIST?
TALK ABOUT MAKING HIS DAY. NO WONDER HE'S ALL EXCITED.
TO THINK SOMEBODY WOULD BE IMPRESSED BY THAT LAME ASSISTED DUNK SHOT.
AAAGH! YOU JUST MADE ME REMEMBER HOW STUPID THE ASSISTANT LOOKED!!
GOSH, THOUGH, THAT GIRL SEIKO...
SHE SEEMS SO SWEET AND INNOCENT, BUT SHE COMES ON REALLY STRONG.
THAT WAS THE FIRST TIME I EVER SAW ANYONE KISSING, IN THE FLESH.
OH!

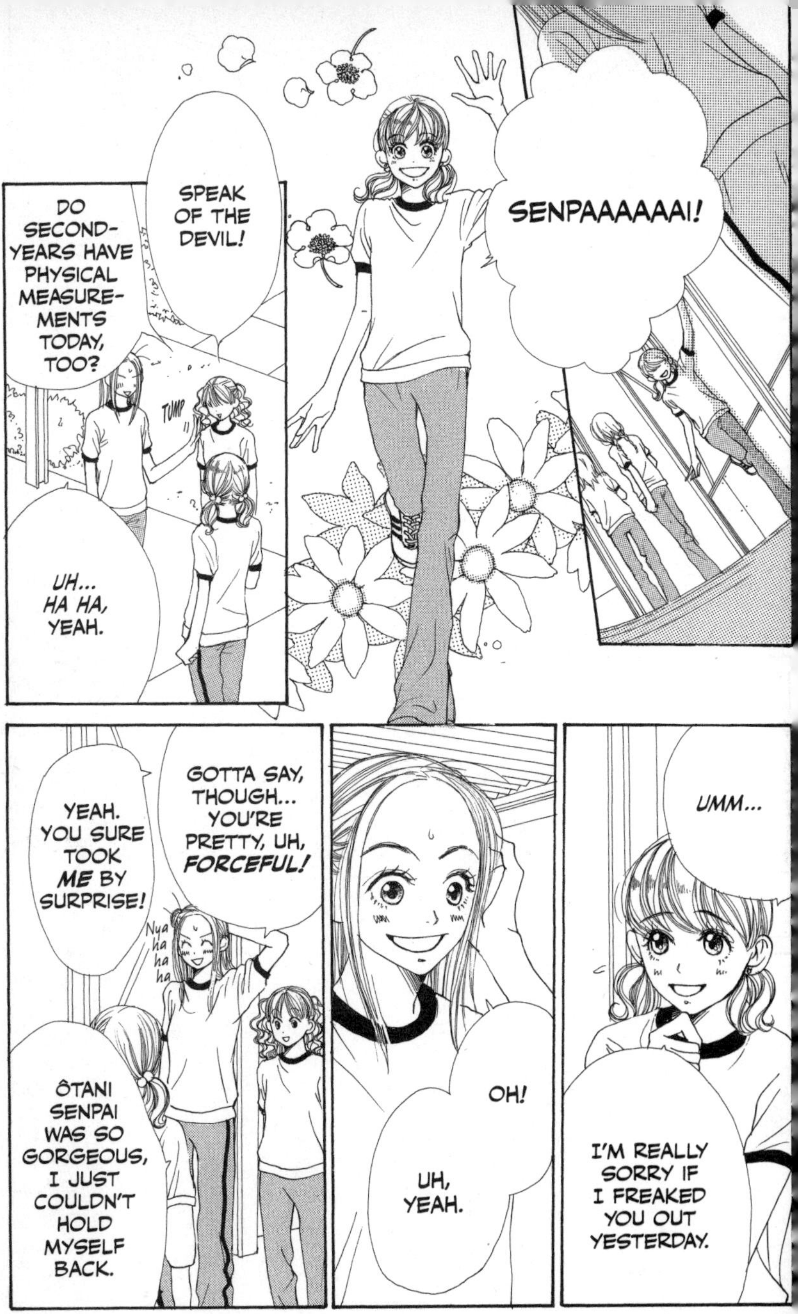
SENPAAAAAAI!
SPEAK OF THE DEVIL!
DO SECOND-YEARS HAVE PHYSICAL MEASUREMENTS TODAY, TOO?
TUMP
UH... HA HA, YEAH.
UMM...
I'M REALLY SORRY IF I FREAKED YOU OUT YESTERDAY.
OH!
UH, YEAH.
GOTTA SAY, THOUGH... YOU'RE PRETTY, UH, *FORCEFUL!*
YEAH. YOU SURE TOOK *ME* BY SURPRISE!
Nya ha ha ha
ÔTANI SENPAI WAS SO GORGEOUS, I JUST COULDN'T HOLD MYSELF BACK.

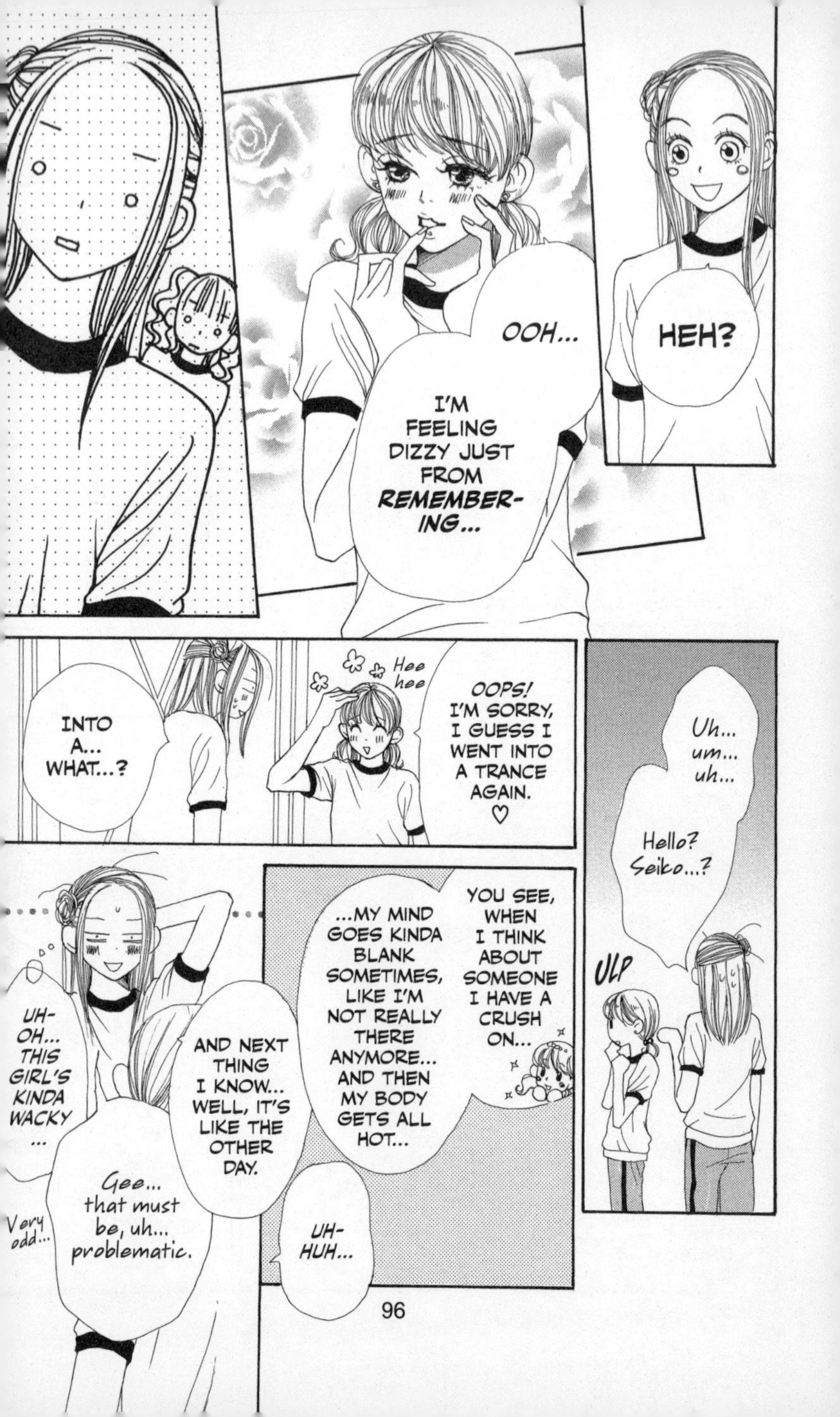
HEH?
OOH...
I'M FEELING DIZZY JUST FROM *REMEMBERING...*
Uh... um... uh...
Hello? Seiko...?
ULP
OOPS! I'M SORRY, I GUESS I WENT INTO A TRANCE AGAIN. ♡
Hee hee
INTO A... WHAT...?
YOU SEE, WHEN I THINK ABOUT SOMEONE I HAVE A CRUSH ON...
...MY MIND GOES KINDA BLANK SOMETIMES, LIKE I'M NOT REALLY THERE ANYMORE... AND THEN MY BODY GETS ALL HOT...
UH-HUH...
AND NEXT THING I KNOW... WELL, IT'S LIKE THE OTHER DAY.
UH-OH... THIS GIRL'S KINDA WACKY...
Gee... that must be, uh... problematic.
Very odd...

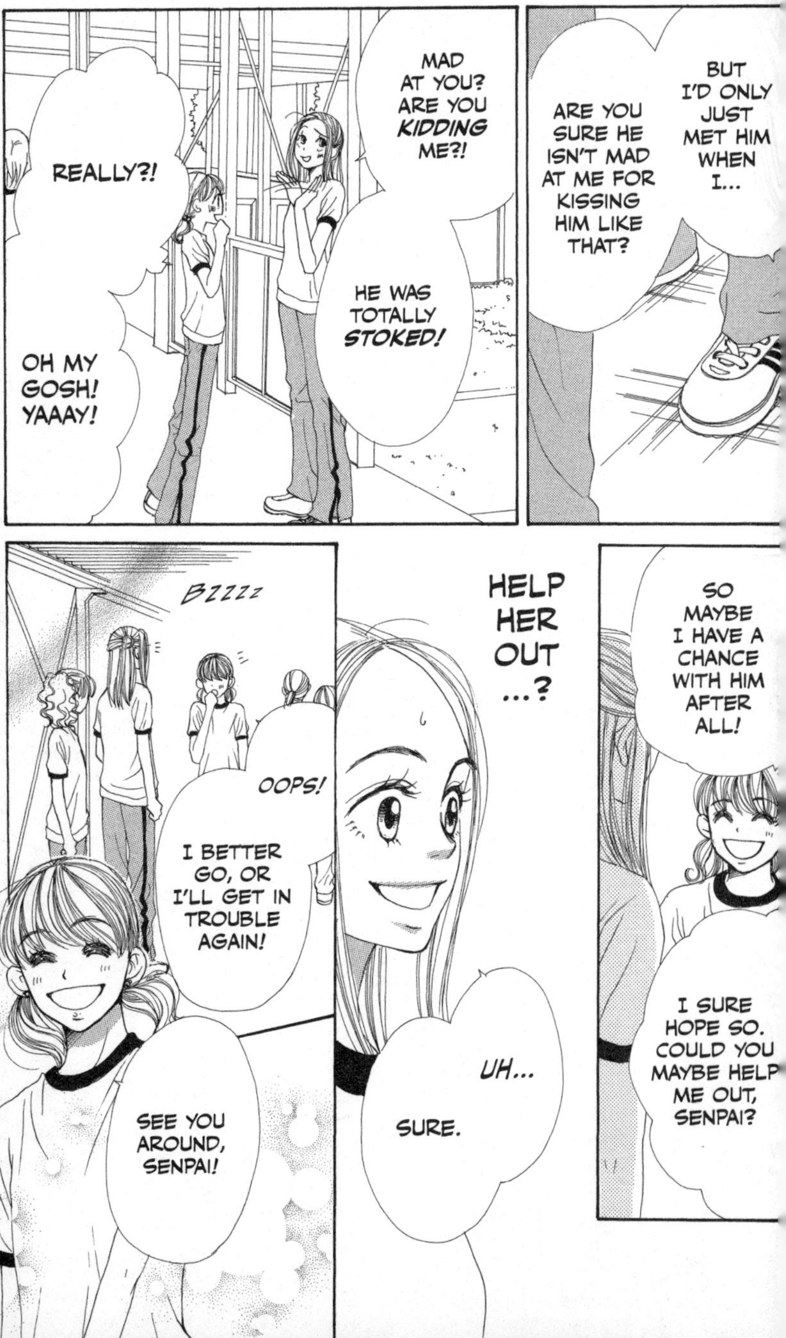
BUT I'D ONLY JUST MET HIM WHEN I...
ARE YOU SURE HE ISN'T MAD AT ME FOR KISSING HIM LIKE THAT?
MAD AT YOU? ARE YOU *KIDDING* ME?!
HE WAS TOTALLY *STOKED!*
REALLY?!
OH MY GOSH! YAAAY!
SO MAYBE I HAVE A CHANCE WITH HIM AFTER ALL!
I SURE HOPE SO. COULD YOU MAYBE HELP ME OUT, SENPAI?
HELP HER OUT ...?
UH...
SURE.
BZZZZ
OOPS!
I BETTER GO, OR I'LL GET IN TROUBLE AGAIN!
SEE YOU AROUND, SENPAI!

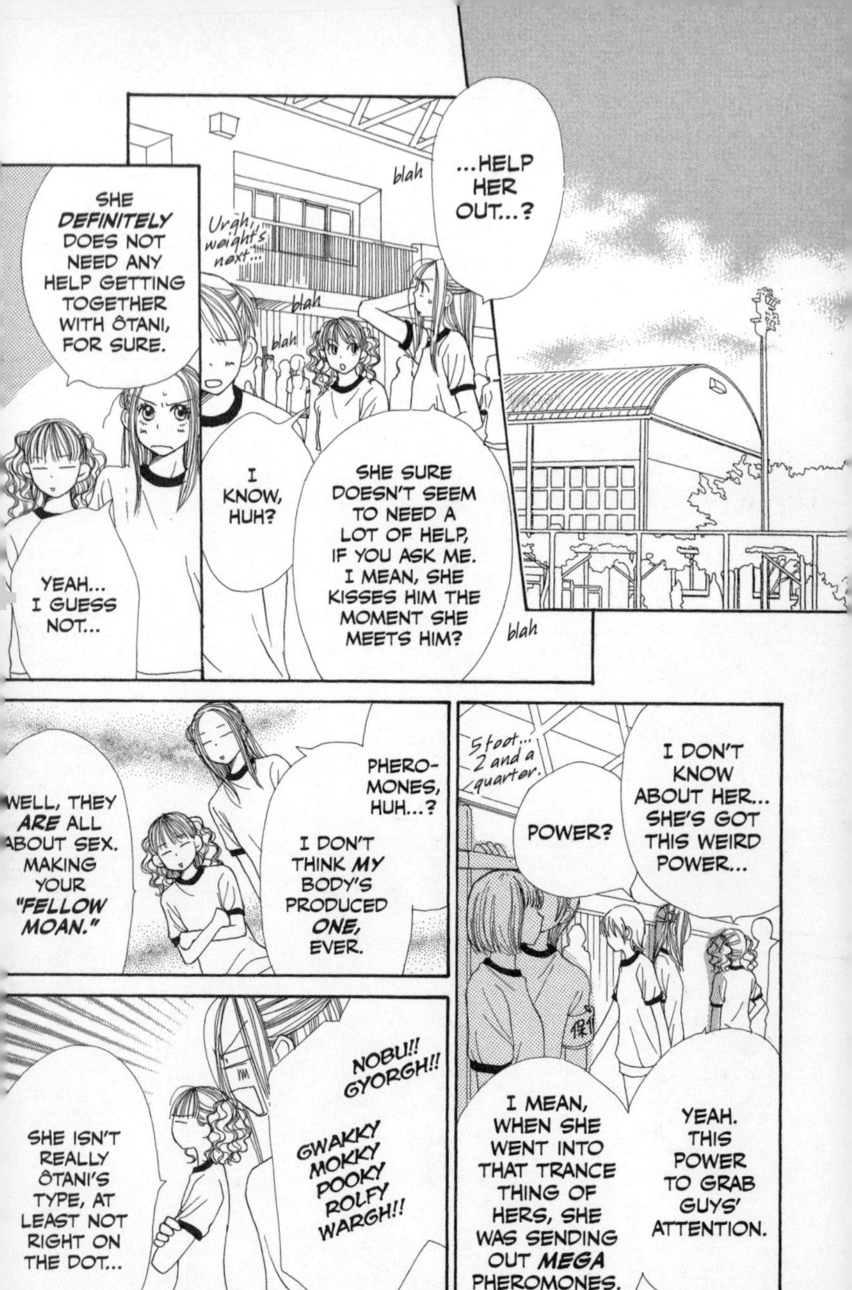
...HELP HER OUT...?
blah
Urgh, weight's next...
blah
blah
SHE SURE DOESN'T SEEM TO NEED A LOT OF HELP, IF YOU ASK ME. I MEAN, SHE KISSES HIM THE MOMENT SHE MEETS HIM?
blah
I KNOW, HUH?
SHE *DEFINITELY* DOES NOT NEED ANY HELP GETTING TOGETHER WITH ÔTANI, FOR SURE.
YEAH... I GUESS NOT...
5 foot... 2 and a quarter.
I DON'T KNOW ABOUT HER... SHE'S GOT THIS WEIRD POWER...
POWER?
YEAH. THIS POWER TO GRAB GUYS' ATTENTION.
I MEAN, WHEN SHE WENT INTO THAT TRANCE THING OF HERS, SHE WAS SENDING OUT *MEGA* PHEROMONES.
PHERO-MONES, HUH...?
I DON'T THINK *MY* BODY'S PRODUCED *ONE,* EVER.
WELL, THEY *ARE* ALL ABOUT SEX. MAKING YOUR *"FELLOW MOAN."*
NOBU!! GYORGH!!
GWAKKY MOKKY POOKY ROLFY WARGH!!
SHE ISN'T REALLY ÔTANI'S TYPE, AT LEAST NOT RIGHT ON THE DOT...

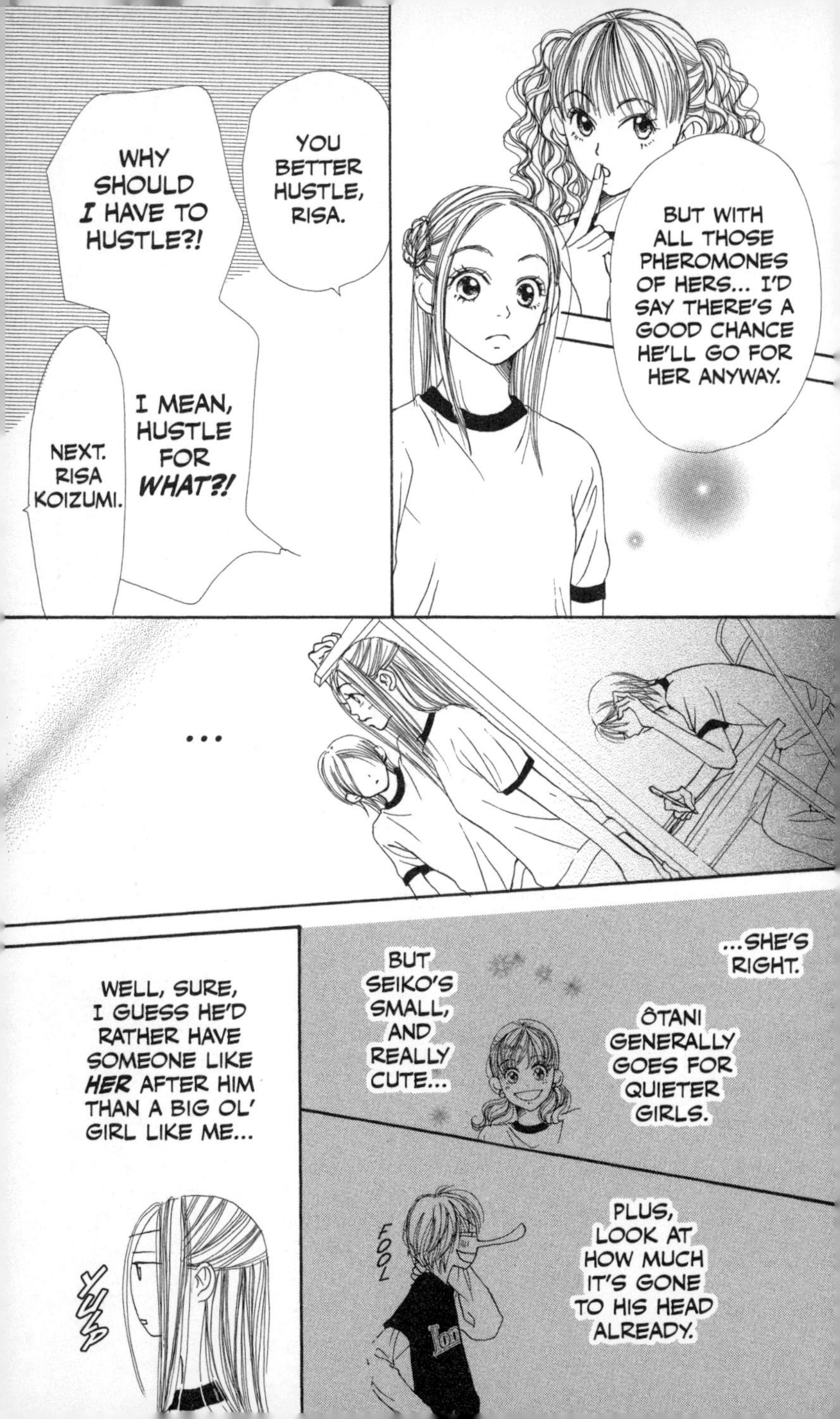
BUT WITH ALL THOSE PHEROMONES OF HERS... I'D SAY THERE'S A GOOD CHANCE HE'LL GO FOR HER ANYWAY.
YOU BETTER HUSTLE, RISA.
WHY SHOULD *I* HAVE TO HUSTLE?!
I MEAN, HUSTLE FOR ***WHAT?!***
NEXT. RISA KOIZUMI.
...
...SHE'S RIGHT.
ÔTANI GENERALLY GOES FOR QUIETER GIRLS.
BUT SEIKO'S SMALL, AND REALLY CUTE...
PLUS, LOOK AT HOW MUCH IT'S GONE TO HIS HEAD ALREADY.
FOOL
WELL, SURE, I GUESS HE'D RATHER HAVE SOMEONE LIKE ***HER*** AFTER HIM THAN A BIG OL' GIRL LIKE ME...
YUP

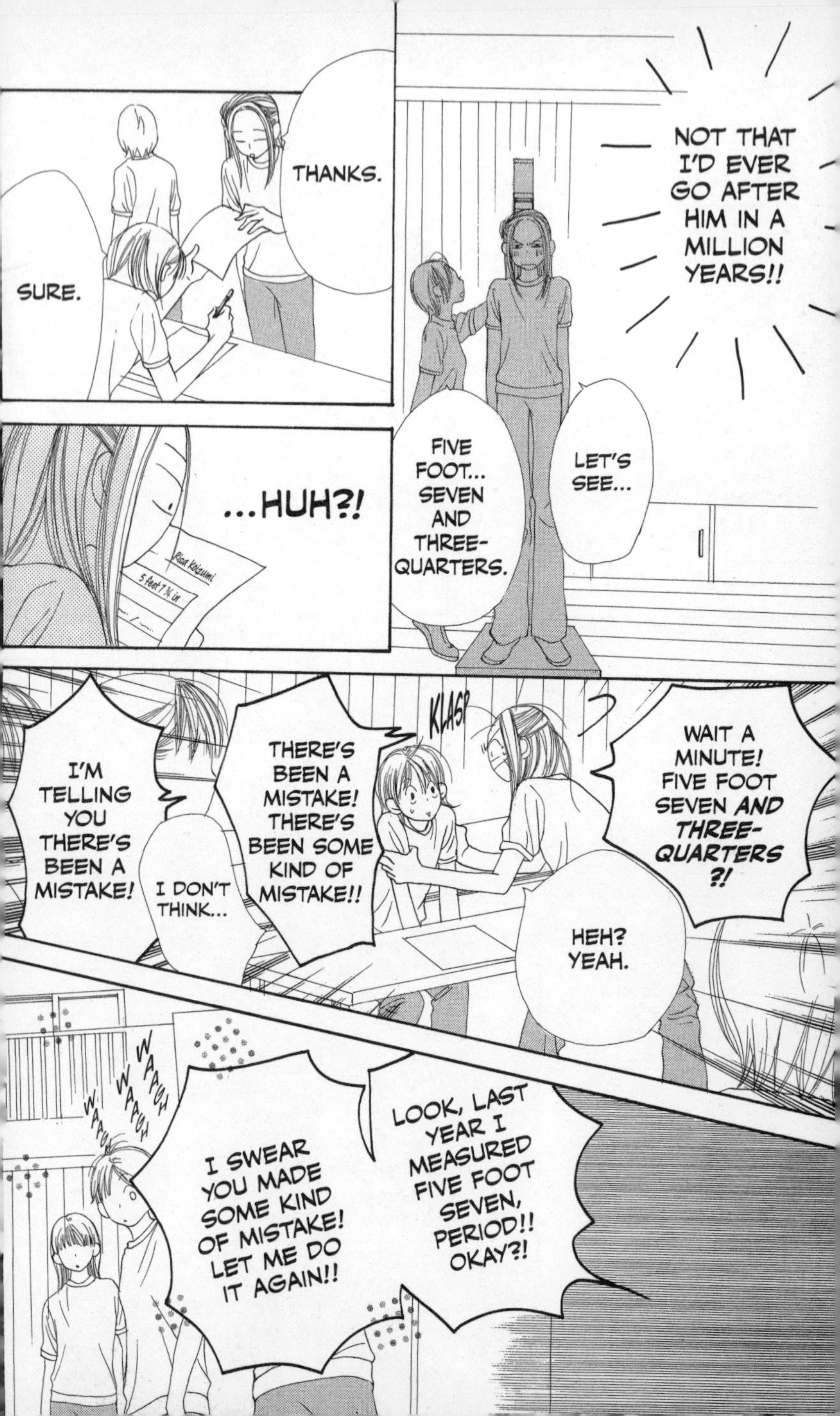
NOT THAT I'D EVER GO AFTER HIM IN A MILLION YEARS!!
LET'S SEE...
FIVE FOOT... SEVEN AND THREE-QUARTERS.
THANKS.
SURE.
...HUH?!
Risa Koizumi
5 feet 7 ¾ in
WAIT A MINUTE! FIVE FOOT SEVEN *AND THREE-QUARTERS* ?!
HEH? YEAH.
KLASP
THERE'S BEEN A MISTAKE! THERE'S BEEN SOME KIND OF MISTAKE!!
I DON'T THINK...
I'M TELLING YOU THERE'S BEEN A MISTAKE!
LOOK, LAST YEAR I MEASURED FIVE FOOT SEVEN, PERIOD!! OKAY?!
I SWEAR YOU MADE SOME KIND OF MISTAKE! LET ME DO IT AGAIN!!
WAPPUH
WAPPUH
WAPPUH

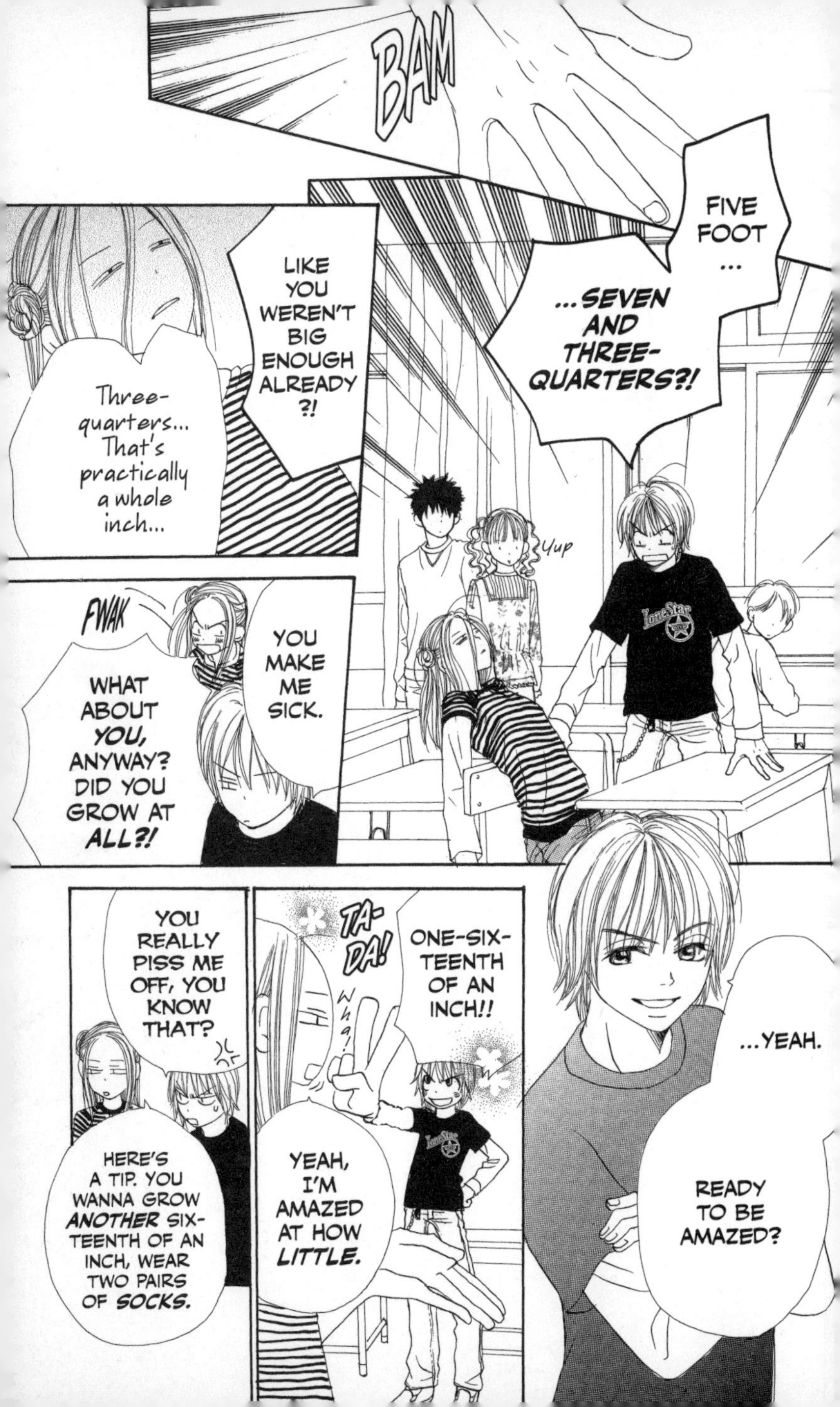
BAM
FIVE FOOT ...
...SEVEN AND THREE-QUARTERS?!
Yup
LIKE YOU WEREN'T BIG ENOUGH ALREADY?!
Three-quarters... That's practically a whole inch...
YOU MAKE ME SICK.
FWAK
WHAT ABOUT YOU, ANYWAY? DID YOU GROW AT ALL?!
...YEAH.
READY TO BE AMAZED?
TA-DA!
ONE-SIXTEENTH OF AN INCH!!
Wha!
YEAH, I'M AMAZED AT HOW LITTLE.
YOU REALLY PISS ME OFF, YOU KNOW THAT?
HERE'S A TIP. YOU WANNA GROW ANOTHER SIXTEENTH OF AN INCH, WEAR TWO PAIRS OF SOCKS.

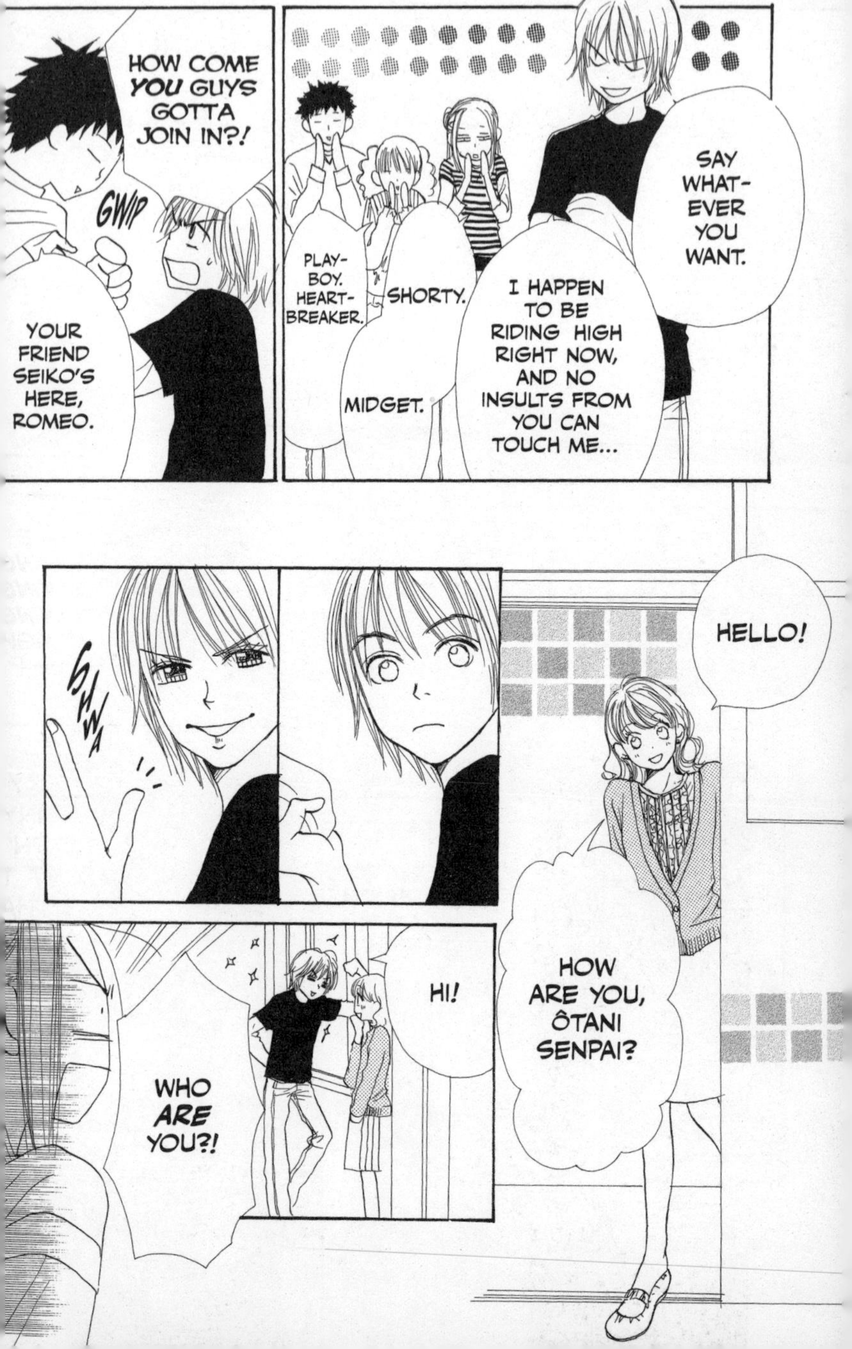
SAY WHAT-EVER YOU WANT.
I HAPPEN TO BE RIDING HIGH RIGHT NOW, AND NO INSULTS FROM YOU CAN TOUCH ME...
SHORTY.
PLAY-BOY. HEART-BREAKER.
MIDGET.
HOW COME YOU GUYS GOTTA JOIN IN?!
GWIP
YOUR FRIEND SEIKO'S HERE, ROMEO.
HELLO!
HOW ARE YOU, ÔTANI SENPAI?
SHWA
HI!
WHO ARE YOU?!

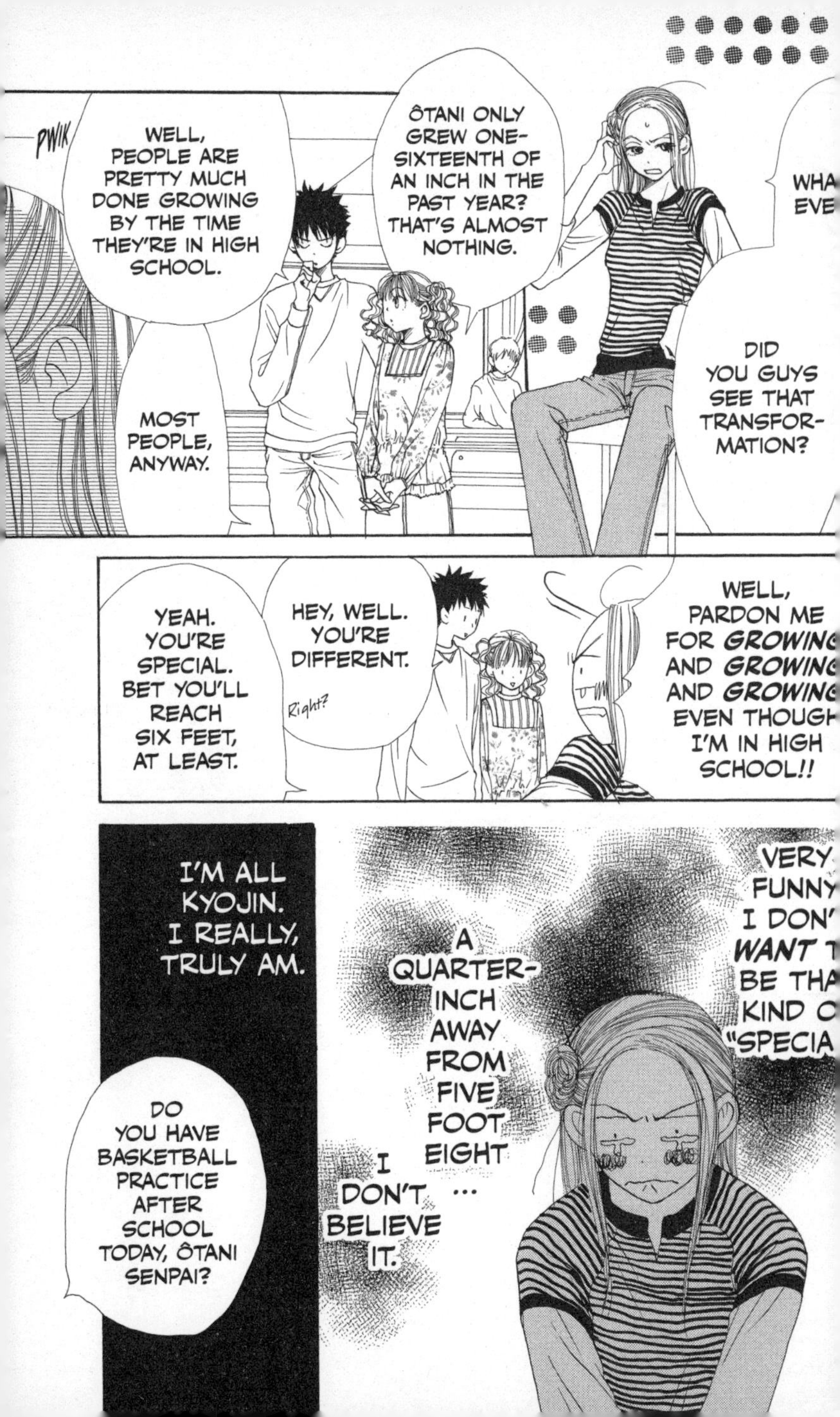
WHA EVE
DID YOU GUYS SEE THAT TRANSFORMATION?
ÔTANI ONLY GREW ONE-SIXTEENTH OF AN INCH IN THE PAST YEAR? THAT'S ALMOST NOTHING.
PWIK
WELL, PEOPLE ARE PRETTY MUCH DONE GROWING BY THE TIME THEY'RE IN HIGH SCHOOL.
MOST PEOPLE, ANYWAY.
WELL, PARDON ME FOR *GROWING* AND *GROWING* AND *GROWING* EVEN THOUGH I'M IN HIGH SCHOOL!!
HEY, WELL. YOU'RE DIFFERENT.
Right?
YEAH. YOU'RE SPECIAL. BET YOU'LL REACH SIX FEET, AT LEAST.
VERY FUNNY I DON'T *WANT* BE THA KIND O "SPECIA
A QUARTER-INCH AWAY FROM FIVE FOOT EIGHT...
I DON'T BELIEVE IT.
I'M ALL KYOJIN. I REALLY, TRULY AM.
DO YOU HAVE BASKETBALL PRACTICE AFTER SCHOOL TODAY, ÔTANI SENPAI?

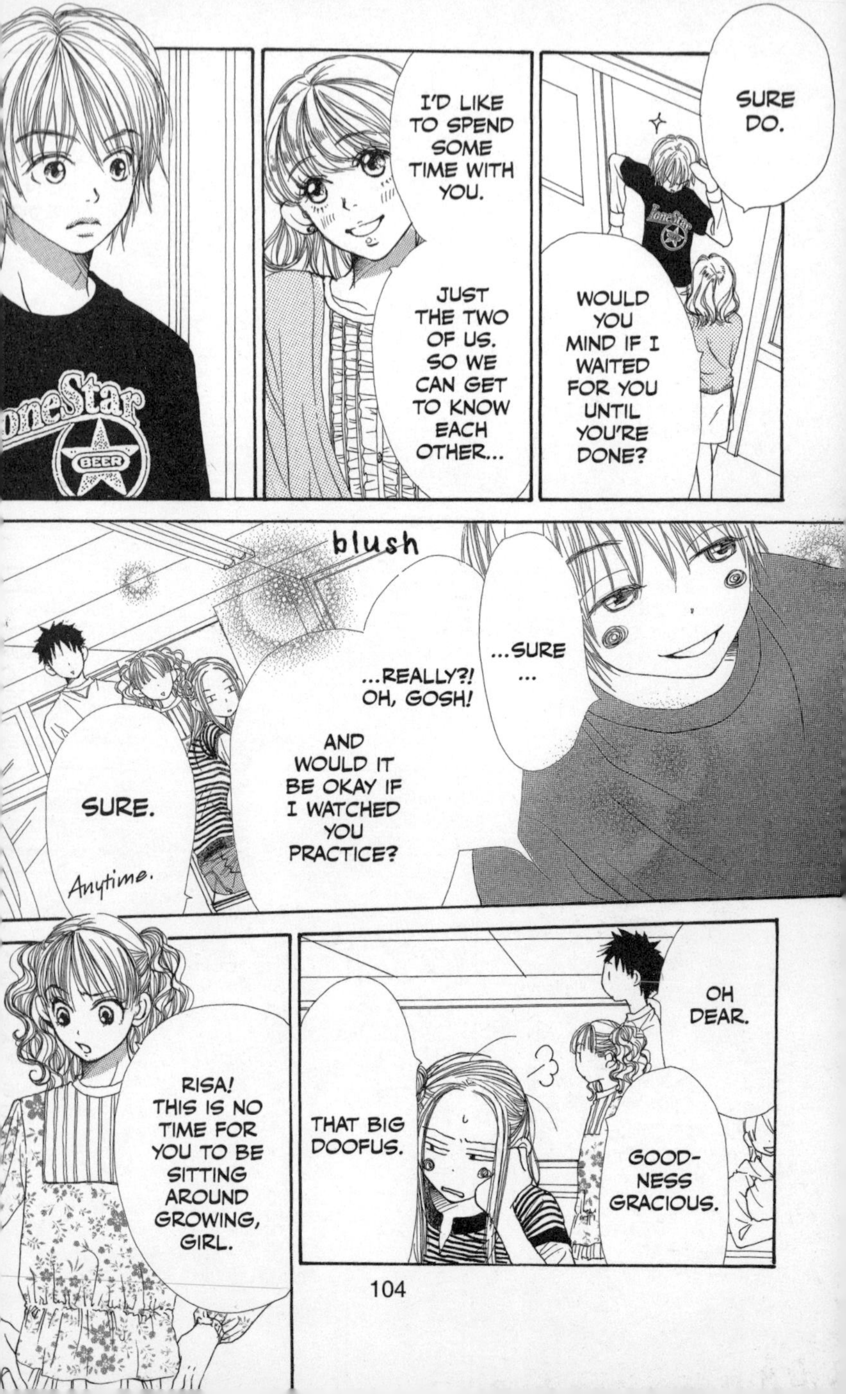
SURE DO.
WOULD YOU MIND IF I WAITED FOR YOU UNTIL YOU'RE DONE?
I'D LIKE TO SPEND SOME TIME WITH YOU.
JUST THE TWO OF US. SO WE CAN GET TO KNOW EACH OTHER...
blush
...SURE ...
...REALLY?! OH, GOSH!
AND WOULD IT BE OKAY IF I WATCHED YOU PRACTICE?
SURE.
Anytime.
OH DEAR.
GOODNESS GRACIOUS.
THAT BIG DOOFUS.
RISA! THIS IS NO TIME FOR YOU TO BE SITTING AROUND GROWING, GIRL.

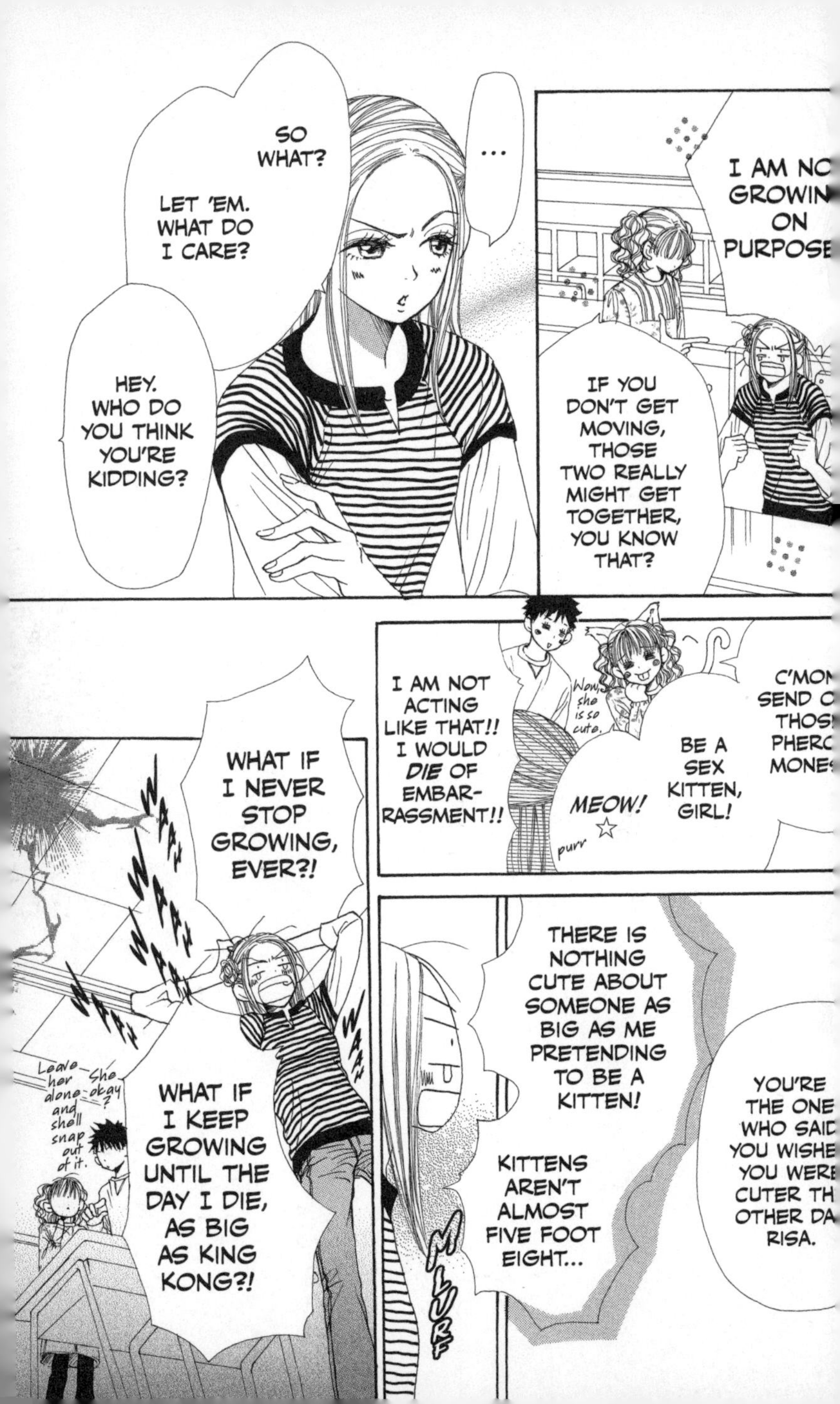

I AM NO
GROWIN
ON
PURPOSE
IF YOU DON'T GET MOVING, THOSE TWO REALLY MIGHT GET TOGETHER, YOU KNOW THAT?
...
SO WHAT?
LET 'EM. WHAT DO I CARE?
HEY. WHO DO YOU THINK YOU'RE KIDDING?
C'MON
SEND O
THOS
PHERO
MONES
BE A SEX KITTEN, GIRL!
MEOW! ☆
purr
Wow, she is so cute.
I AM NOT ACTING LIKE THAT!! I WOULD *DIE* OF EMBAR-RASSMENT!!
YOU'RE THE ONE WHO SAID YOU WISHE YOU WERE CUTER TH OTHER DA RISA.
THERE IS NOTHING CUTE ABOUT SOMEONE AS BIG AS ME PRETENDING TO BE A KITTEN!
KITTENS AREN'T ALMOST FIVE FOOT EIGHT...
MYURF
WHAT IF I NEVER STOP GROWING, EVER?!
WAAAH
WHAT IF I KEEP GROWING UNTIL THE DAY I DIE, AS BIG AS KING KONG?!
She okay?
Leave her alone and she'll snap out of it.

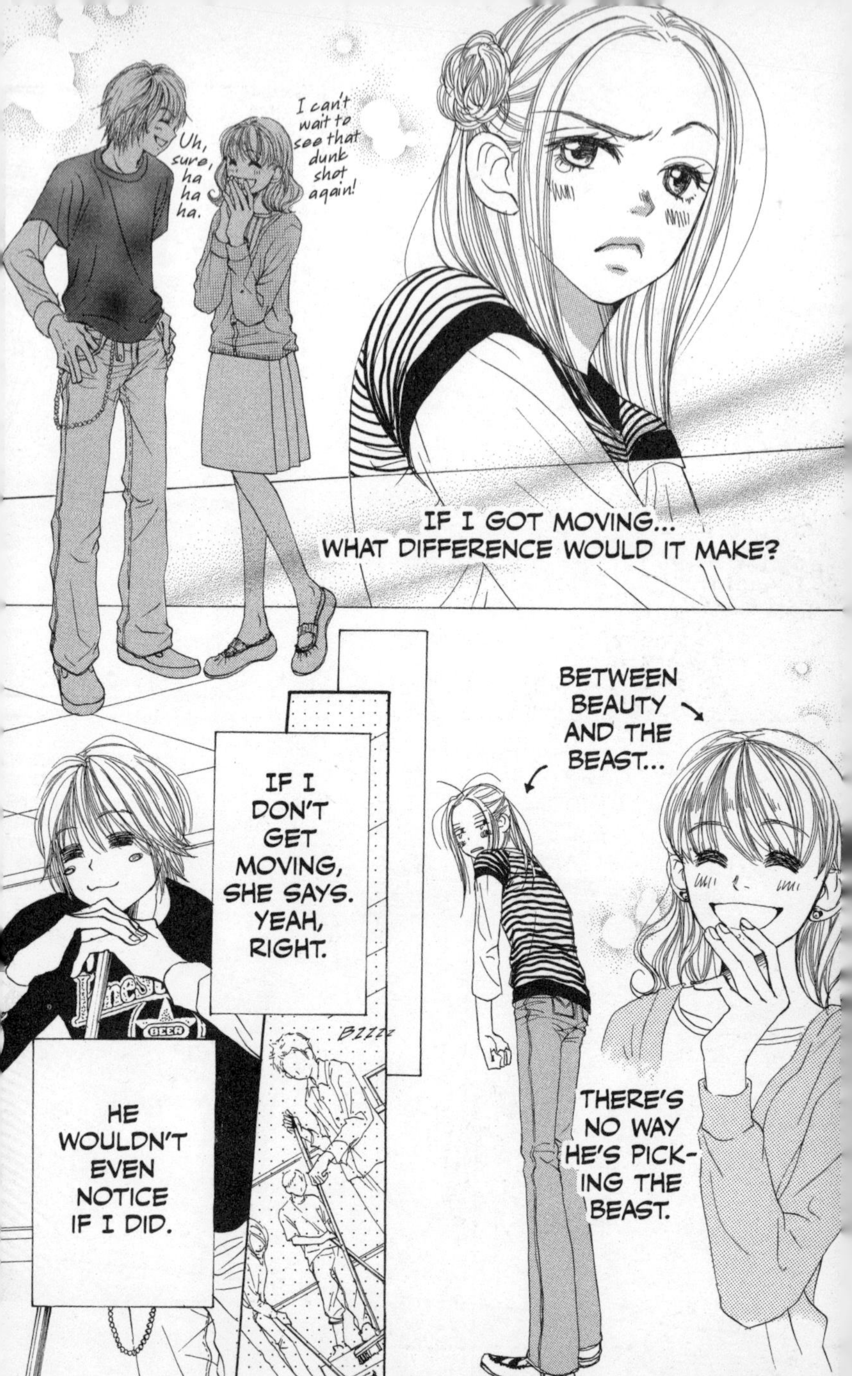
IF I GOT MOVING... WHAT DIFFERENCE WOULD IT MAKE?
I can't wait to see that dunk shot again!
Uh, sure, ha ha ha.
BETWEEN BEAUTY AND THE BEAST...
THERE'S NO WAY HE'S PICKING THE BEAST.
IF I DON'T GET MOVING, SHE SAYS. YEAH, RIGHT.
BZZZZ
HE WOULDN'T EVEN NOTICE IF I DID.

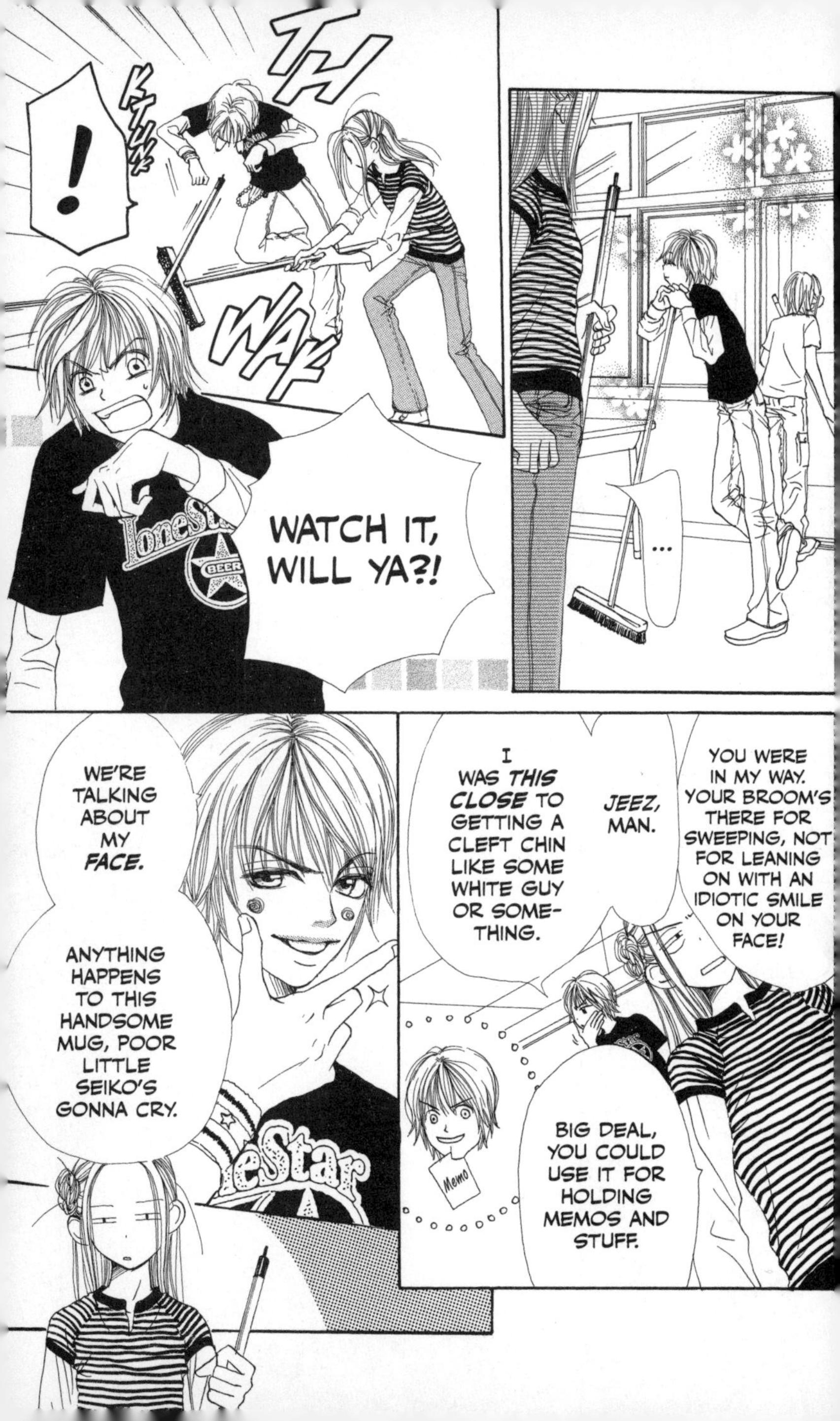
...
TH
!
WAK
WATCH IT, WILL YA?!
YOU WERE IN MY WAY. YOUR BROOM'S THERE FOR SWEEPING, NOT FOR LEANING ON WITH AN IDIOTIC SMILE ON YOUR FACE!
JEEZ, MAN.
I WAS THIS CLOSE TO GETTING A CLEFT CHIN LIKE SOME WHITE GUY OR SOME-THING.
BIG DEAL, YOU COULD USE IT FOR HOLDING MEMOS AND STUFF.
Memo
WE'RE TALKING ABOUT MY FACE.
ANYTHING HAPPENS TO THIS HANDSOME MUG, POOR LITTLE SEIKO'S GONNA CRY.

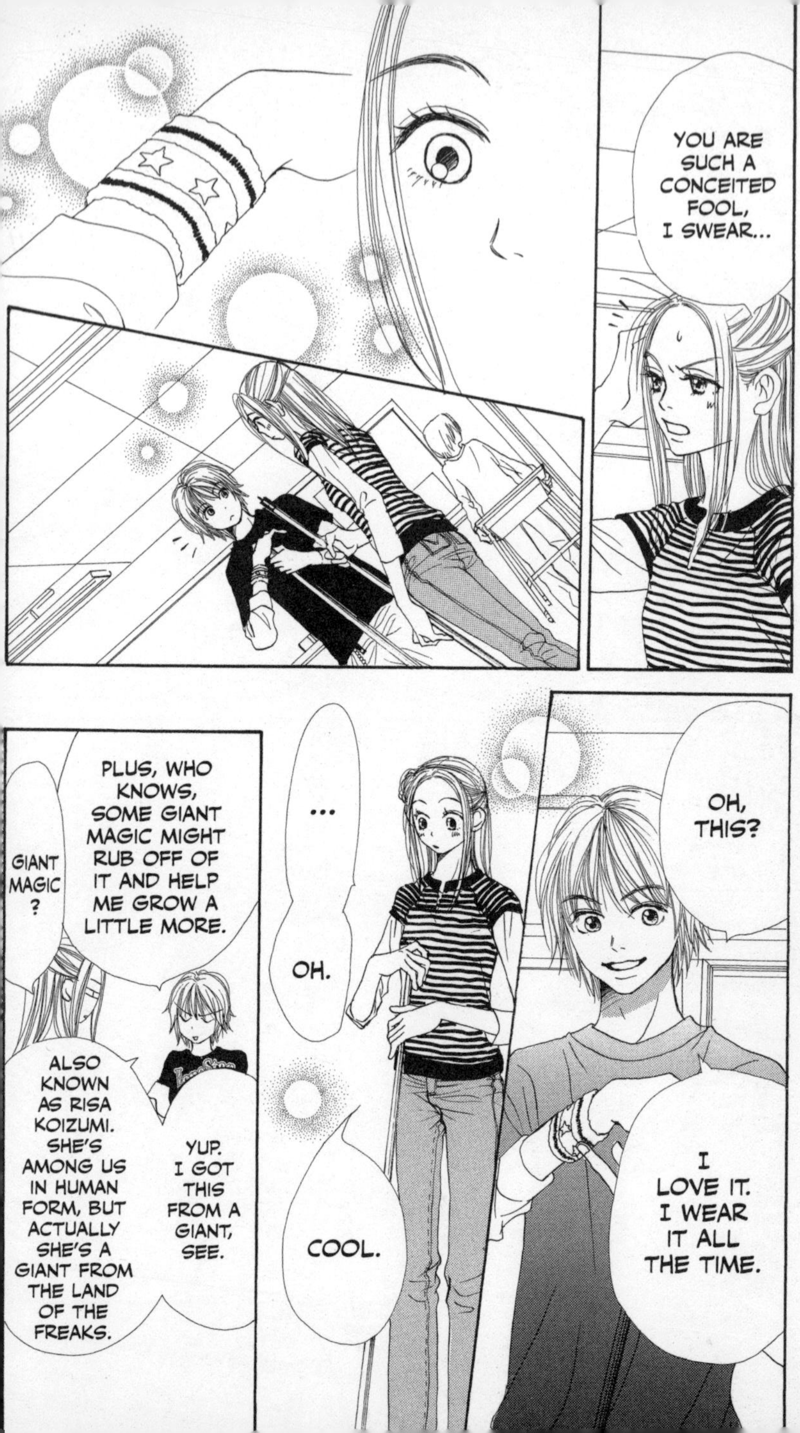
YOU ARE SUCH A CONCEITED FOOL, I SWEAR...
OH, THIS?
I LOVE IT. I WEAR IT ALL THE TIME.
...
OH.
COOL.
PLUS, WHO KNOWS, SOME GIANT MAGIC MIGHT RUB OFF OF IT AND HELP ME GROW A LITTLE MORE.
GIANT MAGIC?
YUP. I GOT THIS FROM A GIANT, SEE.
ALSO KNOWN AS RISA KOIZUMI. SHE'S AMONG US IN HUMAN FORM, BUT ACTUALLY SHE'S A GIANT FROM THE LAND OF THE FREAKS.

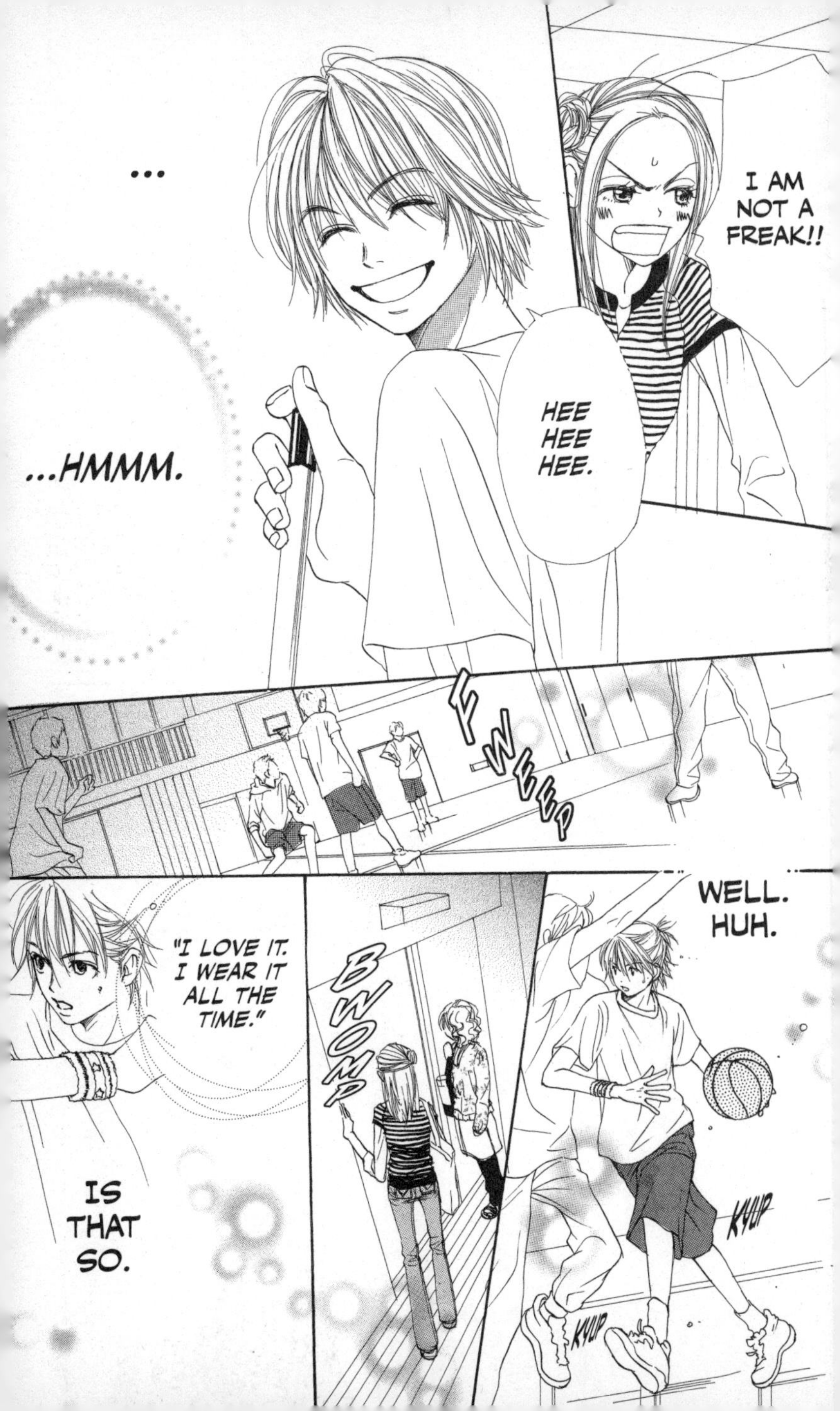

I AM NOT A FREAK!!
HEE HEE HEE.
...
...HMMM.
FWEEP
WELL. HUH.
KYUP
KYUP
BWOMP
"I LOVE IT. I WEAR IT ALL THE TIME."
IS THAT SO.

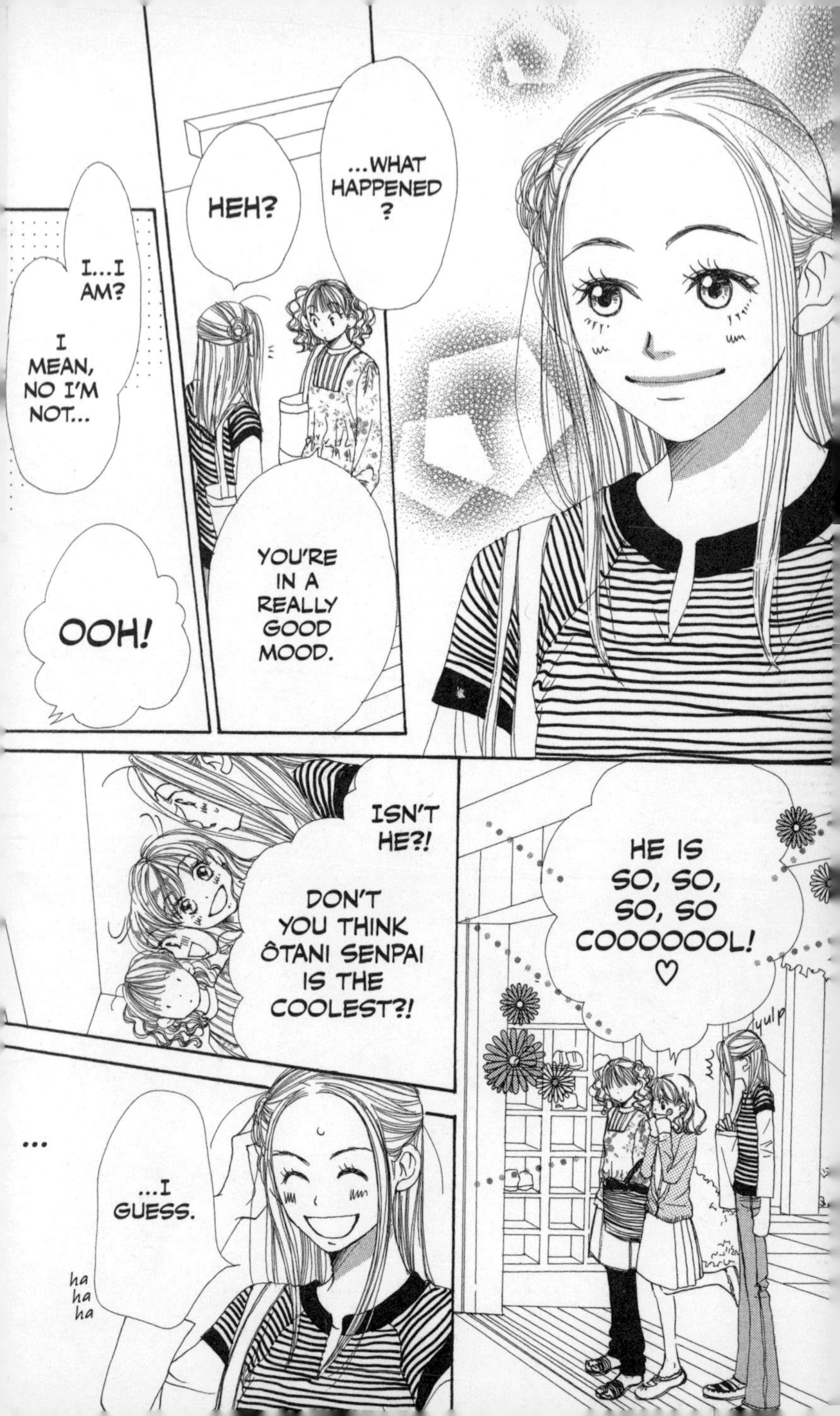
...WHAT HAPPENED?
HEH?
YOU'RE IN A REALLY GOOD MOOD.
I...I AM?
I MEAN, NO I'M NOT...
OOH!
HE IS SO, SO, SO, SO COOOOOOL! ♡
yulp
ISN'T HE?!
DON'T YOU THINK ÔTANI SENPAI IS THE COOLEST?!
...
...I GUESS.
ha ha ha

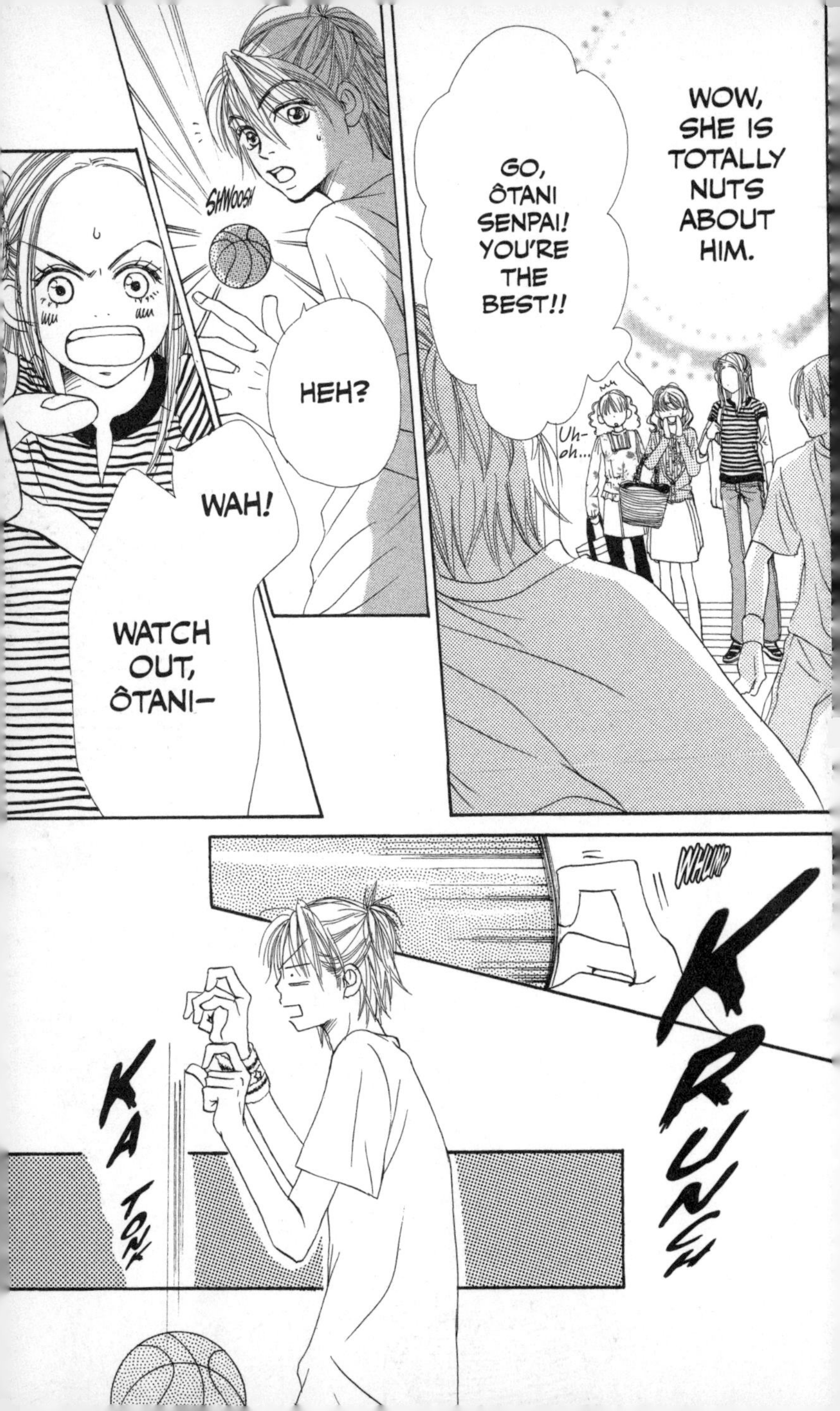
WOW, SHE IS TOTALLY NUTS ABOUT HIM.
GO, ÔTANI SENPAI! YOU'RE THE BEST!!
Uh-oh...
SHWOOSH
HEH?
WAH!
WATCH OUT, ÔTANI–
WHUMP
KRUNCH
KA TONK

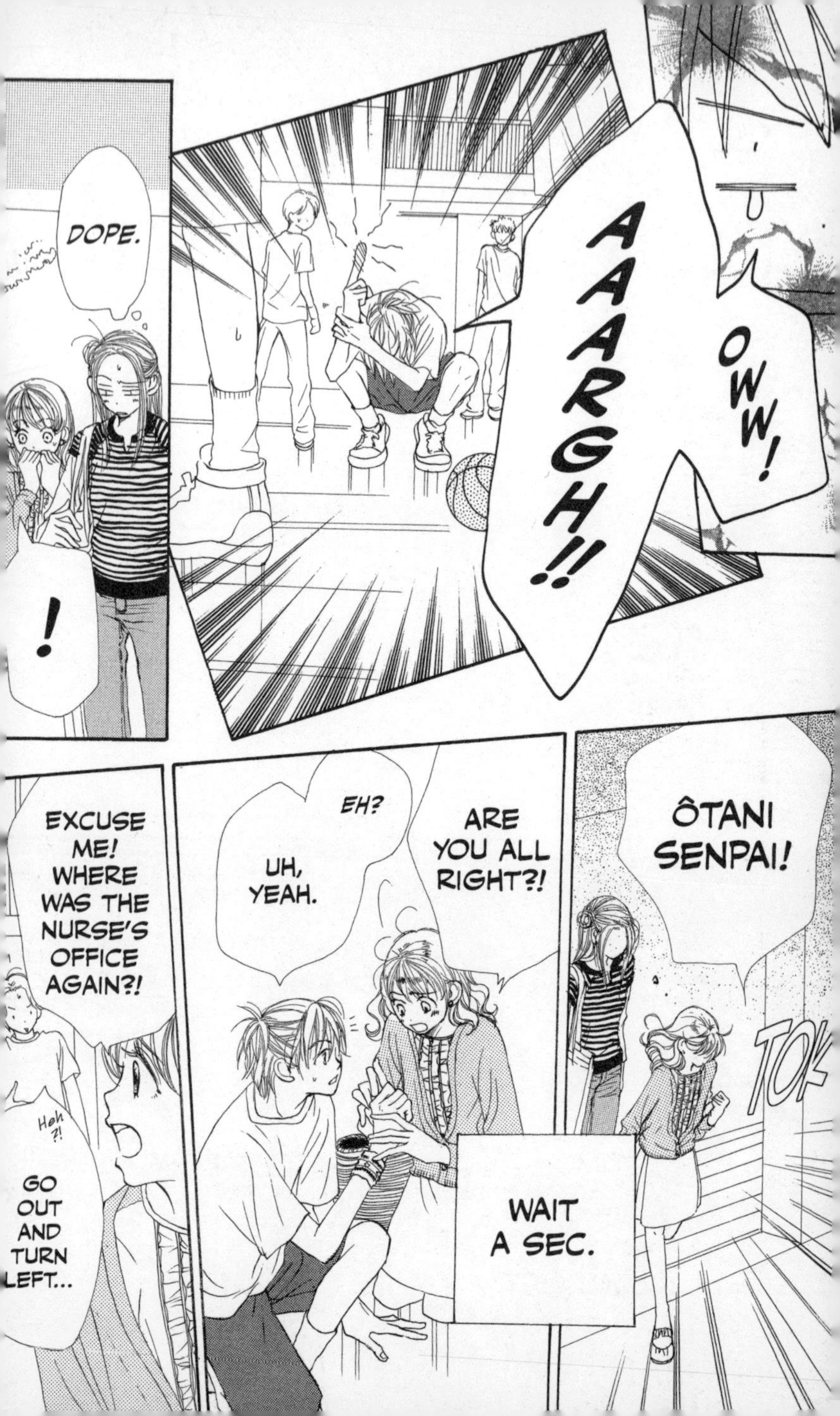
OWW!
AAARGH!!
DOPE.
!
ÔTANI SENPAI!
TOK
ARE YOU ALL RIGHT?!
EH?
UH, YEAH.
WAIT A SEC.
EXCUSE ME! WHERE WAS THE NURSE'S OFFICE AGAIN?!
Heh?!
GO OUT AND TURN LEFT...

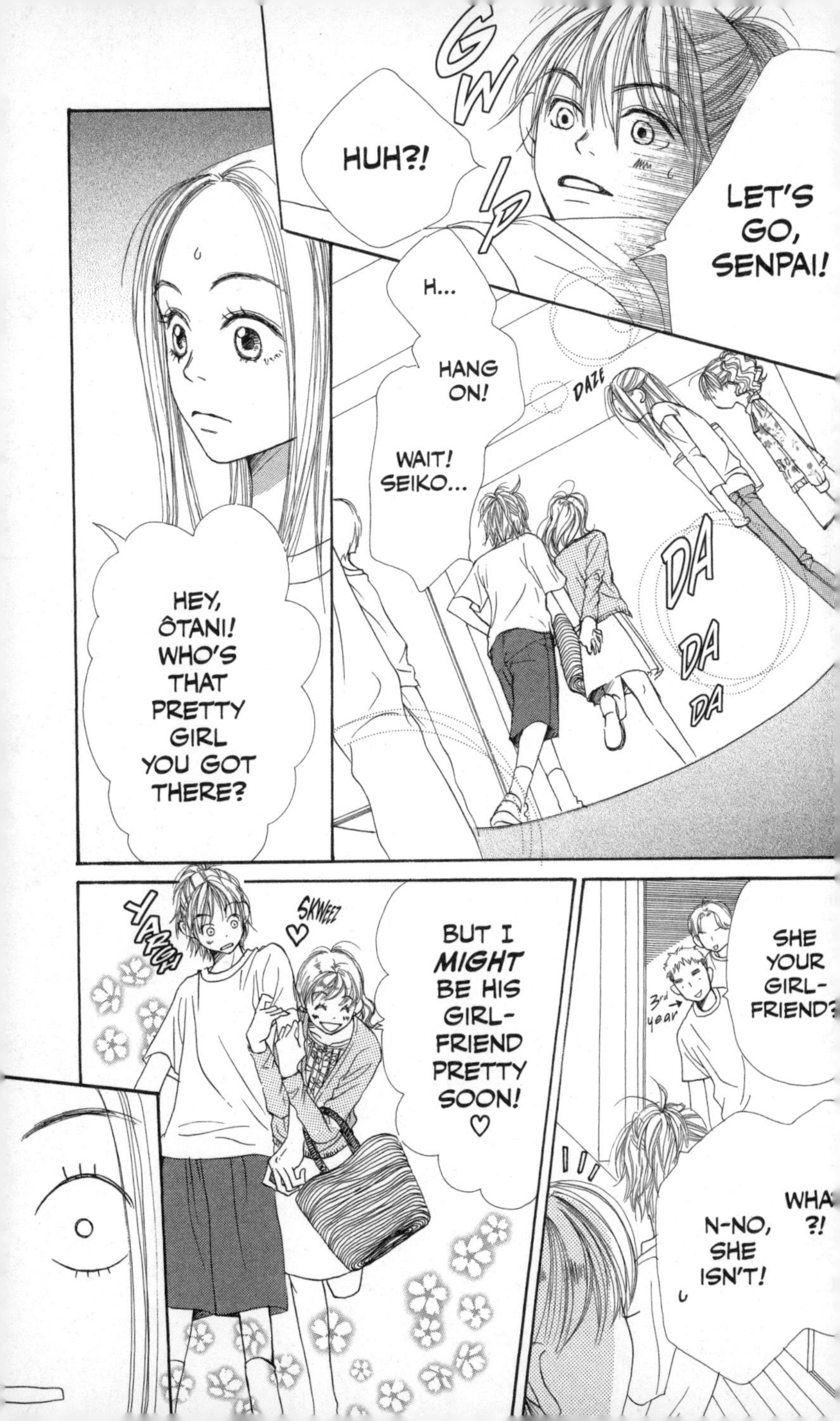
LET'S GO, SENPAI!
GWIP
HUH?!
DA DA DA
DAZE
H...
HANG ON!
WAIT! SEIKO...
HEY, ÔTANI! WHO'S THAT PRETTY GIRL YOU GOT THERE?
SHE YOUR GIRL-FRIEND?
3rd year
WHA?!
N-NO, SHE ISN'T!
BUT I MIGHT BE HIS GIRL-FRIEND PRETTY SOON! ♡
SKWEEZ
YANK

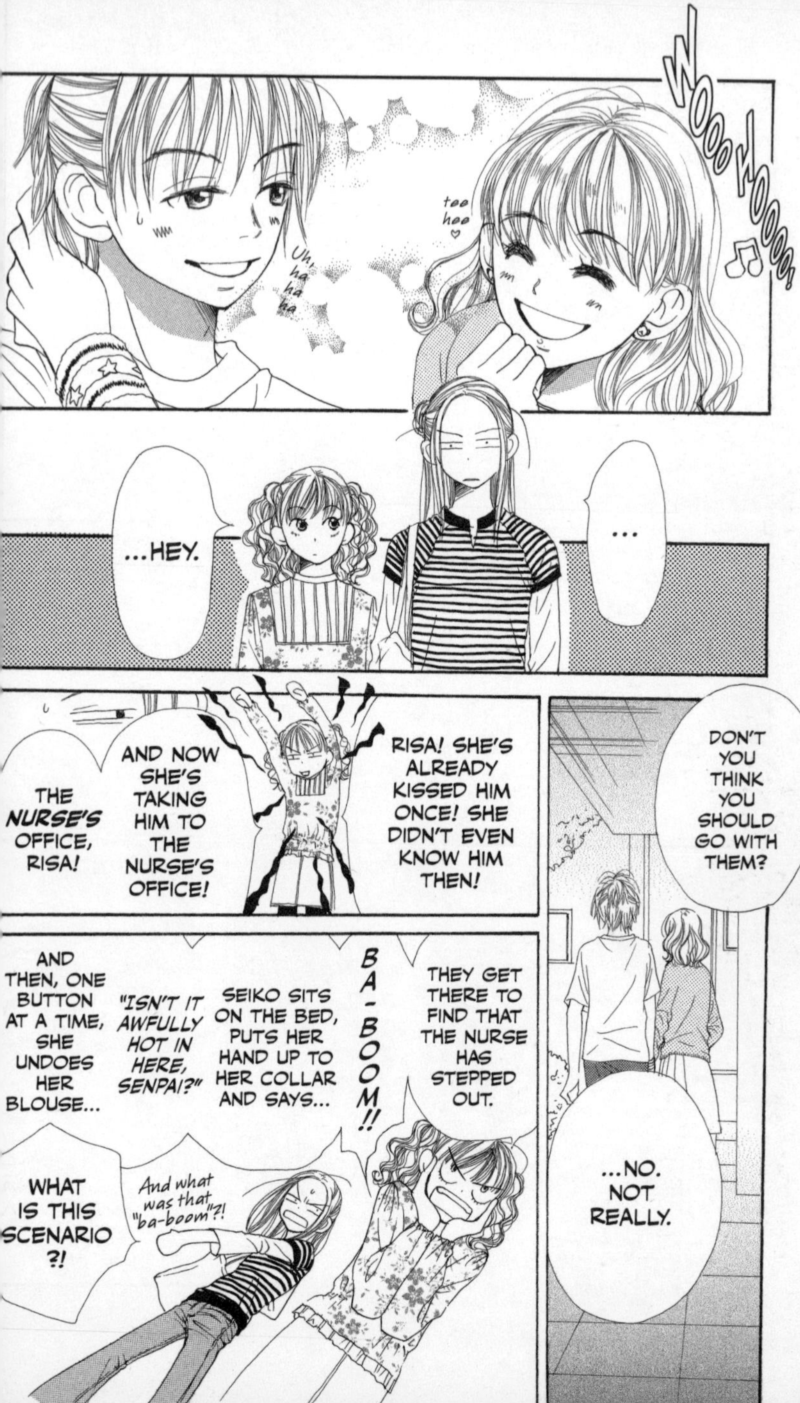
WOOO WOOOO♫
tee hee ♡
Uh, ha ha ha
...
...HEY.
DON'T YOU THINK YOU SHOULD GO WITH THEM?
...NO. NOT REALLY.
RISA! SHE'S ALREADY KISSED HIM ONCE! SHE DIDN'T EVEN KNOW HIM THEN!
AND NOW SHE'S TAKING HIM TO THE NURSE'S OFFICE!
THE *NURSE'S* OFFICE, RISA!
THEY GET THERE TO FIND THAT THE NURSE HAS STEPPED OUT.
BA-BOOOM!!
SEIKO SITS ON THE BED, PUTS HER HAND UP TO HER COLLAR AND SAYS...
"ISN'T IT AWFULLY HOT IN HERE, SENPAI?"
AND THEN, ONE BUTTON AT A TIME, SHE UNDOES HER BLOUSE...
And what was that "ba-boom"?!
WHAT IS THIS SCENARIO?!

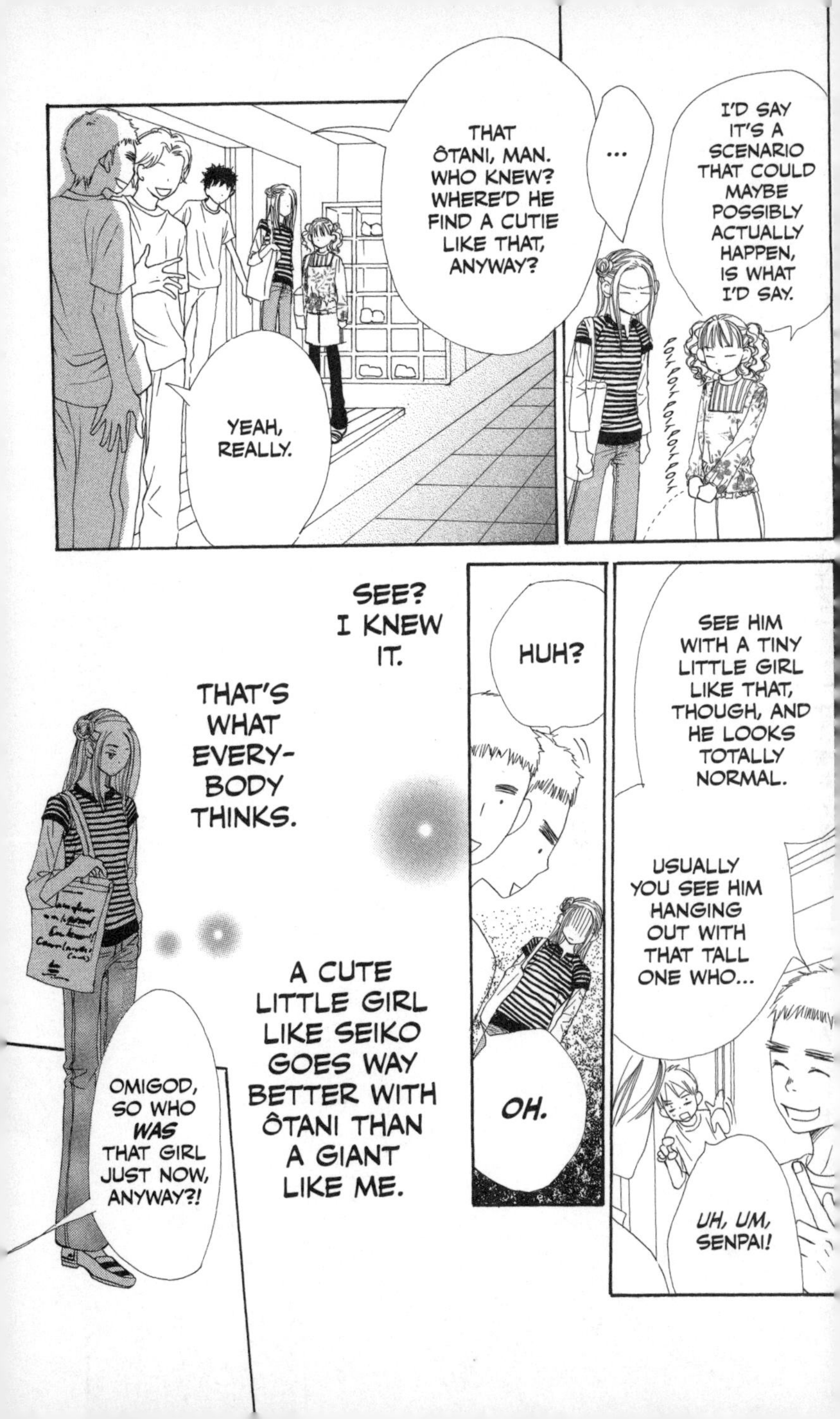
...
I'D SAY IT'S A SCENARIO THAT COULD MAYBE POSSIBLY ACTUALLY HAPPEN, IS WHAT I'D SAY.
THAT ÔTANI, MAN. WHO KNEW? WHERE'D HE FIND A CUTIE LIKE THAT, ANYWAY?
YEAH, REALLY.
SEE HIM WITH A TINY LITTLE GIRL LIKE THAT, THOUGH, AND HE LOOKS TOTALLY NORMAL.
USUALLY YOU SEE HIM HANGING OUT WITH THAT TALL ONE WHO...
UH, UM, SENPAI!
HUH?
OH.
SEE? I KNEW IT.
THAT'S WHAT EVERY-BODY THINKS.
A CUTE LITTLE GIRL LIKE SEIKO GOES WAY BETTER WITH ÔTANI THAN A GIANT LIKE ME.
OMIGOD, SO WHO WAS THAT GIRL JUST NOW, ANYWAY?!

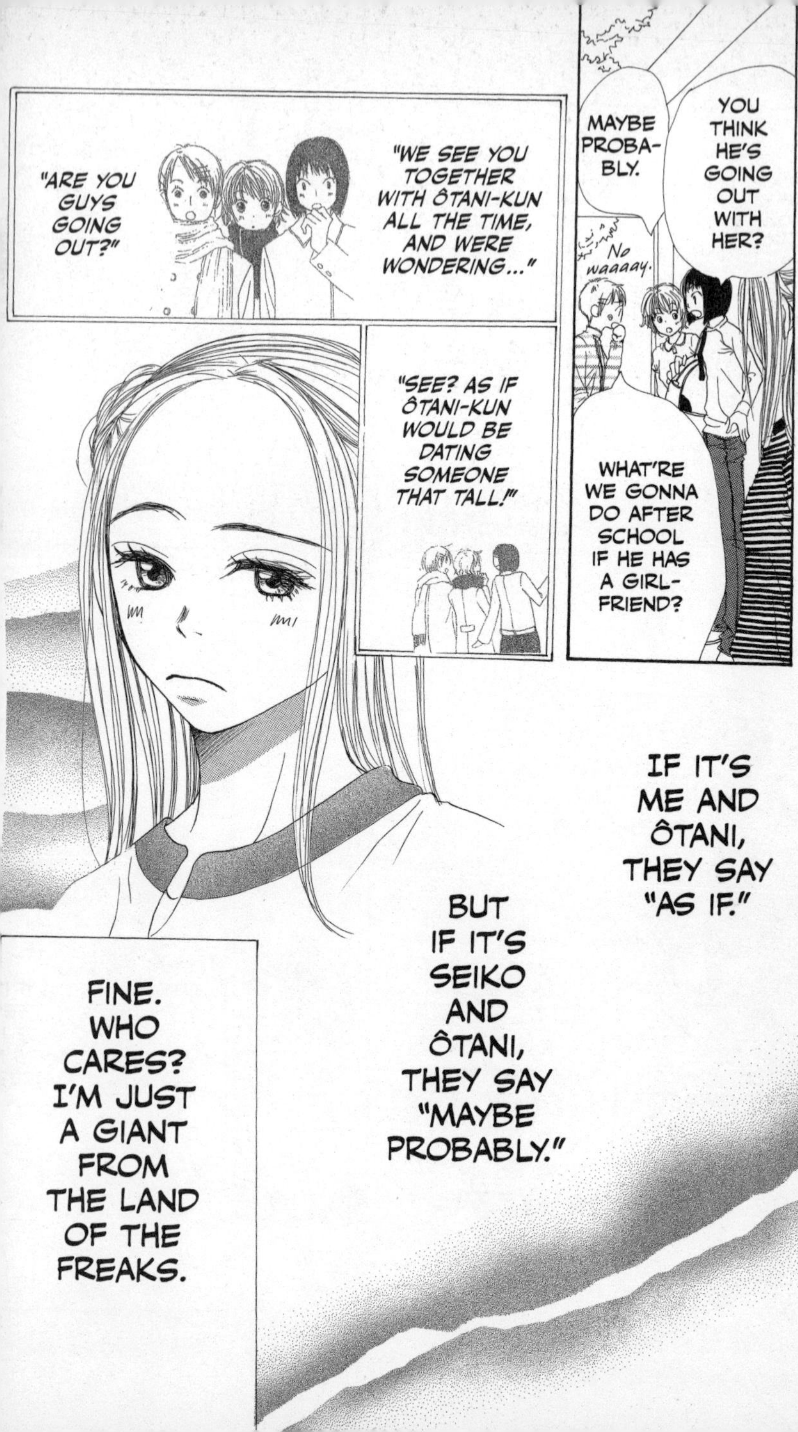
YOU THINK HE'S GOING OUT WITH HER?
MAYBE PROBA-BLY.
No waaaay.
WHAT'RE WE GONNA DO AFTER SCHOOL IF HE HAS A GIRL-FRIEND?
"WE SEE YOU TOGETHER WITH ÔTANI-KUN ALL THE TIME, AND WERE WONDERING..."
"ARE YOU GUYS GOING OUT?"
"SEE? AS IF ÔTANI-KUN WOULD BE DATING SOMEONE THAT TALL!"
IF IT'S ME AND ÔTANI, THEY SAY "AS IF."
BUT IF IT'S SEIKO AND ÔTANI, THEY SAY "MAYBE PROBABLY."
FINE. WHO CARES? I'M JUST A GIANT FROM THE LAND OF THE FREAKS.

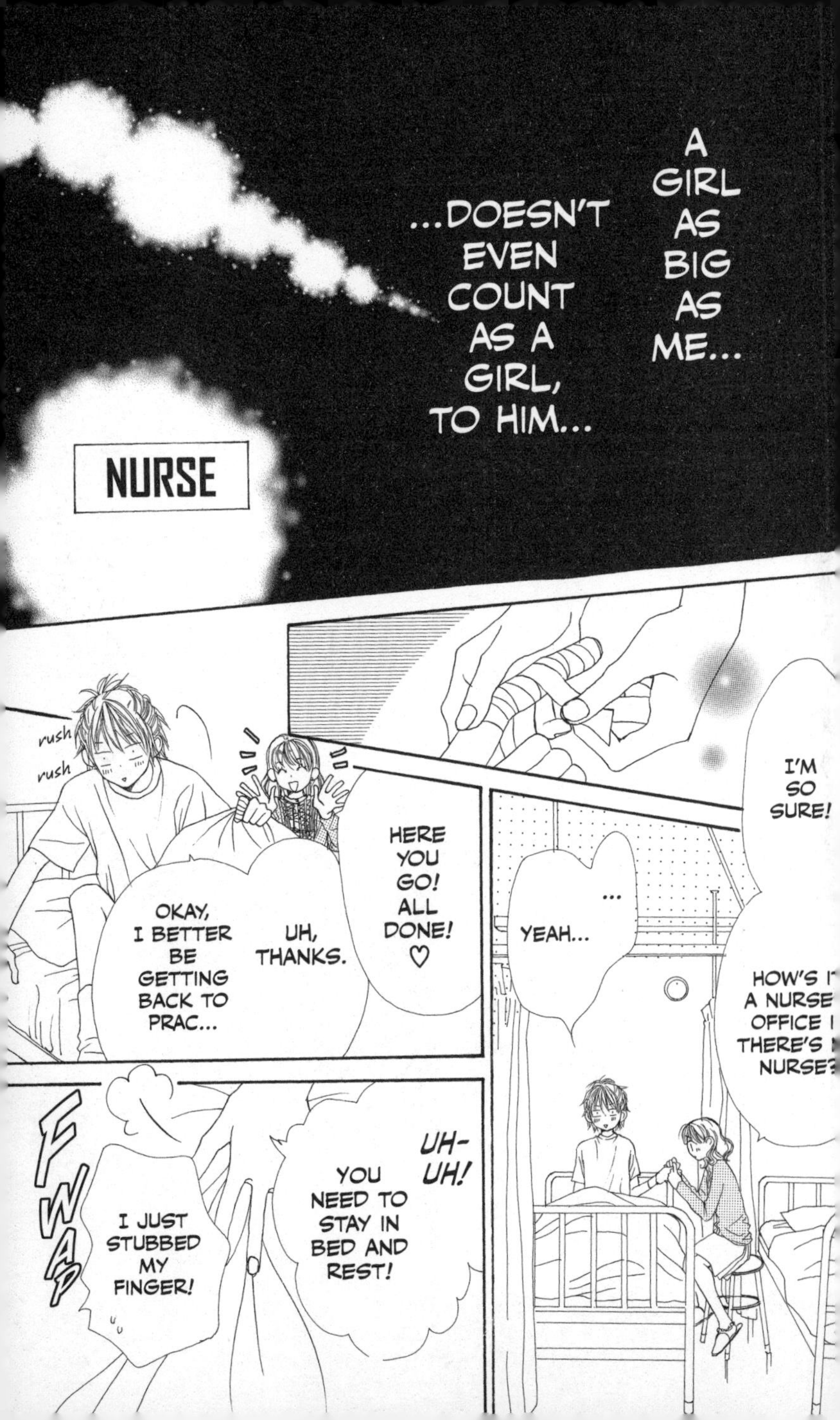
A GIRL AS BIG AS ME...
...DOESN'T EVEN COUNT AS A GIRL, TO HIM...
NURSE
I'M SO SURE!
HOW'S IT A NURSE OFFICE I THERE'S NURSE?
...
YEAH...
HERE YOU GO! ALL DONE! ♡
UH, THANKS.
OKAY, I BETTER BE GETTING BACK TO PRAC...
rush
rush
UH-UH!
YOU NEED TO STAY IN BED AND REST!
I JUST STUBBED MY FINGER!
FWAP

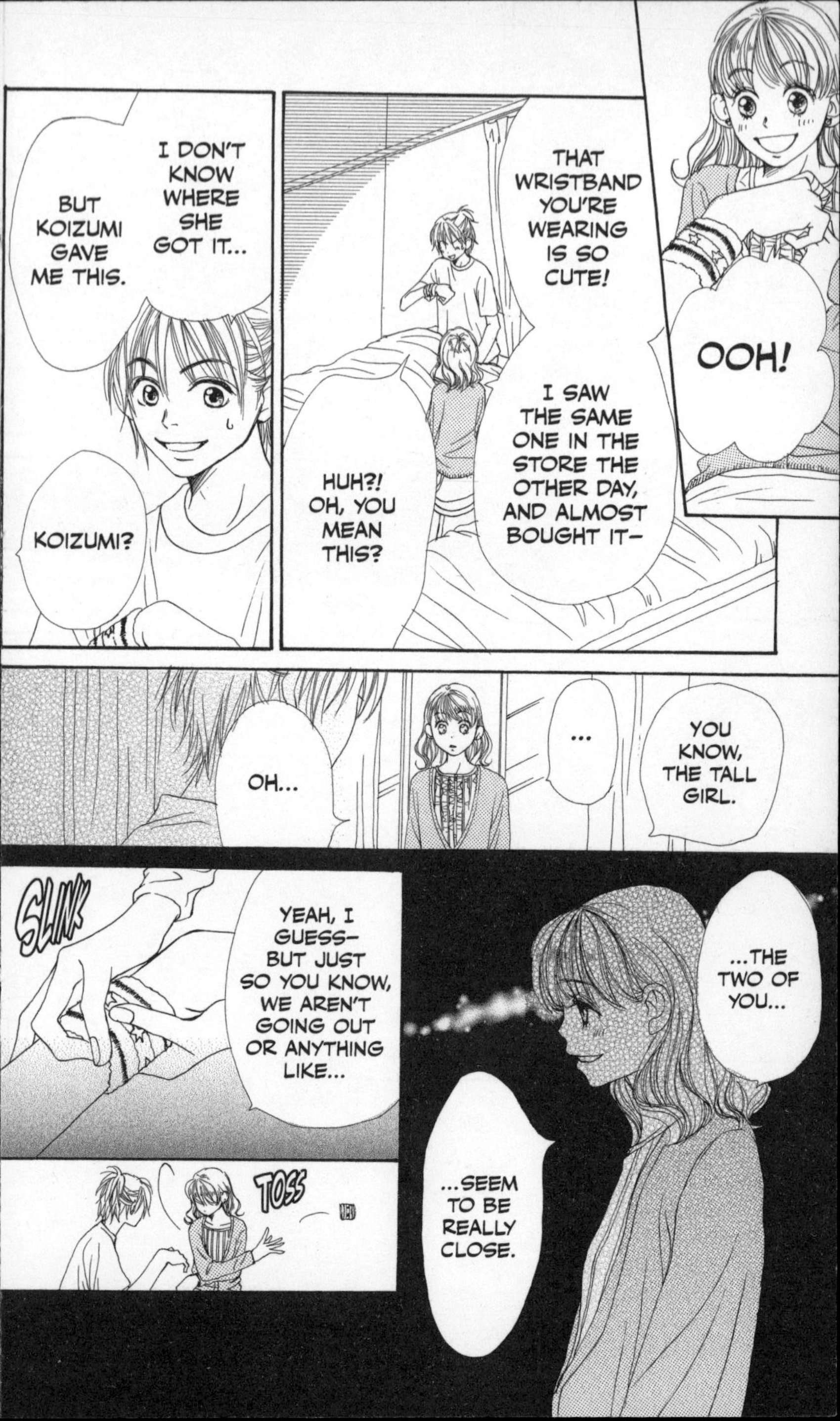
OOH!
THAT WRISTBAND YOU'RE WEARING IS SO CUTE!
I SAW THE SAME ONE IN THE STORE THE OTHER DAY, AND ALMOST BOUGHT IT–
HUH?! OH, YOU MEAN THIS?
I DON'T KNOW WHERE SHE GOT IT...
BUT KOIZUMI GAVE ME THIS.
KOIZUMI?
YOU KNOW, THE TALL GIRL.
...
OH...
...THE TWO OF YOU...
...SEEM TO BE REALLY CLOSE.
SLINK
YEAH, I GUESS– BUT JUST SO YOU KNOW, WE AREN'T GOING OUT OR ANYTHING LIKE...
TOSS

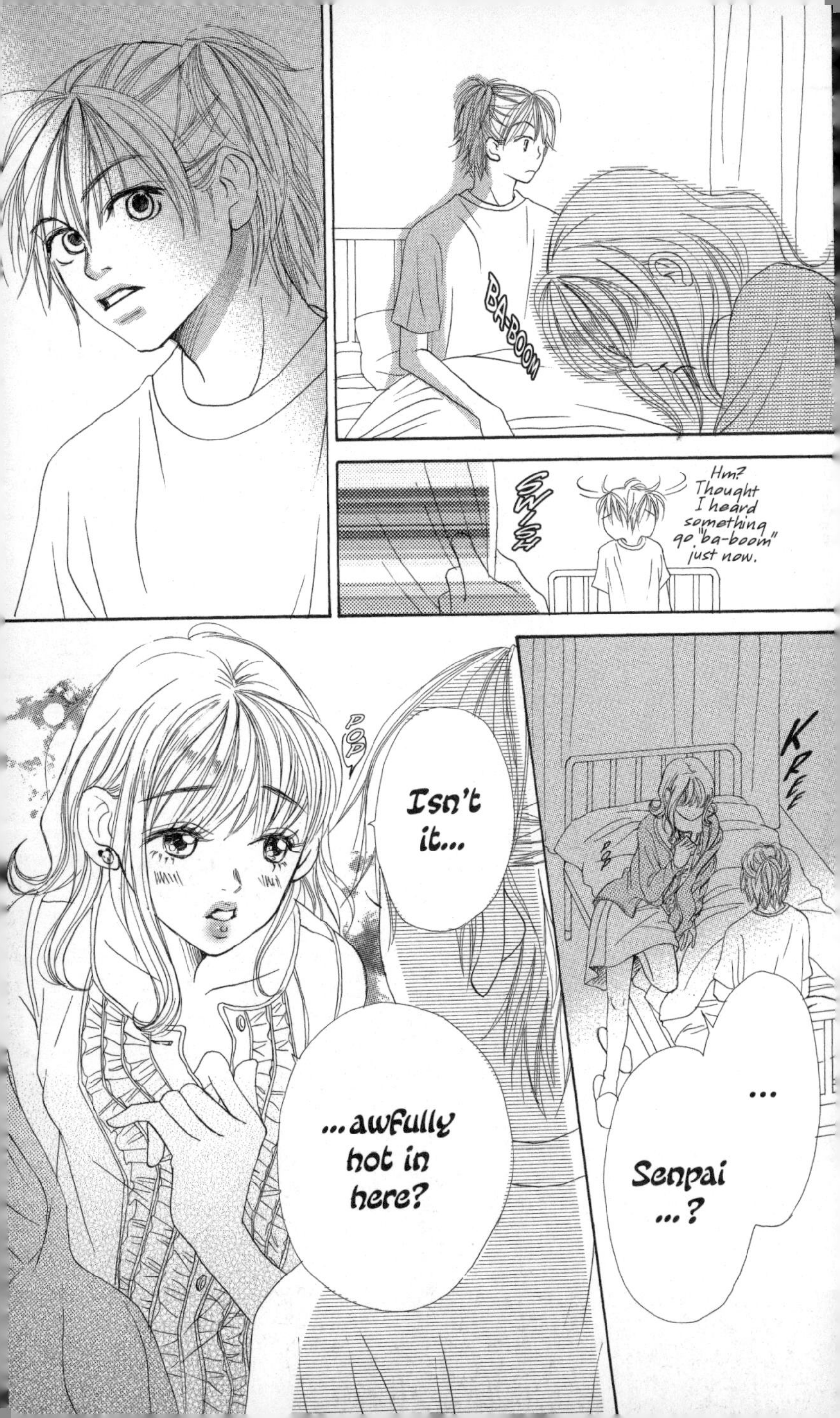
BA-BOOM
SWISH
Hm? Thought I heard something go "ba-boom" just now.
KRI
...
Senpai ...?
POP
Isn't it...
...awfully hot in here?

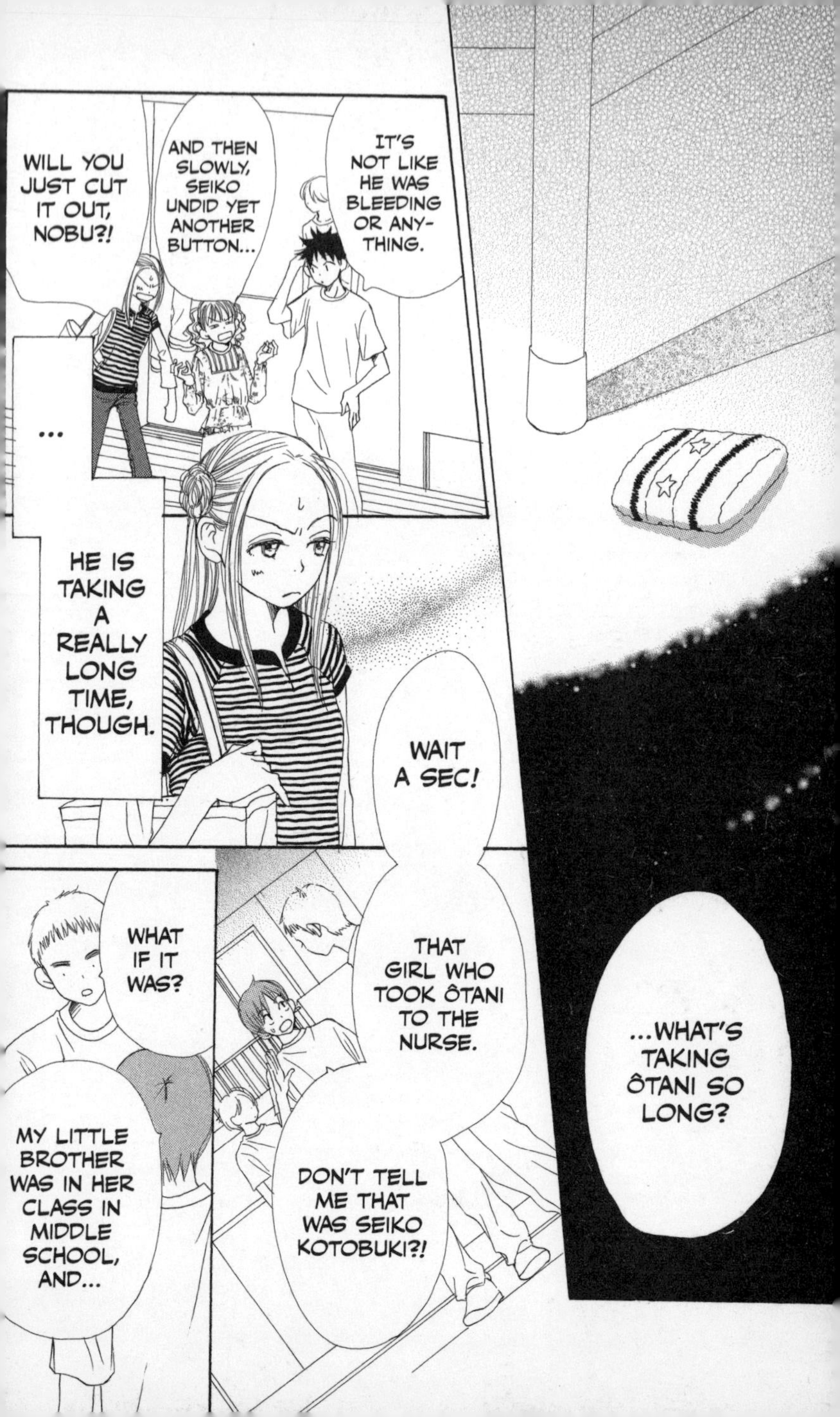
...WHAT'S TAKING ÔTANI SO LONG?
IT'S NOT LIKE HE WAS BLEEDING OR ANYTHING.
AND THEN SLOWLY, SEIKO UNDID YET ANOTHER BUTTON...
WILL YOU JUST CUT IT OUT, NOBU?!
...
HE IS TAKING A REALLY LONG TIME, THOUGH.
WAIT A SEC!
THAT GIRL WHO TOOK ÔTANI TO THE NURSE.
DON'T TELL ME THAT WAS SEIKO KOTOBUKI?!
WHAT IF IT WAS?
MY LITTLE BROTHER WAS IN HER CLASS IN MIDDLE SCHOOL, AND...

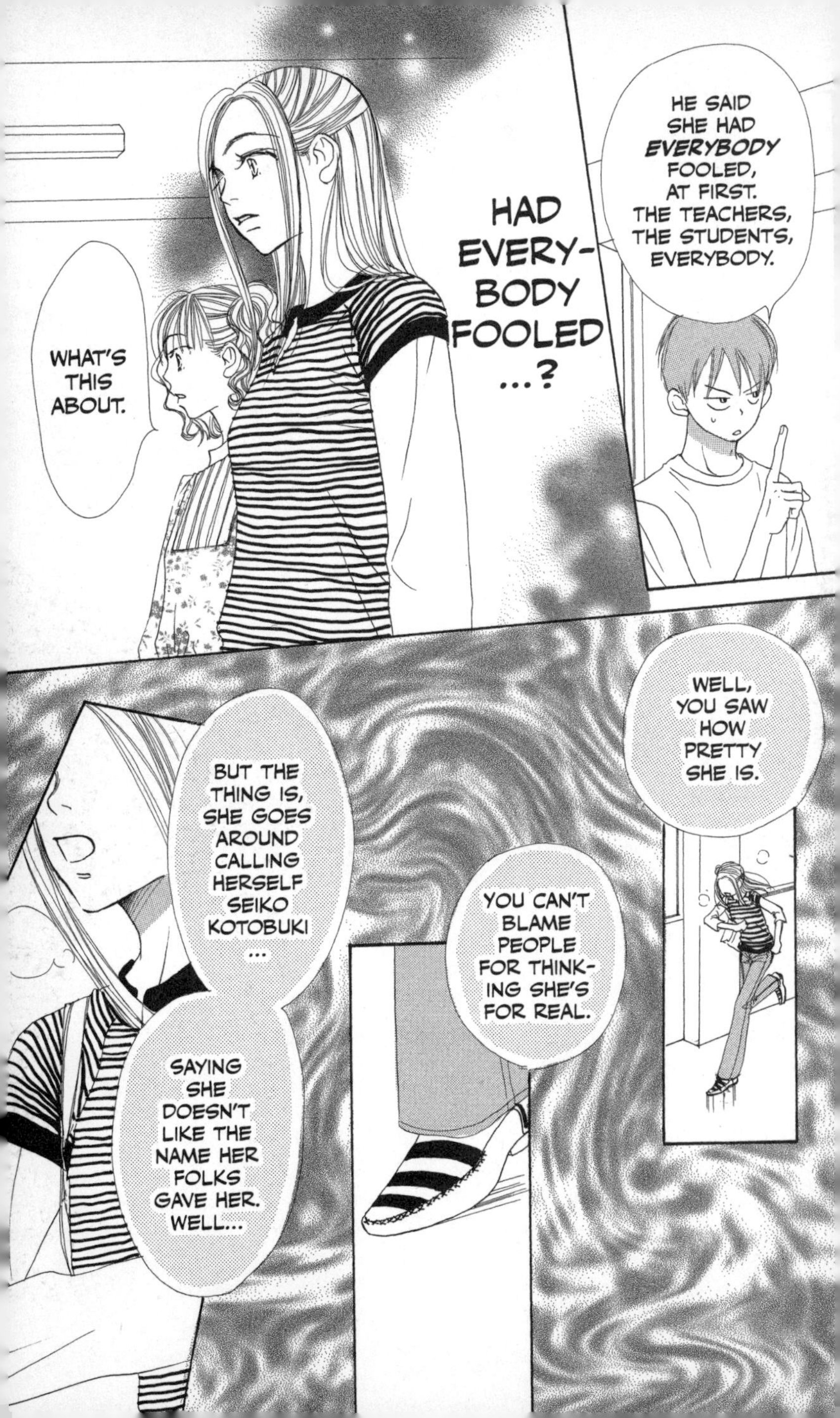
HE SAID SHE HAD *EVERYBODY* FOOLED, AT FIRST. THE TEACHERS, THE STUDENTS, EVERYBODY.
HAD EVERY-BODY FOOLED ...?
WHAT'S THIS ABOUT.
WELL, YOU SAW HOW PRETTY SHE IS.
YOU CAN'T BLAME PEOPLE FOR THINK-ING SHE'S FOR REAL.
BUT THE THING IS, SHE GOES AROUND CALLING HERSELF SEIKO KOTOBUKI ...
SAYING SHE DOESN'T LIKE THE NAME HER FOLKS GAVE HER. WELL...

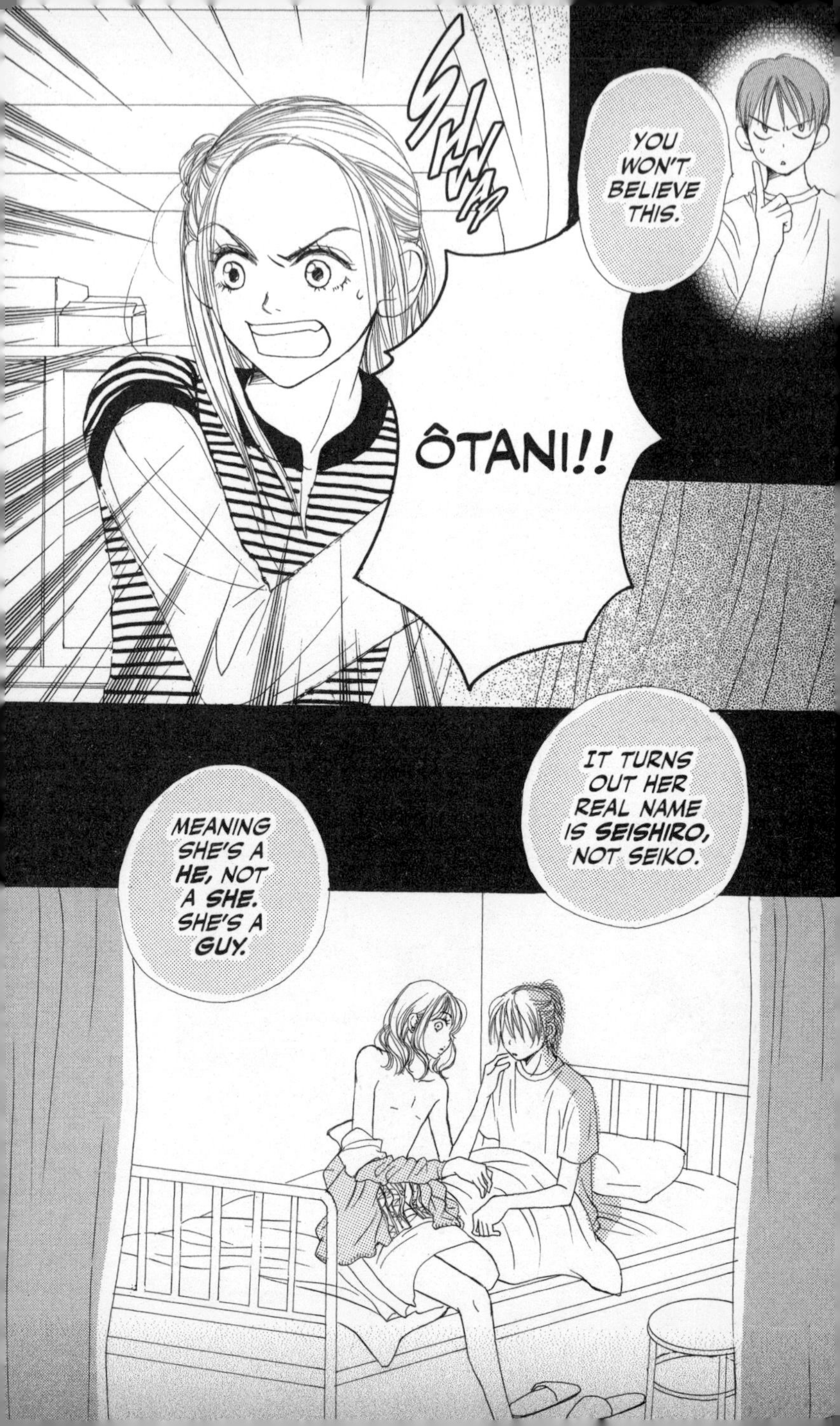
YOU WON'T BELIEVE THIS.
SHWA
ÔTANI!!
IT TURNS OUT HER REAL NAME IS SEISHIRO, NOT SEIKO.
MEANING SHE'S A HE, NOT A SHE. SHE'S A GUY.

OH NO...

O... ÔTANI ...!

BUMF

YIPES

EEK!

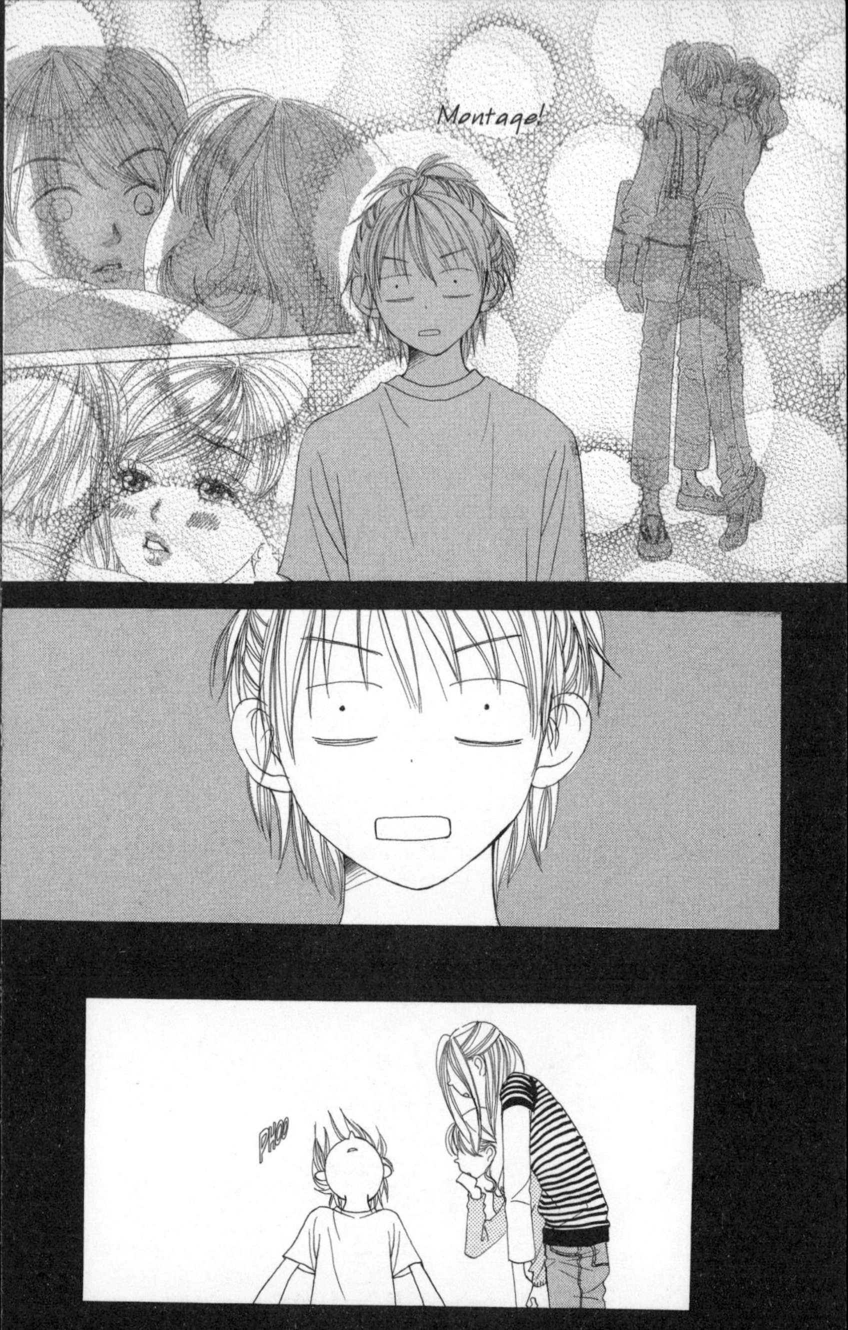
Montage!
PHOO

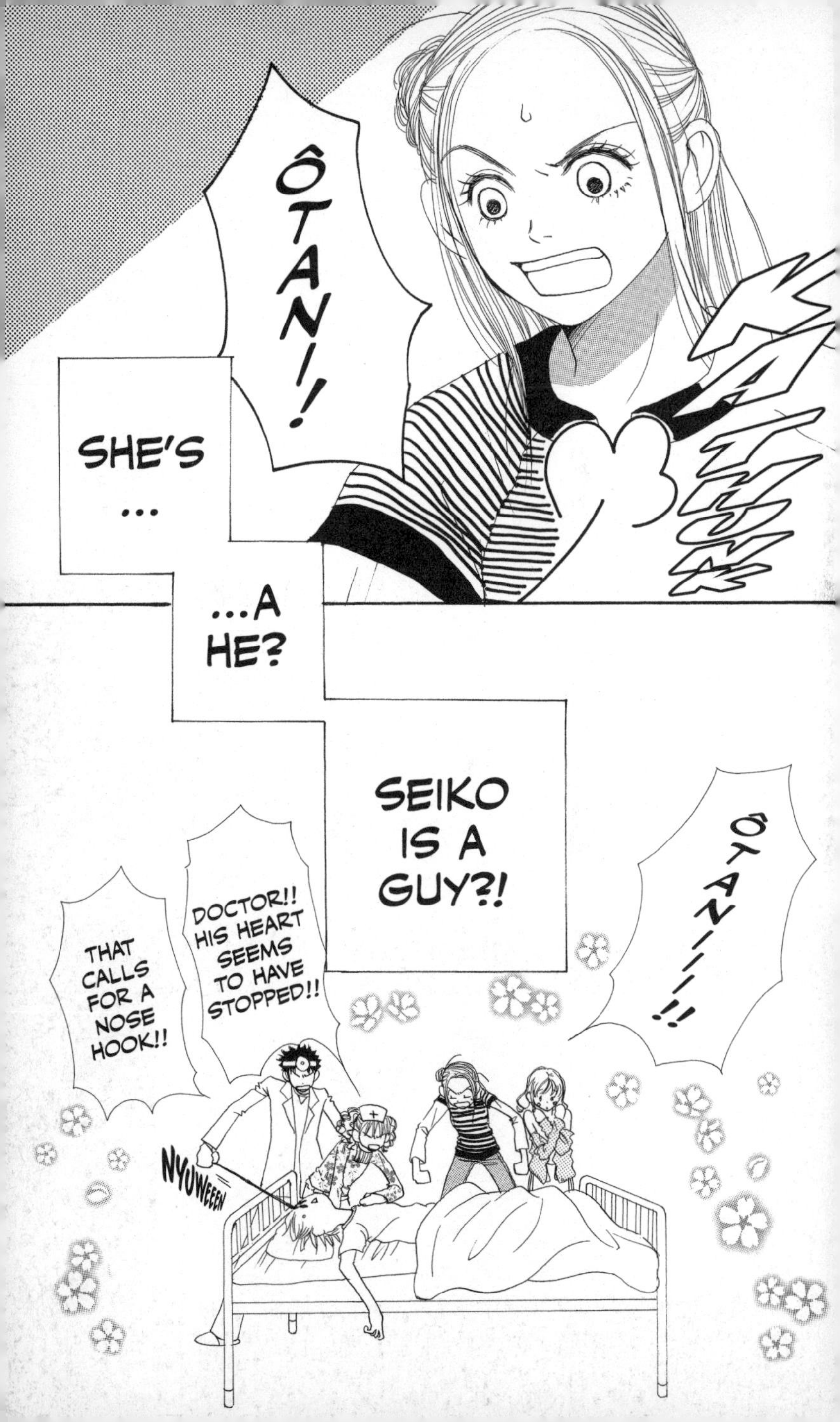
ÔTANI!!
SHE'S ...
...A HE?
SEIKO IS A GUY?!
ÔTANI——!!
DOCTOR!! HIS HEART SEEMS TO HAVE STOPPED!!
THAT CALLS FOR A NOSE HOOK!!
NYUWEEEN

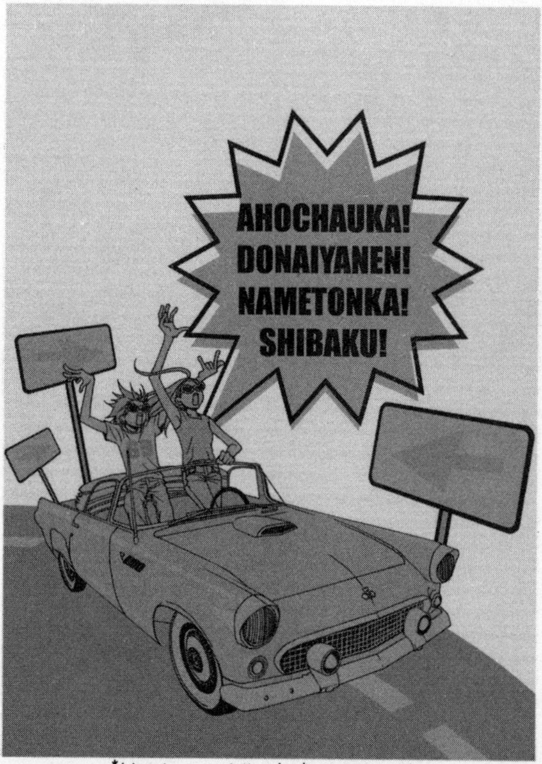
AHOCHAUKA!
DONAIYANEN!
NAMETONKA!
SHIBAKU!
*You're an idiot! What of it?!
Are you messing with me?! I'm gonna tell you off!

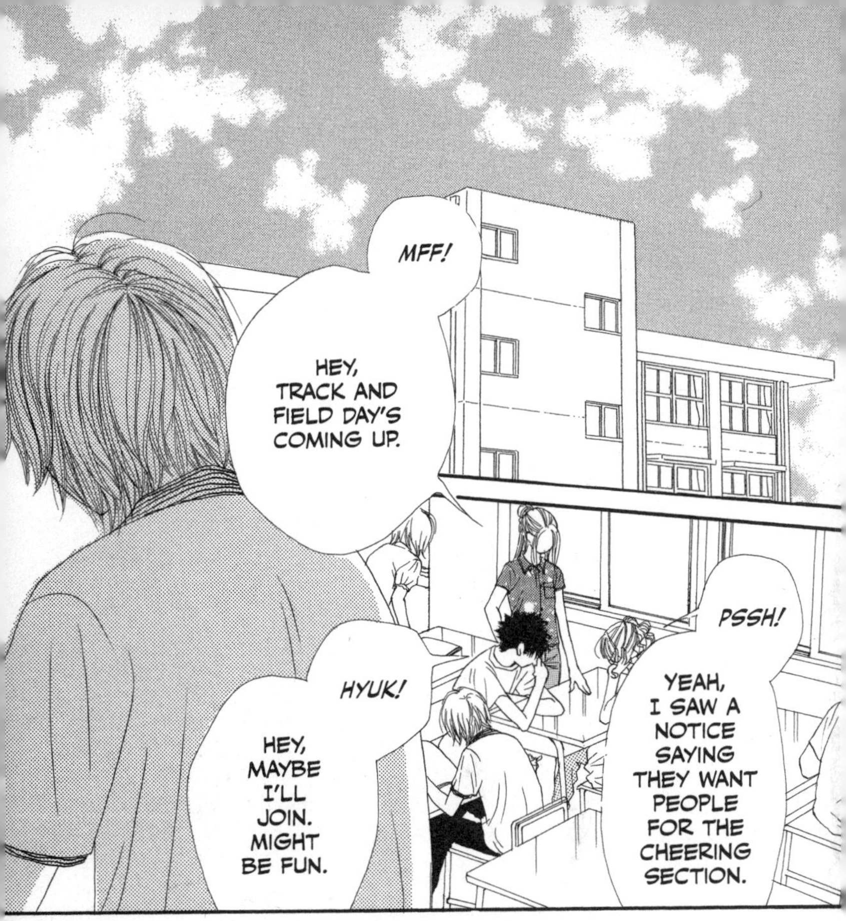
MFF!
HEY, TRACK AND FIELD DAY'S COMING UP.
PSSH!
YEAH, I SAW A NOTICE SAYING THEY WANT PEOPLE FOR THE CHEERING SECTION.
HYUK!
HEY, MAYBE I'LL JOIN. MIGHT BE FUN.

CHAPTER 12

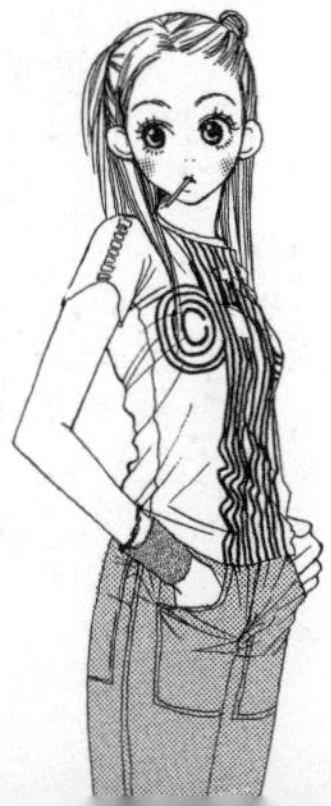

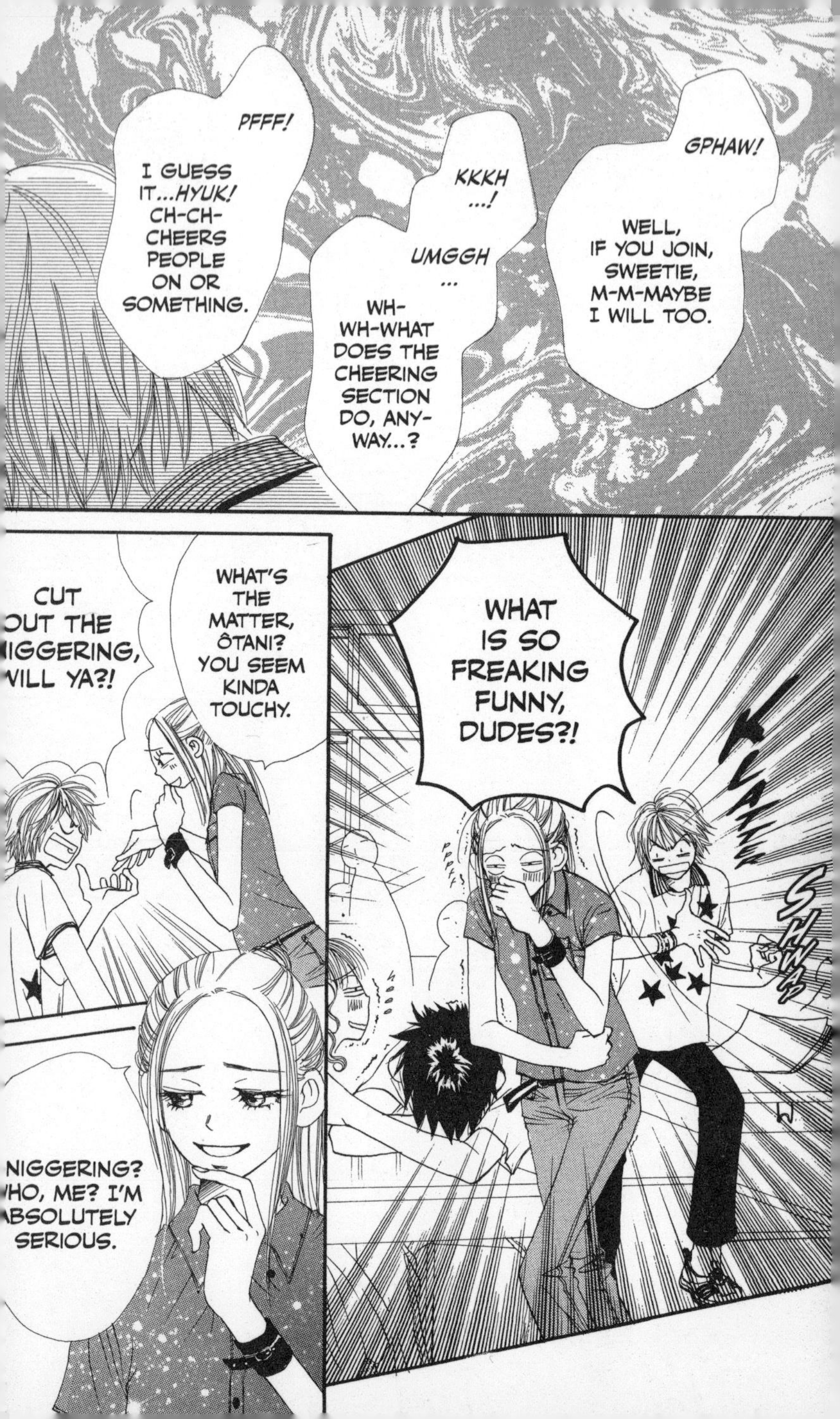
GPHAW!
WELL, IF YOU JOIN, SWEETIE, M-M-MAYBE I WILL TOO.
KKKH ...!
UMGGH ...
WH-WH-WHAT DOES THE CHEERING SECTION DO, ANY-WAY...?
PFFF!
I GUESS IT...HYUK! CH-CH-CHEERS PEOPLE ON OR SOMETHING.
WHAT IS SO FREAKING FUNNY, DUDES?!
WHAT'S THE MATTER, ÔTANI? YOU SEEM KINDA TOUCHY.
CUT OUT THE IGGERING, VILL YA?!
NIGGERING? HO, ME? I'M BSOLUTELY SERIOUS.

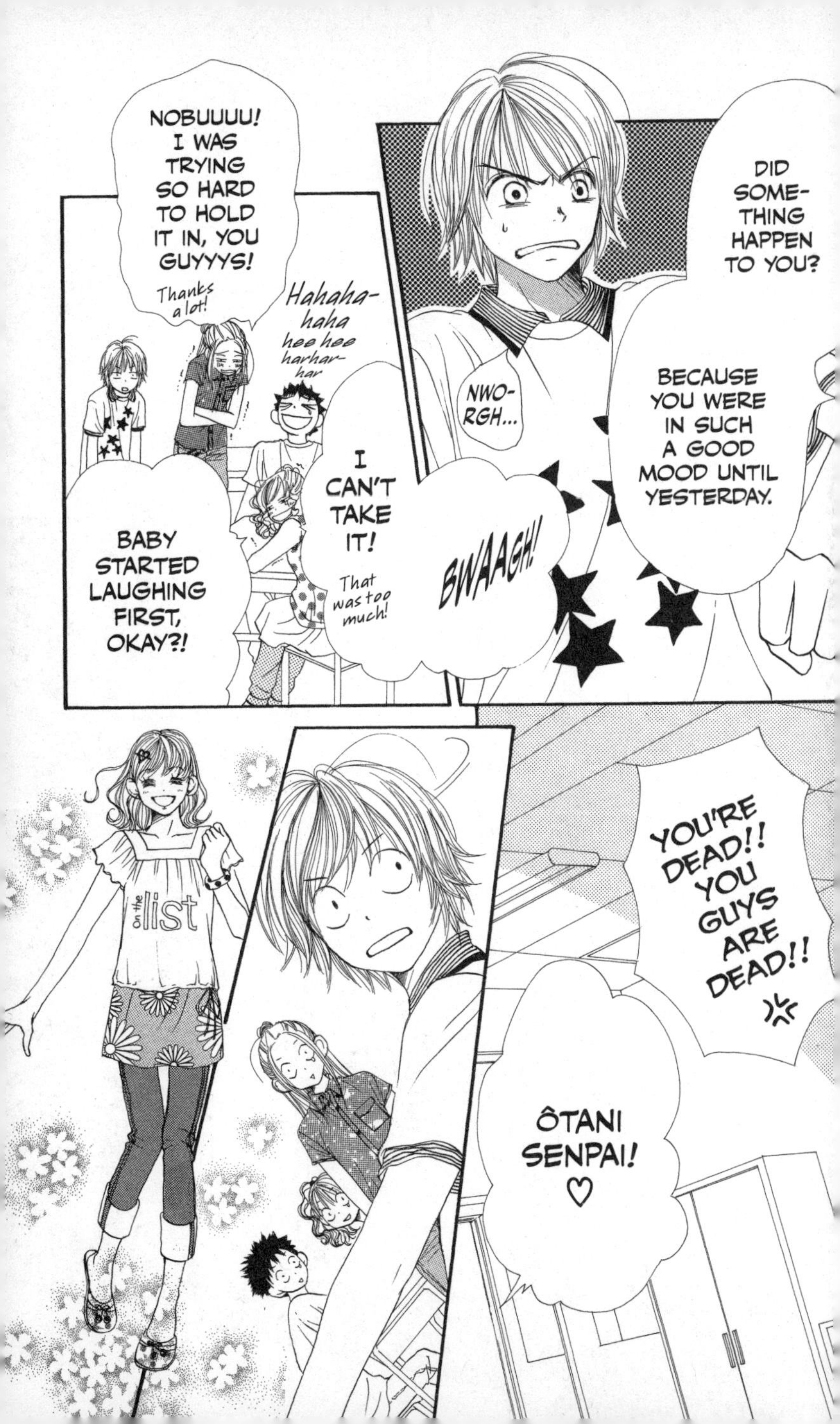
DID SOMETHING HAPPEN TO YOU?
BECAUSE YOU WERE IN SUCH A GOOD MOOD UNTIL YESTERDAY.
NWORGH...
BWAAGH!
NOBUUUU! I WAS TRYING SO HARD TO HOLD IT IN, YOU GUYYYS!
Thanks a lot!
Hahahahaha hee hee harharhar
I CAN'T TAKE IT!
That was too much!
BABY STARTED LAUGHING FIRST, OKAY?!
YOU'RE DEAD!! YOU GUYS ARE DEAD!!
ÔTANI SENPAI! ♡
on the list

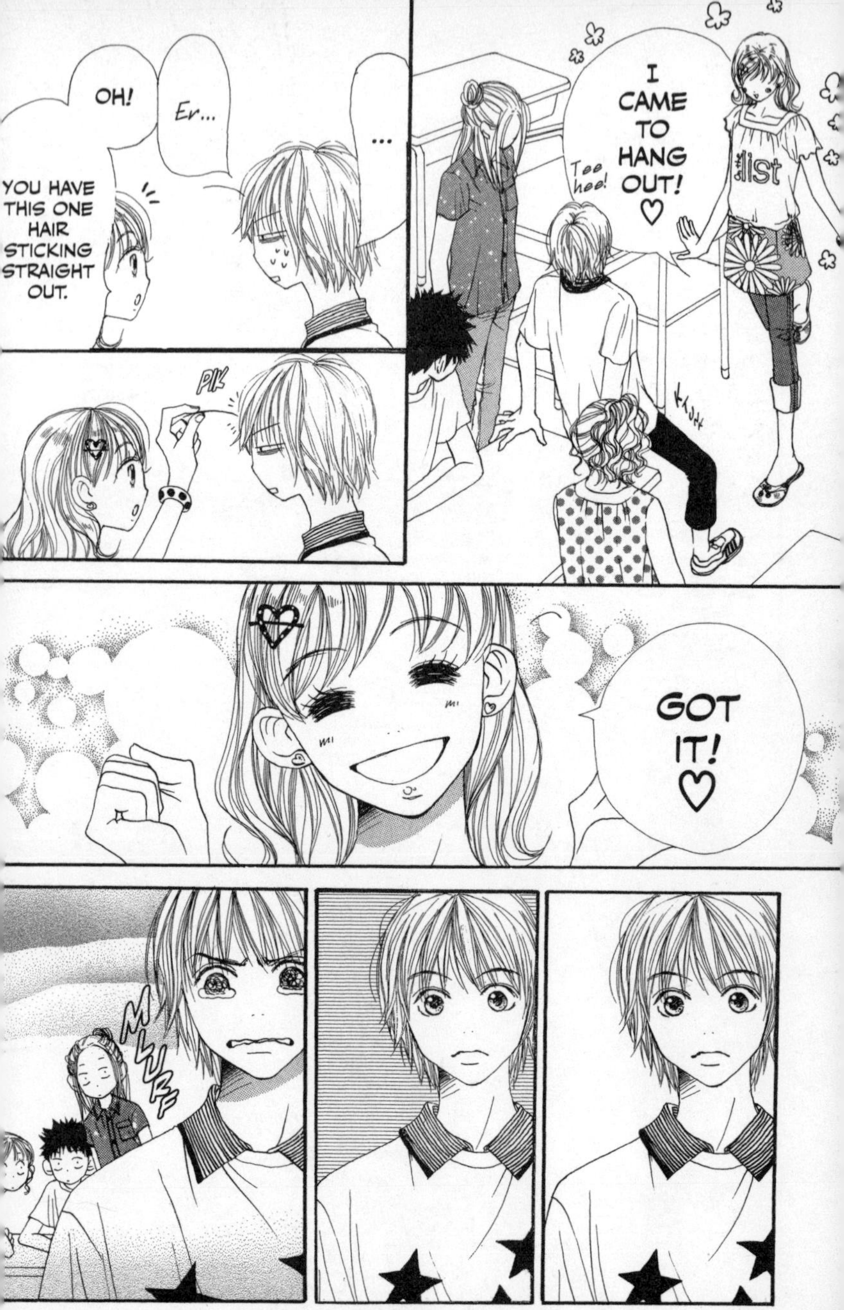
Tee hee!
I CAME TO HANG OUT! ♡
...
Er...
OH!
YOU HAVE THIS ONE HAIR STICKING STRAIGHT OUT.
PIK
GOT IT! ♡
MUFF

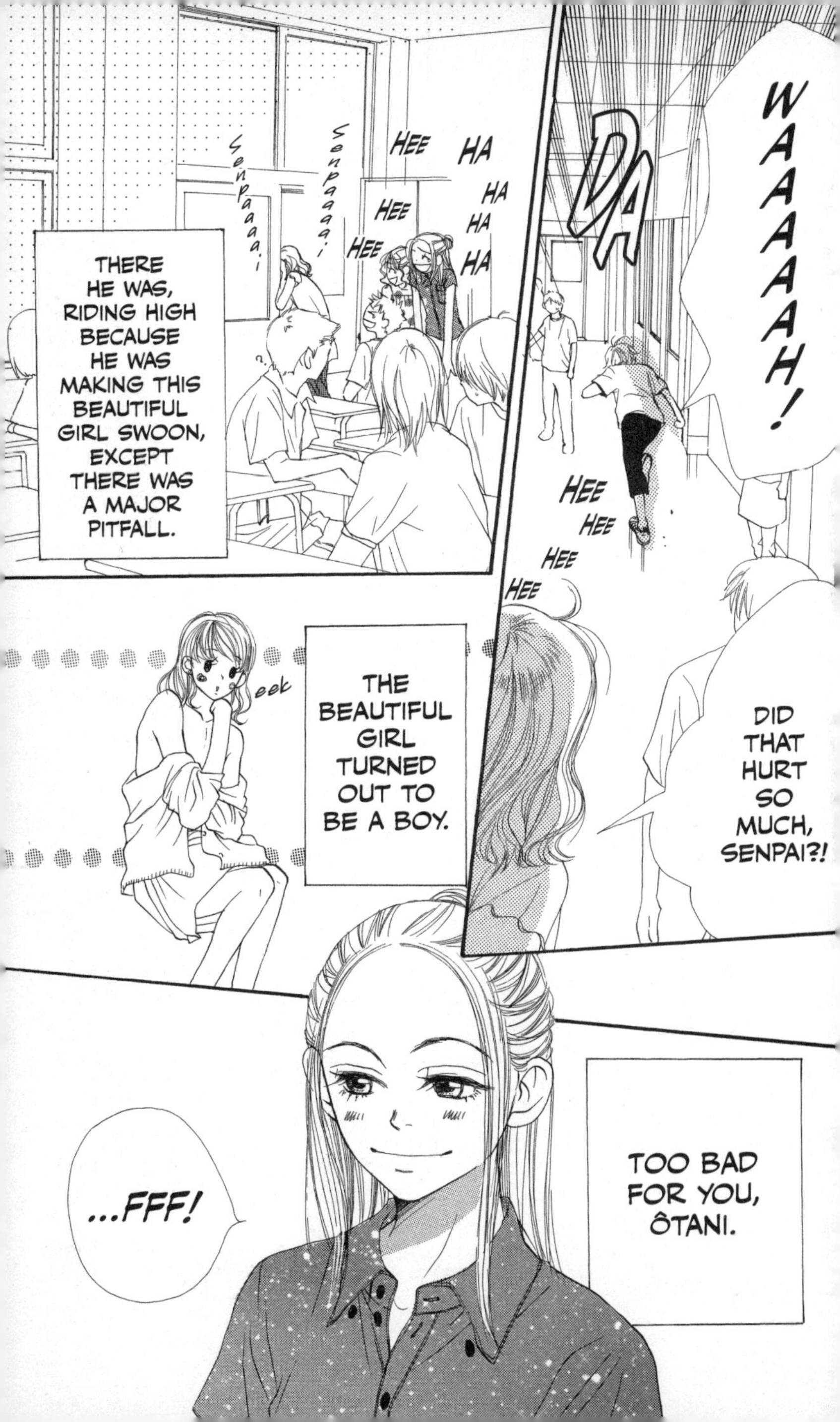
WAAAAAAH!
DA
HEE HEE HEE HEE
THERE HE WAS, RIDING HIGH BECAUSE HE WAS MAKING THIS BEAUTIFUL GIRL SWOON, EXCEPT THERE WAS A MAJOR PITFALL.
HA HA HA HA
HEE HEE HEE
Senpaaaai
Senpaaaai
DID THAT HURT SO MUCH, SENPAI?!
THE BEAUTIFUL GIRL TURNED OUT TO BE A BOY.
eek
TOO BAD FOR YOU, ÔTANI.
...FFF!

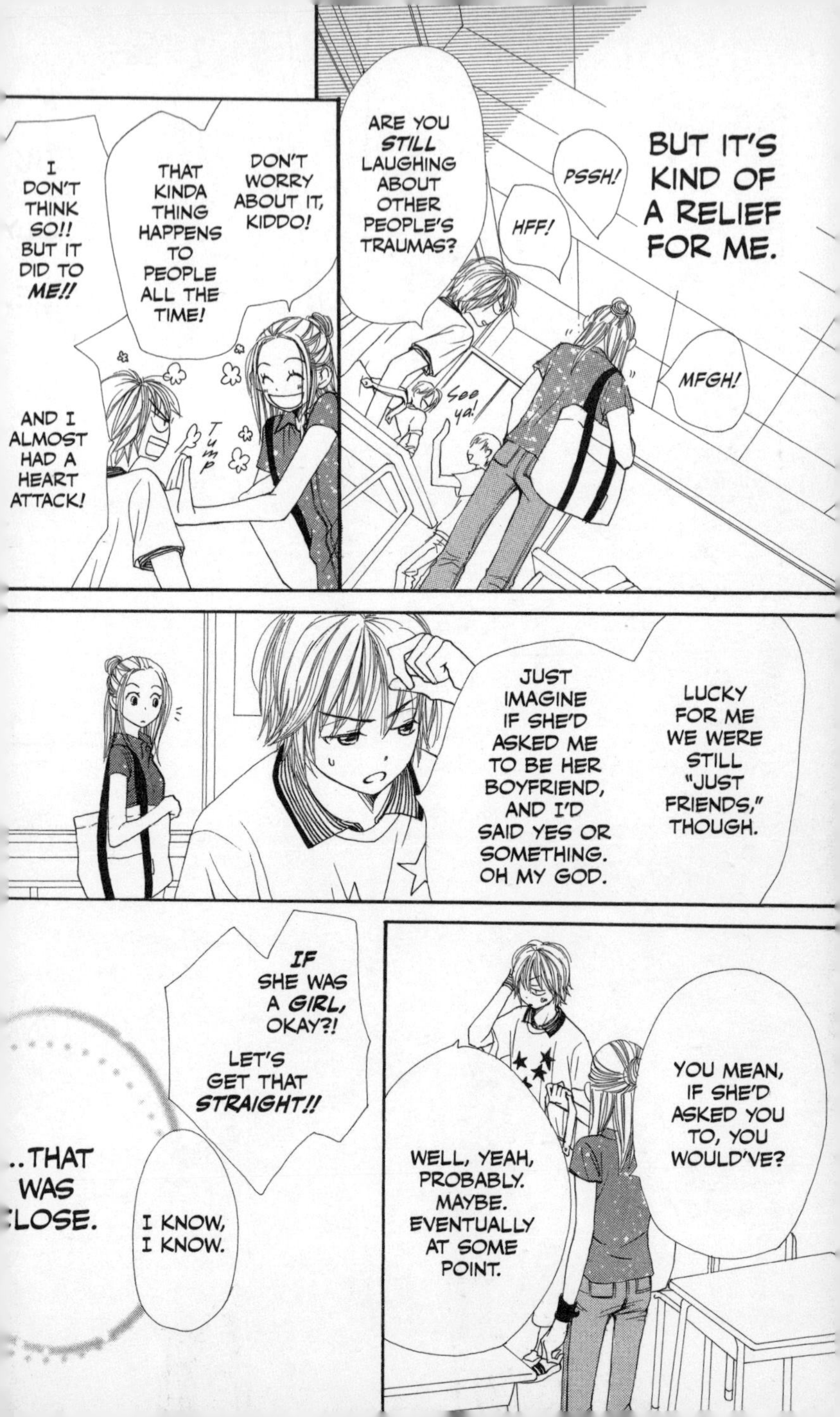
BUT IT'S KIND OF A RELIEF FOR ME.
PSSH!
HFF!
ARE YOU STILL LAUGHING ABOUT OTHER PEOPLE'S TRAUMAS?
MFGH!
See ya!
DON'T WORRY ABOUT IT, KIDDO!
THAT KINDA THING HAPPENS TO PEOPLE ALL THE TIME!
I DON'T THINK SO!! BUT IT DID TO ME!!
Tump
AND I ALMOST HAD A HEART ATTACK!
LUCKY FOR ME WE WERE STILL "JUST FRIENDS," THOUGH.
JUST IMAGINE IF SHE'D ASKED ME TO BE HER BOYFRIEND, AND I'D SAID YES OR SOMETHING. OH MY GOD.
YOU MEAN, IF SHE'D ASKED YOU TO, YOU WOULD'VE?
WELL, YEAH, PROBABLY. MAYBE. EVENTUALLY AT SOME POINT.
IF SHE WAS A GIRL, OKAY?!
LET'S GET THAT STRAIGHT!!
I KNOW, I KNOW.
..THAT WAS CLOSE.

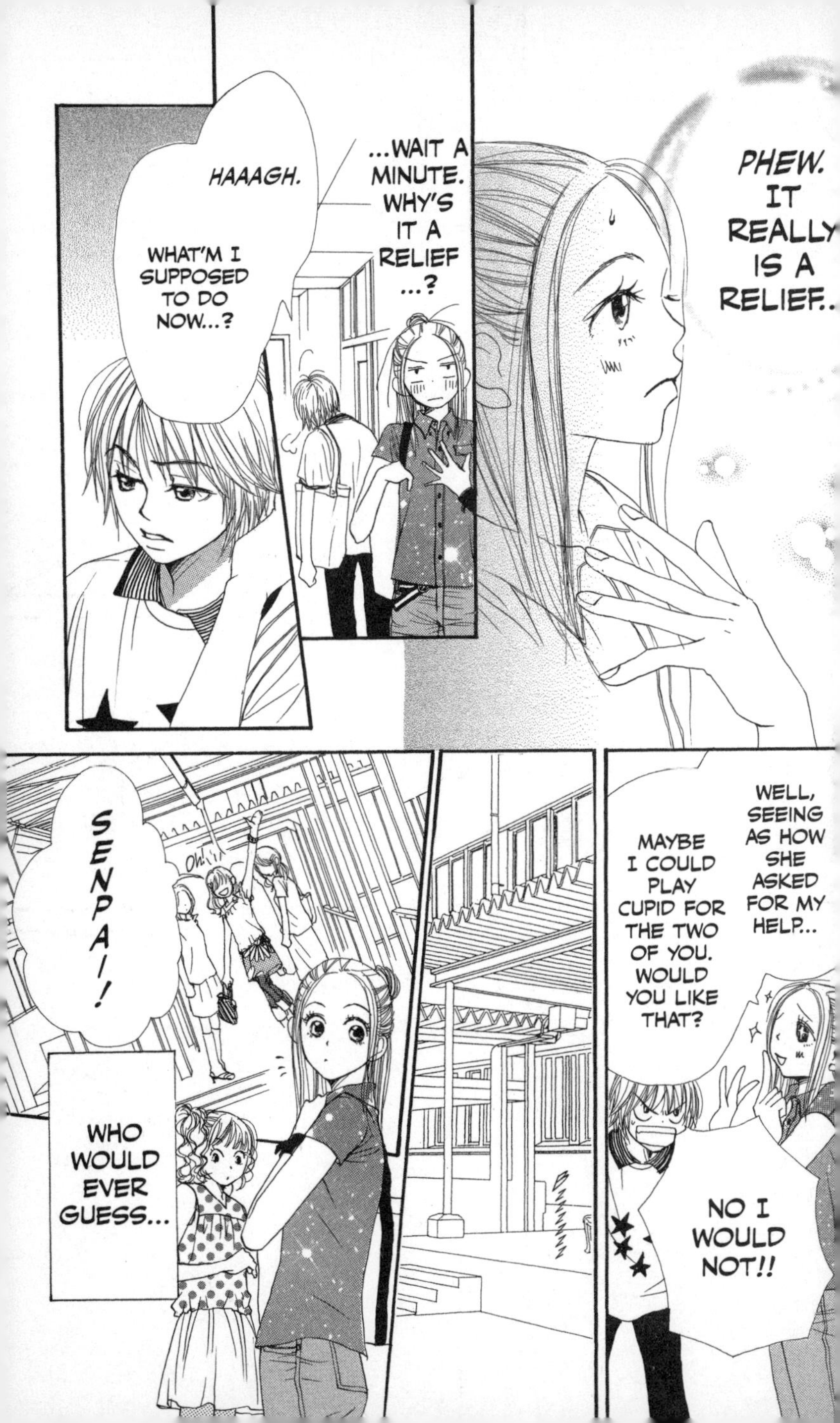
PHEW. IT REALLY IS A RELIEF...
...WAIT A MINUTE. WHY'S IT A RELIEF...?
HAAAGH.
WHAT'M I SUPPOSED TO DO NOW...?
WELL, SEEING AS HOW SHE ASKED FOR MY HELP...
MAYBE I COULD PLAY CUPID FOR THE TWO OF YOU. WOULD YOU LIKE THAT?
NO I WOULD NOT!!
SENPAI!
OH!
WHO WOULD EVER GUESS...

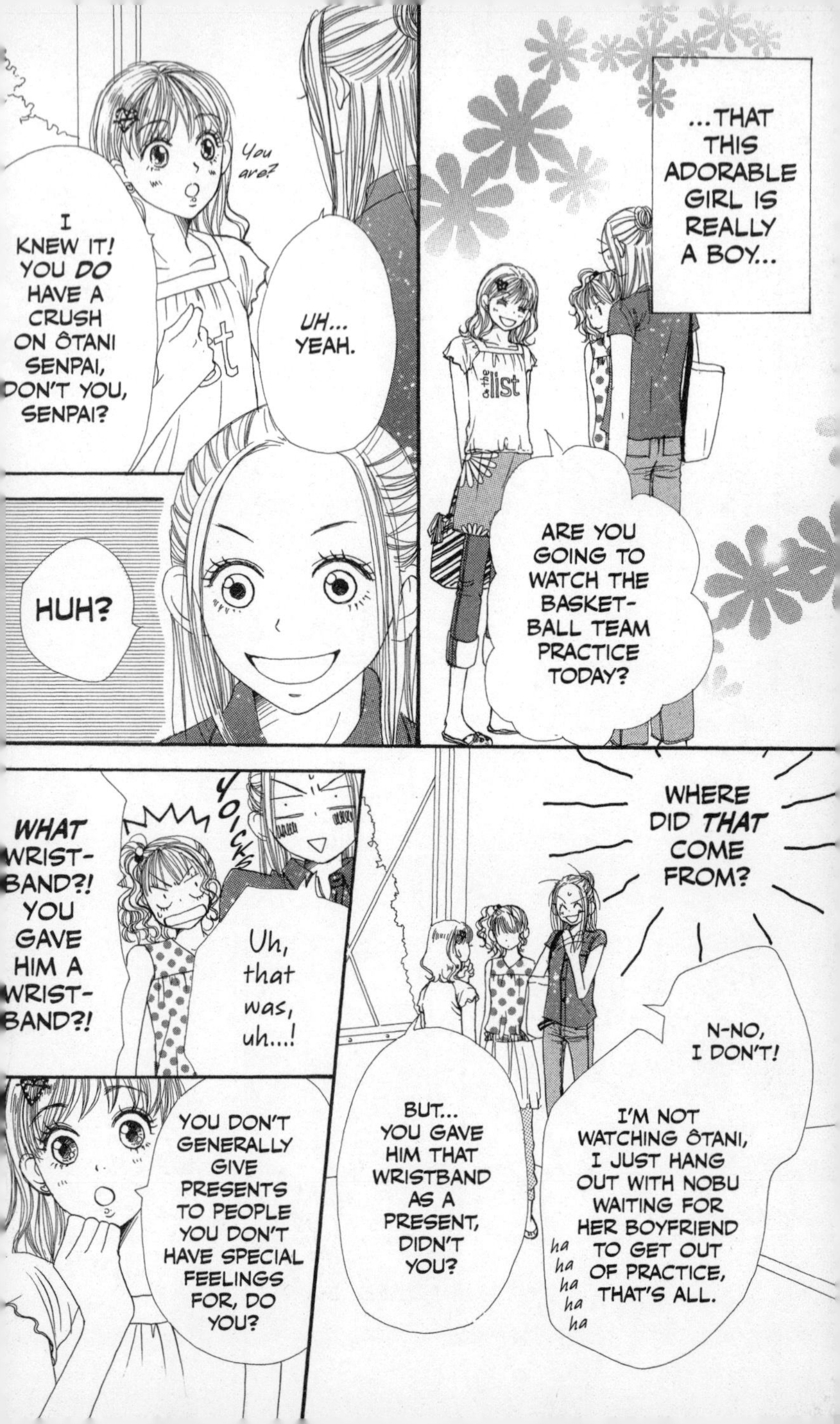

...THAT THIS ADORABLE GIRL IS REALLY A BOY...
ARE YOU GOING TO WATCH THE BASKET-BALL TEAM PRACTICE TODAY?
UH... YEAH.
You are?
I KNEW IT! YOU DO HAVE A CRUSH ON ÔTANI SENPAI, DON'T YOU, SENPAI?
HUH?
WHERE DID THAT COME FROM?
N-NO, I DON'T!
I'M NOT WATCHING ÔTANI, I JUST HANG OUT WITH NOBU WAITING FOR HER BOYFRIEND TO GET OUT OF PRACTICE, THAT'S ALL.
ha ha ha ha ha
BUT... YOU GAVE HIM THAT WRISTBAND AS A PRESENT, DIDN'T YOU?
YOICKS
Uh, that was, uh...!
WHAT WRIST-BAND?! YOU GAVE HIM A WRIST-BAND?!
YOU DON'T GENERALLY GIVE PRESENTS TO PEOPLE YOU DON'T HAVE SPECIAL FEELINGS FOR, DO YOU?

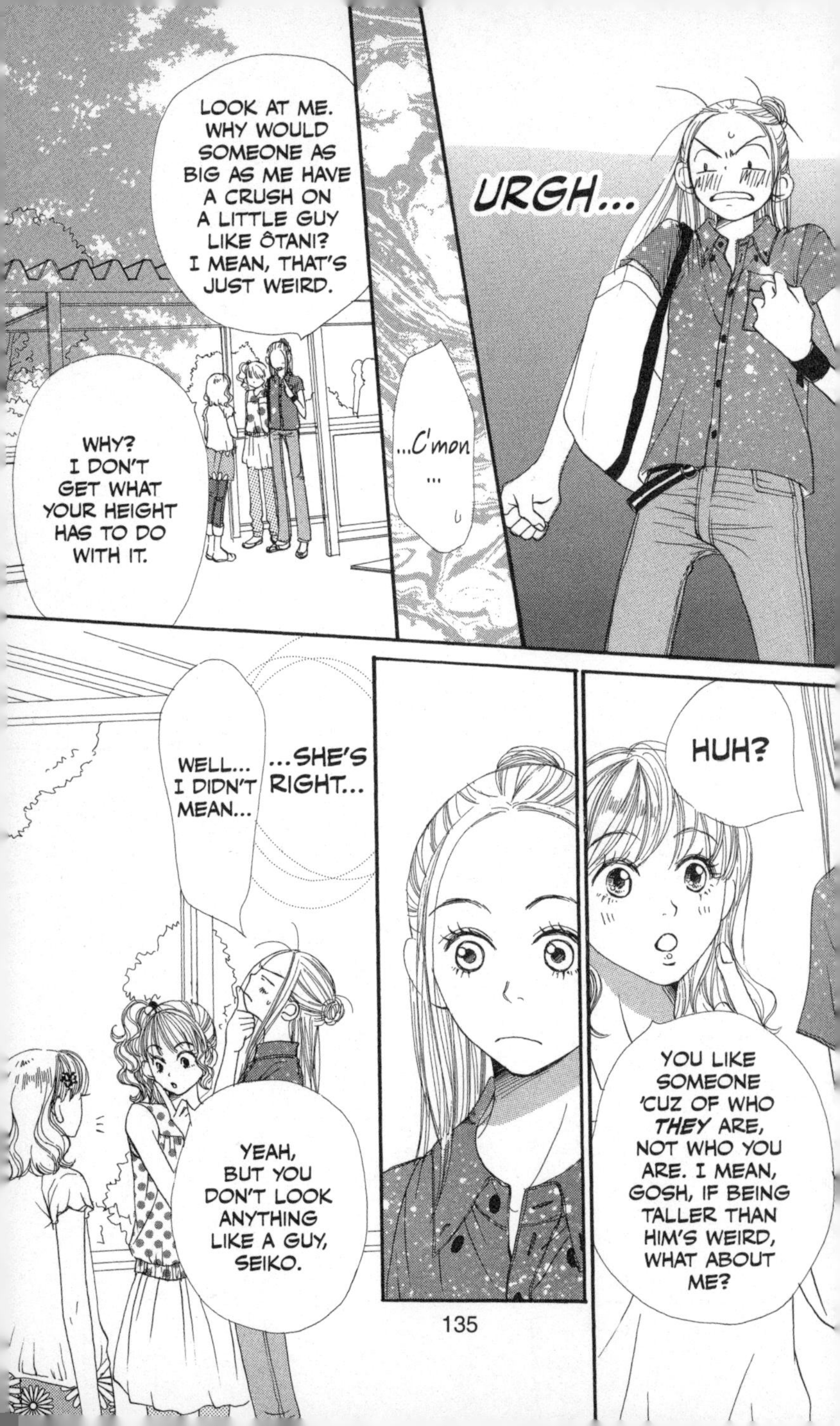
URGH...
...C'mon...
LOOK AT ME. WHY WOULD SOMEONE AS BIG AS ME HAVE A CRUSH ON A LITTLE GUY LIKE ÔTANI? I MEAN, THAT'S JUST WEIRD.
WHY? I DON'T GET WHAT YOUR HEIGHT HAS TO DO WITH IT.
HUH?
YOU LIKE SOMEONE 'CUZ OF WHO THEY ARE, NOT WHO YOU ARE. I MEAN, GOSH, IF BEING TALLER THAN HIM'S WEIRD, WHAT ABOUT ME?
...SHE'S RIGHT...
WELL... I DIDN'T MEAN...
YEAH, BUT YOU DON'T LOOK ANYTHING LIKE A GUY, SEIKO.

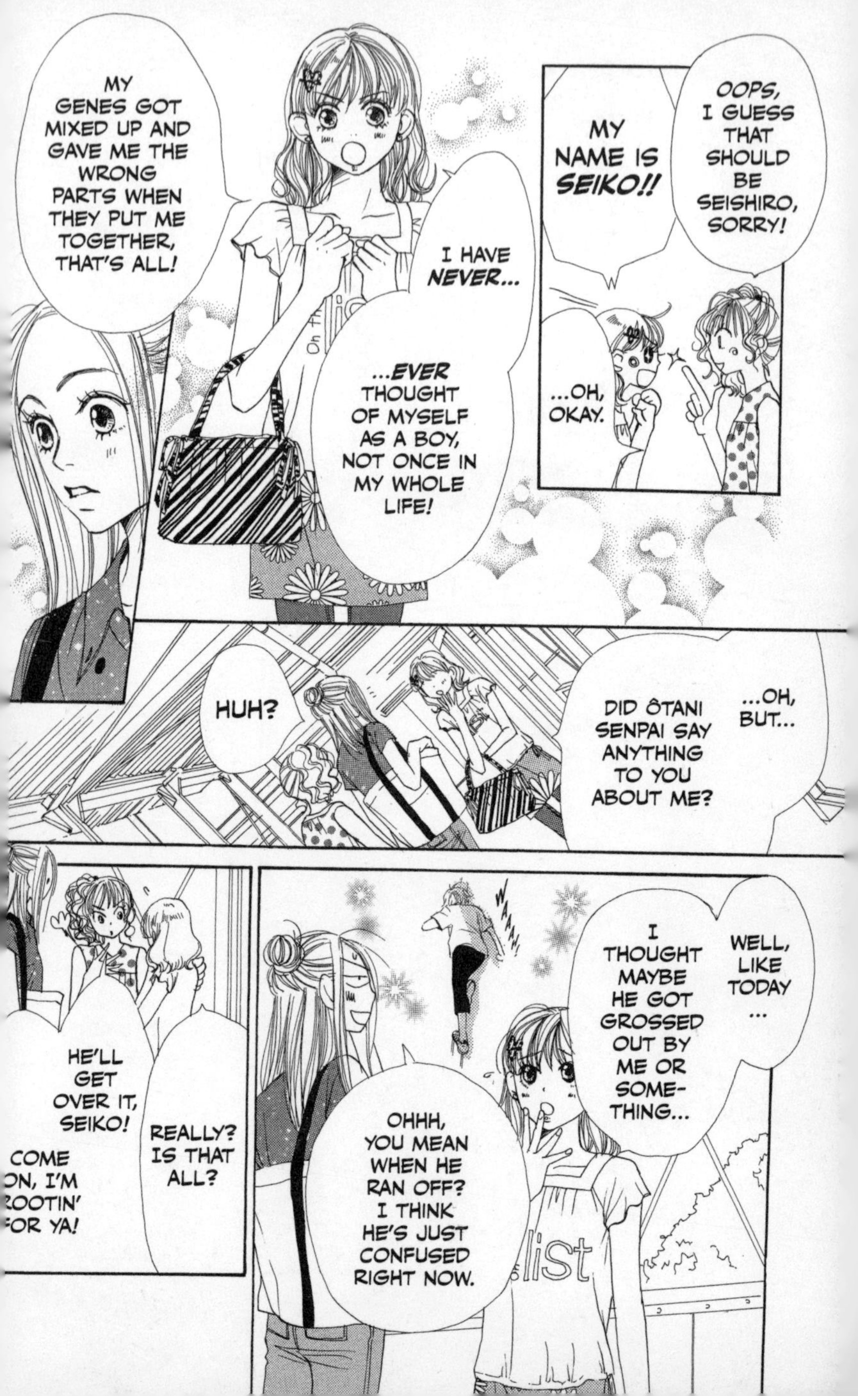
OOPS, I GUESS THAT SHOULD BE SEISHIRO, SORRY!
MY NAME IS *SEIKO!!*
...OH, OKAY.
I HAVE *NEVER...*
...*EVER* THOUGHT OF MYSELF AS A BOY, NOT ONCE IN MY WHOLE LIFE!
MY GENES GOT MIXED UP AND GAVE ME THE WRONG PARTS WHEN THEY PUT ME TOGETHER, THAT'S ALL!
...OH, BUT...
DID ÔTANI SENPAI SAY ANYTHING TO YOU ABOUT ME?
HUH?
WELL, LIKE TODAY...
I THOUGHT MAYBE HE GOT GROSSED OUT BY ME OR SOME-THING...
WAAAH!
OHHH, YOU MEAN WHEN HE RAN OFF? I THINK HE'S JUST CONFUSED RIGHT NOW.
REALLY? IS THAT ALL?
HE'LL GET OVER IT, SEIKO!
COME ON, I'M ROOTIN' FOR YA!

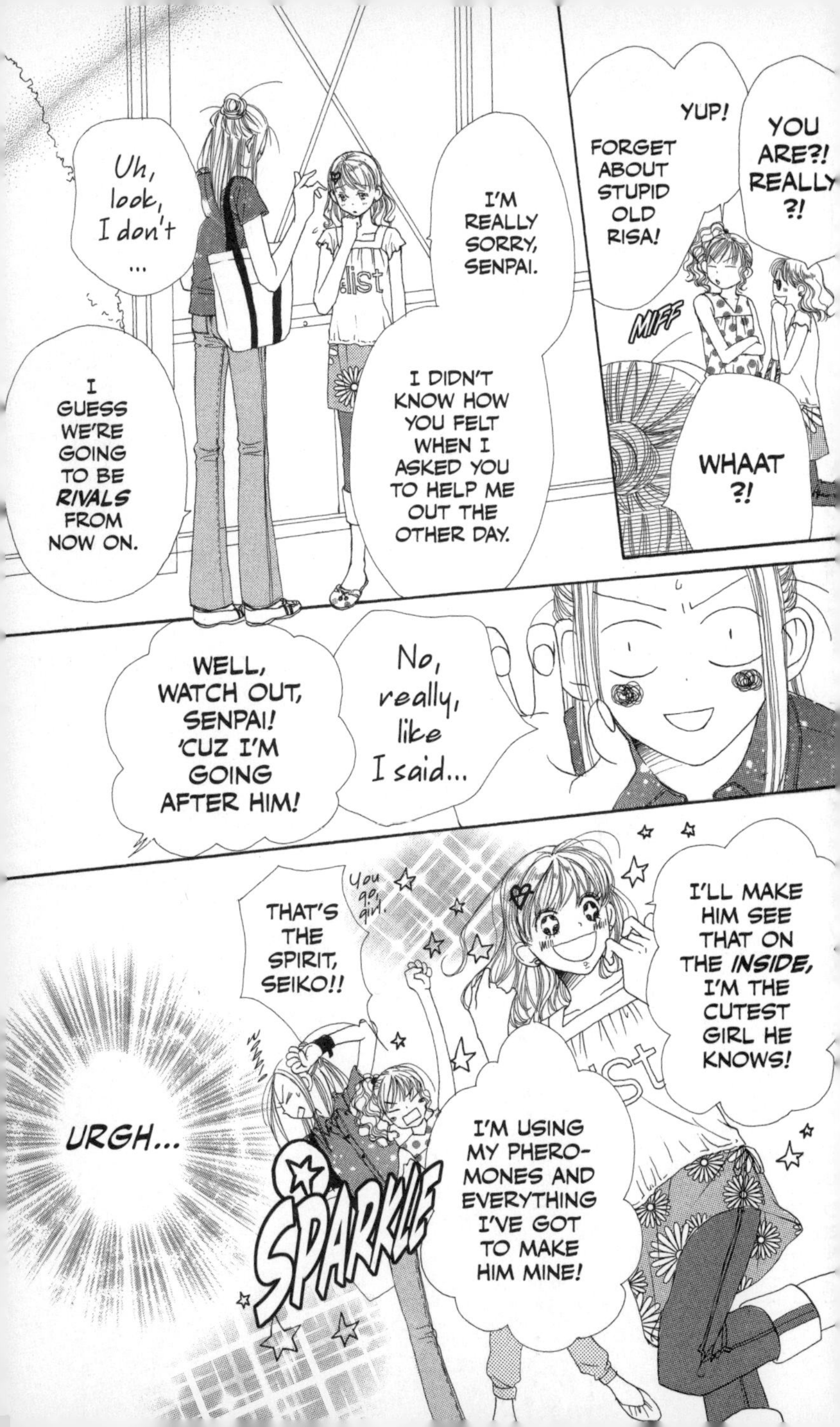
YOU ARE?! REALLY?!
YUP!
FORGET ABOUT STUPID OLD RISA!
MIFF
WHAAT?!
I'M REALLY SORRY, SENPAI.
Uh, look, I don't ...
I DIDN'T KNOW HOW YOU FELT WHEN I ASKED YOU TO HELP ME OUT THE OTHER DAY.
I GUESS WE'RE GOING TO BE *RIVALS* FROM NOW ON.
No, really, like I said...
WELL, WATCH OUT, SENPAI! 'CUZ I'M GOING AFTER HIM!
I'LL MAKE HIM SEE THAT ON THE *INSIDE*, I'M THE CUTEST GIRL HE KNOWS!
You go, girl.
THAT'S THE SPIRIT, SEIKO!!
I'M USING MY PHERO-MONES AND EVERYTHING I'VE GOT TO MAKE HIM MINE!
SPARKLE
URGH...

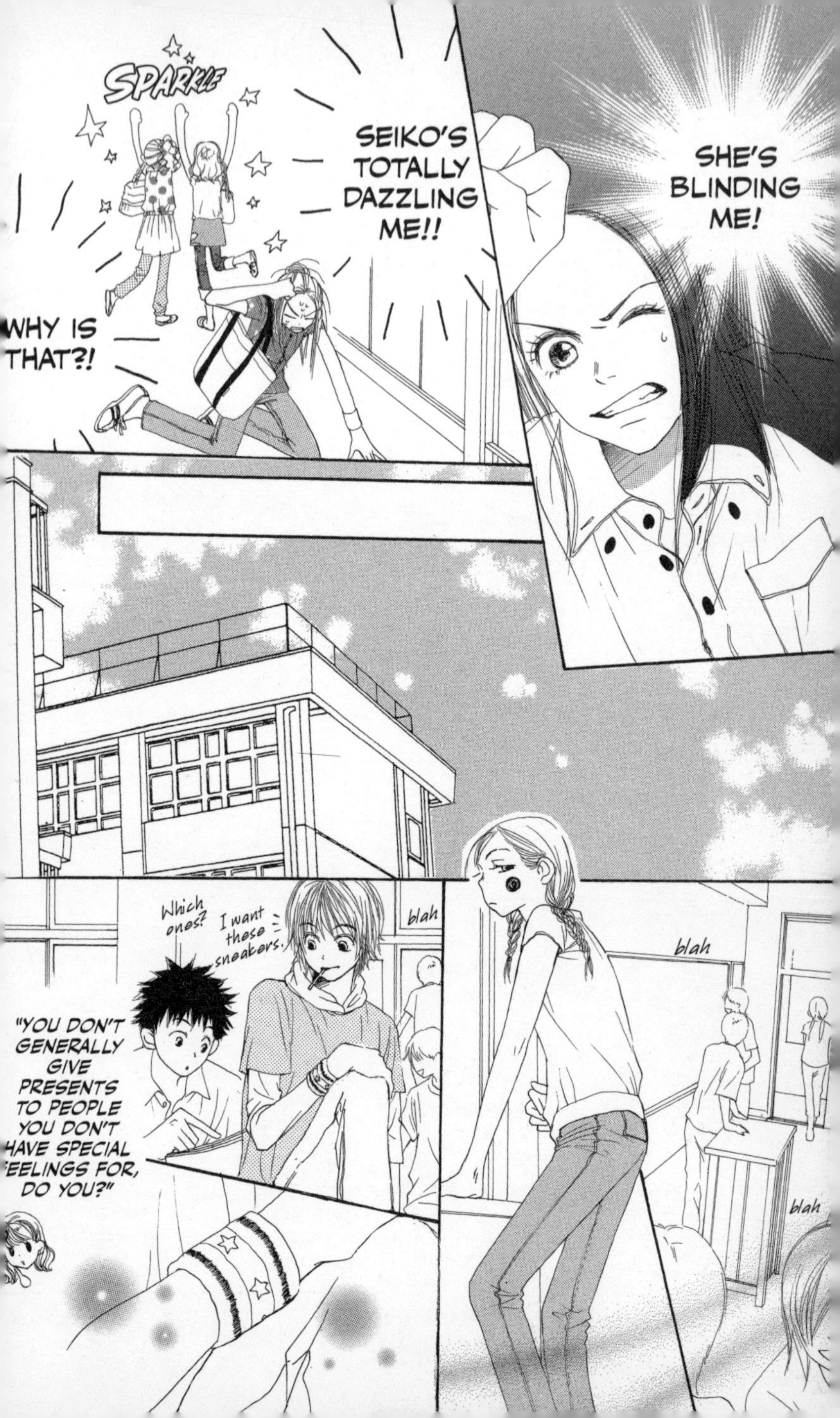
SHE'S BLINDING ME!
SEIKO'S TOTALLY DAZZLING ME!!
SPARKLE
WHY IS THAT?!
blah
blah
blah
I want these sneakers.
Which ones?
"YOU DON'T GENERALLY GIVE PRESENTS TO PEOPLE YOU DON'T HAVE SPECIAL FEELINGS FOR, DO YOU?"

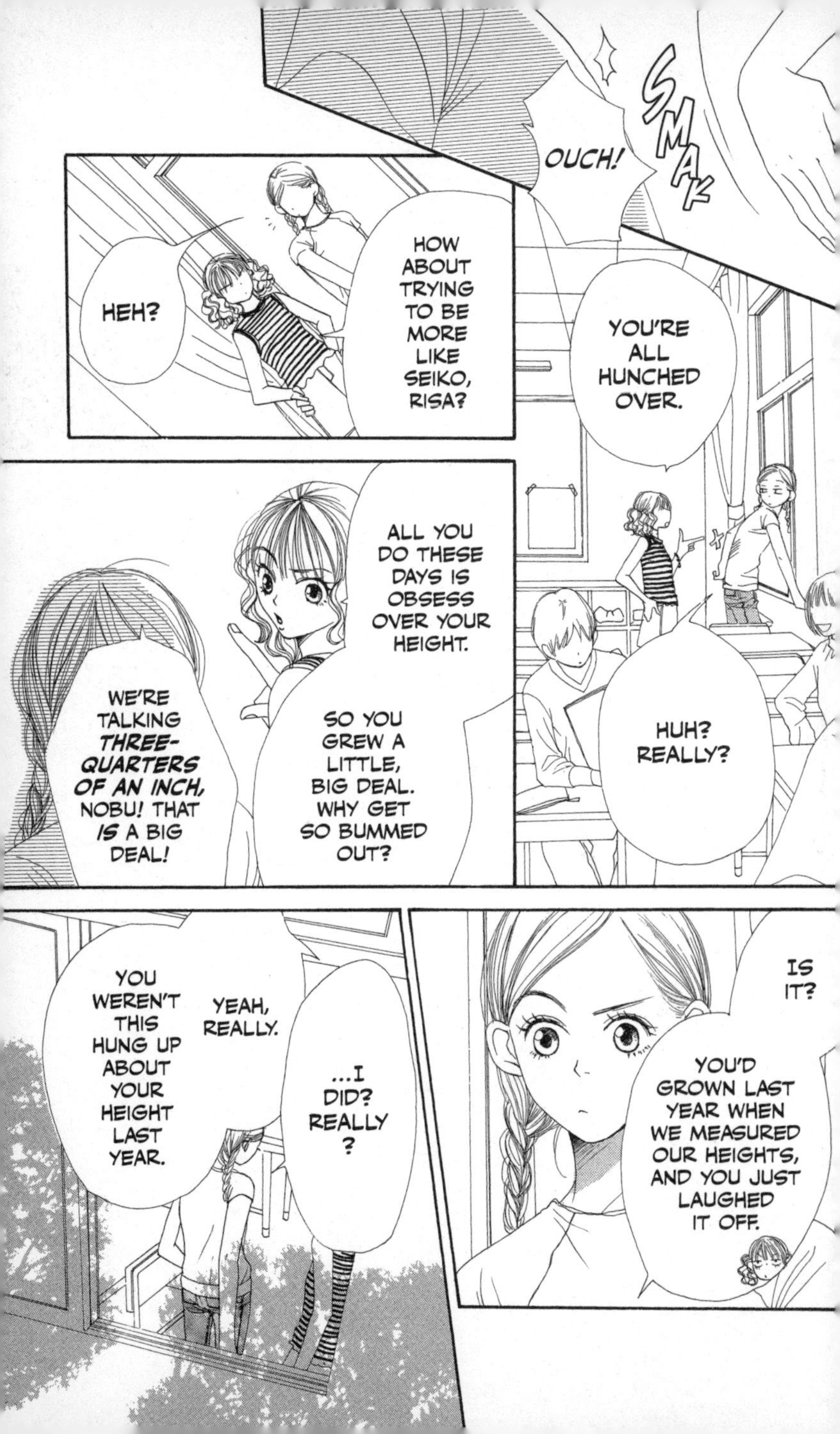
SMAK
OUCH!
YOU'RE ALL HUNCHED OVER.
HUH? REALLY?
HOW ABOUT TRYING TO BE MORE LIKE SEIKO, RISA?
HEH?
ALL YOU DO THESE DAYS IS OBSESS OVER YOUR HEIGHT.
SO YOU GREW A LITTLE, BIG DEAL. WHY GET SO BUMMED OUT?
WE'RE TALKING *THREE-QUARTERS OF AN INCH,* NOBU! THAT *IS* A BIG DEAL!
IS IT?
YOU'D GROWN LAST YEAR WHEN WE MEASURED OUR HEIGHTS, AND YOU JUST LAUGHED IT OFF.
...I DID? REALLY?
YEAH, REALLY.
YOU WEREN'T THIS HUNG UP ABOUT YOUR HEIGHT LAST YEAR.

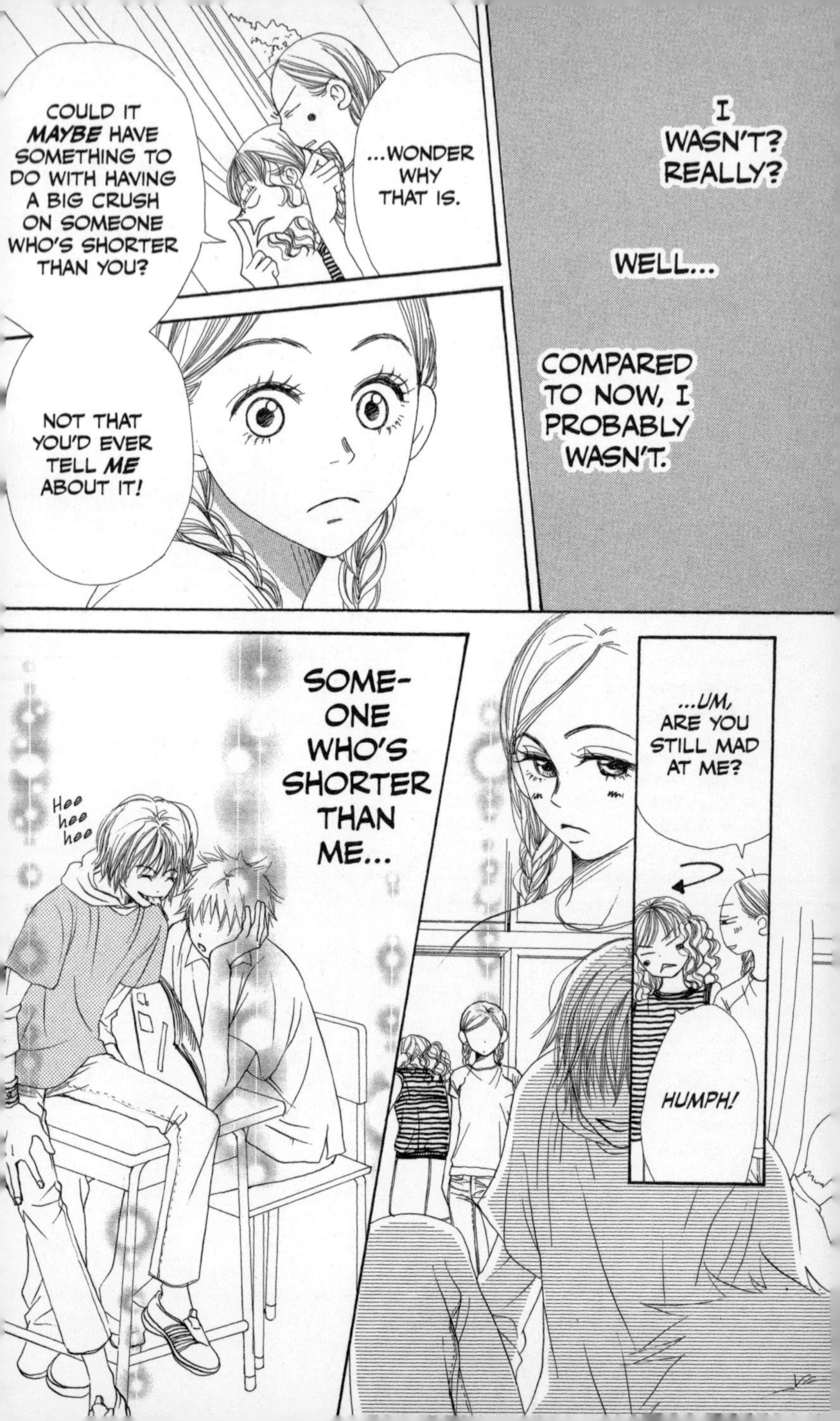
I WASN'T? REALLY?
WELL...
COMPARED TO NOW, I PROBABLY WASN'T.
...WONDER WHY THAT IS.
COULD IT *MAYBE* HAVE SOMETHING TO DO WITH HAVING A BIG CRUSH ON SOMEONE WHO'S SHORTER THAN YOU?
NOT THAT YOU'D EVER TELL *ME* ABOUT IT!
...UM, ARE YOU STILL MAD AT ME?
HUMPH!
SOME-ONE WHO'S SHORTER THAN ME...
Hee hee hee

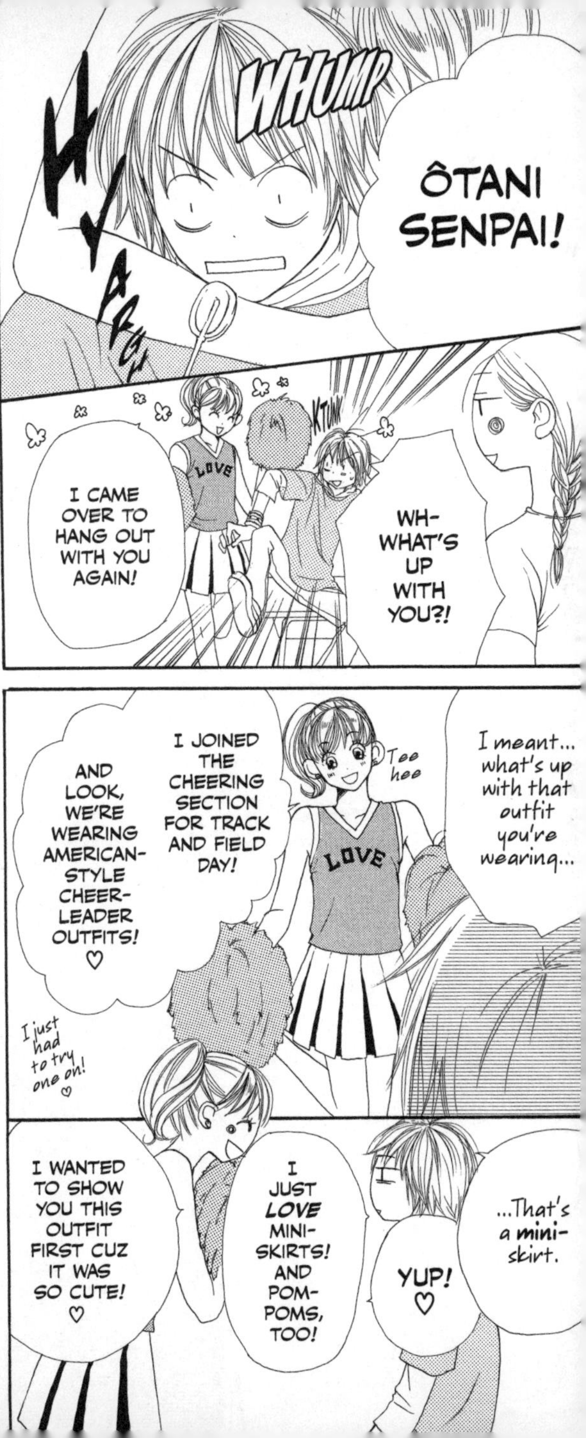
WHUMP
ÔTANI SENPAI!
KTUNK
WH- WHAT'S UP WITH YOU?!
I CAME OVER TO HANG OUT WITH YOU AGAIN!
I meant... what's up with that outfit you're wearing...
Tee hee
I JOINED THE CHEERING SECTION FOR TRACK AND FIELD DAY!
AND LOOK, WE'RE WEARING AMERICAN-STYLE CHEER-LEADER OUTFITS! ♡
I just had to try one on! ♡
...That's a mini-skirt.
YUP! ♡
I JUST LOVE MINI-SKIRTS! AND POM-POMS, TOO!
I WANTED TO SHOW YOU THIS OUTFIT FIRST CUZ IT WAS SO CUTE! ♡

4

This is the last one of these spaces for this volume, but this time we have a special bonus section for you at the end. Some folks who just happened to be over at my house for a visit got shanghaied into it, too. Please give it a little peek...

Well, then, I sure hope to meet you again in Vol. 4! There's still a bit left of this silly volume, so stick around to the end, if you please.

Umph.

Aya
Sept. 2002

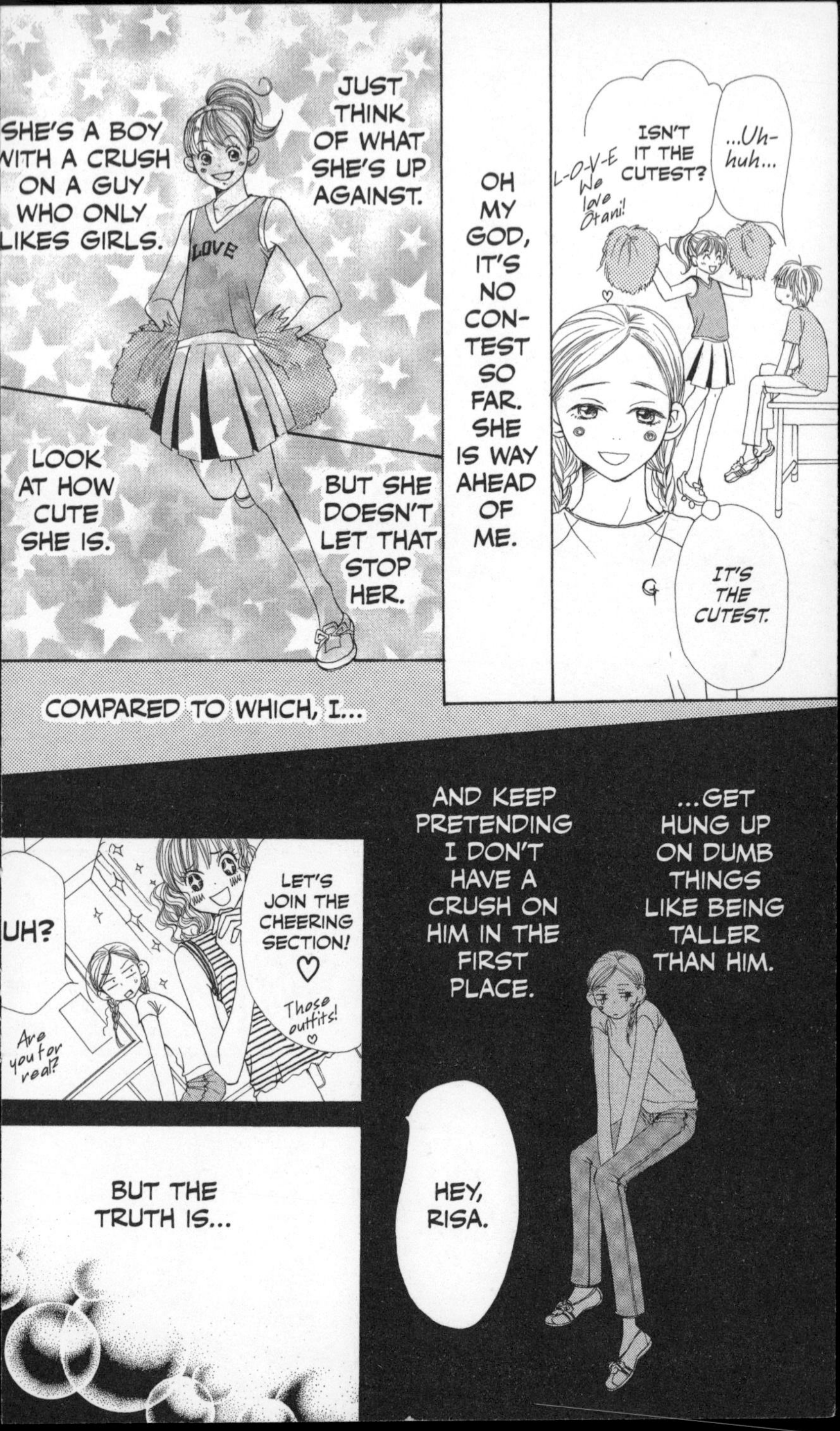
ISN'T IT THE CUTEST?
...Uh-huh...
L-O-V-E We love Otani!
IT'S THE CUTEST.
OH MY GOD, IT'S NO CONTEST SO FAR. SHE IS WAY AHEAD OF ME.
JUST THINK OF WHAT SHE'S UP AGAINST.
SHE'S A BOY WITH A CRUSH ON A GUY WHO ONLY LIKES GIRLS.
LOVE
BUT SHE DOESN'T LET THAT STOP HER.
LOOK AT HOW CUTE SHE IS.
COMPARED TO WHICH, I...
...GET HUNG UP ON DUMB THINGS LIKE BEING TALLER THAN HIM.
AND KEEP PRETENDING I DON'T HAVE A CRUSH ON HIM IN THE FIRST PLACE.
HEY, RISA.
LET'S JOIN THE CHEERING SECTION! ♡
Those outfits! ♡
UH?
Are you for real?
BUT THE TRUTH IS...

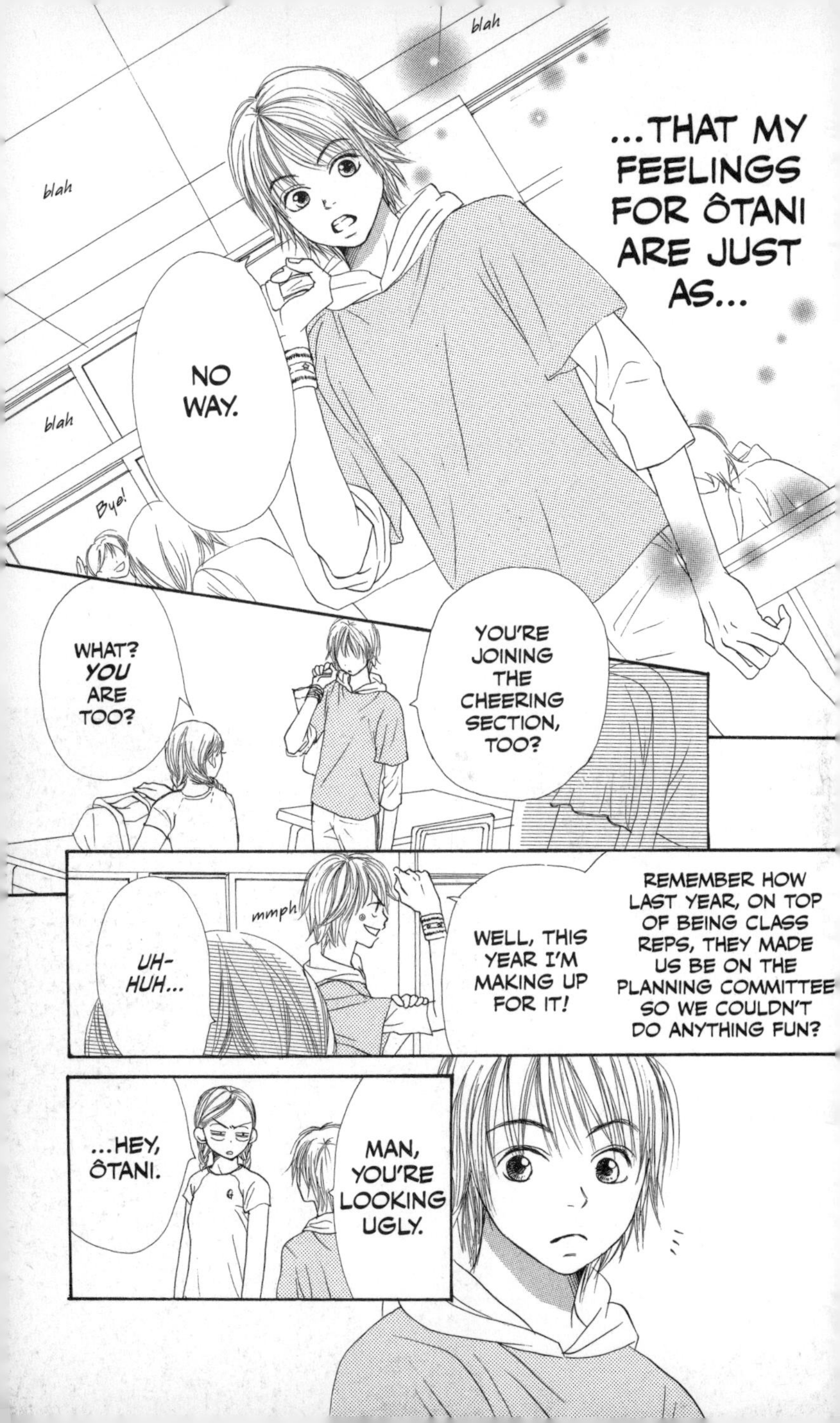
...THAT MY FEELINGS FOR ÔTANI ARE JUST AS...
blah
NO WAY.
blah
blah
Bye!
YOU'RE JOINING THE CHEERING SECTION, TOO?
WHAT? *YOU* ARE TOO?
REMEMBER HOW LAST YEAR, ON TOP OF BEING CLASS REPS, THEY MADE US BE ON THE PLANNING COMMITTEE SO WE COULDN'T DO ANYTHING FUN?
WELL, THIS YEAR I'M MAKING UP FOR IT!
mmph
UH-HUH...
MAN, YOU'RE LOOKING UGLY.
...HEY, ÔTANI.

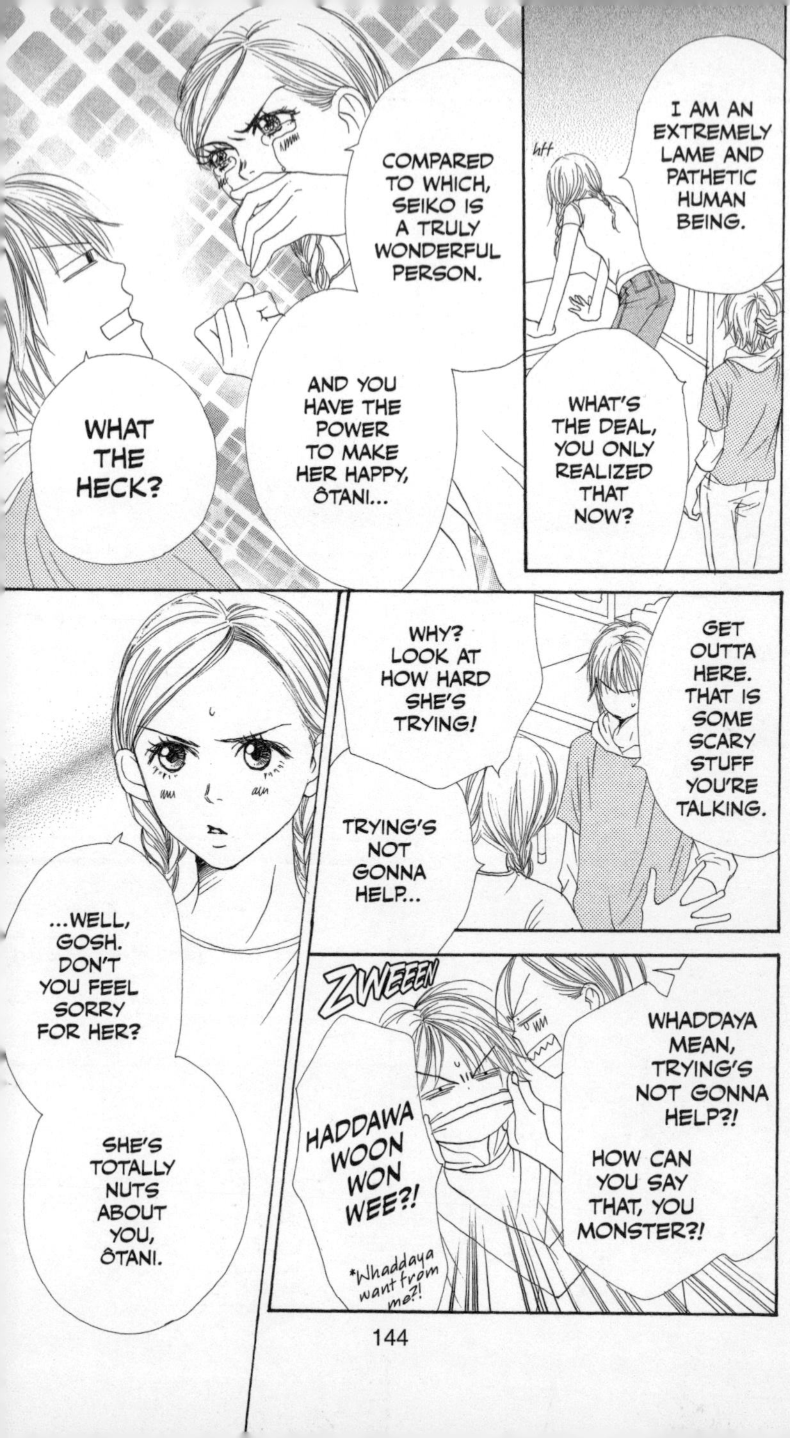
I AM AN EXTREMELY LAME AND PATHETIC HUMAN BEING.
hff
WHAT'S THE DEAL, YOU ONLY REALIZED THAT NOW?
COMPARED TO WHICH, SEIKO IS A TRULY WONDERFUL PERSON.
AND YOU HAVE THE POWER TO MAKE HER HAPPY, ŌTANI...
WHAT THE HECK?
GET OUTTA HERE. THAT IS SOME SCARY STUFF YOU'RE TALKING.
WHY? LOOK AT HOW HARD SHE'S TRYING!
TRYING'S NOT GONNA HELP...
WHADDAYA MEAN, TRYING'S NOT GONNA HELP?!
HOW CAN YOU SAY THAT, YOU MONSTER?!
ZWEEEEN
HADDAWA WOON WON WEE?!
*Whaddaya want from me?!
...WELL, GOSH. DON'T YOU FEEL SORRY FOR HER?
SHE'S TOTALLY NUTS ABOUT YOU, ŌTANI.

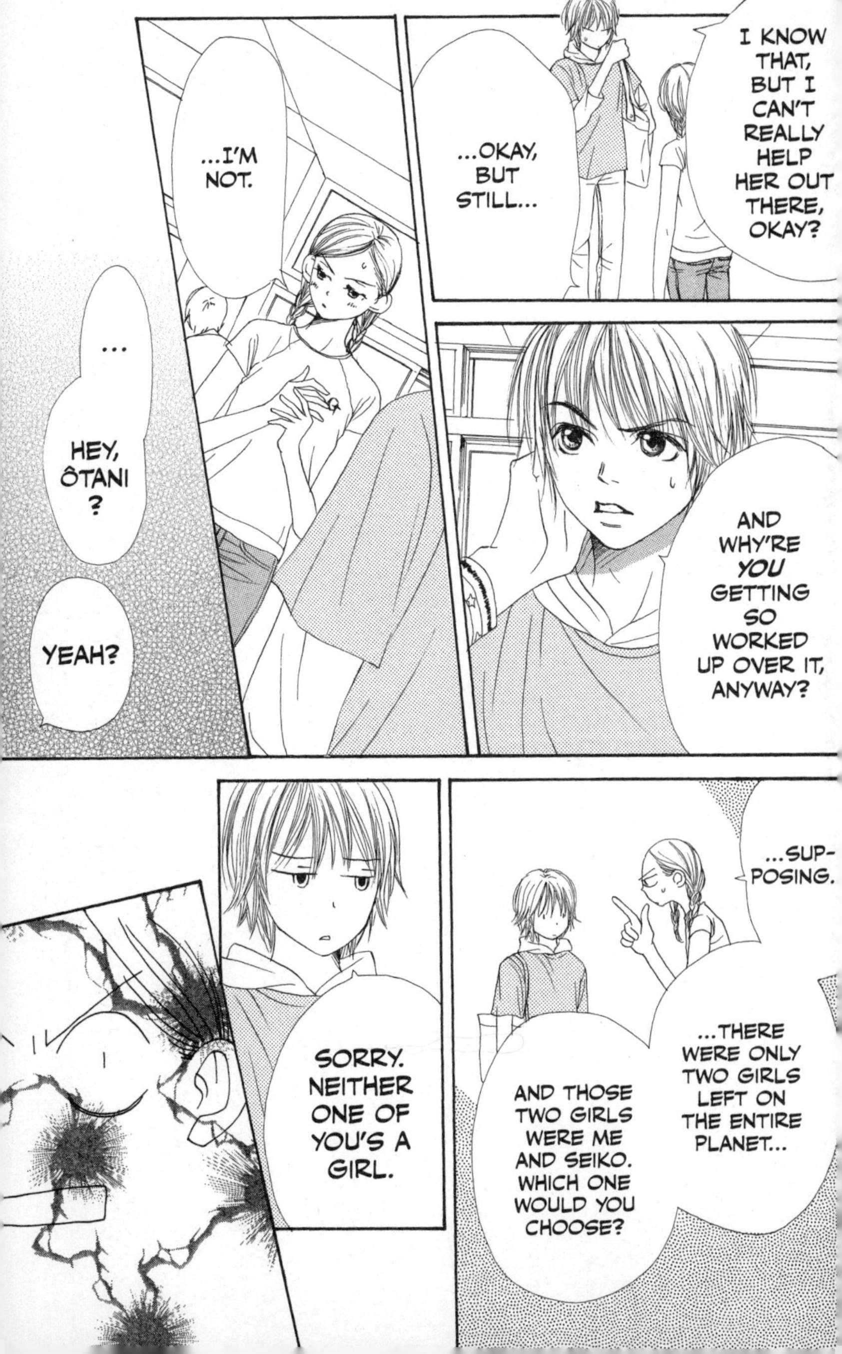
I KNOW THAT, BUT I CAN'T REALLY HELP HER OUT THERE, OKAY?
...OKAY, BUT STILL...
AND WHY'RE *YOU* GETTING SO WORKED UP OVER IT, ANYWAY?
...I'M NOT.
...
HEY, ÔTANI?
YEAH?
...SUP-POSING.
...THERE WERE ONLY TWO GIRLS LEFT ON THE ENTIRE PLANET...
AND THOSE TWO GIRLS WERE ME AND SEIKO. WHICH ONE WOULD YOU CHOOSE?
SORRY. NEITHER ONE OF YOU'S A GIRL.

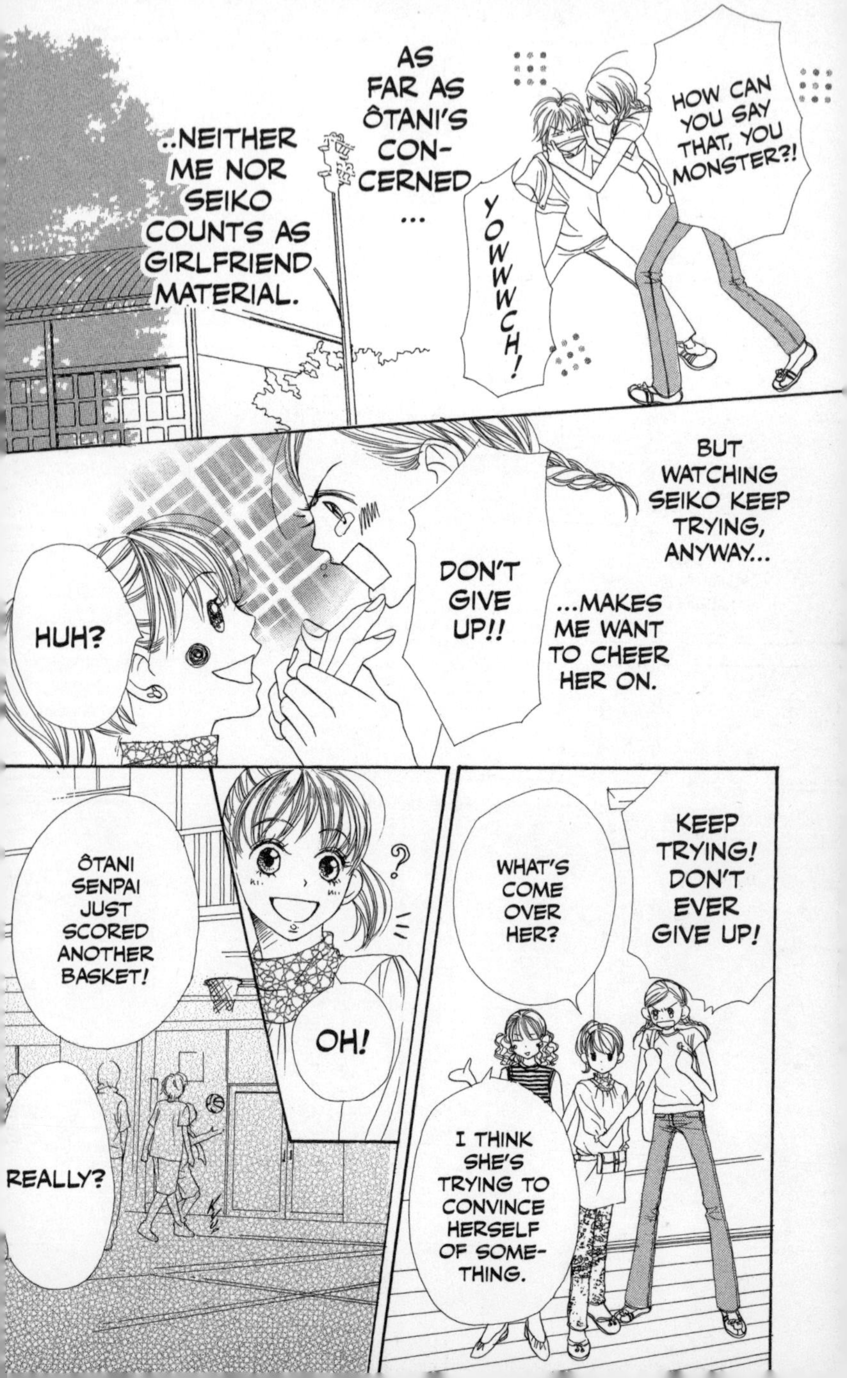
HOW CAN YOU SAY THAT, YOU MONSTER?!
YOWWWCH!
AS FAR AS ÔTANI'S CON-CERNED...
..NEITHER ME NOR SEIKO COUNTS AS GIRLFRIEND MATERIAL.
BUT WATCHING SEIKO KEEP TRYING, ANYWAY...
...MAKES ME WANT TO CHEER HER ON.
DON'T GIVE UP!!
HUH?
KEEP TRYING! DON'T EVER GIVE UP!
WHAT'S COME OVER HER?
I THINK SHE'S TRYING TO CONVINCE HERSELF OF SOME-THING.
?
OH!
ÔTANI SENPAI JUST SCORED ANOTHER BASKET!
REALLY?

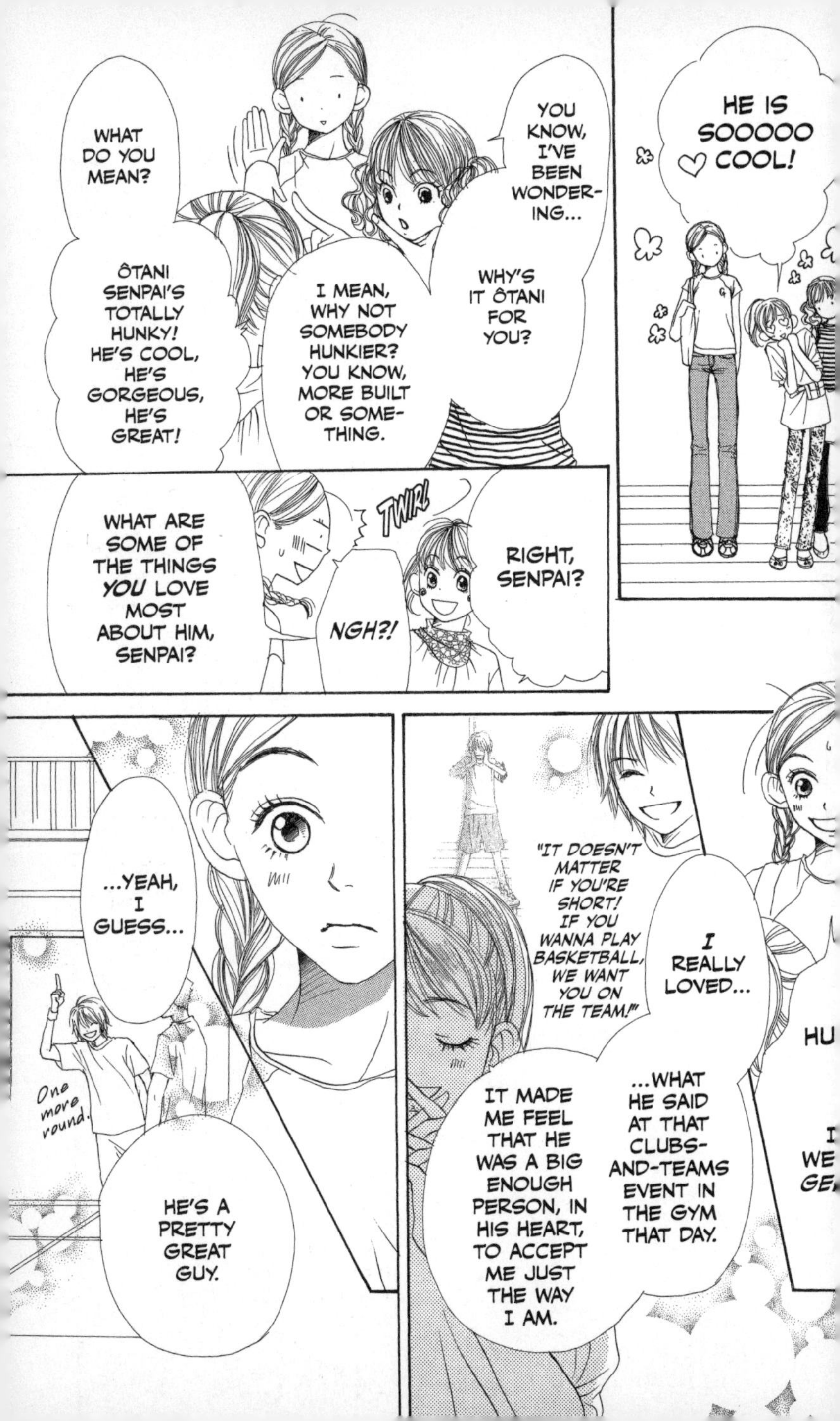
HE IS SOOOOO COOL!
YOU KNOW, I'VE BEEN WONDERING...
WHY'S IT ÔTANI FOR YOU?
WHAT DO YOU MEAN?
I MEAN, WHY NOT SOMEBODY HUNKIER? YOU KNOW, MORE BUILT OR SOMETHING.
ÔTANI SENPAI'S TOTALLY HUNKY! HE'S COOL, HE'S GORGEOUS, HE'S GREAT!
RIGHT, SENPAI?
TWIRL
NGH?!
WHAT ARE SOME OF THE THINGS *YOU* LOVE MOST ABOUT HIM, SENPAI?
HU
I WE GE.
I REALLY LOVED...
...WHAT HE SAID AT THAT CLUBS-AND-TEAMS EVENT IN THE GYM THAT DAY.
"IT DOESN'T MATTER IF YOU'RE SHORT! IF YOU WANNA PLAY BASKETBALL, WE WANT YOU ON THE TEAM!"
IT MADE ME FEEL THAT HE WAS A BIG ENOUGH PERSON, IN HIS HEART, TO ACCEPT ME JUST THE WAY I AM.
...YEAH, I GUESS...
HE'S A PRETTY GREAT GUY.
One more round.

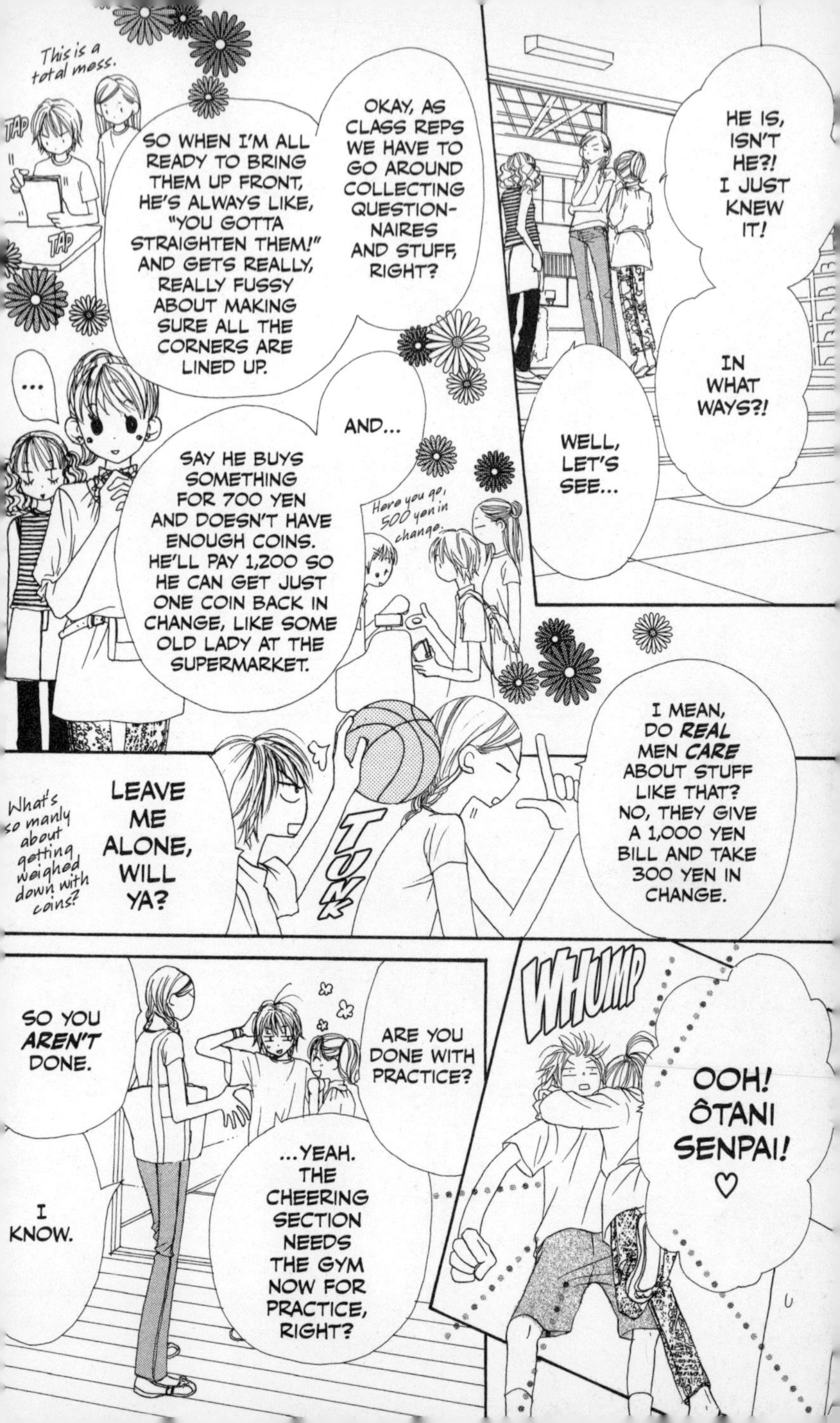

HE IS, ISN'T HE?! I JUST KNEW IT!
IN WHAT WAYS?!
WELL, LET'S SEE...
OKAY, AS CLASS REPS WE HAVE TO GO AROUND COLLECTING QUESTION-NAIRES AND STUFF, RIGHT?
SO WHEN I'M ALL READY TO BRING THEM UP FRONT, HE'S ALWAYS LIKE, "YOU GOTTA STRAIGHTEN THEM!" AND GETS REALLY, REALLY FUSSY ABOUT MAKING SURE ALL THE CORNERS ARE LINED UP.
This is a total mess.
TAP
TAP
...
AND...
SAY HE BUYS SOMETHING FOR 700 YEN AND DOESN'T HAVE ENOUGH COINS. HE'LL PAY 1,200 SO HE CAN GET JUST ONE COIN BACK IN CHANGE, LIKE SOME OLD LADY AT THE SUPERMARKET.
Here you go, 500 yen in change.
I MEAN, DO *REAL* MEN *CARE* ABOUT STUFF LIKE THAT? NO, THEY GIVE A 1,000 YEN BILL AND TAKE 300 YEN IN CHANGE.
TUNK
LEAVE ME ALONE, WILL YA?
What's so manly about getting weighed down with coins?
WHUMP
OOH! ÔTANI SENPAI! ♡
ARE YOU DONE WITH PRACTICE?
SO YOU *AREN'T* DONE.
...YEAH. THE CHEERING SECTION NEEDS THE GYM NOW FOR PRACTICE, RIGHT?
I KNOW.

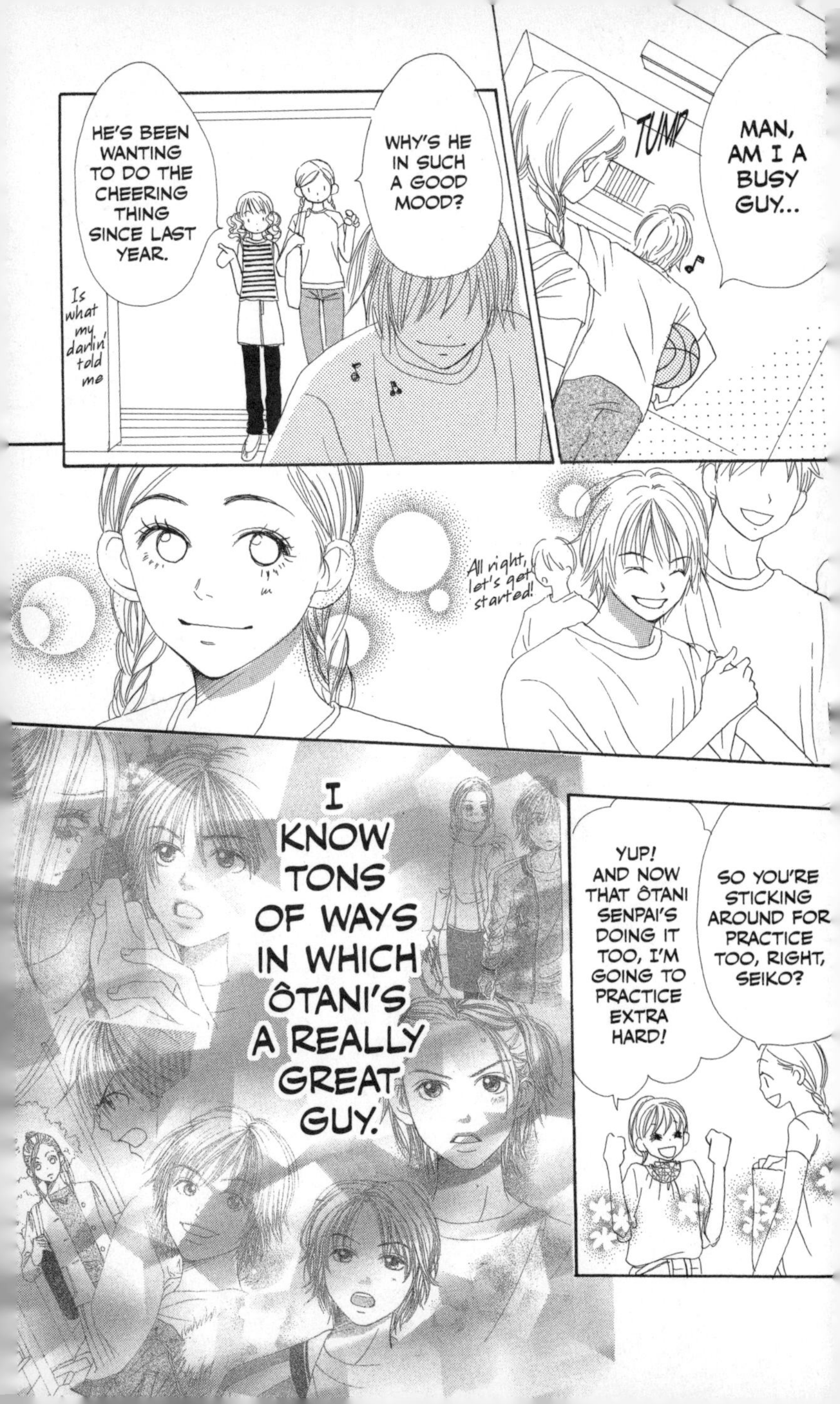
TUMP
MAN, AM I A BUSY GUY...
WHY'S HE IN SUCH A GOOD MOOD?
HE'S BEEN WANTING TO DO THE CHEERING THING SINCE LAST YEAR.
Is what my darlin' told me
All right, let's get started!
SO YOU'RE STICKING AROUND FOR PRACTICE TOO, RIGHT, SEIKO?
YUP! AND NOW THAT ÔTANI SENPAI'S DOING IT TOO, I'M GOING TO PRACTICE EXTRA HARD!
I KNOW TONS OF WAYS IN WHICH ÔTANI'S A REALLY GREAT GUY.

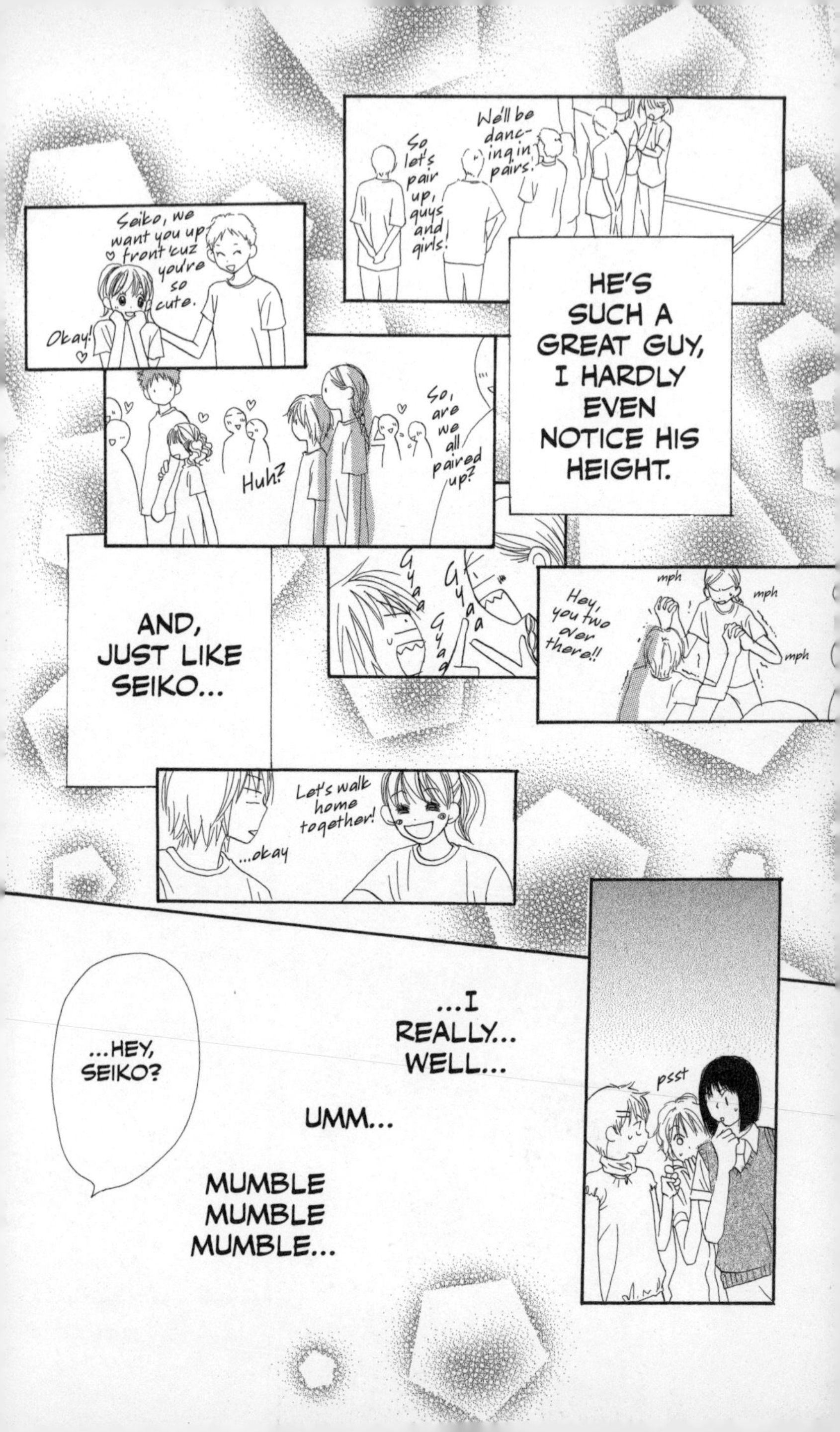

We'll be danc-ing in pairs!
So let's pair up, guys and girls!
Seiko, we want you up front 'cuz you're so cute.
Okay!
HE'S SUCH A GREAT GUY, I HARDLY EVEN NOTICE HIS HEIGHT.
So, are we all paired up?
Huh?
mph
mph
Hey, you two over there!!
mph
Gyaa
Gyaa
Gyaa
AND, JUST LIKE SEIKO...
Let's walk home together!
...okay
psst
...I REALLY... WELL...
UMM...
MUMBLE MUMBLE MUMBLE...
...HEY, SEIKO?

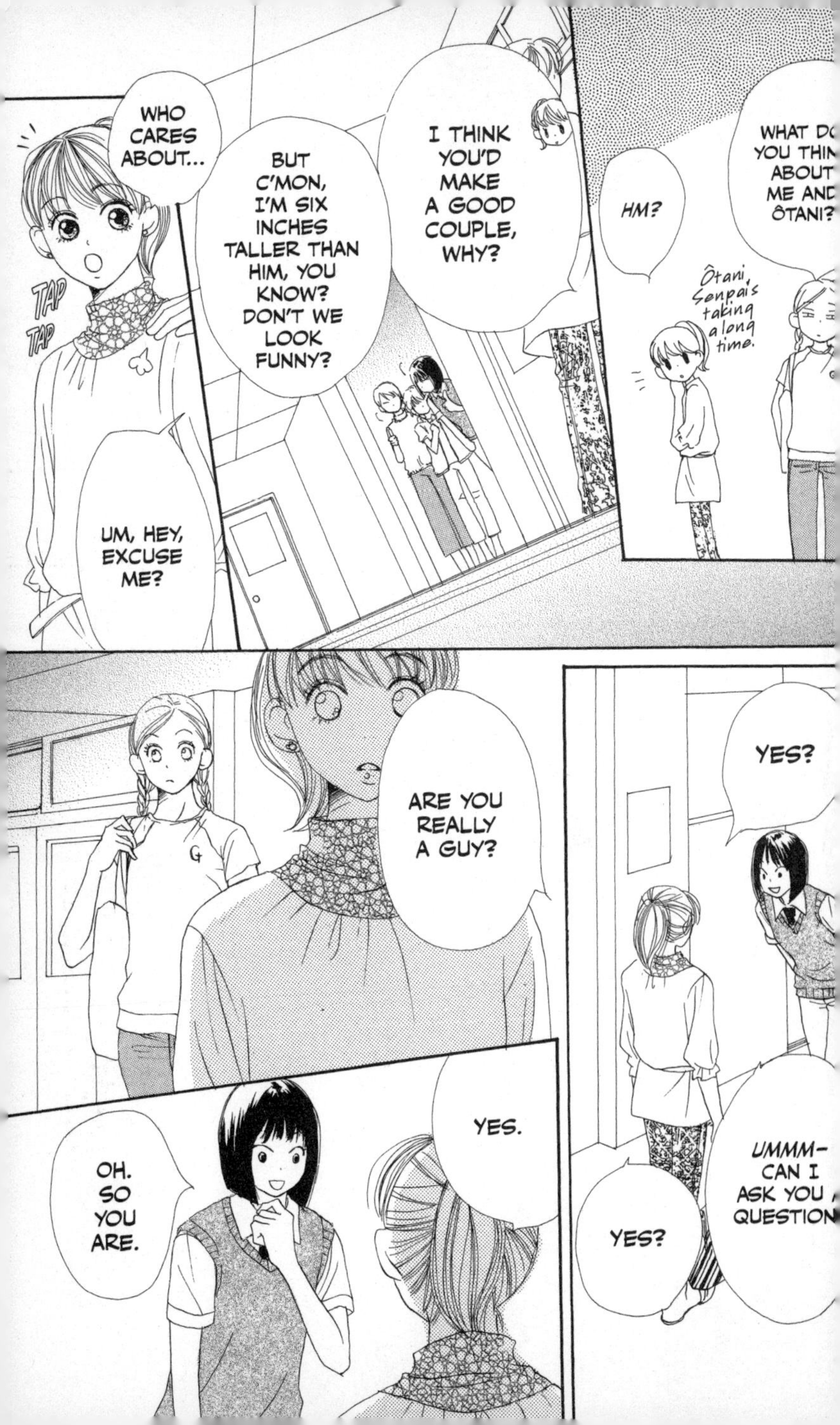
WHAT DO YOU THIN ABOUT ME AND ŌTANI?
HM?
Ōtani Senpai's taking a long time.
I THINK YOU'D MAKE A GOOD COUPLE, WHY?
BUT C'MON, I'M SIX INCHES TALLER THAN HIM, YOU KNOW? DON'T WE LOOK FUNNY?
WHO CARES ABOUT...
TAP TAP
UM, HEY, EXCUSE ME?
YES?
UMMM— CAN I ASK YOU QUESTION
YES?
ARE YOU REALLY A GUY?
YES.
OH. SO YOU ARE.

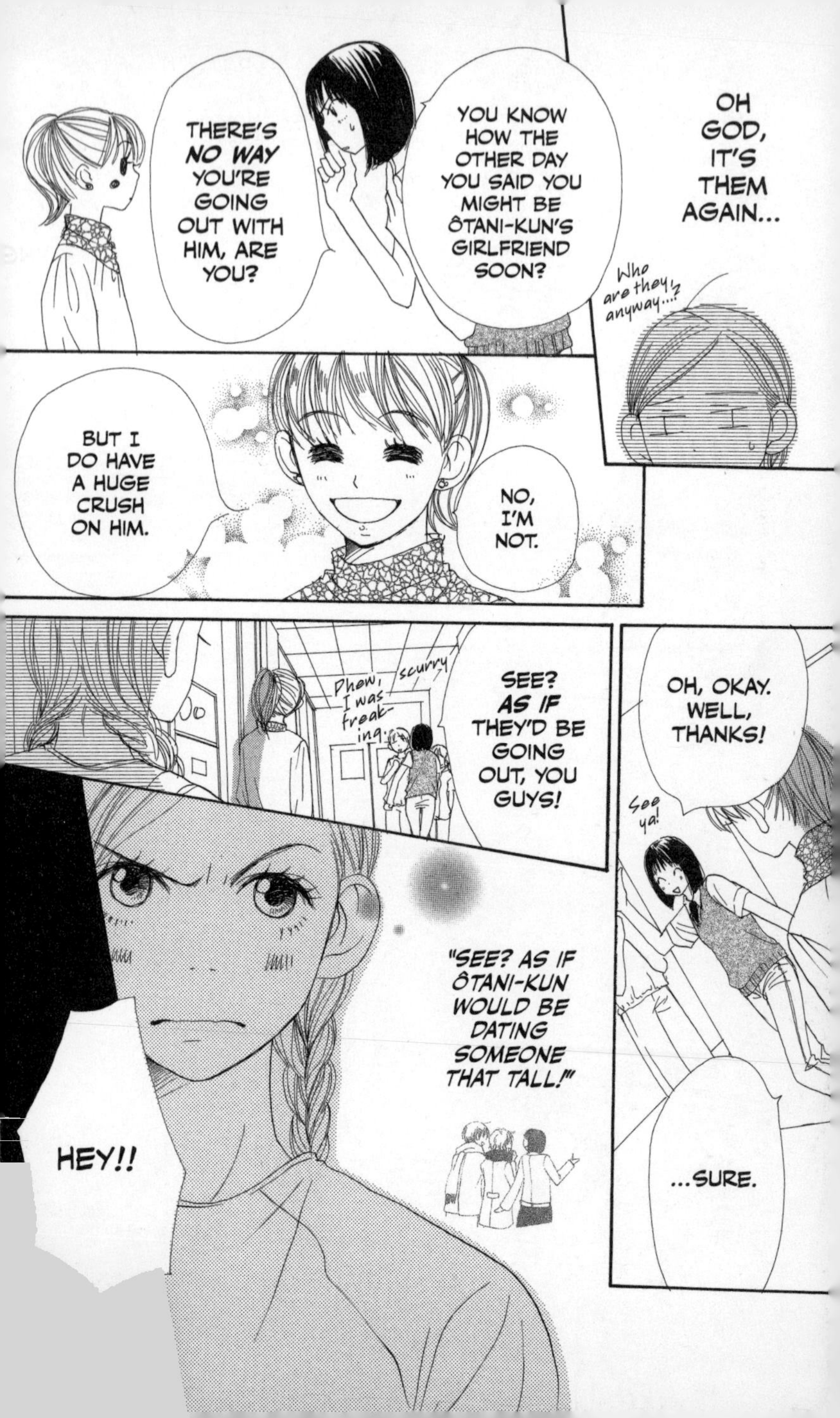
OH GOD, IT'S THEM AGAIN...
Who are they anyway...?
YOU KNOW HOW THE OTHER DAY YOU SAID YOU MIGHT BE ÔTANI-KUN'S GIRLFRIEND SOON?
THERE'S NO WAY YOU'RE GOING OUT WITH HIM, ARE YOU?
NO, I'M NOT.
BUT I DO HAVE A HUGE CRUSH ON HIM.
OH, OKAY. WELL, THANKS!
See ya!
...SURE.
SEE? AS IF THEY'D BE GOING OUT, YOU GUYS!
scurry
Phew, I was freaking.
"SEE? AS IF ÔTANI-KUN WOULD BE DATING SOMEONE THAT TALL!"
HEY!!

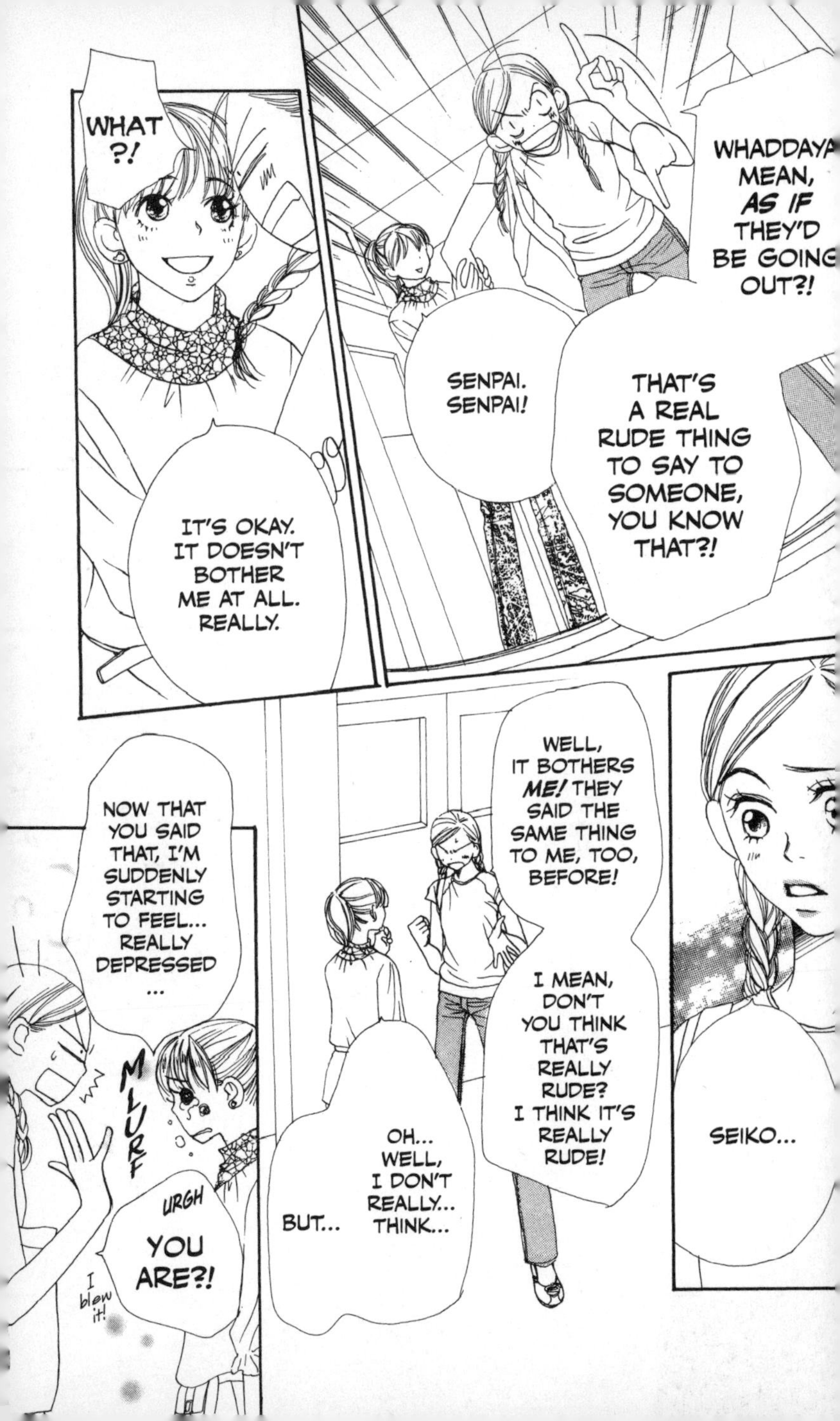
WHADDAYA MEAN, *AS IF* THEY'D BE GOING OUT?!
THAT'S A REAL RUDE THING TO SAY TO SOMEONE, YOU KNOW THAT?!
SENPAI. SENPAI!
WHAT?!
IT'S OKAY. IT DOESN'T BOTHER ME AT ALL. REALLY.
SEIKO...
WELL, IT BOTHERS *ME!* THEY SAID THE SAME THING TO ME, TOO, BEFORE!
I MEAN, DON'T YOU THINK THAT'S REALLY RUDE? I THINK IT'S REALLY RUDE!
OH... WELL, I DON'T REALLY... THINK...
BUT...
NOW THAT YOU SAID THAT, I'M SUDDENLY STARTING TO FEEL... REALLY DEPRESSED ...
MLURF
URGH
YOU ARE?!
I blew it!

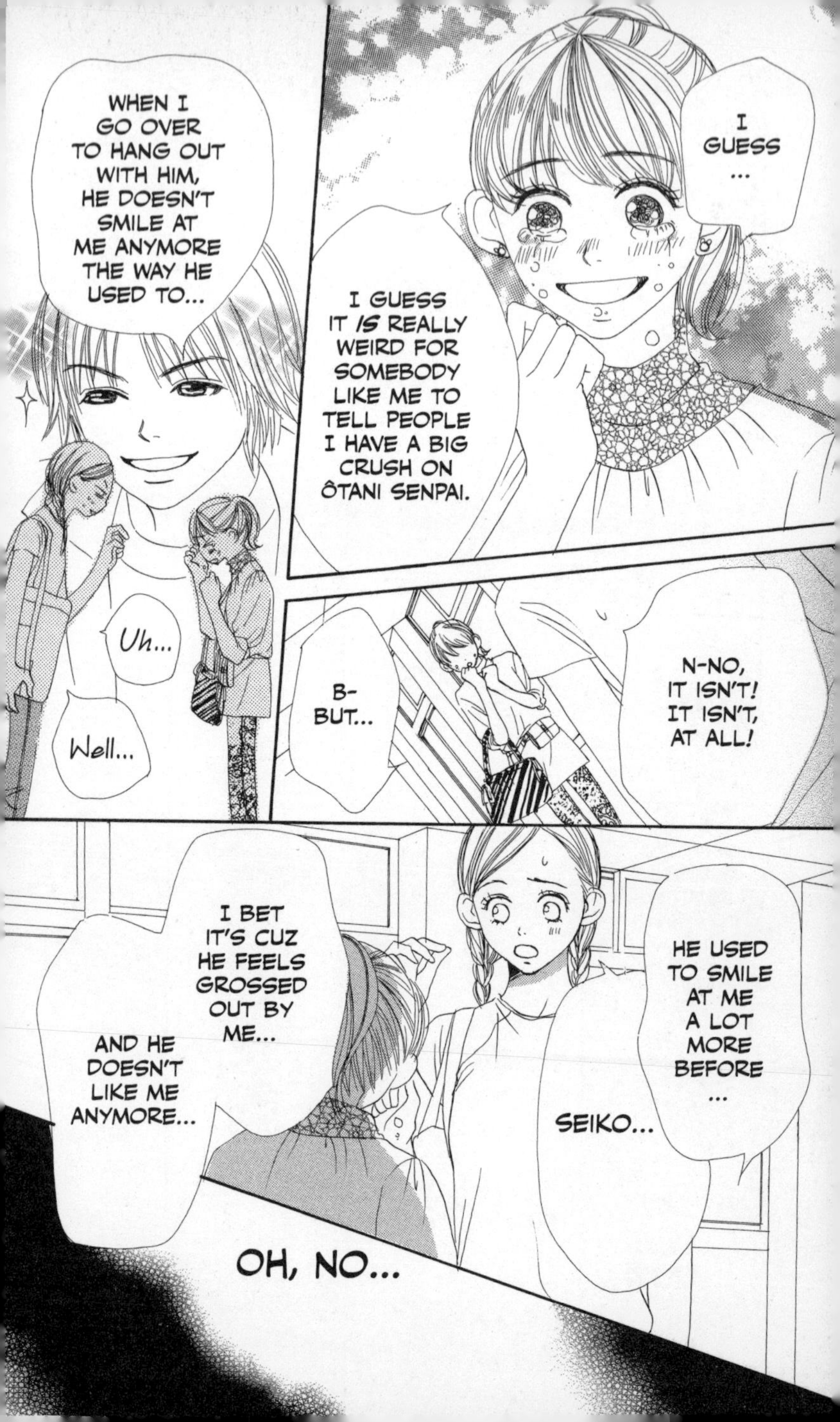
I GUESS ...
I GUESS IT *IS* REALLY WEIRD FOR SOMEBODY LIKE ME TO TELL PEOPLE I HAVE A BIG CRUSH ON ÔTANI SENPAI.
N-NO, IT ISN'T! IT ISN'T, AT ALL!
B-BUT...
WHEN I GO OVER TO HANG OUT WITH HIM, HE DOESN'T SMILE AT ME ANYMORE THE WAY HE USED TO...
Uh...
Well...
HE USED TO SMILE AT ME A LOT MORE BEFORE ...
SEIKO...
I BET IT'S CUZ HE FEELS GROSSED OUT BY ME...
AND HE DOESN'T LIKE ME ANYMORE...
OH, NO...

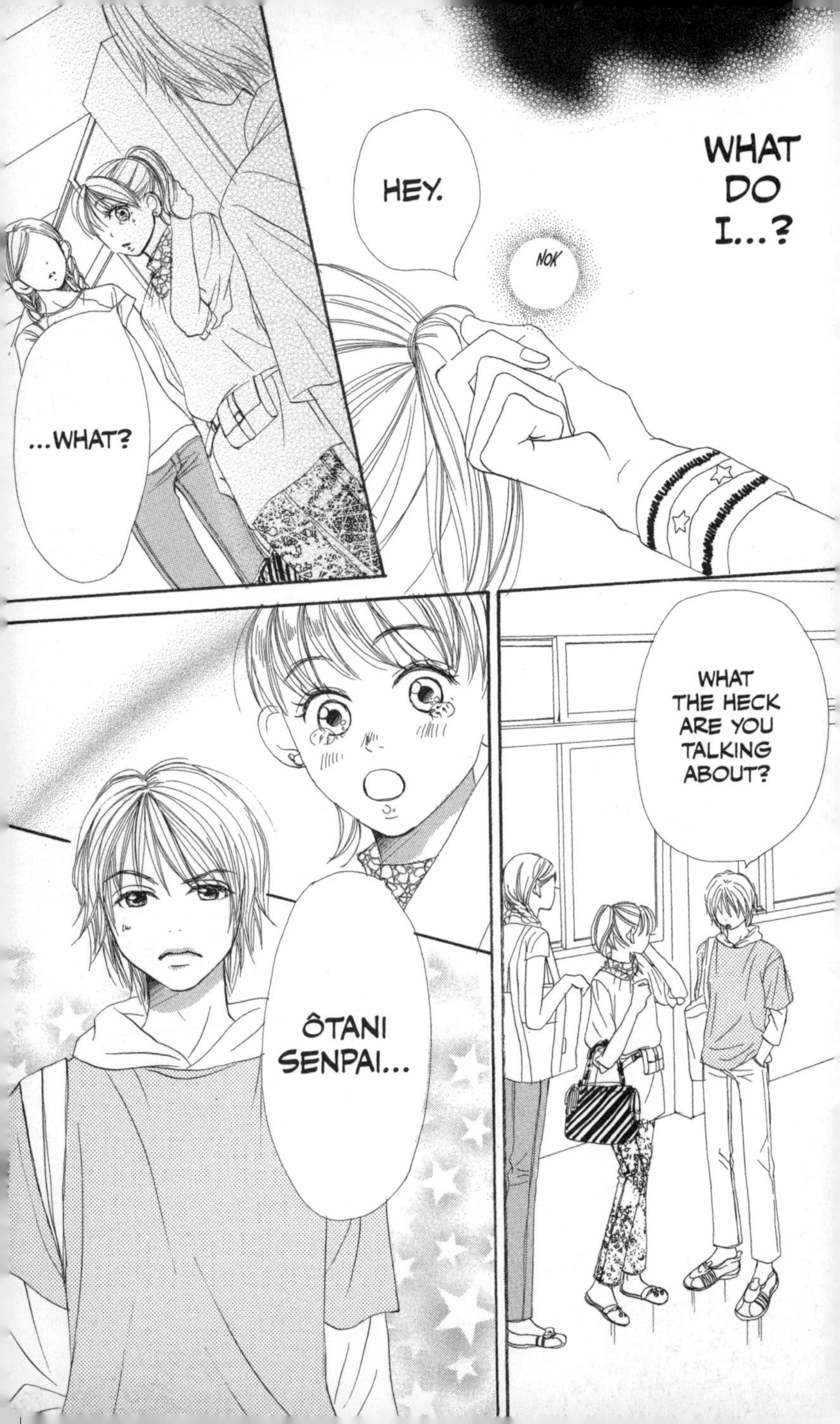
WHAT DO I...?
HEY.
NOK
...WHAT?
WHAT THE HECK ARE YOU TALKING ABOUT?
ÔTANI SENPAI...

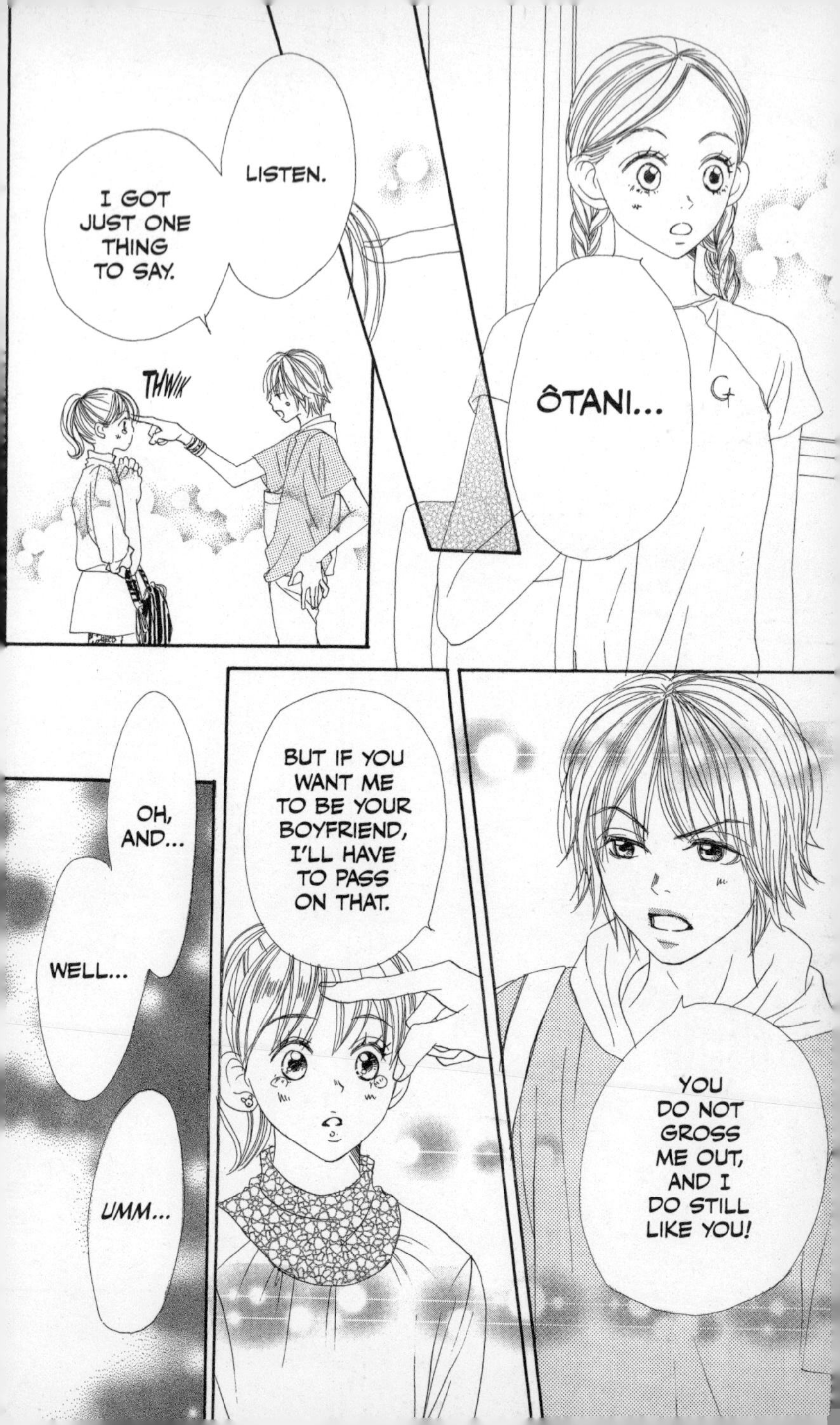
ÔTANI...
LISTEN.
I GOT JUST ONE THING TO SAY.
THWIK
YOU DO NOT GROSS ME OUT, AND I DO STILL LIKE YOU!
BUT IF YOU WANT ME TO BE YOUR BOYFRIEND, I'LL HAVE TO PASS ON THAT.
OH, AND...
WELL...
UMM...

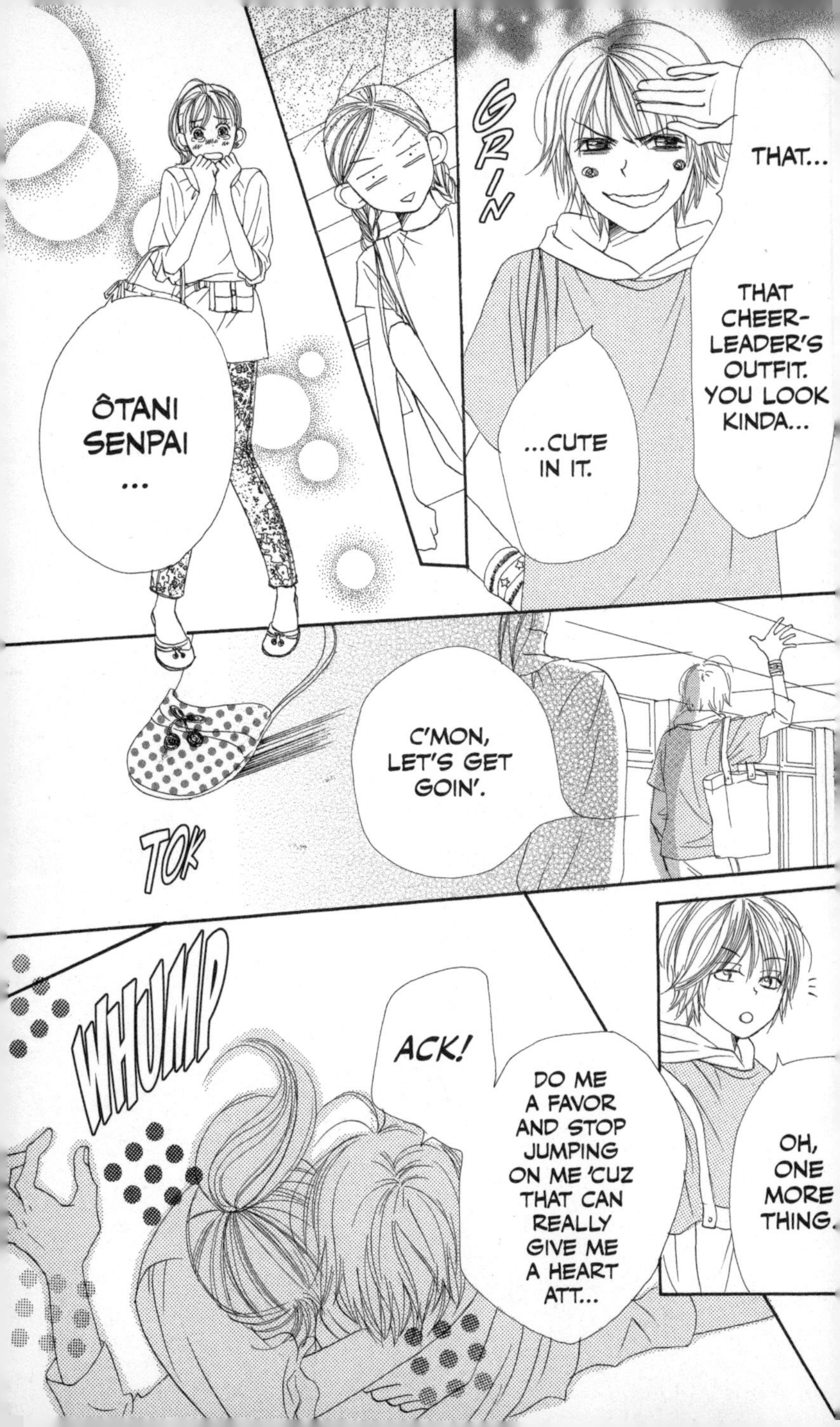
THAT...
THAT CHEER-LEADER'S OUTFIT. YOU LOOK KINDA...
GRIN
...CUTE IN IT.
ÔTANI SENPAI ...
C'MON, LET'S GET GOIN'.
TOK
OH, ONE MORE THING.
DO ME A FAVOR AND STOP JUMPING ON ME 'CUZ THAT CAN REALLY GIVE ME A HEART ATT...
ACK!
WHUMP

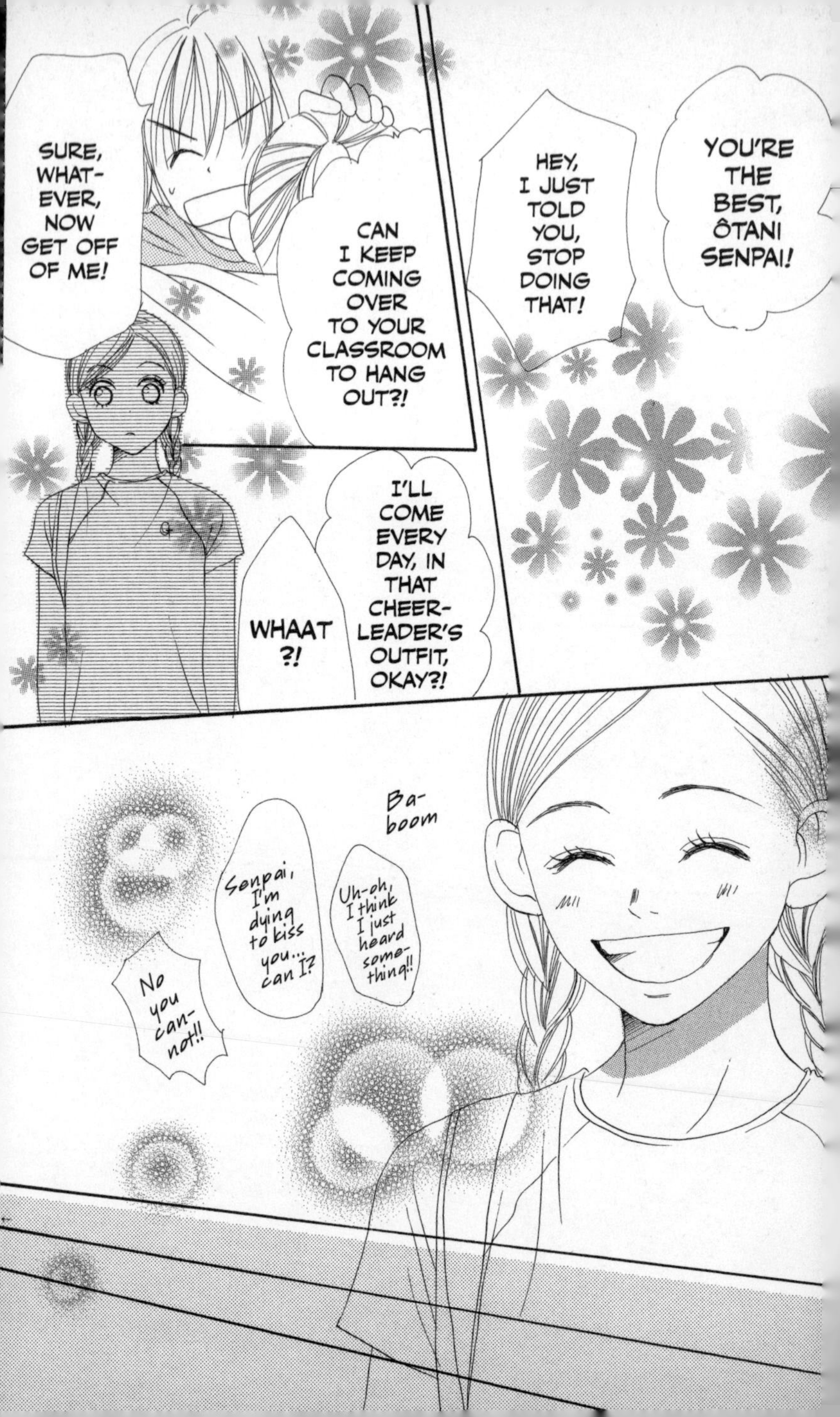
YOU'RE THE BEST, ÔTANI SENPAI!
HEY, I JUST TOLD YOU, STOP DOING THAT!
CAN I KEEP COMING OVER TO YOUR CLASSROOM TO HANG OUT?!
SURE, WHAT-EVER, NOW GET OFF OF ME!
I'LL COME EVERY DAY, IN THAT CHEER-LEADER'S OUTFIT, OKAY?!
WHAAT ?!
Ba-boom
Uh-oh, I think I just heard some-thing!!
Senpai, I'm dying to kiss you... can I?
No you can-not!!

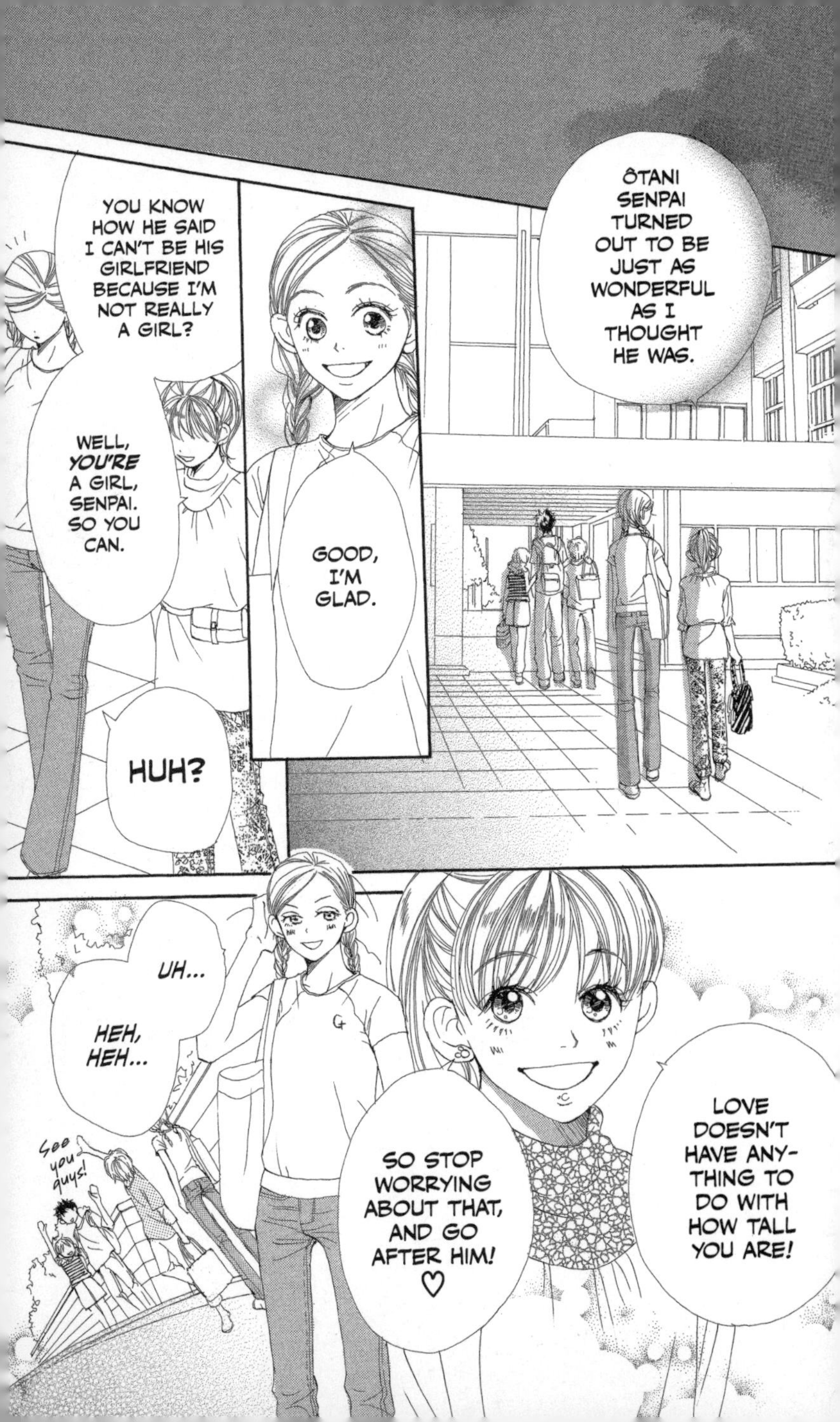
ŌTANI SENPAI TURNED OUT TO BE JUST AS WONDERFUL AS I THOUGHT HE WAS.
GOOD, I'M GLAD.
YOU KNOW HOW HE SAID I CAN'T BE HIS GIRLFRIEND BECAUSE I'M NOT REALLY A GIRL?
WELL, *YOU'RE* A GIRL, SENPAI. SO YOU CAN.
HUH?
LOVE DOESN'T HAVE ANY-THING TO DO WITH HOW TALL YOU ARE!
SO STOP WORRYING ABOUT THAT, AND GO AFTER HIM! ♡
UH...
HEH, HEH...
See you guys!

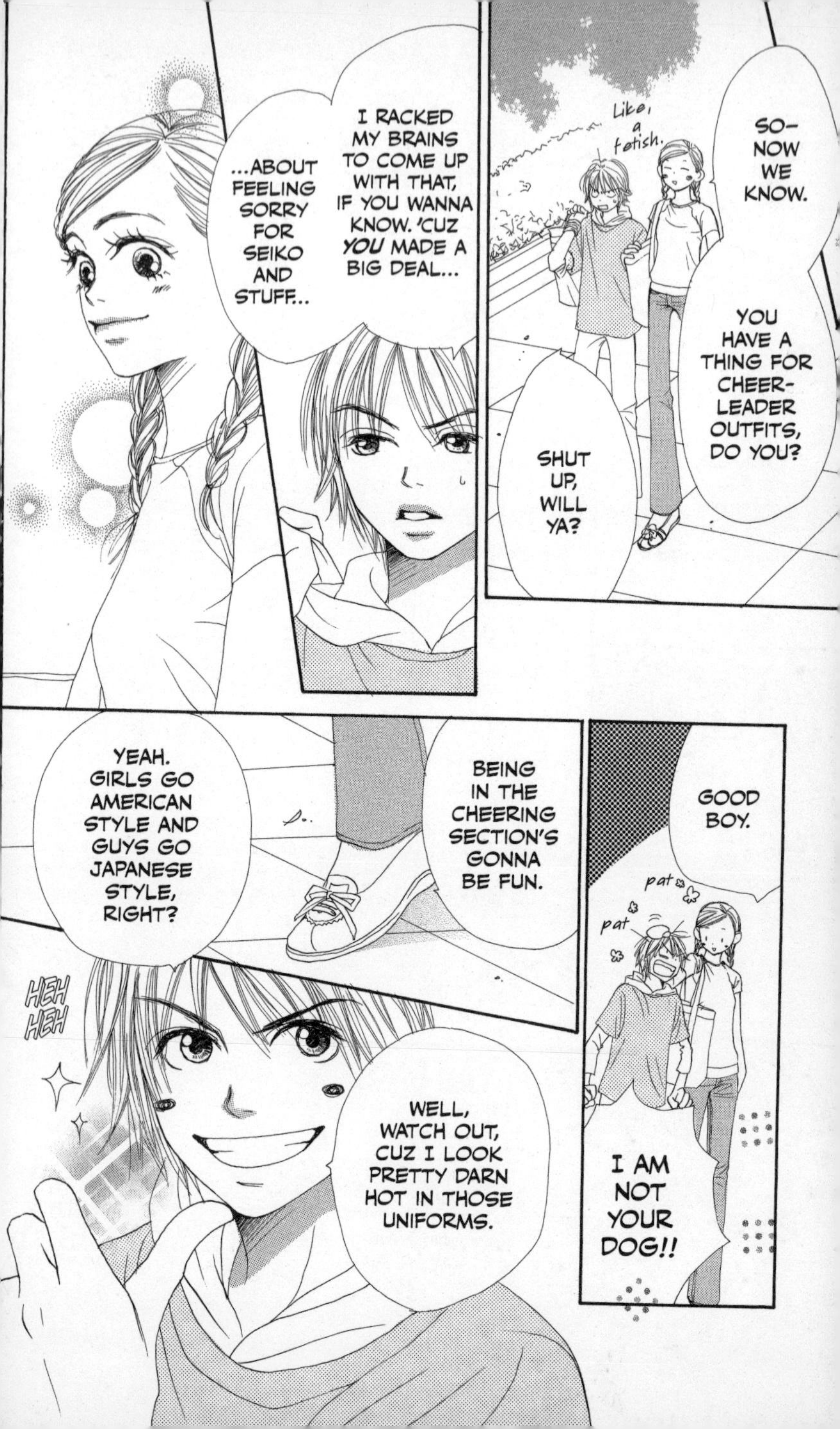
SO— NOW WE KNOW.
Like, a fetish.
YOU HAVE A THING FOR CHEER-LEADER OUTFITS, DO YOU?
SHUT UP, WILL YA?
I RACKED MY BRAINS TO COME UP WITH THAT, IF YOU WANNA KNOW. 'CUZ *YOU* MADE A BIG DEAL...
...ABOUT FEELING SORRY FOR SEIKO AND STUFF...
GOOD BOY.
pat
pat
I AM NOT YOUR DOG!!
BEING IN THE CHEERING SECTION'S GONNA BE FUN.
YEAH. GIRLS GO AMERICAN STYLE AND GUYS GO JAPANESE STYLE, RIGHT?
HEH HEH
WELL, WATCH OUT, CUZ I LOOK PRETTY DARN HOT IN THOSE UNIFORMS.

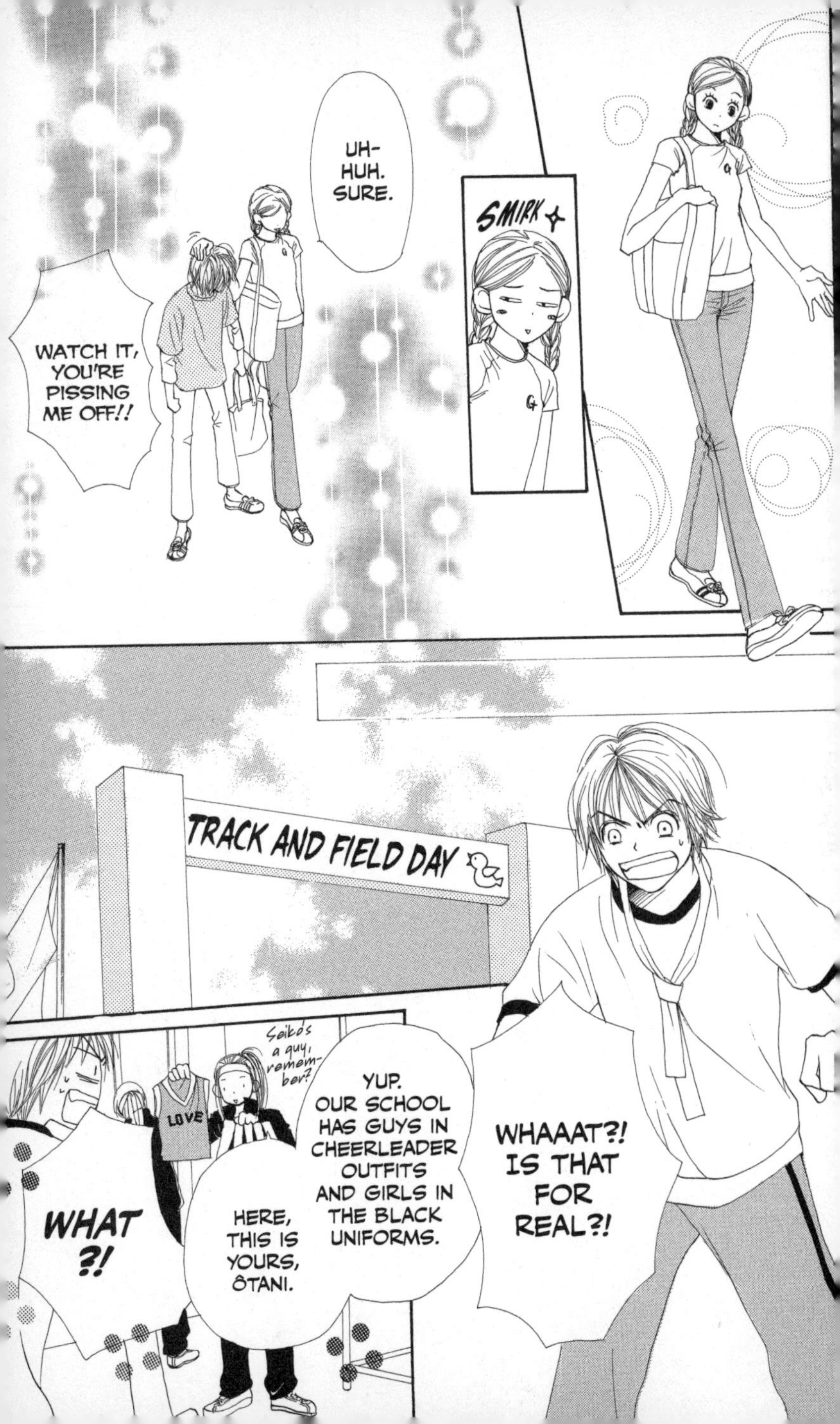
SMIRK
UH-HUH. SURE.
WATCH IT, YOU'RE PISSING ME OFF!!
TRACK AND FIELD DAY
WHAAAT?! IS THAT FOR REAL?!
YUP. OUR SCHOOL HAS GUYS IN CHEERLEADER OUTFITS AND GIRLS IN THE BLACK UNIFORMS.
Seiko's a guy, remember?
HERE, THIS IS YOURS, ŌTANI.
LOVE
WHAT?!

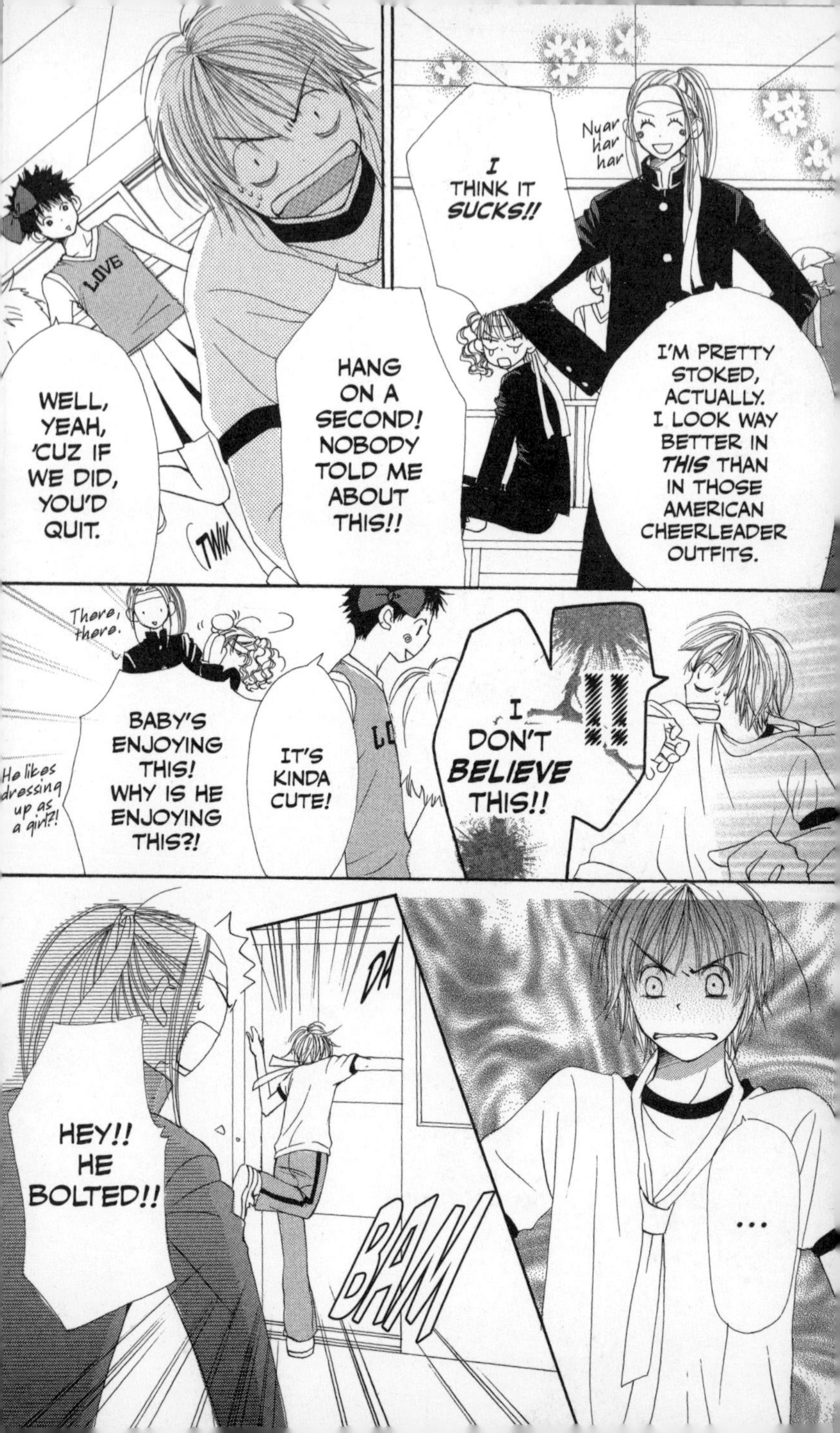

Nyar har har
I THINK IT SUCKS!!
I'M PRETTY STOKED, ACTUALLY. I LOOK WAY BETTER IN THIS THAN IN THOSE AMERICAN CHEERLEADER OUTFITS.
HANG ON A SECOND! NOBODY TOLD ME ABOUT THIS!!
WELL, YEAH, 'CUZ IF WE DID, YOU'D QUIT.
TWIK
!!
I DON'T BELIEVE THIS!!
IT'S KINDA CUTE!
There, there.
BABY'S ENJOYING THIS! WHY IS HE ENJOYING THIS?!
He likes dressing up as a girl?!
...
DA
HEY!! HE BOLTED!!
BAM

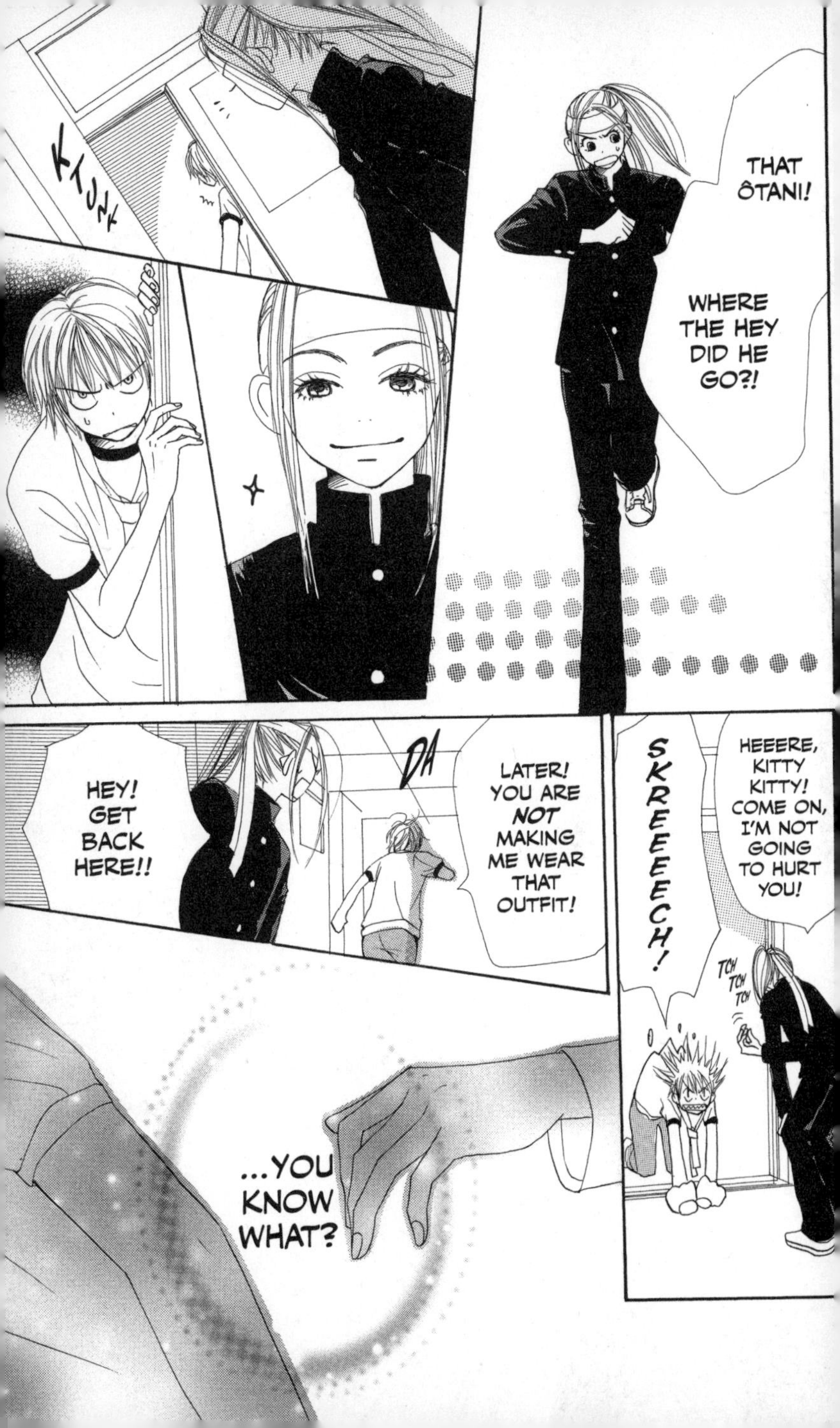
THAT STANI!
WHERE THE HEY DID HE GO?!
KTUNK
SKREEEEECH!
HEEERE, KITTY KITTY! COME ON, I'M NOT GOING TO HURT YOU!
TCH TCH TCH
DA
LATER! YOU ARE *NOT* MAKING ME WEAR THAT OUTFIT!
HEY! GET BACK HERE!!
...YOU KNOW WHAT?

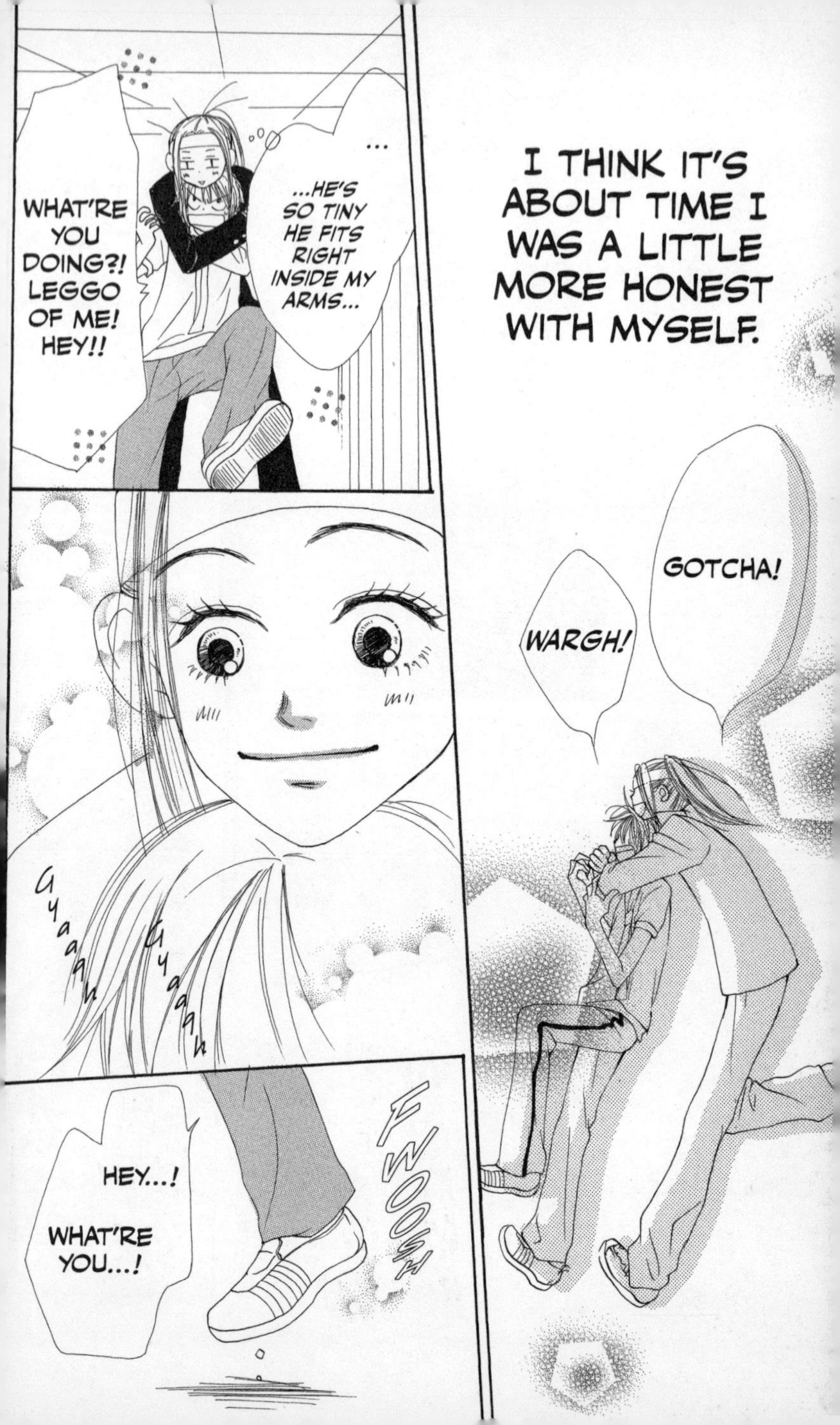
I THINK IT'S ABOUT TIME I WAS A LITTLE MORE HONEST WITH MYSELF.
GOTCHA!
WARGH!
...
...HE'S SO TINY HE FITS RIGHT INSIDE MY ARMS...
WHAT'RE YOU DOING?! LEGGO OF ME! HEY!!
Gyaaah
Gyaaah
FWOOOSH
HEY...!
WHAT'RE YOU...!

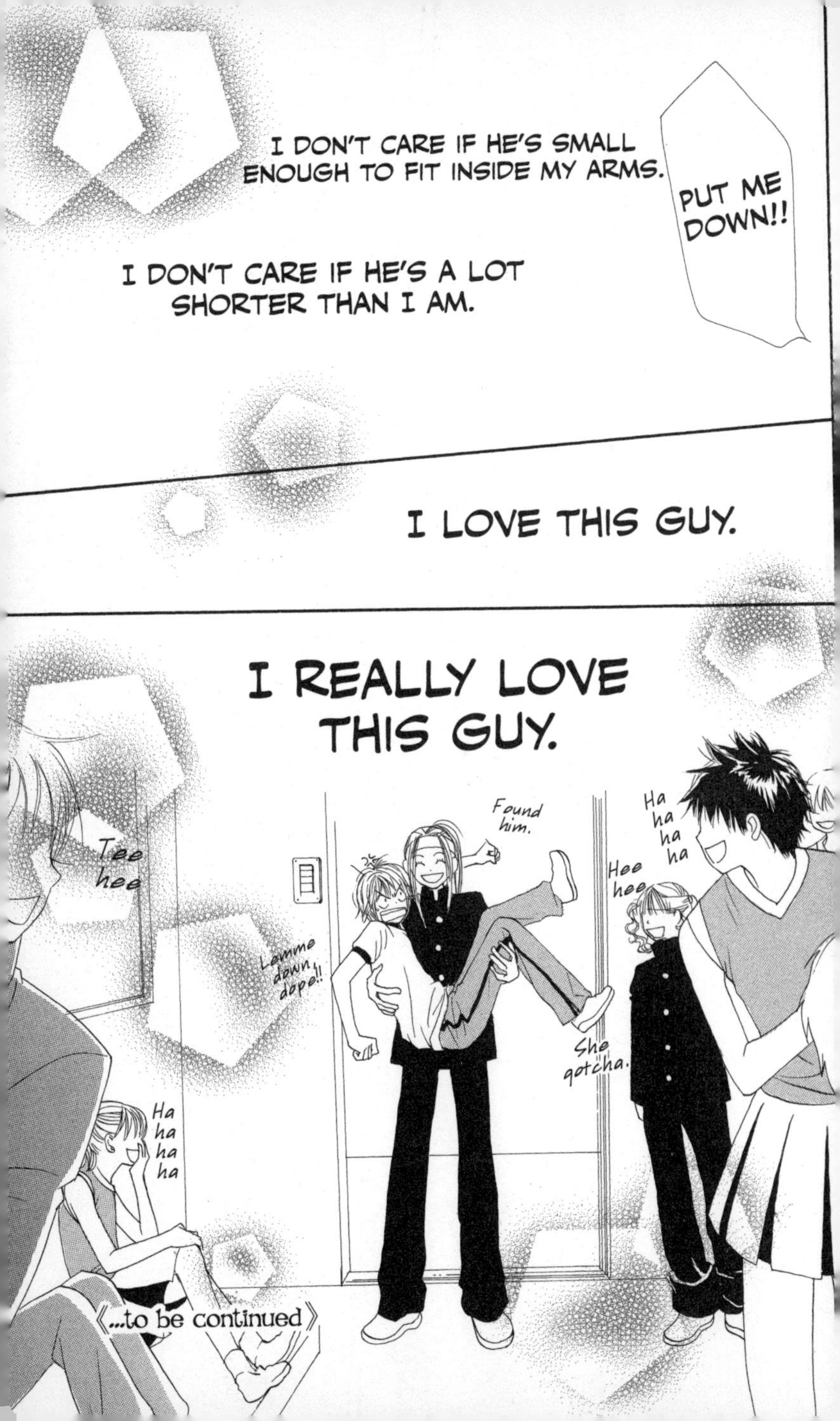
PUT ME DOWN!!
I DON'T CARE IF HE'S SMALL ENOUGH TO FIT INSIDE MY ARMS.
I DON'T CARE IF HE'S A LOT SHORTER THAN I AM.
I LOVE THIS GUY.
I REALLY LOVE THIS GUY.
Ha ha ha ha
Found him.
Hee hee
She gotcha.
Lemme down, dope!!
Tee hee
Ha ha ha ha
《...to be continued》

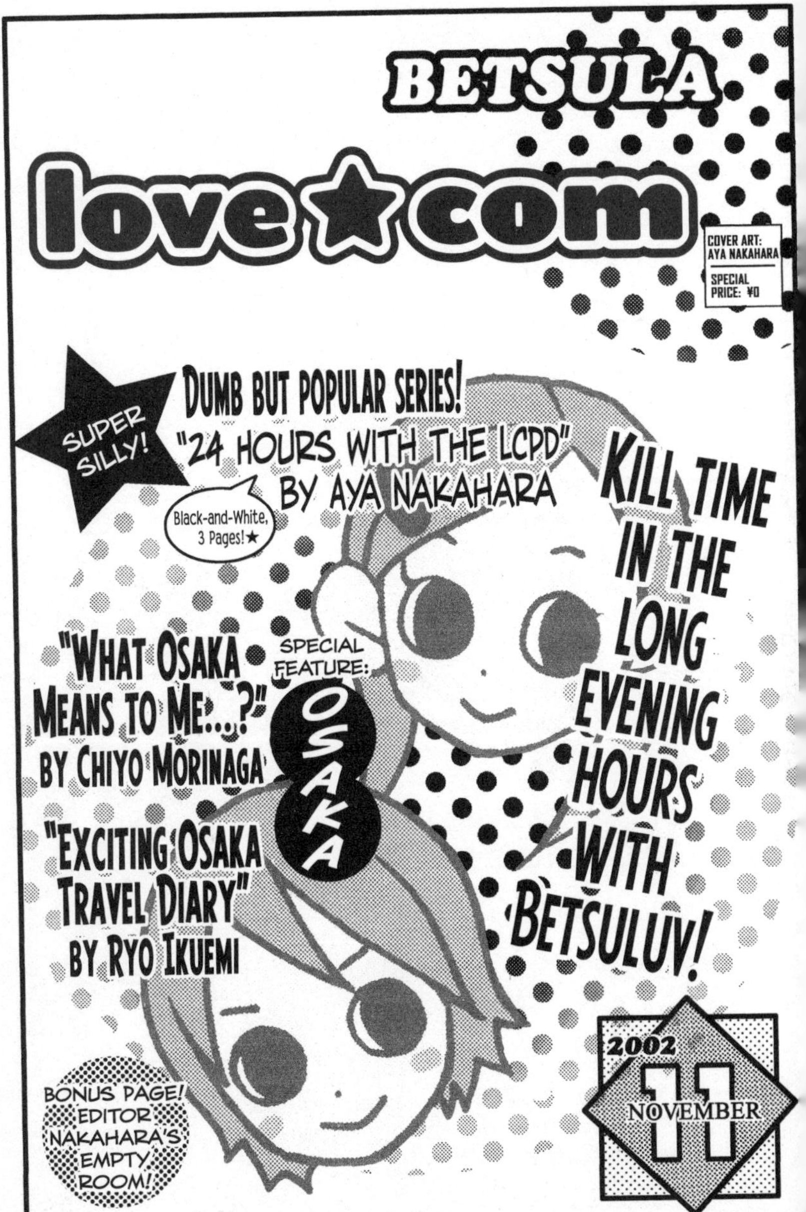
BETSULA
love★com
COVER ART: AYA NAKAHARA
SPECIAL PRICE: ¥0
SUPER SILLY!
DUMB BUT POPULAR SERIES!
"24 HOURS WITH THE LCPD"
BY AYA NAKAHARA
Black-and-White, 3 Pages!★
KILL TIME IN THE LONG EVENING HOURS WITH BETSULUV!
SPECIAL FEATURE:
OSAKA
"WHAT OSAKA MEANS TO ME...?"
BY CHIYO MORINAGA
"EXCITING OSAKA TRAVEL DIARY"
BY RYO IKUEMI
BONUS PAGE! EDITOR NAKAHARA'S EMPTY ROOM!
2002
11
NOVEMBER

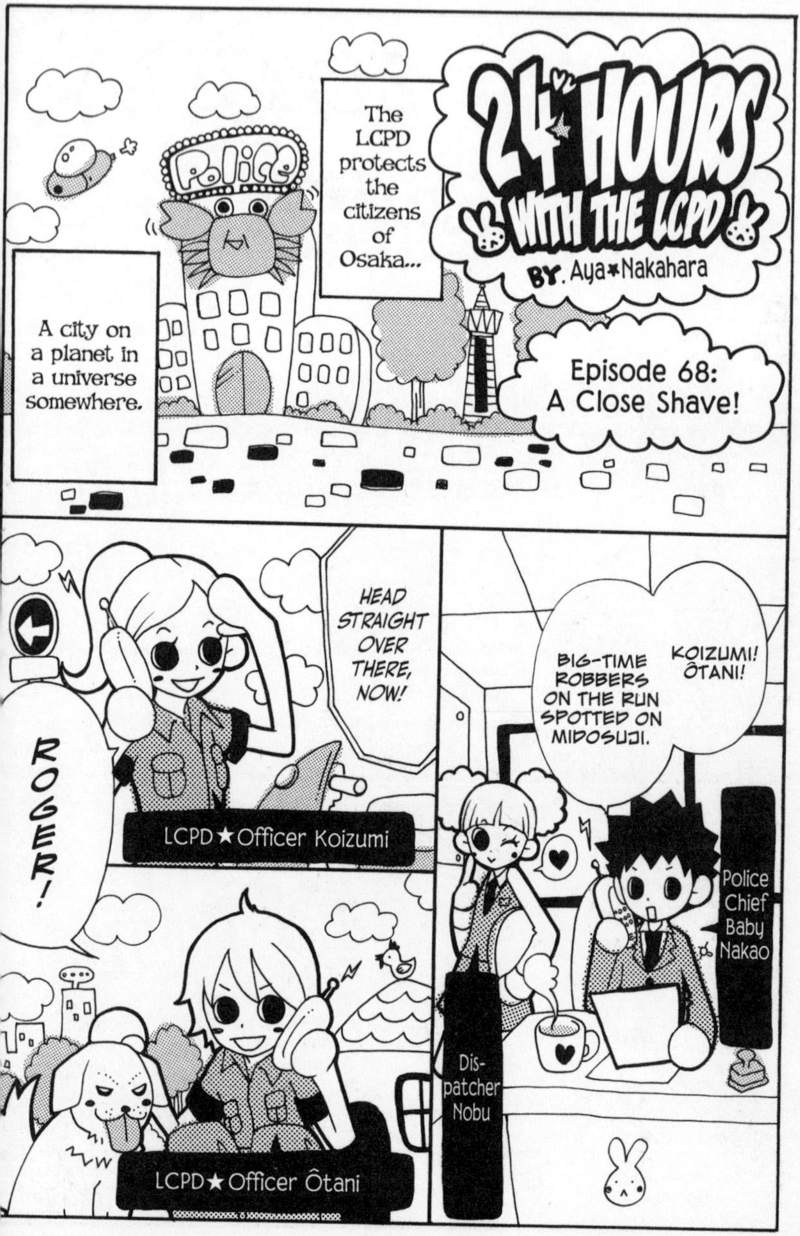
24 HOURS WITH THE LCPD
BY. Aya★Nakahara
Episode 68: A Close Shave!
The LCPD protects the citizens of Osaka...
A city on a planet in a universe somewhere.
KOIZUMI! ÔTANI!
BIG-TIME ROBBERS ON THE RUN SPOTTED ON MIDOSUJI.
Police Chief Baby Nakao
Dis-patcher Nobu
HEAD STRAIGHT OVER THERE, NOW!
LCPD★Officer Koizumi
ROGER!
LCPD★Officer Ôtani

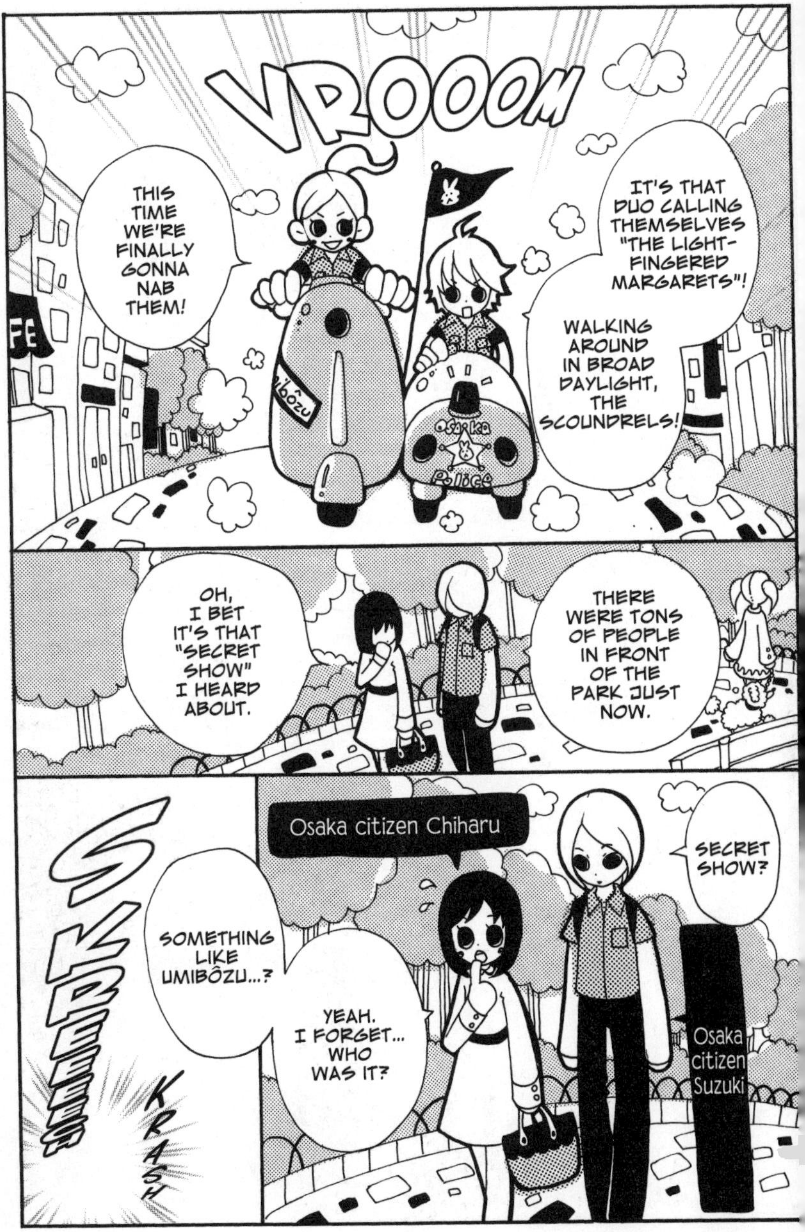
VROOOM
IT'S THAT DUO CALLING THEMSELVES "THE LIGHT-FINGERED MARGARETS"!
WALKING AROUND IN BROAD DAYLIGHT, THE SCOUNDRELS!
THIS TIME WE'RE FINALLY GONNA NAB THEM!
THERE WERE TONS OF PEOPLE IN FRONT OF THE PARK JUST NOW.
OH, I BET IT'S THAT "SECRET SHOW" I HEARD ABOUT.
SECRET SHOW?
Osaka citizen Suzuki
Osaka citizen Chiharu
YEAH. I FORGET... WHO WAS IT?
SOMETHING LIKE UMIBÔZU...?
SKREEEEE
KRASH

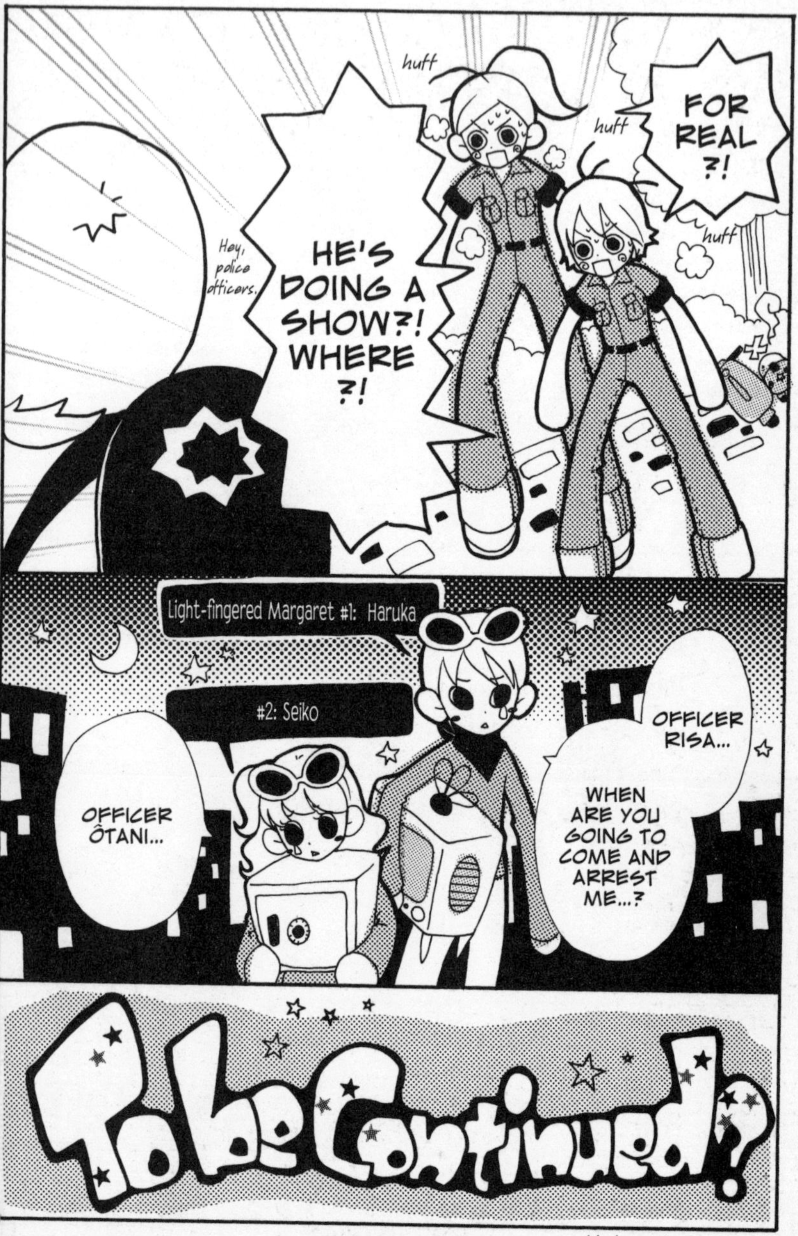

FOR REAL ?!
huff
huff
huff
HE'S DOING A SHOW?! WHERE ?!
Hey, police officers.
OFFICER RISA...
WHEN ARE YOU GOING TO COME AND ARREST ME...?
Light-fingered Margaret #1: Haruka
#2: Seiko
OFFICER ÔTANI...
To be Continued?!

No it won't.

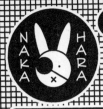

born in OSAKA

THE EDITOR'S EMPTY ROOM

Hello. This is Aya Nakahara, editor-in-chief of Bessatsu Love☆Com. Boy, was I in trouble... lots of empty pages to fill ha ha ha ha. But luckily for me, some fabulous visitors came by my house... so I took them captive!

Love☆Com is...well...a manga where all the characters talk for no good reason in a heavy Osaka dialect, so I asked them to write about Osaka. Yes I did. I was born and raised in Osaka, so I use the Osaka dialect when I talk. There are variations, though, depending on your neighborhood and age...the Osaka dialect I use in Love☆Com is kinda heavy and cliched, sorta, because a) I live smack in the middle of the city, and b) I've always loved stand-up comedy and used to tape comedy acts (mostly Downtown) to listen to on my way to and from school every day, yes I was an odd child...but anyway.

When you do a manga in Osaka dialect it's always introduced as "An Osaka dialect love comedy!" so how come if someone does a manga in Hokkaido dialect it's never introduced as "A Hokkaido dialect love story!"? How come?

Be that as it may, I love Osaka. I sure am glad I was born in this here place.

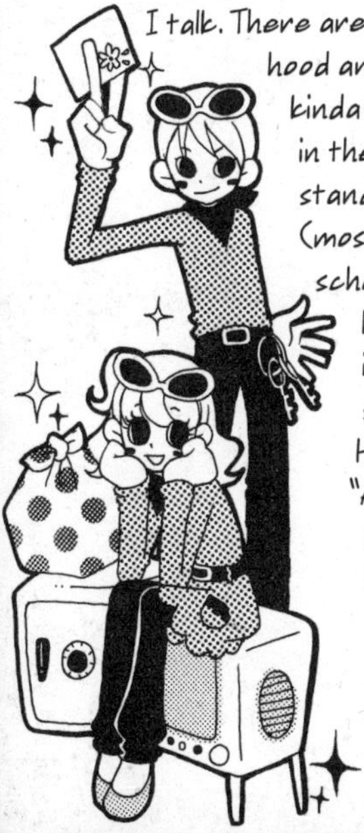

Enough already!

Go to the next page, hurry!

At sonic speed!

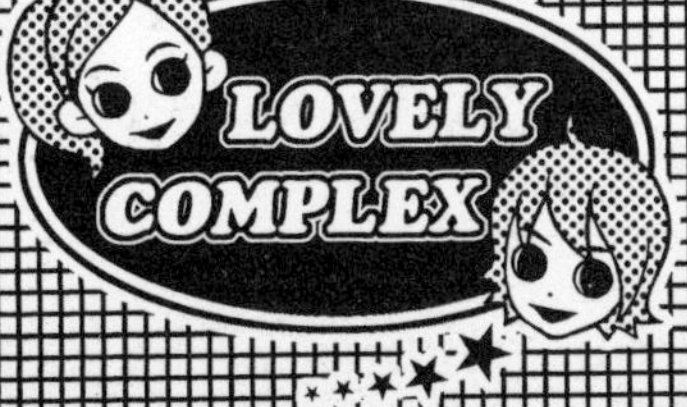
LOVELY
COMPLEX

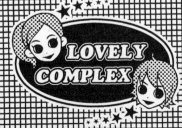

GUEST from Iwamizawa

• Welcome to OSAKA

Chiyo Morinaga

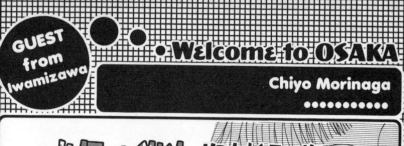

WHAT OSAKA MEANS TO ME...?

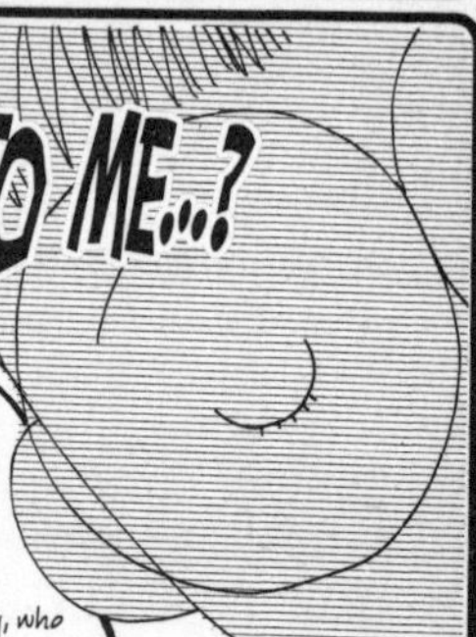

munch

Umm...let's see...what did I do in Osaka...? Wait, is it okay for this to be all writing and no pictures? I guess so. So, it's September 2002 and I'm writing this on my third visit to Osaka. Well, I'm being made to write it. So anyway, the first time I came Aya helped me with my manga. I got the table dirty. I noticed that Osaka mosquitoes are huge. They were so huge I started to think the mosquitoes I'd known till then weren't even mosquitoes at all. Scary. Okay, who cares about mosquitoes..? Oh, and the places that Aya took me to that time for Osaka delicacies okonomiyaki and udon, saying how good they were, well I went back to Hokkaido and found the same places there. Like, these were supposed to be special only-in-Osaka restaurants? My second visit I just spent the whole time helping Aya out with her manga... Gotta admit I was kinda shocked by the way she just slapped on whatever screen tone happened to be lying around, and then smiled and said, "all done!" That's right, everybody, Nakahara Sensei just uses any old screen tone. That's a lie. Aya's dog is named Kozaru-san ("little monkey") and is kinda lethargic but fluffy. He wears a scarf around his neck. Very stylish. This time, on my third visit, I finally made it to Universal Studios Japan. I had to go on "Back to the Future" by myself because both Aya and Ikuemi Sensei said they'd get sick. (waited in line for 10 minutes) It was fun! So we had a great time and came home and when we got inside it smelled like poop... cuz as it turned out Ikuemi Sensei had stepped in some doggy-doo. So had I, a little. Poop, yuck... very stinky... Aya loves hard-boiled eggs. Osaka's so hot you could die. Hokkaido gets so much snow you could die. We have a snow festival, even. Oh, we went to Tsutenkaku tower in Osaka. We went at night, ran up to the top, took a picture and came home. It was kinda scary. Aya had her clothes on back-to-front.

munch

munch munch

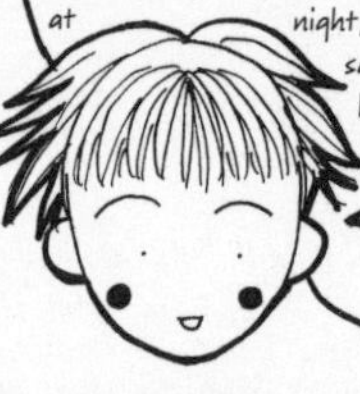

It's not gonna fit... Oh, one more thing. Aya gets flimsier and flimsier every time I see her. Next time I'm going to give her some of my bulk. I bought contacts lately so here I tried drawing myself without glasses.

WITH GRATITUDE FROM THE EDITOR-IN-CHIEF

Sorry about the okonomiyaki and udon places. hee hee. As for screen tone, I do not just use "whatever's lying around." You gotta use instinct with these things, okay? If you paste, then remove, paste then remove again like Chiyo, the whole day is over! Oh, and let me just say that even though Chiyo's two years older than me, she got seriously miffed because I wouldn't go on "Back to the Future" with her, like, grow up, sister! very cute, actually. Osaka mosquitoes are so big? Hope they don't keep you from coming for another visit!

GUEST from Sapporo

Welcome to OSAKA

Ryo Ikuemi

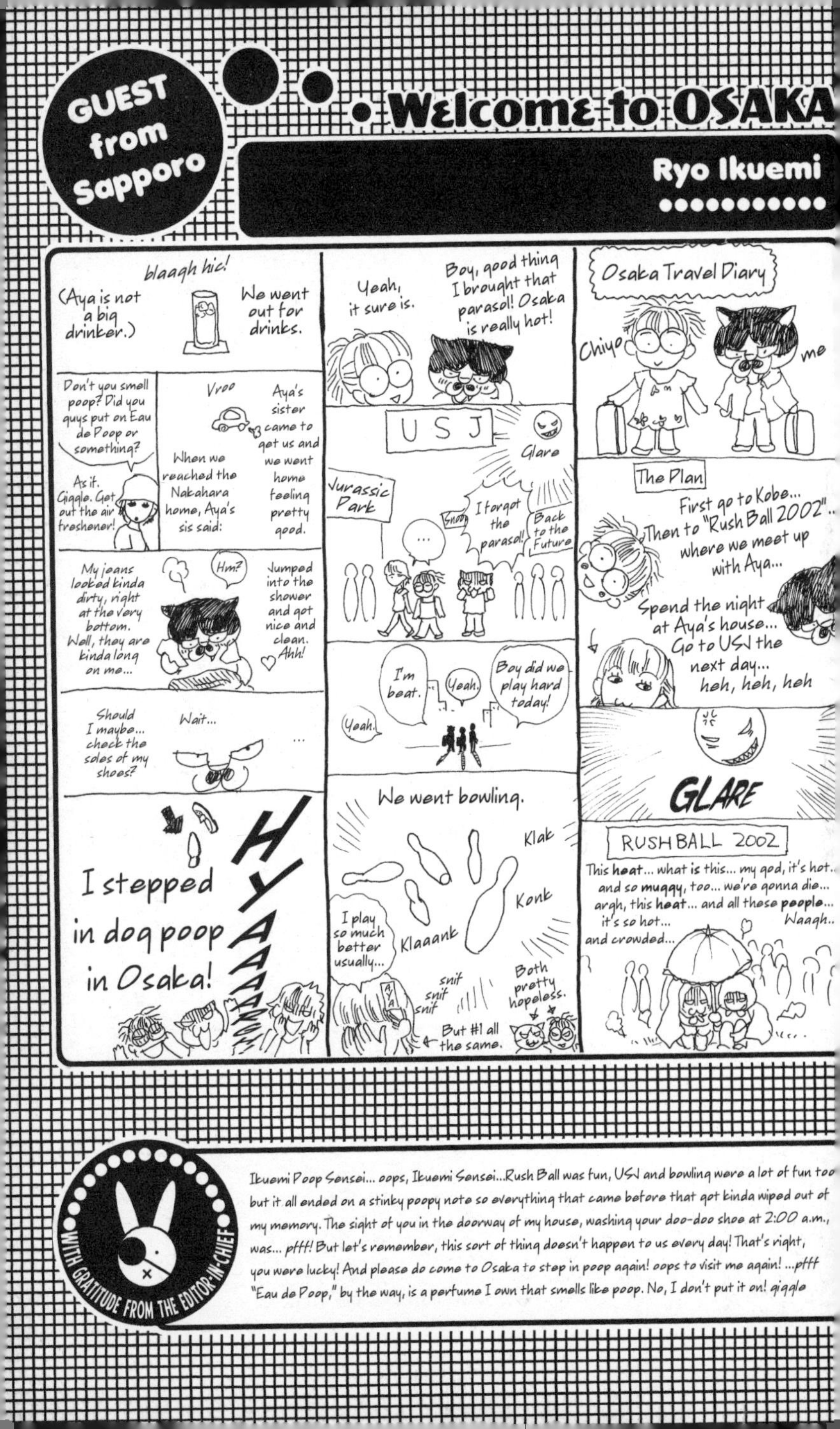
Osaka Travel Diary
Chiyo
me
The Plan
First go to Kobe... Then to "Rush Ball 2002"... where we meet up with Aya...
Spend the night at Aya's house... Go to USJ the next day... heh, heh, heh
GLARE
RUSHBALL 2002
This heat... what is this... my god, it's hot... and so muggy, too... we're gonna die... argh, this heat... and all these people... it's so hot... and crowded...
Waaagh...
Boy, good thing I brought that parasol! Osaka is really hot!
Yeah, it sure is.
USJ
Glare
Jurassic Park
I forgot the parasol!
Back to the Future
Snoo
...
Boy did we play hard today!
Yeah.
I'm beat.
Yeah.
We went bowling.
Klak
Konk
Klaaank
I play so much better usually...
Both pretty hopeless.
snif snif snif
AYA
But #1 all the same.
We went out for drinks.
blaagh hic!
(Aya is not a big drinker.)
Aya's sister came to get us and we went home feeling pretty good.
Vroo
When we reached the Nakahara home, Aya's sis said:
Don't you smell poop? Did you guys put on Eau de Poop or something?
As if. Giggle. Get out the air freshener!
Jumped into the shower and got nice and clean. Ahh!
Hm?
My jeans looked kinda dirty, right at the very bottom. Well, they are kinda long on me...
Wait...
...
Should I maybe... check the soles of my shoes?
HYAAAAAAGH!
I stepped in dog poop in Osaka!

WITH GRATITUDE FROM THE EDITOR-IN-CHIEF

Ikuemi Poop Sensei... oops, Ikuemi Sensei...Rush Ball was fun, USJ and bowling were a lot of fun too but it all ended on a stinky poopy note so everything that came before that got kinda wiped out of my memory. The sight of you in the doorway of my house, washing your doo-doo shoe at 2:00 a.m., was... pfff! But let's remember, this sort of thing doesn't happen to us every day! That's right, you were lucky! And please do come to Osaka to step in poop again! oops to visit me again! ...pfff "Eau de Poop," by the way, is a perfume I own that smells like poop. No, I don't put it on! giggle

Special Thanks
Ryo Ikuemi
Chiyo Morinaga
Rumiko Sawada
Nana Ikebe
Yuko Idomoto
Hikari Katayama
Yoshiyuki Yamamoto
Keisuke Araki
Nakahara Family
Betsuma Family
and You.

glossary

Page 34, panel 3: Yakuza
Member of Japanese organized crime. Yakuza organizations historically arose from various feudal sources, as well as the peddlers (*tekiya*) and gamblers (*bakuto*) of the 18th century. *Gurentai* are the most modern addition to the yakuza world, and they are like Western street gangs.

Page 65, panel 5: Senpai
A term of respect for someone with seniority in an organization, such as clubs, schools, and offices.

Page 91, sidebar, Ulfuls:
A rock band from Osaka that debuted in the early 1990s. They are Tortoise Matsumoto as lead singer, Keisuke Ulful on guitar, John B. Chopper on bass, and Sankon Jr. on drums. http://www.ulfuls.com/

Page 91, sidebar: Rush Ball
Rush Ball is an outdoor music festival in Osaka that started in 1999 with just seven bands. By 2006, it had expanded into three concerts sharing the Rush Ball name, and over 30 artists.

Page 91, sidebar: Tamio Okuda
A J-pop star who debuted in 1988 as a member of the band Unicorn. He moved on to a solo career in 1992 when the band broke up, and has recently rejoined The Band Has No Name, which was inactive for 15 years.

glossary

Page 91, sidebar: Bump of Chicken
A J-rock band formed by childhood friends Motoo Fujiwara (lead singer), Hiroaki Masukawa (guitar), Yoshifumi Naoi (bass), and Hideo Masu (drums). They won their first music competition at age 17 in 1996 and released their first album in 1999.
http://www.bumpofchicken.com/

Page 91, sidebar: Tokyo Ska Paradise
Ten-piece orchestra from Tokyo's underground scene started in 1985 by Asa-Chang. In its more than 20 years of performing, "Skapara" has produced 18 albums and shuffled seven members.
http://www.tokyoska.net/index.html

Page 93, panel 4: Ôtani's big nose
In Japanese, someone who's very boastful or vain is described as being a Tengu. A Tengu is a mountain spirit who has wings and a long nose.

Page 125, panel 2: Nose Hook
Used in the very Japanese nose bondage, where a hook on a leather strap pulls the nostrils up and open to give a pig-like appearance.

Page 160, panel 5: Japanese-style cheerleading
Japanese cheerleader squads are traditionally male. They wear *gakuran*, black uniforms with gold buttons, and wave Japanese fans around in both hands while shouting and squatting sumo-style.

Err...once again we're having *Love★Com* goods produced to give away to readers, and this time they are the little buttons that I sneaked onto Risa's cap on the cover of this volume. The Umibôzu badge, with the character *umi* [sea], was just the kanji on a white background at first, but with the help of the designer who always helps me out, it's turned into a really cool button. These buttons haven't appeared in the story so far, but I did work them into the manga itself, as you'll see in future volumes! (*hee hee hee*)

Aya Nakahara won the 2003 Shogakukan manga award for her breakthrough hit *Love★Com*, which was made into a major motion picture and a PS2 game in 2006. She debuted with *Haru to Kuuki Nichiyou-bi* in 1995, and her other works include *HANADA* and *Himitsu Kichi*.

LOVE★COM VOL 3
The Shojo Beat Manga Edition

STORY AND ART BY
AYA NAKAHARA

Translation & English Adaptation/Pookie Rolf
Touch-up Art & Lettering/Gia Cam Luc
Cover Design/Amy Martin
Interior Design/Yuki Ameda
Editor/Pancha Diaz

Editor in Chief, Books/Alvin Lu
Editor in Chief, Magazines/Marc Weidenbaum
VP of Publishing Licensing/Rika Inouye
VP of Sales/Gonzalo Ferreyra
Sr. VP of Marketing/Liza Coppola
Publisher/Hyoe Narita

Printed in Canada

Published by VIZ Media, LLC
P.O. Box 77010
San Francisco, CA 94107

Shojo Beat Manga Edition
10 9 8 7 6 5 4 3 2 1
First printing, November 2007

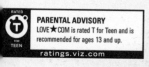

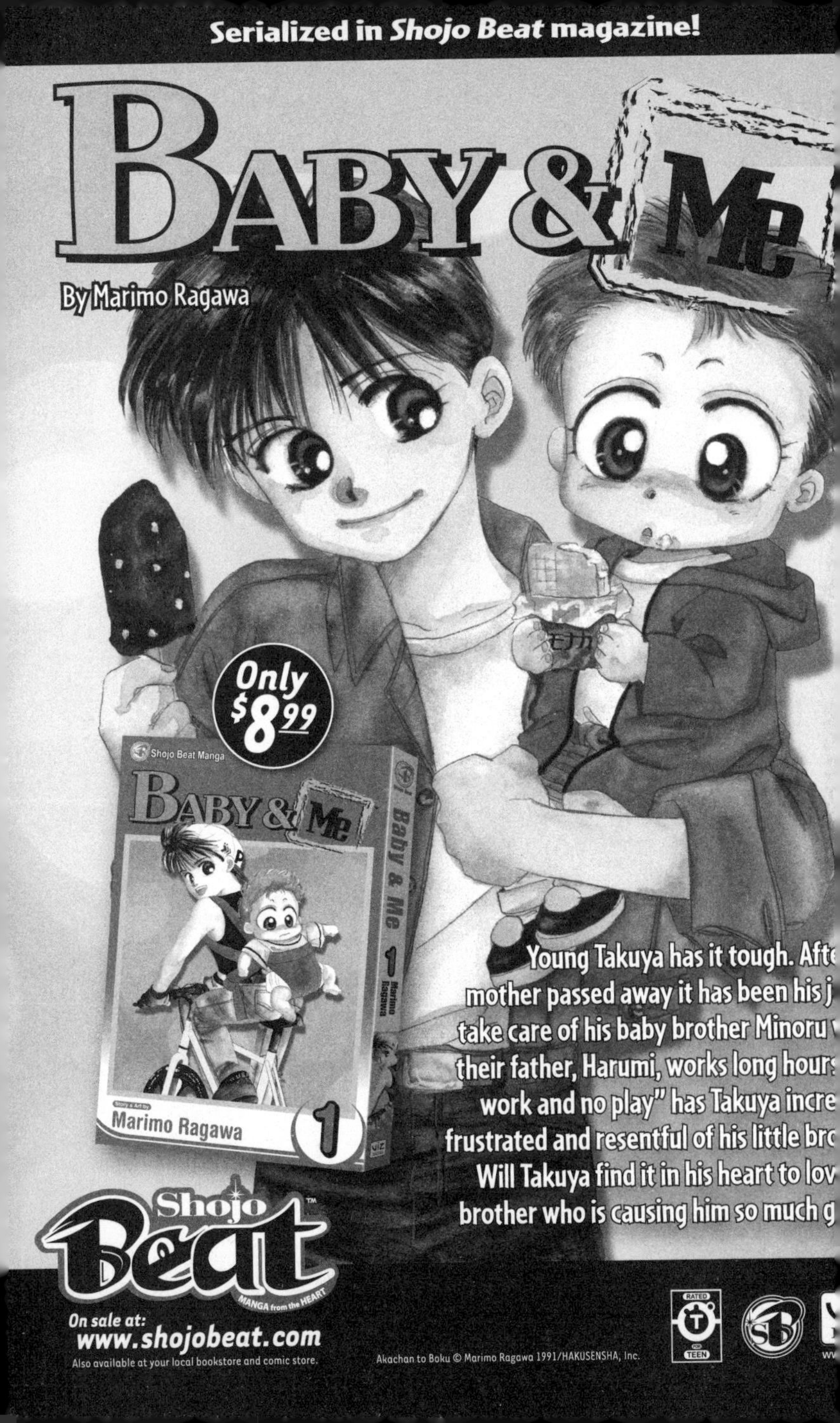
Serialized in Shojo Beat magazine!
BABY & Me
By Marimo Ragawa
Only $8.99
Shojo Beat Manga
BABY & Me
Baby & Me 1 Marimo Ragawa
Marimo Ragawa
1
Young Takuya has it tough. Afte
mother passed away it has been his j
take care of his baby brother Minoru
their father, Harumi, works long hours
work and no play" has Takuya incre
frustrated and resentful of his little bro
Will Takuya find it in his heart to lov
brother who is causing him so much g
Shojo Beat™
MANGA from the HEART
On sale at:
www.shojobeat.com
Also available at your local bookstore and comic store.
Akachan to Boku © Marimo Ragawa 1991/HAKUSENSHA, Inc.
RATED T TEEN

Tell us what you think about Shojo Beat Manga!

Our survey is now available online. Go to:

shojobeat.com/mangasurvey

Help us make our product offerings better!

Love. Laugh. Live

In addition to hundreds of pages of manga each month, **Shojo Beat** will bring you the latest in Japa
fashion, music, art, and culture—plus shopping, how-tos, industry updates, interviews, and much m

DON'T YOU WANT TO HAVE THIS MUCH FU

Subscribe Now!
Fill out the coupon
on the other side

Or go to:
www.shojobeat.com

Or call toll-fre
800-541-787

Crimson Hero ™
by MITSUBA TAKANASHI

Backstage Prince ™
by KANOKO SAKURAKOJI

VAMPIRE KNIGHT ™
by MATSURI HINO

BABY & Me ™
by MARIMO RAGAWA

**Absol
Boyfr**
by YUU W